MESSAGE FROM A KILLER

When I reached my door, I discovered a note taped to it. My name, done in beautiful, heavily inked calligraphy, lay scrawled across the surface. An apprehensive coldness ran through me. The note read:

You are a beautiful woman, Georgina. Beautiful enough, I think, to even tempt angels into falling—something that doesn't happen nearly as often as it should anymore. Beauty such as yours is effortless, however, when you can make it anything you like. Your large friend, unfortunately, doesn't have such luxury, which is a damned shame after what happened today. Fortunately, he works in the right business to correct any damage to his appearance.

I stared at the note like something that might bite me. Ripping it off the door, I hurried into my apartment and picked up the phone. I dialed Hugh's number without hesitation. He was the only one the note could be referring to.

After three rings, an unknown female voice answered.

"Is Hugh Mitchell there?"

There was a long pause. "He . . . can't talk right now. Who is this, please?"

"This is Georgina Kincaid. I'm his friend."

"I've heard him talk about you, Georgina. This is Samantha."

The name didn't mean anything to me, nor did I have the patience for this runaround. "Well, can I please talk to him, then?"

"No . . . " Her voice sounded strained, upset. "Georgina, something bad happened today . . ."

Books by Richelle Mead

SUCCUBUS BLUES

SUCCUBUS ON TOP

SUCCUBUS DREAMS

SUCCUBUS HEAT

STORM BORN

THORN QUEEN

Published by Kensington Publishing Corporation

SUCCUBUS
BLUES

RICHELLE MEAD

KENSINGTON BOOKS
http://www.kensingtonbooks.com

KENSINGTON BOOKS are published by

Kensington Publishing Corp.
119 West 40th Street
New York, NY 10018

All Kensington titles, imprints, and distributed lines are available at special quantity discounts for bulk purchases for sales promotion, premiums, fund-raising, educational, or institutional use.

Special book excerpts or customized printings can also be created to fit specific needs. For details, write or phone the office of the Kensington Special Sales Manager: Attn.: Special Sales Department. Kensington Publishing Corp., 119 West 40th Street, New York, NY 10018. Phone: 1-800-221-2647.

Kensington and the K logo Reg. U.S. Pat. & TM Off.

ISBN-13: 978-0-7582-4270-9
ISBN-10: 0-7582-4270-0

First Kensington Books Trade Paperback Printing: March 2007
First Kensington Books Mass-Market Paperback Printing:
September 2009

10 9 8 7 6 5 4 3 2 1

Printed in the United States of America

For my wonderful parents, Richard and Brenda.

*After filling my childhood with
mythology books and romance novels,
you guys had to have seen this coming.*

Acknowledgments

First and foremost, I have to thank all the friends and family who continually supported me and loved me throughout my writing adventures. In particular, this book could never have been written without my husband, Michael. Considering how often we talked about Georgina and her neuroses in our household, you might as well be married to her too. I love you.

Gratitude must also go to the Original Richelle Fan Club: Michael, David, Christina, and Marcee. You guys dutifully accepted every page I thrust at you and faithfully humored my demands for instantaneous feedback. Your enthusiasm and encouragement kept me going. Don't worry—*Harbinger* will get published one day. Honest. I mean it.

Finally, I need to give a shout-out to the literary and publishing folks who kept me on-track: Kate McKean, Jim McCarthy, and John Scognamiglio. Thank you so much for your guidance and advice.

Chapter 1

Statistics show that most mortals sell their souls for five reasons: sex, money, power, revenge, and love. In that order.

I suppose I should have been reassured, then, that I was out here assisting with *numero uno,* but the whole situation just made me feel . . . well, sleazy. And coming from me, that was something.

Maybe I just can't empathize anymore, I mused. *It's been too long. When I was a virgin, people still believed swans could impregnate girls.*

Nearby, Hugh waited patiently for me to overcome my reticence. He stuffed his hands into well-pressed khakis, leaning his large frame against his Lexus. "I don't see what the big deal is. You do this all the time."

That wasn't exactly true, but we both knew what he meant. Ignoring him, I instead made a great show of studying my surroundings, not that that improved my mood. The suburbs always dragged me down. Identical houses. Perfect lawns. Far too many SUVs. Somewhere in the night, a dog refused to stop yapping.

"I don't do *this*," I said finally. "Even I have standards."

Hugh snorted, expressing his opinion of my standards. "Okay, if it makes you feel better, don't think of this in terms of damnation. Think of it as a charity case."

"A charity case?"

"Sure."

He pulled out his Pocket PC, looking briskly business-like, despite the unorthodox setting. Not that I should have been surprised. Hugh was a professional imp, a master at getting mortals to sell their souls, an expert in contracts and legal loopholes that would have made any lawyer wince in envy.

He was also my friend. It sort of gave new meaning to the *With friends like these . . .* adage.

"Listen to these stats," he continued. "Martin Miller. Male, of course. Caucasian. Nonpracticing Lutheran. Works over at a game store in the mall. Lives in the basement here—his parents' house."

"Jesus."

"Told you."

"Charity or no, it still seems so . . . extreme. How old is he again?"

"Thirty-four."

"Ew."

"Exactly. If you were that old and hadn't gotten any, you might seek desperate measures too." He glanced down at his watch. "So are you going to do this or not?"

No doubt I was keeping Hugh from a date with some hot woman half his age—by which I meant, of course, the age Hugh looked. In reality, he was pushing a century.

I set my purse on the ground and gave him a warning glance. "You owe me."

"I do," he conceded. This wasn't my usual gig, thank goodness. The imp normally "outsourced" this kind of thing but had run into some kind of scheduling problem tonight. I couldn't imagine who he normally got to do this.

I started toward the house, but he stopped me. "Georgina?"

"Yeah?"

"There's . . . one other thing . . ."

I turned back around, not liking the tone in his voice. "Yes?"

"He, um, sort of had a special request."

I raised an eyebrow and waited.

"You see, uh, he's really into the whole, like, evil thing. You know, figures if he sold his soul to the devil—so to speak—then he should lose his virginity to a, I don't know, demoness or something."

I swear, even the dog stopped barking at that. "You're joking."

Hugh didn't respond.

"I'm not a—no. No way am I going to—"

"Come *on*, Georgina. It's nothing. A flourish. Smoke and mirrors. Please? Just do this for me?" He turned wistful, cajoling. Hard to resist. Like I said, he was good at his job. "I'm really in a tight spot . . . if you could help me out here . . . it would mean so much . . ."

I groaned, unable to refuse the pathetic look on his broad face. "If anyone finds out about this—"

"My lips are sealed." He actually had the audacity to make a sealing motion.

Bending down, resigned, I unfastened the straps on my shoes.

"What are you doing?" he asked.

"These are my favorite Bruno Maglis. I don't want them absorbed when I change."

"Yeah, but . . . you can just shape-shift them back."

"They won't be the same."

"They will. You can make them anything you want. This is just silly."

"Look," I demanded, "do you want to stand out here arguing shoes, or do you want me to go make a man of your virgin?"

Hugh clamped his mouth shut and gestured toward the house.

I padded away in the grass, the blades tickling my bare feet. The back patio leading to the basement was open, just as Hugh had promised. I let myself into the sleeping house, hoping they didn't have a dog, blearily wondering how I'd reached this low point in my existence. Adjusting to the darkness, my eyes soon discerned the features of a comfortable, middle-class family room: sofa, television, bookshelves. A stairwell rose to the left, and a hallway veered to the right.

I turned down the hall, letting my appearance shape-shift as I walked. The sensation was so familiar, so second nature to me, that I didn't even need to see my exterior to know what was happening. My petite frame grew taller, the slim build still staying slim but taking on a leaner, harder edge. My skin paled to death white, leaving no memory of its faint tan. The hair, already to my midback, stayed the same length but darkened to jet black, the fine waviness turning straight and coarse. My breasts—impressive by most standards—became larger still, rivaling those of the comic book heroines this guy had undoubtedly grown up with.

As for my outfit . . . well, away went the cute Banana Republic slacks and blouse. Thigh-high black leather boots appeared on my legs, paired with a matching halter top and a skirt I never could have bent over in. Spiky wings, horns, and a whip completed the package.

"Oh Lord," I muttered, accidentally taking in the whole effect in a small decorative mirror. I hoped none of the local demonesses ever found about this. They were really quite classy.

Turning from the taunting mirror, I stared down the hall

at my destination: a closed door with a yellow MEN AT WORK sign attached to it. I thought I could hear the faint sounds of a video game bleeping from beyond, though such noises silenced immediately when I knocked.

A moment later, the door opened, and I stood facing a five-foot-eight guy with shoulder-length, dirty blond hair rapidly receding on top. A large, hairy belly peeped out from underneath his Homer Simpson T-shirt, and he held a bag of potato chips in one hand.

The bag dropped to the floor when he saw me.

"Martin Miller?"

"Y-yes," he gasped out.

I cracked the whip. "You ready to play with me?"

Exactly six minutes later, I left the Miller residence. Apparently thirty-four years doesn't do much for one's stamina.

"Whoa, that was fast," Hugh noted, seeing me walk across the front yard. He was leaning against the car again, smoking a cigarette.

"No shit. Got another one of those?"

He grinned and handed over his own cigarette, giving me a once-over. "Would you be offended if I said the wings kind of get me hot?"

I took the cigarette, narrowing my eyes at him as I inhaled. A quick check ascertained no one else was around, and I shape-shifted back to my usual form.

"You owe me big," I reminded him, putting the shoes back on.

"I know. Of course, some might argue you owe me. You got a nice fix from it. Better than you're used to."

I couldn't deny that, but I didn't have to feel good about it either. Poor Martin. Geek or no, committing his soul to eternal damnation was a helluva price to pay for six minutes.

"You wanna get a drink?" Hugh offered.

"No, it's too late. I'm going home. Got a book to read."

"Ah, of course. When's the big day?"

"Tomorrow," I proclaimed.

The imp chuckled at my hero worship. "He just writes mainstream fiction, you know. He's hardly Nietzsche or Thoreau."

"Hey, one doesn't have to be surreal or transcendental to be a great writer. I should know; I've seen a few over the years."

Hugh grunted at my imperious air, giving me a mock bow. "Far be it from me to argue with a lady about her age."

I gave him a quick kiss on the cheek, then walked two blocks to where I had parked. I was unlocking the car door when I felt it: the warm, tingling feeling indicative of another immortal nearby. *Vampire,* I registered, only a millisecond before he appeared beside me. Damn, they moved fast.

"Georgina, my belle, my sweet succubus, my goddess of delight," he intoned, placing his hands over his heart dramatically.

Great. Just what I needed. Duane was quite possibly the most obnoxious immortal I'd ever met. He kept his blond hair shaved to a close buzz, and as usual, he demonstrated terrible taste in both fashion and deodorant.

"Go away, Duane. I have nothing to say to you."

"Oh come on," he crooned, his hand snaking out to hold the door as I tried to open it. "Even you can't play coy this time. Look at you. You're positively glowing. Good hunting, eh?"

I scowled at the reference to Martin's life energy, knowing it must be wreathing me. Obstinately, I tried to pry my door open against Duane's hold. No luck.

"He'll be out for days, from the looks of it," the vampire added, peering at me closely. "Still, I imagine whoever he was enjoyed the ride—both on you and to hell." He gave me a lazy smile, just barely revealing his pointed teeth. "He must have been someone pretty good for you to look as hot as you do now. What happened? I thought you only fucked the scum of the earth. The real assholes."

"Change of policy. I didn't want to give you false hope."

He shook his head appreciatively. "Oh Georgina, you never disappoint—you and your witticisms. But then, I've always found whores know how to make good use of their mouths, on or off the job."

"Let go," I snapped, tugging harder at the door.

"Why the hurry? I have a right to know what you and the imp were doing over here. The Eastside is my turf."

"We don't have to abide by your 'turf' rules, and you know it."

"Still, common courtesy dictates when you're in the neighborhood—literally, in this case—you at least say hello. Besides, how come we never hang out? You owe me some quality time. You spend enough time with those other losers."

The losers he referred to were my friends and the only decent vampires I'd ever met. Most vampires—like Duane—were arrogant, devoid of social skills, and obsessed with territoriality. Not unlike a lot of mortal men I'd met.

"If you don't let me go, you're going to learn a whole new definition of 'common courtesy.'"

Okay, it was a stupid, faux action-movie line, but it was the best I could come up with on the spot. I made my voice sound as menacing as possible, but it was pure bravado, and he knew it. Succubi were gifted with charisma and shape-shifting; vampires had super strength and speed. What this meant was that one of us mingled better at parties, and the other could break a man's wrist with a handshake.

"Are you actually threatening me?" He ran a playful hand along my cheek, making the hairs on my neck stand on end—in a bad way. I squirmed. "That's adorable. And kind of arousing. I actually think I'd like to see you on the offensive. Maybe if you'd just behave like a good girl—*ow!* You little bitch!"

With both of his hands occupied, I had seized my window of opportunity. A quick burst of shape-shifting, and sharp, three-inch claws appeared on my right hand. I swiped them across his cheek. His superior reflexes didn't let me get very far with the gesture, but I did draw blood before he gripped my wrist and slammed it against the car.

"What's the matter? Not offensive enough for you?" I managed through my pain. More bad movie lines.

"Cute, Georgina. Very cute. We'll see how cute you are by the time I—"

Headlights glimmered in the night as a car turned the corner on the next block and headed toward us. In that split second, I could see the indecision on Duane's face. Our tête-à-tête would undoubtedly be noticed by the driver. While Duane could easily kill an intervening mortal—hell, it was what he did for a living—having the kill linked to his harassment of me would not look good to our superiors. Even an asshole like Duane would think twice before stirring up that kind of paperwork.

"We aren't finished," he hissed, releasing my wrist.

"Oh, I think we are." I could feel braver now that salvation was on the way. "The next time you come near me's going to be the last."

"I'm quaking in terror," he simpered. His eyes gleamed once in the darkness, and then he was gone, moving off into the night just as the car drove past. Thank God for whatever liaison or ice cream run had pulled that driver out tonight.

Not wasting any more time, I got into my car and drove off, anxious to be back in the city. I tried to ignore the shaking of my hands on the wheel, but the truth of the matter was, Duane terrified me. I had told him off plenty of times in the presence of my immortal friends, but taking him on alone on a dark street was an entirely different matter, especially since all my threats had been empty ones.

I actually abhorred violence in all its forms. I suppose this came from living through periods of history fraught with levels of cruelty and brutality no one in the modern world could even comprehend. People like to say we live in violent times now, but they have no idea. Sure, there had been a certain satisfaction centuries ago in seeing a rapist castrated swiftly and promptly for his crimes, without endless courtroom drama or an early release for "good behavior." Unfortunately, those who deal in revenge and vigilantism rarely know where to draw the line, so I'd take the bureaucracy of the modern judicial system any day.

Thinking back to how I'd presumed the fortuitous driver was on an ice cream run, I decided a little dessert would do me some good too. Once I was safely back in Seattle, I stopped in a 24-hour grocery store, discovering some marketing mastermind had created tiramisu-flavored ice cream. Tiramisu and ice cream. The ingenuity of mortals never failed to amaze me.

As I was about to pay, I passed a display of flowers. They were cheap and a little tattered, but I watched as a young man came in and nervously scanned them over. At last he selected some autumn-colored mums and carried them off. My eyes followed him wistfully, half-jealous of whatever girl would be getting those.

As Duane had noted, I usually fed off losers, guys I didn't have to feel guilty about hurting or rendering unconscious for a few days. Those kind did not send flowers and usually avoided most romantic gestures altogether. As for the guys who did send flowers, well, I avoided them. For their own good. That was out of character for a succubus, but I was too jaded to care about propriety anymore.

Feeling sad and lonely, I picked up a bouquet of red carnations for myself and paid for it and the ice cream.

When I arrived home, my phone was ringing. Setting down my goods, I glanced at the Caller-ID. *Caller unknown.*

"My lord and master," I answered. "What a perfect ending to a perfect night."

"Save your quips, Georgie. Why were you fucking with Duane?"

"Jerome, I—what?"

"He just called. Said you were unduly hassling him."

"Hassling? Him?" Outrage surged inside me. "He started it! He came up to me and—"

"Did you hit him?"

"I . . ."

"Did you?"

I sighed. Jerome was the archdemon of the greater Seattle hierarchy of evil, as well as my supervisor. It was his job to manage all of us, make sure we did our duties, and keep us in line. Like any lazy demon, however, he preferred we create as little work for him as possible. His annoyance was almost palpable through the phone line.

"I *did* sort of hit him. Actually, it was more of a swipe."

"I see. A swipe. And did you threaten him too?"

"Well, yes, I guess, if you want to argue semantics, but Jerome, come on! He's a vampire. I can't touch him. You know that."

The archdemon hesitated, apparently considering the outcome of me going head-to-head with Duane. I must have lost in the hypothetical battle because I heard Jerome exhale a moment later.

"Yes. I suppose. But don't provoke him anymore. I've got enough to work on right now without you children having catfights."

"Since when do you work?" Children indeed.

"Good night, Georgie. Don't tangle with Duane again."

The phone disconnected. Demons weren't big on small talk.

I hung up, feeling highly offended. I couldn't believe Duane had tattled on me and then made me out to be the bad guy. Worse, Jerome seemed to have believed it. At least at first. That probably hurt me most of all because, my slacker-succubus habits aside, I'd always enjoyed a kind of indulgent, teacher's pet role with the archdemon.

Seeking consolation, I carried the ice cream off to my bedroom, shedding my clothes for a loose nightshirt. Aubrey, my cat, stood up from where she'd been sleeping at the foot of my bed and stretched. Solid white save for some black smudges on her forehead, she squinted green eyes at me in greeting.

"I can't go to bed," I told her, stifling a yawn. "I have to read first."

I curled up with the pint and my book, recalling again how I'd finally be meeting my favorite author at the signing tomorrow. Seth Mortensen's writing always spoke to me, awakening something inside I hadn't even known was asleep. His current book, *The Glasgow Pact,* couldn't ease the guilt I felt over what had happened with Martin, but it filled an aching emptiness in me nonetheless. I marveled that mortals, living so short a time, could create such wonderful things.

"I never created anything when I was a mortal," I told Aubrey when I'd finished five pages.

She rubbed against me, purring sympathetically, and I had just enough presence of mind to put the ice cream away before collapsing back into bed and falling asleep.

Chapter 2

The phone jolted me to consciousness the next morning. Dim, murky light filtered in through my sheer curtains, signifying some freakishly early hour. Around here, however, that amount of light could have indicated anything from sunrise to high noon. After four rings, I finally deigned to answer, accidentally knocking Aubrey out of the bed. She landed with an indignant *mhew* and stalked off to clean herself.

"Hello?"

"Yo, Kincaid?"

"No." My response came swift and certain. "I'm not coming in."

"You don't even know I'm going to ask that."

"Of course I know. There's no other reason you'd be calling me this early, and I'm not going to do it. It's my day off, Doug."

Doug, the other assistant manager at my day job, was a pretty nice guy, but he couldn't keep a poker face—or voice—to save his life. His cool demeanor immediately gave way to desperation. "Everyone called in sick today, and now we're strapped. You have to do it."

"Well, I'm sick too. Believe me, you don't want me there."

Okay, I wasn't exactly sick, but I was still sporting a residual afterglow from being with Martin. Mortals would not "see" it as Duane had per se, but they would sense it and be drawn to it—men and women alike—without even knowing why. My confinement today would prevent any foolish, lovesick behavior. It was very kind of me, really.

"Liar. You're never sick."

"Doug, I was already planning on coming back tonight for the signing. If I work a shift today too, I'll be there all day. That's sick and twisted."

"Welcome to my world, babe. We have no alternative, not if you really care about the fate of the store, not if you truly care about our customers and their happiness . . ."

"You're losing me, cowboy."

"So," he continued, "the question is, are you going to come here willingly, or do I have to walk over there and drag you out of bed myself? Frankly, I wouldn't mind the latter."

I did a mental eye roll, chiding myself for the billionth time about living two blocks from work. His rambling about the bookstore's suffering had been effective, as he'd known it would. I operated under the mistaken belief that the place couldn't survive without me.

"Well, rather than risk any more of your attempts at witty, sexual banter, I suppose I'll have to come over there. But Doug . . ." My voice turned hard.

"Yeah?"

"Don't put me on the registers or anything."

I heard hesitation on his end.

"Doug? I'm serious. Not the main registers. I don't want to be around a lot of customers."

"All right," he said at last. "Not the main registers."

"Promise?"

"I promise."

A half hour later, I stepped outside my door to walk the two blocks to the bookstore. Long clouds hung low, darkening the sky, and a faint chill touched the air, forcing some of my fellow pedestrians to don a coat. I had opted for none, finding my khaki slacks and brown chenille sweater more than sufficient. The clothing, just like the lip gloss and eyeliner I'd carefully applied this morning, were real; I had not shape-shifted into them. I enjoyed the routine nature of applying cosmetics and matching articles of clothing, though Hugh would have claimed I was just being weird again.

Emerald City Books & Café was a sprawling establishment, occupying almost a full block in Seattle's Queen Anne neighborhood. It sat two stories high, with the café portion dominating a second-floor corner viewing the Space Needle. A cheerful green awning hung over the main door, protecting those customers waiting for the store to open. I walked around them and entered through a side door, using my staff key.

Doug assaulted me before I'd taken two steps inside. "It's about time. We . . ." He paused and did a double-take, reexamining me. "Wow. You look . . . really nice today. Did you do something different?"

Only a thirty-four-year-old virgin, I thought.

"You're just imagining things because you're so happy I'm here to fix your staffing problem. What am I doing? Stock?"

"I, er, no." Doug struggled to snap out of his haze, still looking me up and down in a way I found disconcerting. His interest in dating me was no secret, nor was my continual rejection. "Come on, I'll show you."

"I told you—"

"It's not the main registers," he promised me.

What "it" turned out to be was the espresso counter in our upstairs café. Bookstore staff hardly ever subbed up here, but it wasn't unheard of.

Bruce, the café manager, popped up from where he'd been kneeling behind the counter. I often thought Doug and Bruce could be twins in a mixed-race, alternate-reality sort of way. Both had long, scraggly ponytails, and both wore a good deal of flannel in tribute to the grunge era neither had fully recovered from. They differed mainly in their coloring. Doug was Japanese-American, black-haired with flawless skin; Bruce was Mr. Aryan Nation, all blond hair and blue eyes.

"Hey Doug, Georgina," heralded Bruce. His eyes widened at me. "Whoa, you look great today."

"Doug! This is just as bad. I told you I didn't want any customers."

"You told me not the main registers. You didn't say anything about this one."

I opened my mouth to protest, but Bruce interrupted. "Come on, Georgina, I had Alex call in sick today, and Cindy actually quit." Seeing my stony expression, he quickly added, "Our registers are almost identical to yours. It'll be easy."

"Besides"—Doug raised his voice to a fair imitation of our manager's—"'assistant managers are supposed to be able to fill in for anybody around here.'"

"Yeah, but the café—"

"—is still part of the store. Look, I've got to go open. Bruce'll show you what you need to know. Don't worry, it'll be fine." He hastily darted off before I could refuse again.

"Coward!" I yelled after him.

"It really won't be that bad," Bruce reiterated, not understanding my dismay. "You just take the money, and I'll make the espresso. Let's practice on you. You want a white chocolate mocha?"

"Yeah," I conceded. Everyone I worked with knew about that particular vice. I usually managed to take down three of them a day. Mochas that was, not coworkers.

Bruce walked me through the necessary steps, showing me how to mark up the cups and find what I needed to push on the register's touch-screen interface. He was right. It wasn't so bad.

"You're a natural," he assured me later, handing over my mocha.

I grunted in response and consumed my caffeine, thinking I could handle anything so long as the mochas kept coming. Besides, this really couldn't be as bad as the main registers. The café probably did no business this time of day.

I was wrong. Minutes after opening, we had a line of five people.

"Large latte," I repeated back to my first customer, carefully punching in the information.

"Already got it," Bruce told me, starting the beverage before I even had a chance to label the cup. I happily took the woman's money and moved on to my next order.

"A large skinny mocha."

"Skinny's just another word for nonfat, Georgina."

I scrawled NF on the cup. No worries. We could do this.

The next customer wandered up and stared at me, momentarily bedazzled. Coming to her senses, she shook her head and blurted out a torrent of orders.

"I need one small drip coffee, one large nonfat vanilla latte, one small double cappuccino, and one large decaf latte."

Now I felt bedazzled. How had she remembered all those? And honestly, who ordered drip anymore?

On and on the morning went, and despite my misgivings, I soon felt myself perking up and enjoying the experience. I couldn't help it. It was how I worked, how I carried myself through life. I liked trying new things—even something as banal as ringing up espresso. People could be silly, certainly, but I enjoyed working with the public most of the time. It was how I had ended up in customer service.

And once I overcame my sleepiness, my inborn succubus charisma kicked in. I became the star of my own personal stage show, bantering and flirting with ease. When combined with the Martin-induced glamour, I became downright irresistible. While this did result in a number of proffered dates and pickup lines, it also saved me from the repercussions of any mistakes. My customers found no wrong with me.

"That's all right, dear," one older woman assured me upon discovering I'd accidentally ordered her a large cinnamon mocha instead of a nonfat, decaf latte. "I really need to branch out into new drinks anyway."

I smiled back winningly, hoping she wasn't diabetic.

Later on, a guy came up carrying a copy of Seth Mortensen's *The Glasgow Pact*. It was the first sign I'd seen of tonight's momentous event.

"Are you going to the signing?" I asked as I rang up his tea. Bleh. Caffeine-free.

He studied me for a pregnant moment, and I braced myself for a pass.

Instead the guy said mildly, "Yeah, I'll be there."

"Well, make sure you think up good questions for him. Don't ask the same ones everyone else does."

"What do you mean?"

"Oh, you know, the usual. 'Where do you get your ideas

from?' and 'Are Cady and O'Neill ever going to get to-gether?' "

The guy considered this as I made change. He was cute, in a disheveled sort of way. He had brown hair with a red-dish-gold gleam to it, said gleam being more noticeable in the shadow of facial hair crossing his lower face. I couldn't quite decide if he'd intentionally grown a beard or just for-gotten to shave. Whatever it was, it had grown in more or less evenly and, when combined with the Pink Floyd T-shirt he wore, presented the image of a sort of hippie-lumberjack.

"I don't think the 'usual questions' make them any less meaningful to the one doing the asking," he decided at last, seeming shy about contradicting me. "To a fan, each ques-tion is new and unique."

He stepped aside so I could wait on another customer. I continued the conversation as I took the next order, unwill-ing to pass up the opportunity to discuss Seth Mortensen in-telligently.

"Forget the fans. What about poor Seth Mortensen? He probably wants to impale himself each time he gets one of those."

" 'Impale' is kind of a strong word, don't you think?"

"Absolutely not. The guy's brilliant. Hearing idiotic ques-tions must bore him to tears."

A bemused smile played across the man's mouth, and his steady brown eyes weighed me carefully. When he realized he was staring so openly, he glanced away, embarrassed. "No. If he's out touring, he cares about his fans. He doesn't mind the repetitive questions."

"He's not out touring for altruism. He's out touring be-cause the publicists at his publishing house are making him tour," I countered. "Which is also a waste of time, by the way."

He dared a look back at me. "Touring is? You don't want to meet him?"

"I—well, yes, of course I do. It's just, that . . . okay. Look, don't get me wrong. I worship the ground this guy walks on. I'm excited to meet him tonight. I'm dying to meet him tonight. If he wanted to carry me off and make me his love slave, I'd do it, so long as I got advance copies of his books. But this touring thing . . . it takes time. Time that would be better spent writing the next book. I mean, haven't you seen how long his books take to come out?"

"Yeah. I've noticed."

Just then, a previous customer returned, complaining he'd gotten caramel syrup instead of caramel sauce. Whatever that meant. I offered a few smiles and sweet apologies, and he soon didn't care about the caramel sauce or anything else. By the time he left my register, the Mortensen fan guy was gone too.

When I finally finished my shift around five, Doug came to meet me.

"I heard some interesting things about your performance up here."

"I hear interesting things about your 'performance' all the time, Doug, but you don't hear me making jokes about it."

He bandied with me a bit more and finally released me to get ready for the signing, but not before I'd made him humbly acknowledge how much he owed me for my kindness today. Between him and Hugh, I was accruing favors all over the place.

I practically ran the two blocks home, anxious to grab some dinner and figure out what I wanted to wear. My exhilaration was growing. In an hour or so, I'd be meeting my all-time favorite author. Could life get any better? Humming to myself, I took the stairs two at a time and produced my keys with a flourish that only I noticed or appreciated.

As I opened the door, a hand suddenly grabbed me and pulled me roughly inside, into the darkness of my apartment. I yelped in surprise and fear as I was shoved up against the door, slamming it shut. The lights burst on suddenly and unexpectedly, and the faint smell of sulfur wafted through the air. Although the brightness made me wince, I could see well enough to recognize what was going on.

Hell hath no fury like a pissed-off demon.

Chapter 3

Of course, I should clarify at this point that Jerome doesn't look like a demon, at least not in the traditional red skin and horns sense. Maybe he does on another plane of existence, but like Hugh, me, and all the other immortals walking the earth, Jerome wore a human guise now.

One that looked like John Cusack.

Seriously. No joke. The archdemon always claimed he didn't even know who the actor was, but none of us bought that.

"Ow," I said irritably. "Let me go."

Jerome released his grasp, but his dark eyes still glinted dangerously. "You look good," he said after a moment, seeming surprised by the admission.

I tugged at my sweater, straightening it from where his hand had crumpled it. "You have a funny way of showing your admiration."

"Really good," he continued thoughtfully. "If I didn't know any better, I'd say you—"

"—shine," murmured a voice behind the demon. "You

shine, Daughter of Lilith, like a star in the night sky, like a diamond glittering on the bleakness of eternity."

I started in surprise. Jerome cut a sharp glance to the speaker, not liking his monologue interrupted. I also glared, not liking an uninvited angel in my apartment. Carter only smiled at both of us.

"As I was saying," snapped Jerome, "you look like you've been with a good mortal."

"I did a favor for Hugh."

"So this isn't the start of a new and improved habit?"

"Not on the salary you pay me."

Jerome grunted, but it was all part of a routine between us. He would berate me for not taking my job seriously, I'd give a few witty quips in return, and the status quo would resume. Like I said, I was something of a teacher's pet.

Looking at him now, however, I could see no more jokes would follow. The charm that had so enthralled my customers today had no effect on these two. Jerome's face was drawn and serious, as was Carter's, despite the angel's usual sardonic half-smile.

Jerome and Carter hung out together regularly, especially when alcohol was involved. This baffled me since they were supposedly locked in some sort of great, cosmic struggle. I'd once asked Jerome if Carter was a fallen angel, which had elicited a good laugh from the demon. When he'd recovered from the hilarity, he'd told me no, Carter hadn't fallen. If he had, he wouldn't technically be an angel anymore. I hadn't really found that answer satisfying and finally decided the two must stay together because there was no one else in this area who could relate to an existence stretching back to the beginning of time and creation. All the rest of us lesser immortals had been human at some point before; greater immortals like Jerome and Carter had not. My centuries were a mere blip on their timeline.

Whatever the reasons for his presence now, I didn't like

Carter. He wasn't obnoxious like Duane, but he always seemed so smug and supercilious. Maybe it was an angel thing. Carter also had the most bizarre sense of humor I'd ever seen. I could never tell if he was making fun of me or not.

"So what can I do for you boys?" I asked, tossing my purse on the counter. "I've got places to be tonight."

Jerome fixed me with a narrow-eyed look. "I want you to tell me about Duane."

"What? I already did. He's an asshole."

"Is that why you had him killed?"

"I—what?"

I froze where I'd been sifting through cupboard contents and slowly turned around to look back at the duo, half expecting some joke. Both faces were in earnest, watching me.

"Killed? How . . . how does that work?"

"You tell me, Georgie."

I blinked, suddenly realizing where this was going. "Are you accusing me of killing Duane? And wait . . . this is stupid. Duane isn't dead. He can't be."

Jerome began pacing, his voice exaggeratedly civil. "Oh, I assure you, he is quite dead. We found him this morning, just before sunrise."

"So what? He died of sun exposure?" That was the only way I'd ever heard a vampire could die.

"No. He died because of the stake wedged into his heart."

"Ew."

"So are you ready to tell me who you got to do it, Georgie?"

"I didn't get anyone to do it! I can't even—I don't even understand what this is about. Duane can't be dead."

"You admitted to me last night you two got in a fight."

"Yes . . ."

"And you threatened him."

"Yeah, but I was joking . . ."

"I think he told me you said something about him never coming near you again?"

"I was angry and upset! He was scaring me. This is crazy. Besides, *Duane can't be dead.*"

That was the only piece of sanity I could cling to in all of this, so I kept repeating it to them and to myself. Immortals were, by definition, immortal. End of story.

"Don't you know anything about vampires?" the arch-demon asked curiously.

"Like that they can't die?"

Amusement flickered in Carter's gray eyes; Jerome found me less funny.

"I'm asking you one last time, Georgina. Did you or did you not have Duane killed? Just answer the question. Yes or no."

"No," I said firmly.

Jerome glanced at Carter. The angel studied me, his lank blond hair falling forward to partially cover his face. I realized then why Carter was along for the ride tonight. Angels can always discern truth from lies. At last, he nodded sharply to Jerome.

"Glad I passed the test," I muttered.

But they weren't paying attention to me anymore.

"Well," observed Jerome grimly, "I guess we know what this means."

"Well, we don't know for sure . . ."

"*I* do."

Carter gave him a meaningful look, and several seconds of silence passed. I'd always suspected the two were communicating mentally in such moments, something we lesser immortals could not do unassisted.

"So Duane's really dead?" I asked.

"Yes," said Jerome, remembering I was there. "Very much so."

"Who killed him then? Now that we've determined it wasn't me?"

The two glanced at each other and shrugged, neither answering. Negligent parents, both of them. Carter pulled out a pack of cigarettes and lit up. Lord, I hated it when they got this way.

Finally Jerome said, "A vampire hunter."

I stared. "Really? Like that girl on TV?"

"Not exactly."

"So where are you going tonight?" asked Carter pleasantly.

"To Seth Mortensen's signing. And don't change the subject. I want to know about this vampire hunter."

"Are you going to sleep with him?"

"I—what?" For half a moment, I thought the angel was asking me about the vampire hunter. "You mean Seth Mortensen?"

Carter exhaled smoke. "Sure. I mean, if I were a succubus obsessed with a mortal author, that's what I'd do. Besides, doesn't your side always want more celebrities?"

"We've already got plenty of celebrities," Jerome said in an undertone.

Sleep with Seth Mortensen? Good grief. It was the most preposterous thing I'd ever heard. It was appalling. If I absorbed his life force, there was no telling how long it'd be until his next book came out.

"No! Of course not."

"Then what are you going to do to get noticed?"

"Noticed?"

"Sure. I mean, the guy probably sees tons of fans on a regular basis. Don't you want to stand out in some way?"

Surprise washed over me. I hadn't even considered that. Should I have? My jaded nature made it difficult to find pleasure in many things nowadays. Seth Mortensen books were one of my few escapes. Should I acknowledge that and attempt to connect with the novels' creator? Earlier today, I'd mocked run-of-the-mill fans. Was I about to become one of them?

"Well . . . I mean, Paige will probably introduce the staff privately to him. I'll sort of stand out then."

"Yes, of course." Carter put out the cigarette in my kitchen sink. "I'm sure he never gets the opportunity to meet bookstore management."

I opened my mouth to protest, but Jerome cut me off. "Enough." He gave Carter another of those meaningful looks. "We need to go."

"I—wait a minute!" Carter had succeeded in derailing me off the topic after all. I couldn't believe it. "I want to know more about this vampire hunter."

"All you need to know is that you should be careful, Georgie. Extremely careful. I am not joking about this."

I swallowed, hearing the iron in the demon's voice. "But I'm not a vampire."

"I don't care. These hunter types sometimes follow vampires around, hoping to find others. You could be implicated by association. Lay low. Avoid being alone. Stay with others—mortal or immortal, it doesn't matter. Maybe you can follow up on your favor for Hugh and score some more souls for our side while you're at it."

I rolled my eyes at that as the two walked to the door.

"I mean it. Be careful. Keep a low profile. Don't get involved with this."

"And," added Carter with a wink, "say hi to Seth Mortensen for me."

With that, the two left, closing the door gently behind them. A formality really, since either of them could have just teleported out. Or blown my door apart.

I turned to Aubrey. She had watched the proceedings cautiously from the back of my sofa, tail twitching.

"Well," I told her, reeling. "What am I supposed to make of that?"

Duane was actually dead? I mean, yeah, he was a bastard, and I had been pretty pissed when I threatened him last night, but I'd never actually wanted him to be *really* dead. And what about this vampire hunter business? Why was I supposed to be careful when—

"Shit!"

I had just glanced at my microwave clock. It coolly informed me I needed to return to the bookstore ASAP. Pushing Duane out of my brain, I dashed to my bedroom and stared at myself in the mirror. Aubrey followed more sluggishly.

What to wear? I could just keep my current outfit. The sweater and khakis combination looked both respectable and subdued, though the color scheme blended a bit too well with my light brown hair. It was a librarian sort of outfit. Did I want to look subdued? Maybe. Like I had told Carter, I really didn't want to do anything that might solicit the romantic interest of my favorite author in the whole world.

Still . . .

Still, I remembered what the angel had said about getting noticed. I didn't want to be just another face in Seth Mortensen's crowd. This was the final stop on his latest tour. No doubt he'd seen thousands of fans in the last month, fans who blurred together into a sea of bland faces, making their inane comments. I had advised the guy at the counter to be innovative with his questions, and I intended to behave the same way with my appearance.

Five minutes later, I stood in front of the mirror once more, this time clad in a silk tank top, deep violet and low-cut, paired with a floral chiffon skirt. The skirt almost covered my thighs and swirled when I spun. It would have made a great dancing outfit. Stepping into strappy brown heels, I glanced over at Aubrey for confirmation.

"What do you think? Too sexy?"

She began cleaning her tail.

"It *is* sexy," I conceded, "but it's classy sexy. The hair helps, I think."

I had pulled my long hair up into a romantic sort of bun, leaving wavy locks to frame my face and enhance my eyes. Momentary shape-shifting made them turn greener than usual. Changing my mind, I let them go back to their normal gold-and-green-flecked hazel.

When Aubrey still refused to acknowledge how awesome I looked, I grabbed my snakeskin coat and glared at her. "I don't care what you think. This outfit was a good call."

I left the apartment with my copy of *The Glasgow Pact* and walked back to work, impervious to the drizzle. Another perk of shape-shifting. Fans milled inside the main retail area, eager to see the man whose latest book still dominated the bestseller lists, even after five weeks. I squeezed past the group, making my way toward the stairs that led to the second floor.

"Young adult books are over there by the wall." Doug's friendly voice drifted nearby. "Let me know if you need anything else."

He turned away from the customer he'd been helping, caught sight of me, and promptly dropped the stack of books he'd been holding.

Customers stepped back, politely watching him kneel down to retrieve the books. I recognized the covers immediately. They were paperbacks of Seth Mortensen's older titles.

"Sacrilege," I commented. "Letting those touch the ground. You'll have to burn them now, like a flag."

Ignoring me, Doug gathered up the books and then ushered me off out of earshot. "Nice of you to go home and change into something more comfortable. Christ, can you even bend over in that?"

"What, do you think I'll have to tonight?"

"Well, that depends. I mean, Warren's here after all."

"Harsh, Doug. Very harsh."

"You bring it on yourself, Kincaid." He gave me a reluctant, appreciative glance just before we started climbing the stairs. "You do look pretty good, though."

"Thanks. I wanted Seth Mortensen to notice me."

"Believe me, unless he's gay, he'll notice you. Probably even then too."

"I don't look too slutty, do I?"

"No."

"Or cheap?"

"No."

"I was going for classy sexy. What do you think?"

"I think I'm done feeding your ego. You already know how you look."

We crested the top of the stairs. A mass of chairs had been set up, covering most of the café's normal seating area and spreading out into part of the gardening and maps section of books. Paige, the store manager and our superior, busily attempted some sort of wiring acrobatics with the microphone and sound system. I didn't know what this building had been used for before Emerald City Books moved in, but it was not an ideal venue for acoustics and large groups.

"I'm going to help her," Doug told me, kindly chivalrous. Paige was three months pregnant. "I'd advise you do something that doesn't involve leaning more than twenty degrees in any one direction. Oh, and if somebody tries to get you to touch your elbows together behind your back, don't fall for it."

I gave him a sharp jab in the ribs, nearly making him lose the books again.

Bruce, still manning the espresso counter, made me my fourth white chocolate mocha of the day, and I wandered over to the geography books to drink it while I waited for things to pick up. Glancing beside me, I recognized the guy

I'd discussed Seth Mortensen with earlier. He still held his copy of *The Glasgow Pact*.

"Hey," I said.

He jumped at the sound of my voice, having been absorbed in a travel book about Texas.

"Sorry," I told him. "Didn't mean to scare you."

"I—no, you d-didn't," he stammered. His eyes assessed me from head to toe in one quick glance, lingering ever so briefly on my hips and breasts but longest on my face. "You changed clothes." Apparently realizing the myriad implications behind such an admission, he added hastily, "Not that that's bad. I mean that's good. Er, well, that is—"

His embarrassment growing, he turned from me and tried to awkwardly replace the Texas book back on the shelf, upside down. I hid my smile. This guy was too adorable. I didn't run into many shy guys anymore. Modern-day dating seemed to demand men make as great a spectacle of themselves as possible, and unfortunately, women seemed to really go for it. Okay, even I went for it sometimes. But shy guys deserved a break too, and I decided a little harmless flirting with him would be good for his ego while I waited for the signing to start. He probably had terrible luck with women.

"Let me do that," I offered, leaning across him. My hands touched his as I took the book from him, replacing it carefully on the shelf, front cover out. "There."

I stepped back as though to admire my handiwork, making sure I stood very close to him, our shoulders nearly touching. "It's important to keep up appearances with books," I explained. "Image goes a long way in this business."

He dared a look over at me, still nervous but steadily recovering his composure. "I go more for content."

"Really?" I repositioned slightly so that we were touching again, the soft flannel of his shirt brushing my bare skin. "Because I could have sworn a moment ago you were pretty caught up in outside appearance."

His eyes shifted down again, but I could see a smile curving his lips. "Well. Some things are so striking, they can't help but draw attention to themselves."

"And doesn't that make you curious about what's inside?"

"Mostly it makes me want to get you some advanced copies."

Advanced copies? What did he—?

"Seth? Seth, where—ah, there you are."

Paige turned down our aisle, Doug following behind. She brightened when she saw me, and I felt my stomach sink out of me and hit the floor with a thud as I put two and two together. No. No. It couldn't be—

"Ah, Georgina. I see you've already met Seth Mortensen."

Chapter 4

"Kill me, Doug. Just kill me now. Put me out of my misery."

My immortality notwithstanding, the sentiment was sincere.

"Christ, Kincaid, what did you say to him?" murmured Doug.

We stood off to the side of Seth Mortensen's audience, along with many others. All the seats had filled up, putting space and visibility at a premium. I was lucky to be with the staff in our reserved section, giving us a perfect view of Seth as he read from *The Glasgow Pact*. Not that I wanted to be in his line of sight. In fact, I really would have preferred that I never come face to face with him again.

"Well," I told Doug, keeping an eye on Paige so as not to draw attention to our whispering, "I ripped on his fans and on how long it takes for his books to come out."

Doug stared at me, his expectations exceeded.

"Then I said—not knowing who he was—that I'd be Seth

Mortensen's love slave in exchange for advanced copies of his books."

I didn't elaborate on my impromptu flirting. To think, I'd imagined I was boosting a shy guy's ego! Good Lord. Seth Mortensen could probably bed a different groupie every night if he wanted.

Not that he seemed like the type. He'd demonstrated much of the same initial nervousness in front of the crowd as he had with me. He grew more comfortable once he started reading, however, warming to the material and letting his voice rise and fall with intensity and wry humor.

"What kind of a fan are you?" Doug asked. "Didn't you know what he looked like?"

"There are never pictures of him in his books! Besides, I thought he'd be older." I guessed now that Seth was in his mid-thirties, a bit older than I looked in this body, but younger than the forty-something writer I'd always imagined.

"Well, look on the bright side, Kincaid. You succeeded in your goal: you got him to notice you."

I stifled a groan, letting my head flop pathetically onto Doug's shoulder.

Paige turned her head and gave us a withering glance. As usual, our manager looked stunning, wearing a red suit that set off her chocolate brown skin. The faintest swellings of pregnancy showed under the jacket, and I couldn't help but feel a tug of jealous longing.

When she had first announced her unplanned pregnancy, she had laughed it off, saying: "Well, you know how these things can just happen."

But I had never known how it could "just happen." I'd tried desperately to get pregnant as a mortal, to no avail, instead becoming an object of pity and carefully hidden—albeit not well enough—jokes. Becoming a succubus had killed whatever lingering chance I might have had at motherhood, though I hadn't realized that at the time. I had sacrificed my body's ability to create in exchange for eternal youth and beauty. One type of immortality traded for another. Long centuries give you a lot of time to accept what you can and can't have, but being reminded of it stings nonetheless.

Giving Paige a smile that promised good behavior, I turned my attention back to Seth. He was just finishing up the reading and moving on to questions. As expected, the first ones asked were, "Where do you get your ideas from?" and "Are Cady and O'Neill ever going to get together?"

He glanced briefly in my direction before answering, and I cringed, recalling my remarks about him impaling himself when those questions were asked. Turning back to his fans, he addressed the first question seriously and dodged the second one.

Everything else he answered succinctly, often in a dry and subtly humorous way. He never spoke any more than he had to, always providing just enough to fulfill the questioner's requirements. The crowd clearly unnerved him, which I found a bit disappointing.

Considering how punchy and clever his books were, I guess I'd expected him to speak in the same way he wrote. I wanted a confident outpouring of words and wit, a charisma to rival my own. He'd had a few good lines earlier while we spoke, I supposed, but he'd taken time to warm up to them and to me.

Of course, it was unfair to make comparisons between us. He had no uncanny knack for dazzling others, nor centuries of practice behind him. Still. I had never imagined a slightly scattered introvert capable of creating my favorite books. Unjust of me, but there it was.

"Everything going okay?" a voice behind us asked.

I looked over and saw Warren, the store's owner and my occasional fuck-buddy.

"Perfectly," Paige told him in her crisp, efficient way. "We'll start the signing in another fifteen minutes or so."

"Good."

His eyes flicked casually over the rest of us staff and then shot back to me. He said nothing, but as he scoured me with that gaze, I could almost feel his hands undressing me. He'd come to expect sex on a regular basis, and usually I didn't fight it since he provided a quick and reliable—albeit small—fix of energy and life. His low moral character erased any guilt I might have for doing so.

After the questions ended, we faced crowd control issues as everyone queued up to get their books signed. I offered to help, but Doug told me they had things under control. So, instead, I stayed out of the way, trying to avoid eye contact with Seth.

"Meet me in my office when this is all over," Warren murmured, coming up to stand close beside me.

He wore a tailored, charcoal gray suit tonight, looking every inch the sophisticated literary tycoon. In spite of my distasteful opinion of a man who cheated on his wife of thirty years with a much younger employee, I still had to acknowledge a certain amount of physical charm and allure to him. After everything that had happened today, though, I was not in the mood to be sprawled across his desk when the store closed.

"I can't," I answered back softly, still watching the signing. "I'm busy afterwards."

"No you aren't. It's not a dancing night."

"No," I agreed. "But I'm doing something else."

"Like what?"

"I have a date." The lie came easily to my lips.

"You do not."

"I do."

"You never date, so don't try that line now. The only appointment you have is with me, back in my office, preferably on your knees." He took a step closer, speaking into my ear so that I could feel the warmth of his breath on my skin. "Jesus, Georgina. You're so fucking hot tonight, I could take you right now. Do you have any idea what you're doing to me in that outfit?"

" 'Doing to you?' I'm not 'doing' anything. It's attitudes like that that result in women being veiled around the world, you know. It's blaming the victim."

He chuckled. "You crack me up, you know that? Do you have any panties on under that?"

"Kincaid? Can you come help us over here?"

I turned and saw Doug frowning at us. It would figure. He wanted my help, now that he saw Warren hitting on me. Who said there was no chivalry left in this world? Doug was one of the few who knew what passed between Warren and me, and he didn't approve. Yet, I wanted the escape, belated or no, and thus temporarily evaded Warren's lust as I walked over to assist with the book sale.

It took almost two hours to shuffle customers through the signing line, and by then, the store was fifteen minutes from closing. Seth Mortensen looked a little tired but seemed to be in good spirits. My stomach flip-flopped inside me when Paige beckoned those of us not involved with closing to come over and talk to him.

She introduced us matter-of-factly. "Warren Lloyd, store owner. Doug Sato, assistant manager. Bruce Newton, café manager. Andy Kraus, sales. And you already know Georgina Kincaid, our other assistant manager."

Seth nodded politely, shaking everyone's hand. When he reached me, I averted my eyes, waiting for him to just move on. When he did not, I mentally cringed, bracing myself for some comment about our previous encounters. Instead, all he said was, "G.K."

I blinked. "Huh?"

"G.K.," he repeated, as though those letters made perfect

sense. When my idiotic expression persisted, he gave a swift head jerk toward one of the promotional flyers for tonight's event. It read:

> If you haven't heard of Seth Mortensen, then you obviously haven't been living on this planet for the last eight years. He's only the hottest thing to hit the mystery/contemporary fiction market, making the competition look like scribbles in a child's picture book. With several bestselling titles to his name, the illustrious Mr. Mortensen writes both self-standing novels and continual installments in the stunningly popular Cady & O'Neill series. *The Glasgow Pact* continues the adventures of these intrepid investigators as they travel abroad this time, continuing to unravel archaeological mysteries and engage in the persistent witty, sexual banter we've come to love them for. Guys, if you can't find your girlfriends tonight, they're here with *The Glasgow Pact*, wishing you were as suave as O'Neill.
> —G.K.

"You're G.K. You wrote the bio."

He looked to me for confirmation, but I couldn't speak, wouldn't utter the clever acknowledgment about to spring from my lips. I was too afraid. After my earlier mishaps, I feared saying the wrong thing.

Finally, confused by my silence, he asked haltingly, "Are you a writer? It's really good."

"No."

"Ah." A few moments passed in cool silence. "Well. I guess some people write the stories, and others live them."

That sounded like a dig of sorts, but I bit my lip on any response, still playing my new ice-bitch role, wanting to defuse the earlier flirtation.

Paige, not understanding the tension between Seth and

me, still felt it and tried to allay it. "Georgina's one of your biggest fans. She was absolutely ecstatic when she found out you were coming here."

"Yeah," added Doug wickedly. "She's practically a *slave* to your books. Ask her how many times she's read *The Glasgow Pact*."

I shot him a murderous look, but Seth's attention focused back on me, genuinely curious. *He's trying to bring back our earlier rapport,* I realized sadly. I couldn't let that happen now.

"How many?"

I swallowed, not wanting to answer, but the weight of all those eyes grew too heavy. "None. I haven't finished it yet." Practiced poise allowed me to utter those words calmly and confidently, hiding my discomfort.

Seth looked puzzled. So did everyone else; they all stared at me, rightfully perplexed. Only Doug knew the joke.

"None?" asked Warren with a frown. "Hasn't it been out for over a month now?"

Doug, the bastard, grinned. "Tell them the rest. Tell them how much you read a day."

I wished then that the floor would open up and swallow me whole, so I could escape this nightmare. As if coming off as an arrogant strumpet in front of Seth Mortensen wasn't bad enough, Doug was now shaming me into confessing my ridiculous habit.

"Five," I finally said. "I only read five pages a day."

"Why?" asked Paige. She had apparently never heard this story.

I could feel my cheeks turning red. Paige and Warren stared at me like I was from another planet while Seth simply continued to remain silent and look thoughtfully distracted. I took a deep breath and spoke in a rush: "Because . . . because it's so good, and because there's only one chance to read a book for the first time, and I want it to last. That experience.

I'd finish it in a day otherwise, and that'd be like . . . like eating a carton of ice cream in one sitting. Too much richness over too quickly. This way, I can draw it out. Make the book last longer. Savor it. I have to since they don't come out that often."

I promptly shut up, realizing I had just insulted Seth's writing prowess . . . again. He made no response to my comment, and I couldn't decipher the expression on his face. Considering, maybe. Once again, I silently begged the floor to consume me and save me from this humiliation. It obstinately refused.

Doug smiled reassuringly at me. He found my habit cute. Paige, who apparently did not, looked as though she shared my wish that I be somewhere else. She cleared her throat politely and started a completely new line of conversation. After that, I scarcely paid attention to what anybody said. All I knew was that Seth Mortensen probably thought I was an erratic nutcase, and I couldn't wait for this night to end.

". . . Kincaid would do it."

The sound of my name brought me back around several minutes later.

"What?" I turned to Doug, the speaker.

"Wouldn't you?" he repeated.

"Wouldn't I what?"

"Show Seth around the city tomorrow." Doug spoke patiently, as if to a child. "Get him acquainted with the area."

"My brother's too busy," explained Seth.

What did his brother have to do with anything? And why did he need to get acquainted with the area?

I faltered, unwilling to admit I'd spaced out just now while wallowing in self-pity.

"I . . ."

"If you don't want to . . ." began Seth hesitantly.

"Of course she does." Doug nudged me. "Come on. Climb out of your hole."

We exchanged smartass looks, worthy of Jerome and Carter. "Yeah, fine. Whatever."

We arranged the logistics of me meeting Seth, and I wondered what I'd gotten myself into. I no longer wanted to stand out. In fact, I would have preferred if he could have just blotted me from his mind forever. Hanging out as we toured Seattle tomorrow didn't seem like the best way to make that happen. If anything, it would probably only result in more foolish behavior on my part.

Conversation finally faded. As we were about to disperse, I suddenly realized something. "Oh. Hey. Mr. Mortensen. Seth."

He turned toward me. "Yeah?"

I frantically tried to say something that would undo the tangled mess of mixed signals and embarrassment he and I had stumbled into. Unfortunately, the only things that came to mind were: *Where do you get your ideas from?* and *Are Cady and O'Neill ever going to get together?* Dismissing such idiocy, I simply shoved my book over to him.

"Can you sign this?"

He took it. "Uh, sure." A pause. "I'll bring it back tomorrow."

Deprive me of my book for the night? Hadn't I suffered enough?

"Can't you just sign it now?"

He shrugged haplessly, as though the matter were out of his control. "I can't think of anything to write."

"Just sign your name."

"I'll bring it back tomorrow," he repeated, walking away with my copy of *The Glasgow Pact* like I hadn't even said anything. Appalled, I seriously considered running over and beating him up for it, but Warren suddenly tugged on my arm.

"Georgina," he said pleasantly as I stared desperately at

my retreating book, "we still need to discuss that matter in my office."

No. No way. I definitely wasn't putting out after this debacle of an evening. Turning slowly toward him, I shook my head. "I told you, I can't."

"Yeah, I know already. Your fictitious date."

"It's not fictitious. It's—"

My eyes desperately scanned for escape as I spoke. While no magical portals appeared in the cookbook section, I suddenly locked gazes with a guy browsing our foreign language books. He smiled curiously at my attention, and in a flash, I made a ballsy choice.

"—with him. It's with him."

I waved my hand at the strange guy and beckoned him over. He looked understandably surprised, setting his book down and walking toward us. When he arrived, I slung my arm around him familiarly, giving him a look that had been known to bring kings to their knees.

"Are you ready to go?"

Mild astonishment flashed in his eyes—which were beautiful, by the way. An intense green-blue. To my relief, he played along and returned my serve masterfully.

"You bet." His own arm snaked around me, his hand resting on my hip with surprising presumption. "I would have been here sooner, but I got held up in traffic."

Cute. I glanced at Warren. "Rain check for our talk?"

Warren looked from me to the guy and then back to me. "Sure. Yes. Of course." Warren had proprietary feelings toward me, but they weren't strong enough for him to challenge a younger competitor.

A few of my coworkers also watched with interest. Like Warren, none of them had ever really seen me date anyone. Seth Mortensen busied himself packing up a briefcase, never meeting my eyes again, for all the world oblivious to my existence. He didn't even respond when I said goodbye. Probably just as well.

My "date" and I left the store, stepping out into the cool night. The precipitation had stopped, but clouds and city lights blotted out the stars. Studying him, I kind of wished maybe we were going out after all.

He was tall—really tall. Probably at least ten inches taller than my diminutive five-four. His hair was black and wavy, brushed away from a deeply tanned face that nearly made those sea-colored eyes glow. He wore a long, black wool coat and a scarf with a black, burgundy, and green plaid pattern.

"Thanks," I said as we paused to stand on the street corner. "You saved me from an . . . unpleasant situation."

"My pleasure." He held out his hand to me. "I'm Roman."

"Nice name."

"I guess. It reminds me of a romance novel."

"Oh?"

"Yeah. No one's really named that in real life. But in romance novels, there are a million of them. 'Roman the Fifth Duke of Wellington.' 'Roman the Terrible yet Dashing and Eerily Attractive Pirate of the High Seas.'"

"Hey, I think I read that last one. I'm Georgina."

"So I see." He nodded toward the staff ID badge I wore around my neck. Probably an excuse to check out my cleavage. "Is that outfit the standard uniform for assistant managers?"

"This outfit's becoming a real pain in the ass actually," I noted, thinking of the various reactions it had elicited.

"You can wear my coat. Where do you want to go tonight?"

"Where do I—? We aren't going out. I told you: you just saved me from a minor entanglement, that's all."

"Hey, that's still got to be worth something," he countered. "A handkerchief? A kiss on the cheek? Your phone number?"

"No!"

"Oh, come on. Did you see how good I was? I didn't miss a beat when you roped me in with that come-hither look of yours."

I couldn't deny that. "All right. It's 555-1200."

"That's the store number."

"How did you know that?"

He pointed to the Emerald City sign behind me. It contained all of the store's contact information. "Because I'm literate."

"Wow. That puts you, like, ten steps above most of the guys that hit on me."

He turned hopeful. "So does that mean we can go out sometime?"

"Nope. I appreciate your help tonight, but I don't date."

"Don't think of it as a date then. Think of it as . . . a meeting of minds."

The way he looked at me suggested he wanted to meet more than just my mind. I shivered involuntarily, but I wasn't cold. In fact, I was starting to feel unnervingly warm.

He unbuttoned his coat. "Here. You're freezing. Wear this while I take you home. My car's around the corner."

"I live within walking distance." His coat was still warm from his body and smelled nice. A combination of cK One and, well, *man*. Yum.

"Then let me walk you home."

His persistence was charming, which was all the more reason I had to end things now. This was exactly the kind of quality guy I needed to avoid.

"Come on," Roman begged when I didn't answer. "This isn't much to ask for. I'm not a stalker or anything. All I want is one walk home. Then you never have to see me again."

"Look, you barely even know me . . ." I paused, reconsidering what he'd said. "Okay."

"Okay what?"

"Okay, you can walk me home."

"Really?" He brightened.

"Yup."

Three minutes later, when we arrived at my apartment building, he threw up his hands in dismay. "That wasn't fair at all. You're practically next door."

" 'One walk home.' That was all you asked for."

Roman shook his head. "Not fair. Not fair at all. But"—he looked up hopefully at my building—"at least I know where you live now."

"Hey! You said you weren't a stalker."

He grinned, gorgeous white teeth flashing against his tanned skin. "It's never too late to start." Leaning down, he kissed my hand and gave me a wink. "Until we meet again, fair Georgina."

He turned and walked off into the Queen Anne night. I watched him go, still feeling his lips on my skin. What an unexpected—and perplexing—twist to the evening.

When he was no longer in sight, I turned around and went into my building. I was halfway up the stairs when I realized I was still wearing his coat. How was I going to get it back to him? *He did that on purpose*, I realized. He let me keep it.

I suddenly knew then that I would be seeing wily Duke Roman again. Probably sooner, rather than later.

Chuckling, I continued on to my apartment, halting after just a few more steps.

"Not again," I muttered in exasperation.

Familiar sensations swirled behind my apartment door. Like a glittering tempest. Like the humming of bees in the air.

There was a group of immortals inside my home.

What the fuck? Did I need to start charging admission to my apartment? Why did everyone suddenly think they could just go right inside when I wasn't there?

It occurred to me then, ever so briefly, that I had *not* sensed Jerome and Carter's presence earlier. They had caught me completely unaware. That was weird, but I had been too distracted by their news to pay much attention to anything else.

Similarly, my current anger did not allow me to further ponder that odd piece of trivia now. I was too annoyed. Slinging my purse over one shoulder, I stormed into my home.

Chapter 5

"**F**or someone who just orchestrated a murder, you're kind of overreacting."

Overreacting? In the last twenty-four hours, I'd had to endure virgins, scary vampires, murder, accusation, and humiliation in front of my favorite author. I really didn't think coming home to a quiet apartment was too much to ask for. Instead, I found three interlopers. Three interlopers who were also my friends, mind you, but that didn't change the principle of the matter.

Naturally, none of them understood why I was so upset.

"You're invading my privacy! And I didn't murder anybody. Why does everyone keep thinking that?"

"Because you said yourself you were going to," explained Hugh. The imp sprawled on my love seat, his relaxed posture indicating I might actually be the one in his home. "I heard it from Jerome."

Across from him, our friend Cody offered me a friendly smile. He was exceptionally young for a vampire and reminded me of the kid brother I'd never had. "Don't worry. He had it coming. We stand by you all the way."

"But I didn't—"

"Is that our illustrious hostess I hear?" called Peter from the bathroom. A moment later, he appeared in the hallway. "You look pretty snazzy for a criminal mastermind."

"I'm not—" My words died on my lips as I caught sight of him. For a moment, all thoughts of murder and apartment intrusion blanked out of my mind. "For God's sake, Peter. What happened to your hair?"

He self-consciously ran a hand over the sharp, half-inch spikes covering his head. I couldn't even imagine how much styling product it must have taken to defy the laws of physics like that. Worse, the tips of the spikes were white-blond, standing out boldly against his normally dark hair color. "Someone I work with helped me with it."

"Someone who hates you?"

Peter scowled. "You are the most uncharming succubus I've ever met."

"I think the spikes really, um, emphasize the shape of your eyebrows," offered Cody diplomatically. "They just take . . . some getting used to."

I shook my head. I liked Peter and Cody. They were the only vampires I'd ever been friends with, but that didn't make them any less trying. Between Peter's assorted neuroses and Cody's dogged optimism, I sometimes felt like the straight man—er, woman—on a sitcom.

"A *lot* of getting used to," I muttered, pulling up a barstool from my kitchen.

"You're one to talk," returned Peter. "You and your wings and whip getup."

My mouth dropped, and I turned an incredulous look on Hugh. He hastily shut the Victoria's Secret catalog he'd been leafing through.

"Georgina—"

"You said you weren't going to tell! You sealed your lips and everything!"

"I, uh . . . it just sort of slipped out."

"Did you really have horns?" asked Peter.

"All right, that's it. I want you all out of here now." I pointed at the door. "I've been through enough today without you three adding to it."

"You haven't even told us about taking the contract out on Duane." Cody's puppy-dog eyes looked at me pleadingly. "We're dying to know."

"Well, Duane's the one who technically did the dying," pointed out Peter in an undertone.

"Watch the snide comments," warned Hugh. "You might be next."

I half expected steam to pour from my ears. "For the last time, I did not kill Duane! Jerome believes me, okay?"

Cody looked thoughtful. "But you did threaten him . . ."

"Yes. And from what I recall, so have all of you at some time or another. This is just a coincidence. I didn't have anything to do with it, and . . ." Something suddenly occurred to me. "Why does everyone keep saying things like 'arranged his death' or 'got someone to murder him'? Why aren't you saying that *I* did it myself?"

"Wait . . . you just said you didn't."

Peter rolled his eyes at Cody before facing me, the older vampire's expression turning serious. Of course, "serious" means all sorts of things when paired with a hairstyle like his. "No one's saying *you* did it because you couldn't have."

"Especially in those shoes." Hugh nodded toward my heels.

"I appreciate your complete lack of faith in my abilities, but isn't it possible I could have, I don't know, taken him by surprise? Hypothetically, I mean."

Peter smiled. "It wouldn't have mattered. Lesser immortals can't kill one another." Seeing my astonished look, he added, "How can you not know that? After living as long as you have?"

Teasing laced his words. There had always been an unspoken mystery between Peter and me concerning which of us was the oldest of the mortals-turned-immortals in our little circle. Neither of us would openly admit our age, so we'd never really determined who had the most centuries. One night, after a bottle of tequila, we'd started playing a "Do you remember when . . ." sort of game. We'd only gotten back as far as the Industrial Revolution before passing out.

"Because no one's ever tried to kill me. So what, are you saying all those turf wars vampires have are for nothing?"

"Well, not for nothing," he said. "We inflict some pretty terrific damage, believe me. But no, no one ever dies. With all the territory disputes, there'd be very few of us left if we could kill each other."

I stayed silent, turning this revelation over in my head. "Then how do—" I suddenly remembered what Jerome had told me. "They get killed by vampire hunters."

Peter nodded.

"What's the deal with them?" I asked. "Jerome wouldn't elaborate."

Hugh was equally interested. "You mean like that one girl on TV? The hot blonde?"

"This is going to be a long night." Peter gave us both scathing looks. "You all need some serious Vampires 101. I don't suppose you're going to offer us anything to drink, Georgina?"

I waved an impatient hand toward the kitchen. "Get whatever you want. I want to know about vampire hunters."

Peter sauntered out of my living room, yelping when he nearly tripped over one of the many stacks of books I had sitting around. I made a mental note to buy a new bookshelf. Scowling, he surveyed my nearly empty refrigerator with disapproval.

"You really need to work on your hosting skills."

"Peter—"

"Now, I keep hearing stories about that other succubus . . . the one in Missoula. What's her name again?"

"Donna," offered Hugh.

"Yeah, Donna. She throws great parties, I hear. Gets them catered. Invites everyone."

"If you guys want to party with all ten people in Montana, then you're welcome to move there. Now stop wasting time."

Ignoring me, Peter eyed the red carnations I'd bought the other night. I'd put them in a vase near the kitchen sink. "Who sent you flowers?"

"No one."

"You sent yourself flowers?" asked Cody, his voice quaking with sympathy.

"No, I just bought them. It's not the same. I didn't—look. Why are we talking about this when there's an alleged vampire killer on the loose? Are you two in danger?"

Peter finally opted for water but tossed beers to Hugh and Cody. "Nope."

"We aren't?" Cody seemed surprised to learn this. His scant years as a vampire practically made him a baby compared to the rest of us. Peter was teaching him "the trade," so to speak.

"Vampire hunters are simply special mortals born with the ability to inflict real damage to vampires. Mortals in general can't touch us, of course. Don't ask me how or why this all works; there's no system as far as I can tell. Most so-called vampire hunters go through life without even realizing they have this talent. The ones who do sometimes decide to make a career out of it. They pop up like this from time to time, picking off the occasional vampire, making a general nuisance of themselves until some enterprising vampire or demon takes them out."

"'Nuisance'?" asked Cody incredulously. "Even after Duane? Aren't you the least bit worried about this person coming after you? After us?"

"No," said Peter. "I am not."

I shared Cody's confusion. "Why not?"

"Because this person, whoever he or she is, is a total amateur." Peter glanced over at Hugh and me. "What did Jerome say about Duane's death?"

Deciding I needed a drink myself, I raided my kitchen liquor cabinet and made a vodka gimlet. "He wanted to know if I did it."

Peter made a dismissive gesture. "No, about how he died."

Hugh frowned, apparently trying to piece together the logic afoot. "He said that Duane had been found dead—with a stake through his heart."

"There. You see?"

Peter looked at us expectantly. We all looked back, baffled.

"I don't get it," I finally said.

Peter sighed, again looking utterly put out. "If you are a mortal who has the semidivine ability to kill a vampire, it doesn't fucking matter how you do it. You can use a gun, a knife, a candlestick, or whatever. The stake through the heart thing is hearsay. If a normal mortal does it to a vampire, it won't do a damned thing except really piss the vampire off. We only hear about it when a vampire hunter does it, so it carries some special superstitious lure, when really, it's only like that egg thing on the equinoxes."

"What?" Hugh looked totally lost.

I rubbed my eyes. "I actually know what he's talking about, as scary as that is to admit. There's this urban myth that eggs balance on their ends during the equinoxes. Sometimes it works, sometimes it doesn't, but the truth is, you'd get the same results any time of the year. People only try it on the equinoxes, however, so that's all anyone notices." I glanced over at Peter. "Your point is that a vampire hunter could kill a vampire in any number of ways, but because the stake gets all the attention, that's what has become the accepted method of . . . 'revocation of immortality.'"

"In people's minds," he corrected. "In reality, it's a pain in the ass to drive a stake through someone's heart. A lot easier to shoot them."

"And so you think this hunter is an amateur because . . ." Cody trailed off, obviously unconvinced by the compelling egg analogy.

"Because any vampire hunter worth his or her snuff knows that and wouldn't use a stake. This person's a total newbie."

"First," I advised Peter, "don't say 'worth his snuff.' That expression's out-of-style and makes you sound dated. Second, maybe this hunter was just trying to be old-school or something. And even if this person is a 'newbie,' does it really matter since they managed to take out Duane?"

Peter shrugged. "He was an arrogant asshole. Vampires can sense vampire hunters at close range. Combined with this one's inexperience, Duane should have never been taken. He was stupid."

I opened my mouth to counter this. I would be among the first to agree that Duane had indeed been both arrogant and an asshole, but stupid he was not. Immortals could not live as long as we did and see as many things as we did without gleaning substantial know-how and street smarts. We grew up quickly, so to speak.

Another question moved to the forefront of my reasoning. "Can these hunters hurt other immortals? Or just vampires?"

"Only vampires, as far as I know."

Something didn't add up here between Peter's comments and Jerome's. I couldn't quite put my finger on what was bothering me exactly, so I kept my misgivings to myself as the others chatted on. The vampire hunter topic soon became passé, once they'd decided—with some disappointment—I hadn't contracted anybody. Cody and Hugh also seemed content to buy Peter's theory that an amateur hunter posed no real threat.

"Be careful, you two," I warned the vampires when they were getting ready to leave. "Newbie or no, Duane is still dead."

"Yes, Mom," answered Peter disinterestedly, putting on his coat.

I gave Cody a sharp look, and he squirmed a bit. He was easier to manipulate than his mentor. "I'll be careful, Georgina."

"Call me if anything weird happens."

He nodded, earning an eye roll from Peter. "Come on," said the older vampire. "Let's get some dinner."

I had to smile at that. While vampires getting dinner might have frightened most people, I knew better. Peter and Cody both hated hunting human victims. They did it on occasion but rarely killed when they did. Most of their sustenance came from extra-rare butcher shop purchases. Like me, they were half-assing their infernal jobs.

"Hugh," I said sharply as he was about to follow the vampires out. "A word, please."

The vampires gave Hugh sympathetic looks before leaving. The imp grimaced, closing the door and facing me.

"Hugh, I gave you that key for emergencies—"

"Vampire murder doesn't constitute an emergency?"

"I'm serious! It's bad enough Jerome and Carter can teleport in here without you deciding to open up my home to God and the world."

"I don't think God was invited tonight."

"And then, you went and told them about the demon-girl outfit . . ."

"Oh come on," he protested. "That was too good to keep to myself. Besides, they're our friends. What's it matter?"

"It matters because you said you weren't going to tell," I growled. "What kind of friend are *you*? Especially after I helped you out last night?"

"Christ, Georgina. I'm sorry. I didn't know you'd take it so personally."

I ran a hand through my hair. "It's not just that. It's . . . I don't know. It's this whole business with Duane. I was thinking about what Jerome told me . . ."

Hugh waited, giving me time to gather my thoughts, sensing I was about to unleash something. My mind pondered the night's unfolding as I studied the imp's large shape beside me. He could be as silly as the vampires sometimes; I didn't know if I could speak seriously to him.

"Hugh . . . how do you know if a demon is lying?"

There was a pause, then he emitted a soft laugh, recognizing the old joke. "His lips are moving." We leaned against my counter, and he studied me from his greater height. "Why? Do you think Jerome's lying to us?"

"Yes, I do." Another pause followed.

"Tell me then."

"Jerome told me to be careful, said I could be mistaken for a vampire."

"He told me the same thing."

"But Peter said vampire hunters can't kill us."

"You ever had a stake driven through your heart? It might not kill you, but I bet you wouldn't like it."

"Fair enough. But Jerome claimed vampire hunters find other vampires by following their prey. That's bullshit. Cody and Peter are the exception. You know how most vampires are—they don't hang out with other vampires. Following one generally won't lead to another."

"Yeah, but he said this one was a newbie."

"Jerome didn't say that. That was Peter's theory based on the stake."

Hugh gave a conciliatory grunt. "Okay. So what do you think is going on?"

"I don't know. I just know these stories are contradicting each other. And Carter seemed awfully involved, like he was in on some secret with Jerome. Why should Carter even care? His side should technically approve of someone picking off our people."

"He's an angel. Isn't he supposed to love everyone, even the damned? Especially when said damned are his drinking buddies."

"I don't know. There's more here than we're being told . . . and Jerome seemed so adamant about me being careful. You too, apparently."

He stayed quiet a few moments before finally saying, "You're a pretty girl, Georgina."

I started. So much for serious talk. "Did you drink more than that beer?"

"I forget, though," he continued, ignoring my question, "that you're also a smart one. I work around shallow women so much—suburban housewives wanting smoother skin and bigger breasts—who have no other concerns but their appearances. It's easy to get caught up in the stereotypes and forget that you have a brain in there too, behind your beautiful face. You see things differently than the rest of us—more clearly, I guess. Sort of a bigger picture kind of thinking. Maybe it's your age—no offense."

"You did drink too much. Besides, I'm not smart enough to figure out what Jerome isn't telling us unless . . . there aren't really succubus or imp hunters out there, are there?"

"Have you ever heard of one?"

"No."

"Neither have I. But I have heard of vampire hunters—independent of pop culture." Hugh reached for his cigarettes and changed his mind, remembering I didn't like smoking in my apartment. "I don't think anyone's going to put a stake through us anytime soon, if that's what's bothering you."

"But you do agree we're being left out of the loop?"

"What else do you expect from Jerome?"

"I think . . . I think I'm going to go see Erik."

"Is he still alive?"

"Last I knew."

"That's a good idea. He knows more about us than we do."

"I'll let you know what I find out."

"Nah. I think I'd rather stay ignorant."

"Fine. Where are you off to now?"

"I've got to go put in some after-hours time with one of the new secretaries, if you catch my meaning." He grinned, dare I say, impishly. "Twenty years old, with breasts that defy gravity. I should know. I helped install them."

I couldn't help but laugh, despite the grim atmosphere. Hugh, like the rest of us, had a day job when not furthering the cause of evil and chaos. In his case, the line between occupations was a little thin: he was a plastic surgeon.

"I can't compete with that."

"Not true. Science can't duplicate your breasts."

"Praise from a true connoisseur. Have fun."

"I will. Watch your back, sweetie."

"You too."

He gave me a quick kiss on the forehead and left. I stood there, alone at last, staring idly at my door and wondering what all this meant. Jerome's warning probably had been overkill, I decided. As Hugh had said, no one had ever heard of imp or succubus hunters.

Still, I clicked my dead bolt and fastened the chain on my door before going to bed. Immortal I might be, but reckless I was not. Well, at least not when it counted.

Chapter 6

I woke up the next day, determined to go see Erik and get the truth about vampire hunters. Then, as I was brushing my teeth, I remembered yesterday's other crisis.

Seth Mortensen.

Swearing, I finished up in the bathroom, earning a disapproving look from Aubrey for my profanity. There was no telling how long this tour thing with him might take. I might have to wait until tomorrow to see Erik, and by then, this vampire hunter or whatever could have struck again.

I set out for Emerald City, wearing the most nonattractive outfit I could muster: jeans and a turtleneck, with my hair pulled severely back. Paige, all smiles, approached me as I waited for Seth in the café. "You should show him Foster's and Puget Sound Books while you're out," she told me conspiratorially.

Still waking up, I took a sip of the mocha Bruce had just made me and tried to reason out her logic. Foster's and Puget Sound Books were competitors of ours, though not major ones. "Those places are dives."

"Exactly." She grinned at me with her even white teeth. "Show him those, and he'll be convinced we're the best place for him to do his writing at."

I studied her, feeling seriously out of the loop. Or maybe I was just distracted still about the Duane thing. It wasn't every day one had his immortality revoked.

"Why . . . would he do his writing here?"

"Because he likes to take his laptop and write in coffee shops."

"Yeah, but he lives in Chicago."

Paige shook her head. "Not anymore. Where were you last night? He's moving here to be closer to his family."

I recalled Seth mentioning his brother, but I had been too caught up in my own mortification to pay much attention. "When?"

"Now, as far as I know. That's why this was his last stop on the tour. He's staying with his brother but plans on finding his own place soon." She leaned close to me, eyes gleaming predatorily. "Georgina, if we have a famous author hanging out here regularly, it'll be good for our image."

Honestly, my immediate concern wasn't where Seth would be writing. What freaked me out was that he would not be departing for a different time zone anytime soon, a time zone where he could then forget about me and let us both get on with our lives. I could run into him every day now. Literally, if Paige's wish was realized.

"Won't that be distracting to his writing if his presence is widely known? Annoying fans and whatnot?"

"We won't let it become a problem. We'll make the most of this and respect his privacy. Careful now, here he comes."

I drank more of my mocha, still marveling at the way Paige's mind worked. She could think of promotional ideas that never would have entered my head. Warren might have been the one to invest capital in this place, but it had been her marketing genius that made it a success.

"Good morning," Seth told us, walking up to the table. He wore jeans, a Def Leppard T-shirt, and a brown corduroy jacket. The lay of his hair did not convince me he'd brushed it this morning.

Paige looked at me pointedly, and I sighed. "Let's go."

Seth silently followed me outside, that awkward tension building between us like a solid barrier. He did not look at me; I did not look at him. It was only when we stood outside on Queen Anne Avenue and I realized I had no plan for today that conversation had to occur.

"Where to start? Seattle, unlike Gaul, is not divided into just three parts."

I made the joke more to myself, but Seth suddenly laughed. *"Seattle peninsula est,"* he observed, playing off my observation.

"Not exactly. Besides, that's Bede, not Caesar."

"I know. But I don't know very much Latin." He gave me that quirky, bemused smile that seemed to be his trademark expression. "Do you?"

"Enough." I wondered how he would react if I mentioned my fluency in Latin dialects from various stages of the Roman Empire. My vague answer must have been interpreted as lack of interest because he looked away, and more silence fell. "Is there anything special you wanted to see?"

"Not really."

Not really. Okay. Well. The sooner we got this started, the sooner it would end and I could see Erik.

"Follow me."

As we drove off, I sort of hoped we might naturally flow into meaningful conversation, in spite of our bad start yesterday. Yet, as we traveled, it seemed clear Seth had no intention of carrying on any discourse. I recalled his nervousness in front of the crowd yesterday and even with some of the bookstore staff. This guy had serious social phobias, I realized, though he had made a valiant effort in shedding them during our initial flirtations. Then, I had gone and turned on the *back-off* vibes, undoubtedly scarring him for life and undoing whatever progress he had made. Way to go, Georgina.

Maybe if I could broach some compelling topics, he would muster his earlier confidence and bring back our rapport—in a platonic way, of course. I attempted to recall my profound questions from last night. And once again, they eluded me, so I switched to mundane ones.

"So your brother lives around here?"

"Yup."

"What part?"

"Lake Forest Park."

"That's a nice area. Are you going to look for a place up there?"

"Probably not."

"Do you have another place in mind then?"

"Not really."

Okay, this wasn't getting us anywhere. Annoyed at how this master of the written word could be so short on spoken ones, I finally decided to cut him out of the conversation altogether. Having him involved was too much work. Instead, I chatted on amiably without him, pointing out the popular spots: Pioneer Square, Pike Place Market, the Fremont Troll. I even showed him the shoddier representatives of our competition, per Paige's instructions. I neglected anything closer to the Space Needle than a brief nod, however. No doubt he'd seen it from Emerald City's windows and could pay the exorbitant fees to visit it up close if he really needed the tourist experience.

We went to the U District for lunch. He followed without protest or comment to my favorite Vietnamese restaurant. Our meal progressed quietly as I took a break from talking, both of us eating noodles and staring out the nearby window to watch the bustle of students and cars.

"This is nice."

It was the most Seth had spoken in a while, and I nearly jumped at the sound of his voice.

"Yeah. This place doesn't look like much, but they make a mean pho."

"No, I meant out there. This area."

I followed his gesture back to University Way, at first seeing nothing more than disgruntled students hauling backpacks around. Then, expanding my search, I became aware of the other small specialty restaurants, the coffee shops, and the used bookstores. It was an eclectic mix, somewhat tattered around the edges, but it had a lot to offer quirky, intellectual types—even famous, introverted writers.

I looked at Seth, who looked back at me expectantly. It was our first direct eye contact all day.

"Are there places to live around here?"

"Sure. If you want to share a house with a bunch of eighteen-year-olds." I paused, thinking that option might not be so unappealing for a guy. "If you want something more substantial in this area, it'll cost you. I guess Cady and O'Neill ensure that's not really an issue, huh? We can drive around and look, if you want."

"Maybe. I'd honestly rather go there first." He pointed across the street, to one of the used bookstores. His eyes flicked back to me uncertainly. "If that's okay with you."

"Let's go."

I loved used bookstores but always felt a little guilty walking into them. Like I was cheating. After all, I worked around bright, crisp books all the time. I could obtain a reprint of almost anything I wanted, brand new. It seemed wrong to take such visceral pleasure from being around old books, from the smell of aged paper, mildew, and dust. Such collections of knowledge, some quite old, always reminded me of times long past and places I'd seen, triggering a tidal wave of nostalgia. These emotions made me feel both old and young. The books aged while I did not.

A gray tabby cat stretched and blinked at us from her spot on the counter as we entered. I stroked her back and said hello to the old man near her. He glanced up briefly from the books he sorted, smiled at us, and returned to his work. Seth stared around at the towering shelves before us, an expression of bliss on his face, and promptly disappeared into them.

I wandered over to nonfiction, wanting to peruse the cookbooks. I had grown up preparing food without microwaves and food processors and decided it was high time to let my culinary knowledge expand into this century.

Finally settling on a Greek cookbook with lots of colored pictures, I dragged myself away a half hour later and looked for Seth. I found him in the children's section, kneeling next to a stack of books, completely absorbed.

I crouched down beside him. "What are you looking at?"

He flinched slightly, startled by my proximity, and tore his gaze away from his find to look at me. This close, I could see that his eyes were actually more of a golden-amber brown, his lashes long enough to make any girl jealous.

"Andrew Lang's fairy books." He held a paperback entitled *The Blue Fairy Book*. On top of the stack near him sat another called *The Orange Fairy Book*, and I could only assume the rest followed color-coded suit. Seth glowed with literary rapture, forgetting his reticence around me. "The 1960s reprints. Not as valuable as, say, editions from the 1800s, but these are the ones my dad had, the ones he used to read to us from. He only had a couple, though; this is the whole set. I'm going to get them and read them to my nieces."

Flipping through the pages of *The Red Fairy Book*, I recognized the titles of many familiar stories, some I hadn't even known were still around. I turned the book over and looked inside the cover but found no price. "How much are they?"

Seth pointed to a small sign near the shelf he'd obtained them from.

"Is that reasonable for these?" I asked.

"It's a little high, but it's worth it to me to get them all in one go."

"No way." I gathered up part of the books, rising. "We'll talk him down."

"Talk him down how?"

My lips turned up in a smile. "With words."

Seth seemed dubious, but the clerk proved an easy target. Most men would eventually cave before an attractive, charismatic woman—let alone a succubus who still sported a residual life force glow. Besides, I had learned bartering at my mother's knee. The guy behind the counter didn't stand a chance. By the time I finished with him, he had happily lowered the price by 25 percent and thrown in my cookbook for free.

Walking back to my car, arms laden with books, Seth kept glancing at me wonderingly. "How did you do that? I've never seen anything like it."

"Lots of practice." A vague answer worthy of one of his.

"Thanks. I wish I could repay the favor."

"Don't worry—hey, you can actually. Would you mind running an errand with me? It's to a bookstore, but it's a scary bookstore."

"Scary how?"

Five minutes later, we were on our way to see my old friend Erik Lancaster. Erik had been ensconced in the Seattle area long before me, and he was a well-known figure to almost every immortal entity around. Versed in mythology and supernatural lore, he regularly proved to be an excellent resource for all things paranormal. If he had noticed that some of his best patrons never aged, he wisely refrained from pointing that out.

The only annoying thing about seeing Erik was that it required a visit to Krystal Starz—a stunning example of New Age spirituality gone wrong. I didn't doubt the place might have had good intentions back when it opened in the 1980s, but the bookstore now touted a barrage of colorful, highly commercial merchandise more weighted in price than any sort of mystical value. Erik, by my estimation, was the only employee with legitimate concern and knowledge of esoteric matters. The best of his coworkers were simply apathetic; the worst were zealots and scam artists.

Pulling up into the store's parking lot, I immediately felt surprise at the number of cars there. This many people at Emerald City would have constituted a signing, but that sort of event seemed odd in the middle of the workday.

A heavy wave of incense poured over us as we entered, and Seth appeared just as surprised as me by all the people and stimuli. "I might be a minute," I told him. "Feel free to look around. Not that there's much here worth seeing."

He melted away, and I turned my attention to a bright-eyed young man standing near the door and directing the crowd around. "Are you here for the Gathering?"

"Um, no," I told him. "I'm looking for Erik."

"Erik who?"

"Lancaster? Older guy? African-American? He works here."

The young lackey shook his head. "There's no Erik here. Not as long as I've been working here." He spoke like he'd founded the store.

"How long has that been?"

"Two months."

I rolled my eyes. A veritable veteran. "Is there a manager around here I can talk to?"

"Well, Helena's here, but she's going to be—ah, there she

is." He gestured to the far side of the store where the woman in question appeared as though summoned.

Ah yes, Helena. She and I had tangled before. Pale-haired, her neck bestrewn with crystals and other arcane symbols, she stood in a doorway marked MEETING ROOM. A teal shawl covered her slim shoulders, and like always, I wondered how old she was. She looked to be in her lower to mid-thirties, but something about her demeanor always made me think she was older. Maybe she'd had a lot of plastic surgery. It would be fitting, really, considering the rest of her trumped-up, artificial persona.

"Everyone? Everyone?" She spoke in this obviously faked, high-pitched voice, meant to sound like a whisper, albeit one that could reach loud volumes. So mostly it came out raspy, like she had a cold. "It's time to start."

The masses—thirty or so, I'd say—moved toward the meeting room, and I followed, blending into the crowd. Some of the people around me looked like Helena: theme-dressed, in either all-black or too-vibrant shades, with a plethora of pentagrams, crystals, and ohms in attendance. Others looked like average people, dressed much like me in my work clothes, trailing along in excited curiosity.

With a frozen, fake smile plastered across her face, Helena beckoned us into the room murmuring, "Welcome, welcome. Feel the energy." When I passed by her, the smile faltered. "I know you."

"Yes."

The smile diminished further. "You're that woman who works at that big bookstore—that big, commercial bookstore." A few people stopped and listened to our exchange, no doubt the reason she refrained from pointing out the last time I was in here, I had called her a hypocrite pushing marked-up crap merchandise.

Compared to certain national chains, I hardly considered

Emerald City commercial. Still, I shrugged in acknowledgment. "Yeah, what can I say, we're part of the problem in corporate America. However, we do sell all the books and tarot cards that you do, often at a discount if you're a member of Emerald City's Frequent Readers Program." I mentioned this last part loudly. Extra advertising never hurt.

Helena's weakening smile disappeared altogether, as did some of her raspy voice. "Is there something I can help you with?"

"I'm looking for Erik."

"Erik doesn't work here anymore."

"Where'd he go?"

"I'm not at liberty to discuss that."

"Why? Are you afraid I'll take my business elsewhere? Believe me, you were never in danger of having it."

She raised delicate fingers to her forehead and studied me seriously, eyes nearly going crossed. "I sense a lot of darkness in your aura. Black and red." Her voice rose, drawing in the attention of her acolytes. "You would benefit greatly from some clearing work. A smoky or rutilated quartz might also help. We have excellent specimens of both for sale here. Either would lighten up your aura."

I couldn't resist a smirk. I believed in auras, knew they were perfectly real. I also knew, however, that my aura looked nothing at all like a mortal one, nor would someone like Helena even be able to see it. Indeed, a true human adept, capable of perceiving such things, would notice that in standing with a group of humans, I would be the only person without a discernible aura. It would be invisible to all, save someone like Jerome or Carter, though some particularly skilled mortal might be able to feel its strength and be understandably cautious. Erik was one such mortal, which was why he always treated me with so much respect. Helena was not.

"Wow," I crooned. "I can't believe you were able to deduce all that without your aura camera." Krystal Starz proudly touted a camera that would photograph your aura for $9.95. "Do I owe you something now?"

She sniffed. "I don't need a camera to see others' auras. I am a Master. Besides, the spirits who have assembled for this Gathering tell me plenty about you."

My smile increased. "What do they say?" I'd had little dealings with spirits or other ethereal beings in my long life, but I would know if any were present.

She closed her eyes, hands to her forehead again, lines of thought creasing her face. The onlookers watched in wonder.

"They tell me that much troubles you. That the indecision and monotony in your life force you to lash out, and so long as you choose the path of darkness and distrust, you will never find peace or light." Her blue eyes opened, caught up in her own otherworldly ecstasy. "They want you to join us. Sit in our circle, feel their healing energy. The spirits will help you to a better life."

"Like they helped you out of the porn industry?"

She froze, paling, and I almost felt bad for a moment. Adepts like Erik weren't the only ones with reputations in the immortal community. A crackpot like Helena was well known too. Someone who had apparently been a fan of hers back in the day had recognized her from a movie and passed on this bit of dirt to the rest of us.

"I don't know what you mean," she finally said, face struggling for control in front of her minions.

"My mistake. You reminded me of someone called Moana Licka. You sort of rub crystals the way she used to rub . . . well, you get the idea."

"You are mistaken," Helena said, voice on the verge of cracking. "Erik no longer works here. Please leave."

Another retort rose to my lips, but then, beyond her, I caught sight of Seth. He had wandered up to the edge of the crowd, observing the spectacle with the others. Seeing him, I suddenly felt foolish, the thrill of humiliating Helena turning cheap and shallow. Embarrassed, I still managed to hold my head high as I withheld my remarks and walked away from her. Seth fell into step beside me.

"Let me guess," I said dryly. "Some people write the stories, and some people live them."

"I think you can't help but make a sensation wherever you go."

I assumed he was being sarcastic. Then, I glanced over and saw his frank expression, neither censuring nor snide. His earnestness was so unexpected that I stumbled slightly, paying more attention to him than where I was going. Having a much-deserved reputation for gracefulness, I recovered almost immediately. Seth, however, instinctually held out a hand to catch me.

As he did, I suddenly had a flash of . . . of something. Like that moment of connection back in the map aisle. Or the surge of fulfillment I got when I read his books. It was brief, fleeting, like maybe it hadn't happened at all. He seemed as surprised as I felt and released my arm tentatively, almost hesitantly. A moment later, a voice behind me broke the spell entirely.

"Excuse me?" Turning, I saw a slim teenage girl with cropped red hair and piercings up and down her ears. "You were looking for Erik, right?"

"Yeah . . ."

"I can tell you where he's at. He left about five months ago to start his own store. It's in Lake City . . . I forget the name. There's a light there, with a grocery store and a big Mexican restaurant . . ."

I nodded. "I know that area. I'll find it. Thanks." I eyed her curiously. "Do you work here?"

"Yeah. Erik was always pretty cool to me, so I'd rather see him get business than this place. I'd have gone with him, but he doesn't really need any other help, so I'm stuck with Nutso in there." She jerked her thumb back in Helena's direction.

The girl had a serious, practical demeanor different from most of this place's employees. I recalled now that I'd seen her helping customers when I'd come in. "Why do you work here if you don't like it?"

"I don't know. I like books, and I need money."

I dug through my purse, searching for one of my rarely used business cards. "Here. You want a new job, come talk to me sometime."

She took the card and read it, surprise filling her features. "Thanks . . . I think."

"Thanks for the info about Erik."

Pausing, I considered further, and dug out another card. "If you've got a friend—anyone else who works here and is like you—give this to them too."

"Is that legal?" asked Seth later.

"Dunno. But we're short-staffed at Emerald City."

I figured a specialty store like Erik's must be closed by now, so instead I turned toward Lake Forest Park to return Seth to his brother's house. I confess, relief flooded me. Being with one's hero was tiring, not to mention every interaction between us swung between wildly opposing poles. I'd probably be safer limiting our relationship to me simply reading his books.

I dropped him off at a cute, suburban home, its front yard littered with children's playthings. I saw no sign of the children themselves, much to my disappointment. Seth gathered up his haul of books, gave me another scattered smile as he voiced his thanks, and disappeared into the house. I was almost back to Queen Anne when I realized I'd forgotten to ask him for my copy of *The Glasgow Pact*.

Annoyed, I entered my building and immediately heard the front desk attendant solicit me. "Miss Kincaid?"

I walked over to him, and he handed me a vase of flowers teeming with shades of purple and dark pink. "These came for you today."

I accepted the vase with delight, inhaling the mingled scents of roses, irises, and stargazer lilies. They had no card. Typical. "Who brought them?"

He gestured beyond me. "That man over there."

Chapter 7

I turned and saw Roman sitting over in a corner of the small lobby. He looked striking in a deep green turtleneck, his dark hair brushed away from his face. He smiled at me when I caught his eye, and I walked over to sit near him.

"Jesus, you really are a stalker."

"Well, well. Aren't you presumptuous. I only came for my coat."

"Ah." I blushed, feeling foolish. "How long have you been waiting?"

"Not too long. I actually tried the bookstore first, thinking that might be a little less stalker-ish."

"It's my day off." I looked down at the riotously colored blossoms in my arms. "Thanks for the flowers. You didn't need to bring them to get your coat back."

Roman shrugged, those blue-green eyes wreaking havoc with me. "True, but I figured they might induce you to go out for a drink tonight."

So he did have another motive. "Not this again—"

"Hey, if you'd wanted to avoid 'this,' you shouldn't have lured me in last night. Now it's too late. You might as well avoid the long, drawn-out pain and get it over with quickly. Sort of like taking off a Band-Aid. Or cutting off a limb."

"Wow. Who says there's no romance left in the world?" In spite of my sarcasm, I found Roman's easy repartee a refreshing change from the halting atmosphere with Seth.

"So, what? Does that mean you finally concede, general? Truly, you've fought a worthy battle in eluding me thus far."

"I don't know. You showed up at my home. I apparently didn't do that much eluding." When he only waited expectantly, my smile faded. I sighed, studying him and trying to figure out his motivations. "Roman, you seem like a nice guy and everything—"

He groaned. "No. Don't start that with me. It's never a good sign when a woman says 'you're a nice guy.' It means she's getting ready to let you down easy."

I shook my head. "I'm just not interested in getting serious with anyone right now, that's all."

"Whoa, 'get serious'? Slow down there, sister. I'm not asking you to marry me or anything. I just want to go out with you sometime, maybe catch a movie, have dinner and drinks, that's it. Kiss at the end of the night if I'm lucky. Hell, if that still freaks you out, we'll just shake hands."

I leaned my head back against the wall, and we stayed like that a moment, each of us sizing up the other. I knew it was perfectly possible for men and women to go out on dates without automatic sex, but my dates generally didn't work that way. My instincts drove me to seek sex out, and looking at him, I realized that urge might be strong independent of any sort of succubus need to feed. I liked the way he looked, the way he dressed, and the way he smelled. I especially liked his goofy attempt at courtship. Unfortunately, I couldn't turn off the destructive succubus absorption, even if I wanted to. It would happen of its own volition, probably strongly with him. Even the kiss he joked about would still steal some of his life away.

"I don't know anything about you," I said finally, realizing I'd been quiet too long.

He smiled lazily. "What do you want to know?"

"Well . . . I don't know. What do you like to do? Do you even have a job? You must have lax hours to be able to hang around me all the time."

"All the time, huh? You're being presumptuous again, but yes, I do work. I teach a couple of community college linguistics classes. Short of when I'm there, I get to make my own hours with grading and stuff."

"Okay. What's your last name?"

"Smith."

"No way."

"Way."

"That hardly goes with Duke Roman." I tried to think of another appropriate screening item. "How long have you lived in Seattle?"

"A few years."

"Hobbies?"

"I've got some." He paused and cocked his head toward me when no more questions came. "Anything else you want to know? Should I dig out my college transcripts perhaps? A full curriculum vitae and background check?"

I waved a hand of dismissal. "I have no use for inconsequential information like that. I only need to know the really important stuff."

"Like?"

"Like . . . what's your favorite song?"

The question obviously caught him by surprise, but he recovered immediately, just as he had last night. I loved that. "The last half of the Beatles' *Abbey Road*."

"The last half of *Abbey Road*?"

"Yeah, there are a bunch of songs, but they sort of blend into one song—"

I cut him off with a quick gesture. "Yeah, yeah, I know the album."

"So?"

"So, that's a pretty good answer." I tugged at my ponytail, wondering how best to navigate this. He nearly had me. "I—no. I'm sorry. I can't. It's just too complicated. Even the one date. It'll turn into a second date, then another, then—"

"You really do jump ahead. What if I gave the super-secret Boy Scout promise to never bother you again after one date?"

"You'd agree to that?" I asked skeptically.

"Sure, if that's what you want. But I don't think you will once you've spent an evening with me."

A suggestive tone in his voice did something to my stomach I hadn't felt in a very long time. Before I could fully process this, my cell phone rang.

"Sorry," I apologized, digging it out of my purse. Glancing at the Caller ID display, I recognized Cody's number. "Yeah?"

"Hey, Georgina. Something weird happened tonight . . ."

Lord. That could mean anything from another death to Peter shaving his head. "Hang on a second."

I stood up and looked at Roman, juggling the vase of flowers as I did. He rose with me, looking concerned. "Is everything okay?"

"Yeah, I mean, no. I mean, I don't know. Look Roman, I need to go upstairs and take this call. I appreciate the flowers, but I just can't get involved right now. I'm sorry. It's not you, it's me. Honestly."

He took a few steps toward me as I started to walk away. "Wait." He dug in his pockets, pulled out a pen and piece of paper. Hastily he scrawled something and handed it to me. I looked down and saw a phone number.

"For when you change your mind."

"I won't."

He simply smiled, inclined his head slightly, and left the lobby. I watched him only a moment before heading upstairs, anxious to hear Cody's news. Once inside, I set the flowers on my counter and put the phone back to my ear.

"Still there?"

"Yeah. Who's Roman and why'd you use the old 'it's not you, it's me' line on him?"

"Never mind. What's going on? Is someone else dead?"

"No . . . no. It's just, something happened, and Peter doesn't think it's a big deal. Hugh said you thought there might be more going on than we think."

"Tell me what happened."

"I think we were followed last night."

Cody related how, not long after leaving my place, he'd kept hearing footsteps following him and Peter on the street. Whenever he'd turned around, no one was there. Peter had written the matter off, as they had sensed no other being present.

"Maybe you don't know what a vampire hunter feels like."

"I'd still have felt something. And Peter certainly would have. Maybe he's right, and I was imagining things. Or maybe it was just a regular mortal, wanting to mug us or something."

I doubted that. We couldn't sense mortals the same way we could sense immortals, but one would be hard-pressed to sneak up on a vampire.

"Thanks for telling me. You did the right thing."

"What should I do now?"

A strange, anxious feeling played through me as I thought about some freak stalking Peter and Cody. Dysfunctional they might have been, but I loved them. They were the closest I had to family anymore. I couldn't let anything happen to them.

"What Jerome said. Be careful. Stay with others. Let me know immediately if anything happens."

"What about you?"

I thought of Erik. "I'm going to clear things up, once and for all."

Chapter 8

Paige was all smiles when I went in for the early shift the next day.

"Nice work with Seth Mortensen," she told me, glancing up from the neatly stacked paperwork on her desk. The desk Doug and I shared in the store's back offices tended to look like an apocalyptic war zone.

"How so?"

"In convincing him to write here."

I blinked. With our assorted U District and Krystal Starz adventures, I'd never said a word about him becoming our resident writer. "Oh?"

"I saw him upstairs in the café just now. He said he had a great time yesterday."

I left her office, baffled, wondering if I'd missed something from yesterday. It hadn't seemed like that stellar of an outing, but I supposed he felt pleased and grateful over the discounted books. Had anything else notable happened?

Unbidden, the memory of touching Seth's hand suddenly

ushed back to me, the odd shockwave of familiarity it had ent through me. No, I decided, that had been nothing. I had magined the moment.

I went up to the café for a mocha, still puzzled. Sure nough, Seth sat in a corner, laptop spread out on the table in ront of him. He looked much the same as yesterday, save hat his shirt today sported Beeker from the Muppets. His ingers moved furiously along the keys, his eyes locked on he screen.

"Hey," I told him.

"Hey."

He offered no more. He didn't even look up.

"Are you working?"

"Yes."

I waited for elaboration, but it never came. So I kept oing.

"So, um, Paige told me you're moving here."

He didn't answer. I didn't even know if he'd heard me. uddenly, he looked up, his eyes sharpening. "Ever been to exas?"

That took me by surprise. "Sure. Which part?"

"Austin. I need to know what the weather's like there."

"When? This time of year?"

"No . . . more like spring or early summer."

I racked my brain. "Hot. Rain and storms. Some humidty. The edge of tornado alley, you know?"

"Ah." Seth turned thoughtful, then nodded smartly and eturned his attention back down. "Cady'll love that. Thanks."

It took me a moment to realize he meant one of his charcters. Nina Cady's dislike of inclement weather was notorius. My stomach suddenly dropped out of me and hit the loor. It was a wonder he didn't hear the *thud*.

"Are you . . . are you . . . writing something with Cady nd O'Neill? Right now?"

"Yeah." He spoke very casually, like we were still discussing weather. "Next book. Well, next-next book. The *next* one's already queued up for publishing. I'm about a quarter through this one."

I stared in awe at the laptop, like it was a divine golden idol from days of old, capable of performing miracles. Providing rain. Feeding the masses. Now I felt speechless. That the next masterpiece was being created right in front of me, that I might say something that could influence it was too much to bear. I swallowed heavily and dragged my eyes away from it, forcing calm. After all, I could hardly be excited about another installment when I had yet to read the current one.

"A Cady and O'Neill book. Wow. That's really—"

"Um, so, I'm kind of busy here. I've got to run with this right now. Sorry."

The words stopped me cold. "What?" Was I being dismissed?

"Can we talk later?"

I *was* being dismissed. I was being dismissed without even being looked at. Heat flushed my cheeks.

"What about my book?" I blurted out ungracefully.

"Huh?"

"*The Glasgow Pact*. Did you sign it?"

"Oh. That."

"What's that mean?"

"I'll send you an e-mail."

"You'll send me—so you don't have my book?"

Seth shook his head and kept working.

"Oh. Okay." I didn't understand the e-mail bit but wasn't going to waste my time begging for his attention. "Well. I'll see you later then. Let us know if you need anything." My voice was stiff and cold, but I doubted he even noticed.

I tried not to storm downstairs. Where did he get off acting like that? Especially after I'd shown him around yesterday. Famous author or no, he didn't have the right to be a jerk to me. I felt humiliated.

Humiliated over what, being ignored? chided a reasonable voice inside me. *It's not like he made a scene. He was just busy. After all, you were the one complaining he didn't write fast enough.*

I ignored the voice and went back to work, still feeling put-out. Business didn't allow me to nurture my wounded ego for long, however, as the afternoon and lack of staff ensured I stayed busy on the floor. The next time I managed to return to my office, it was only to grab my purse at the end of my shift.

As I was about to walk out, I saw a message from Seth in my e-mail's inbox. I moved to the computer and read.

Georgina,

Have you ever paid much attention to real estate agents—the way they dress, the kinds of cars they drive? Truth is stranger than fiction, as they say. Last night, I expressed interest in living in the University District to my brother, and he called up this real estate agent friend of his. She arrived in something like two minutes flat, no small feat I guess, since her office is in West Seattle. She pulled up in a Jaguar, whose shiny whiteness was rivaled only by the day-glow white of her Miss America smile. While gushing nonstop about how exciting it was to have me here, she hacked away at a computer, searching for appropriate residences, typing with nails long enough to impale small children on. (See? I remembered how much you liked the word "impale.")

Each time she found a place that might work, she'd get really excited: "Yes—yes. Oh yes! This is it! This is it! Yes! Yes!" I confess, by the time it was through, I felt kind of sleazy and exhausted, like maybe I should have tossed some cash on the pillow or something. Her theatrics aside, we did end up finding a nice condo not too far from campus, brand new. It was as pricey as you insinuated, but I think it's exactly what I want. Mistee—yes, that's her name—and I are going to look at it later tonight. I'm kind of afraid to see her reaction if I bid on the place. No doubt the thought of the commission will lead straight to multiple orgasms. (And to think, I always thought missionary position was what inhibited women from true fulfillment.)

Anyway, I just wanted to give you the update since you were the one who first showed me the U District. I'm sorry I didn't get a chance to talk earlier; I would have liked to pick your brain about restaurants over there. I still don't know the area that well, and my brother and sister-in-law are too busy with their suburban life to recommend any restaurants that don't serve children's meals.

Well, I guess I should get back to writing, so I can afford said new lodging. Cady and O'Neill are impatient mistresses—er, that is, an impatient mistress and master—as you observed earlier. Speaking of which, I haven't forgotten about your copy of *The Glasgow Pact*. I intended to write something semi-original in it last night, after our nice day together, but the real estate vortex caught me up. My apologies. I'll bring it to you soon.

Later,
Seth

I reread the letter twice. I felt pretty confident that in the short span I'd known Seth, I'd never heard him utter aloud as

many words as he'd just written. Not only that, they were
funny words. Entertaining words. Like a mini Cady and
O'Neill novel, addressed just to me. A far cry from his halting attitude this morning. If he'd said anything remotely
comparable in person, I probably would have passed out.

"Incredible," I muttered to my screen.

Part of me felt mollified by the letter, though another part
felt he still could have been a bit more tactful in his earlier
treatment, busy or no. The rest of me pointed out that all of
these "parts of me" probably should be in therapy, and besides, I really needed to leave and go see Erik about the vampire hunter thing. I quickly sent back a response:

> Thanks for the letter. I suppose I'll make it another
> day without the book. Good luck with the real estate
> agent, and be sure to wear a condom when you make
> an offer. Other good places to eat in that area are Han
> & Sons, the Plum Tomato Café, and Lotus Chinese.
> —Georgina

I left the store, promptly forgetting about Seth, happy
there'd be no traffic this early in the day. Driving up to Lake
City, I easily found the intersection the girl at Krystal Starz
had indicated. Locating the store itself proved more of a
challenge. Strip malls and assorted businesses packed the
area, and I read through myriad billboards and storefronts in
the hopes of finding something promising. Finally, I spotted
a small, dark sign tucked away in the corner of a less-
frequented cluster of stores. ARCANA, LTD. That had to be it.

I parked in front, hoping it was actually open. No one had
posted hours or anything on the door, but it gave way without resistance when I pushed on it. Sandalwood incense
burned in the air around me as I entered, and faint harp
music played from a small CD player set up on the counter. I

couldn't see anyone else in the room, and so I wandered around, admiring the sights. Real books on mythology and religion—not the flashy fluff Krystal Starz sold—lined the walls, and carefully arranged display cases held handcrafted jewelry I recognized from a few different local artists. Assorted ritual items—candles, incense, and statuary—filled in the nooks and crannies, giving the whole place a sort of jumbled, pleasantly lived-in feel.

"Miss Kincaid. It is an honor to see you again."

I spun around from where I had been admiring a White Tara statue. Erik walked into the room, and I reined in my surprise at his appearance. When had he grown so old? He had been old the last time I saw him—dark skin wrinkled, hair gone gray—but I did not remember the slight stoop in his walk, or the hollowed look around his eyes. I tried to remember the last time we'd talked; I hadn't thought it'd been that long. Five years? Ten? With mortals, it was easy to lose track.

"It's good to see you too. You aren't easy to find anymore. I had to go poking around Krystal Starz to figure out what happened to you."

"Ah. I hope the experience wasn't too . . . awkward."

"Nothing I couldn't handle. Besides, I'm glad you got out of there." I looked around at the cluttered, dimly lit shop. "I like this new place."

"It's not much—doesn't bring in much either—but it's mine. It's what I've been saving for, where I'll spend my last years."

I grimaced. "Don't turn melodramatic on me now. You aren't that old."

His smile broadened, his expression turning slightly wry. "Neither are you, Miss Kincaid. Indeed, you are as beautiful as the first time I saw you." He gave me a slight bow, bending lower than someone with his back probably should have. "How may I be of service?"

"I need information."

"Of course." He gestured to a small table near the main counter, currently covered with books and an elaborate candle holder. "Sit and have tea with me, and we'll talk. Unless you are in a hurry?"

"No, I have time."

While Erik fetched the tea, I cleared off the table, setting books in neat stacks on the floor. When he returned with the teapot, we made small talk and sipped our drinks for a bit, but my mind really wasn't into it. My restlessness must have come through loud and clear as my fingers danced along the cup's edge and my toe tapped impatiently.

Finally, I broached my topic. "I need to know about vampire hunters."

For most other people, this would have been a weird request, but Erik only nodded expectantly. "What in particular would you like to know?"

"Anything. Their habits, how to recognize them. Whatever you've got."

He leaned back in his chair, holding the cup delicately. "My understanding is that vampire hunters are born, not made. They are 'gifted,' so to speak, with the ability to kill vampires." He proceeded to relate several other details, most of which matched up with what I'd learned from Peter.

Pondering what Cody had said, about the sense of being followed by someone he could not see, I asked, "Do they have any other special abilities that you know of? Can they go invisible?"

"Not that I know of. Some immortal beings can, of course, but not vampire hunters. They're still just mortals, after all, despite their odd talents."

I nodded, being one such creature who could turn invisible, though I rarely used the power. I toyed with the thought that Cody's phantom might have been an invisible immortal, trying to play a trick, but he still should have sensed the tell-tale signature we all carried. Indeed, he should have sensed a mortal vampire hunter as well. The fact that he had neither seen nor felt anything lent credence to Peter's theory that the stalker had all been in Cody's head.

"Can vampire hunters harm anyone else? Demons . . . or other immortal creatures?"

"It's very hard to do anything tangible to an immortal," he mused. "Certain denizens of good—powerful priests, for example—can drive off demons, but they can't harm them permanently. Likewise, I've heard of mortals capturing supernatural creatures, but doing much more than that . . . I'm not saying it's impossible, just that I've never heard of it. To my offhand knowledge, vampire hunters can only harm vampires. Nothing else."

"I value your offhand knowledge more than most confirmed facts."

He eyed me curiously. "But this isn't the answer you were expecting."

"I don't know. It's pretty much what I've already been told. I was just thinking there might be more."

It was entirely possible that Jerome had been telling the truth, that this was merely a case of a rampant vampire hunter and that his warnings to Hugh and me had been simple courtesies to protect us from discomfort. Still, I couldn't shake the feeling that Jerome had held back information, nor did I really believe Cody to be the kind of person who imagined things.

I must have looked perplexed because Erik offered, somewhat hesitantly it seemed, "I could look into this more for you, if you'd like. Just because I've never heard of something capable of harming other immortals doesn't mean it's out of the realm of existence."

I nodded. "I'd appreciate that. Thank you."

"It's a privilege to be of assistance to someone like you.

And if you like, I could also make other inquiries into vampire hunters in general." He paused again, choosing his words carefully. "Were such a person to be at large, certain signs would show up in the local occult community. Supplies would be bought, questions asked. Such beings do not go unnoticed."

Now I hesitated. Jerome had told us to be careful. I had the feeling he wouldn't appreciate any vigilante work, though speaking with Erik now probably counted as exactly that. Surely it wouldn't matter if I sent out my own feelers. Gathering information was not the same as me personally going out to find this person.

"I'd appreciate that as well. Anything you could find out would be useful." I finished the last of my tea and set the empty cup down. "I should probably leave now."

He rose with me. "Thank you for having tea with me. Being with a woman like you is generally the sort of thing that only happens in a man's dreams."

I laughed gently at the veiled joke, referencing the old story of succubi visiting men in their sleep. "Your dreams are safe, Erik."

He returned my smile. "Come back in a few days, and I'll tell you what I've learned. We'll have tea again."

Glancing around at the empty store, thinking how no customers had shown up during our visit, I suddenly felt the need to give him some business. "Let me buy some of that tea before I go."

He gave me an indulgent look, his dark brown eyes amused like he knew the game I played.

"I always took you for more of a black tea advocate—or at least an admirer of caffeine."

"Hey, even I like to shake things up once in a while. Besides, it was good . . . in an herbal, decaffeinated sort of way."

"I'll pass your compliments on to my friend. She makes the blends, and I sell them for her."

"A lady friend, huh?"

"Just a friend, Miss Kincaid."

He walked over to a shelf behind the register where several varieties of tea lay. Approaching the counter to pay, I admired some of the jewelry under its glass. One piece in particular caught my eye, a three-stranded choker of peach-colored, freshwater pearls, occasionally intermixed with copper beads or pieces of sea green glass. An ankh made of copper hung as its centerpiece.

"Is this from another of your local artisans?"

"An old friend in Tacoma made it." Erik reached into the case and took the choker out for me, laying it on the counter. I ran my hands over the fine, smooth pearls, each one slightly irregular in shape. "He mixed some Egyptian influence in with it, I think, but he wanted to sort of invoke the spirit of Aphrodite and the sea, create something the ancient priestesses might have worn."

"They wore nothing so fine," I murmured, turning over the necklace, noting the high price on its tag. I found myself speaking without conscious thought. "And many of the ancient Greek cities did have Egyptian influence. Ankhs appeared on Cyprian coins, as did Aphrodite."

Touching the copper of the ankh reminded me of another necklace, a necklace long since lost under the dust of time. That necklace had been simpler: only a string of beads etched with tiny ankhs. But my husband had brought it to me the morning of our wedding, sneaking up to our house just after dawn in a gesture uncharacteristically bold for him.

I had chastised him for the indiscretion. "What are you doing? You're going to see me this afternoon . . . and then every day after that!"

"I had to give you these before the wedding." He held up

the string of beads. "They were my mother's. I want you to have them, to wear them today."

He leaned forward, placing the beads around my neck. As his fingers brushed my skin, I felt something warm and tingly run through my body. At the tender age of fifteen, I hadn't exactly understood such sensations, though I was eager to explore them. My wiser self today recognized them as the early stirrings of lust, and . . . well, there had been something else there too. Something else that I still didn't quite comprehend. An electric connection, a feeling that we were bound into something bigger than ourselves. That our being together was inevitable.

"There," he'd said, once the beads were secure and my hair brushed back into place. "Perfect."

He said nothing else after that. He didn't need to. His eyes told me all I needed to know, and I shivered. Until Kyriakos, no man had ever given me a second glance. I was Marthanes' too-tall daughter after all, the one with the sharp tongue who didn't think before speaking. (Shape-shifting would eventually take care of one of those problems but not the other.) But Kyriakos had always listened to me and watched me like I was someone more, someone tempting and desirable, like the beautiful priestesses of Aphrodite who still carried on their rituals away from the Christian priests.

I wanted him to touch me then, not realizing just how much until I caught his hand suddenly and unexpectedly. Taking it, I placed it around my waist and pulled him to me. His eyes widened in surprise, but he didn't pull back. We were almost the same height, making it easy for his mouth to seek mine out in a crushing kiss. I leaned against the warm stone wall behind me so that I was pressed between it and him. I could feel every part of his body against mine, but we still weren't close enough. Not nearly enough.

Our kissing grew more ardent, as though our lips alone might close whatever aching distance lay between us. I moved his hand again, this time to push up my skirt along the side of one leg. His hand stroked the smooth flesh there and, without further urging, slid over to my inner thigh. I arched my lower body toward his, nearly writhing against him now, needing him to touch me everywhere.

"Letha? Where are you at?"

My sister's voice carried over the wind; she wasn't nearby but was close enough to be here soon. Kyriakos and I broke apart, both gasping, pulses racing. He was looking at me like he'd never seen me before. Heat burned in his gaze.

"Have you ever been with anyone before?" he asked wonderingly.

I shook my head.

"How did you . . . I never imagined you doing that . . ."

"I learn fast."

He grinned and pressed my hand to his lips. "Tonight," he breathed. "Tonight we . . ."

"Tonight," I agreed.

He backed away then, eyes still smoldering. "I love you. You are my life."

"I love you too." I smiled and watched him ago. A minute later, I heard my sister again.

"Letha?"

"Miss Kincaid?"

Erik's voice snapped me out of the memory, and suddenly I was back in his store, away from my family's long-since crumbled home. I met his questioning eyes and held up the necklace.

"I'll take this too."

"Miss Kincaid," he said uncertainly, fingering the price tag. "The help I give you . . . there's no need . . . no cost . . ."

"I know," I assured him. "I know. Just add this to my bill. And ask your friend if he can make matching earrings."

I left the store wearing the choker, still thinking about that morning, what it had been like to be touched for the first time, touched only by someone I loved. I exhaled carefully and put it from my mind. Just like I had countless other times.

Chapter 9

Returning to Queen Anne, I discovered I still had a lot of evening left. Unfortunately, I had nothing to do. A succubus without a social life. Very sad. It was made sadder still by the fact that I could have had any number of things to do but had dropped the ball on them. Certainly Doug had asked me out often enough; no doubt he was now enjoying his day off with a more appreciative woman. Roman I had also turned down, beautiful eyes and all. I smiled wistfully, remembering his easy banter and quick, bright charm. He could have been O'Neill, made flesh from Seth's novels.

Thinking of Seth reminded me he still had my book and that I was going on Day 3 without it. I sighed, wanting to know what would happen next, to be lost in the pages of Cady and O'Neill. Now that would have been a way to spend the evening. The bastard. He'd never bring it back. I'd never find out what—

With a groan, I suddenly wanted to smack my forehead for my own stupidity. Did I or did I not work for a large bookstore? After parking my car, I walked over to Emerald

City and found the massive display of *The Glasgow Pact* that was still up from the signing. I grabbed a copy and carried it to the front counter. Beth, one of the cashiers, was momentarily free.

"Will you demagnetize this for me?" I asked her, sliding the book over the counter.

"Sure," she said, running it across the pad. "Are you using your discount on it?"

I shook my head. "I'm not buying it. I'm just borrowing it."

"Can you do that?" She passed the book back to me.

"Sure," I lied. "Managers can."

Minutes later, I showed my prize to an unimpressed Aubrey and turned on the water in my bathtub. While it filled, I checked my messages—none—and sorted through the mail I'd picked up on the way in. Nothing interesting there either. Satisfied nothing else required my attention, I stepped out of my clothes and sank into the watery depths of the tub, careful not to get the book wet. Aubrey, crouching on a nearby counter, watched me with squinty eyes, apparently pondering why anyone would willingly immerse themselves in water ever, let alone for extended periods of time.

I figured I could read more than five pages tonight since I'd been deprived for the last couple of days. When I finished the fifteenth, I discovered I was three pages from the next chapter. Might as well end with a clean break. After I was done, I sighed and leaned back, feeling decadent and spent. Pure bliss. Books were a lot less messy than orgasms.

The next morning, I went to work, happy and refreshed. Paige found me around lunchtime as I sat on the edge of my desk and watched Doug play Mine Sweeper. Seeing her, I leapt from my position while he hastily closed down the game.

Paige ignored him, fixing her eyes on me. "I want you to do something with Seth Mortensen."

Uneasily, I remembered the love slave comment. "Like what?"

"I don't know." She gave a small, unconcerned shrug of the head. "Anything. He's new to town. He doesn't know anyone yet, so his social life is probably dismal."

Recalling his cold reception yesterday and conversational difficulties, I wasn't exactly surprised by this news. "I took him on a tour."

"It's not the same."

"What about his brother?"

"What about him?"

"I'm sure they're doing social things all the time."

"Why are you fighting this? I thought you were a fan."

I was a fan—a major one—but reading his work and interacting with him were proving to be two very different things. *The Glasgow Pact* was amazing, as was the e-mail he'd sent. Spoken conversation was a bit . . . lacking. I couldn't tell Paige this, of course, so she and I went back and forth a bit on the issue while Doug looked on with interest. Finally, I agreed against my better judgment, dreading the prospect of even proposing the venture to Seth, let alone embarking upon it.

When I finally made myself approach him later in the day, I was fully braced for another brush-off. Instead, he turned from his work and smiled at me.

"Hey," he said. His mood seemed so improved that I decided yesterday must have been a fluke.

"Hey. How's it going?"

"Not so well." He tapped the laptop's screen lightly with his fingernail, eyes frowning as he focused on it. "They're being a bit difficult. I just can't quite get the grip I need on this one scene."

Interest swept me. Bad days with Cady and O'Neill. I had always imagined interacting with such characters must be a nonstop thrill. The ultimate job.

"Sounds like you need a break then. Paige is worried about your social life."

His brown eyes glanced back to me. "Oh? How so?"

"She thinks you aren't getting out enough. That you don't know anyone in town yet."

"I know my brother and his family. And Mistee." He paused. "And I know you."

"Good thing, because I'm about to become your cruise director."

Seth's lips quirked slightly, then he shook his head and looked back at the screen. "That's really nice—of you and Paige both—but not necessary."

He wasn't dismissing me as he had yesterday, but I still felt miffed that my generous deal was not being embraced, especially since I was offering it under duress.

"Come on," I said. "What else are you going to do?"

"Write."

I couldn't argue with that. Writing those novels was God's Own Work. Who was I to interfere with their creator? And yet . . . Paige had given a directive. That was nearly a divine commandment in itself. A compromise popped into my head.

"You could do something, I don't know, research-related. For the book. Two birds with one stone."

"I've already got all the research I need for this one."

"What about, uh, ongoing character development? Like . . . going to the planetarium." Cady had a fascination with astronomy. She would often point out constellations and link them to some symbolic story analogous to the novel's plot. "Or . . . or . . . a hockey game? You need fresh ideas for O'Neill's games. You'll run out."

He shook his head. "No I won't. I've never even been to a hockey game to begin with."

"I—what? That's . . . no. Really?"

He shrugged.

"Where . . . do you get the game info from then? The plays?"

"I know the basic rules. I pick up pieces on the Internet, patch it together."

I stared, feeling betrayed. O'Neill was absolutely obsessed with the Detroit Red Wings. That passion shaped his personality and was reflected in his actions: fast, skilled, and at times brutal. Believing Seth to be meticulous about every detail, I had naturally assumed he must know everything about hockey to have written such a defining trait into his protagonist.

Seth watched me, confused by whatever stunned look I wore.

"We're going to a hockey game," I stated.

"No, we—"

"We *are* going to a hockey game. Hang on a sec."

I ran back downstairs, kicked Doug off our computer, and got the information I needed. It was just as I'd suspected. The Thunderbirds' season had just started.

"Six-thirty," I told Seth, minutes later. "Meet me at Key Arena, at the main window. I'll buy the tickets."

He looked dubious.

"Six-thirty," I repeated. "This'll be great. It'll give you a break and let you actually see what the game's like. Besides, you said you were blocked today."

Not only that, it would fulfill my obligation to Paige in a way that didn't require much talking. The stadium would be too loud, and we'd be too busy watching to need conversation.

"I don't know where Key Arena is."

"You can walk to it from here. Just keep heading for the Space Needle. They're both part of the Seattle Center."

"I—"

"So when are you meeting me?" There was a warning note in my voice, daring him to cross me.

He grimaced. "Six-thirty."

After work, I set off to run my own errands. I had nothing new to work on with the vampire hunter enigma until Erik got back to me. Unfortunately, the mundane world still had its own share of requirements, and I spent most of my evening taking care of miscellany. Like restocking my supply of cat food, coffee, and Grey Goose. And checking out the new line of lip glosses at the MAC counter. I even remembered to pick up a cheap, assemble-it-yourself bookshelf for the fire-hazard stacks of books in my living room.

My productivity knew no bounds.

For dinner, I grabbed Indian food and managed to land at Key Arena precisely at six-thirty. I didn't see Seth anywhere but didn't panic just yet. The Seattle Center was not easy to navigate; he was probably still wandering around the Needle, trying to make his way over here.

I bought the tickets and sat down on one of the large cement steps. The air had turned chilly tonight, and I snuggled into my heavy fleece pullover, shape-shifting it a bit thicker. While waiting, I people-watched. Couples, groups of guys, and excited children were all turning out for Seattle's fierce little team. They made for interesting viewing.

When six-fifty rolled around, I started getting nervous. We had ten more minutes, and I worried Seth might have gotten seriously lost. I pulled out my cell phone and dialed the store, wondering if he was there. Nope, they told me, but Paige did have his cell number. I tried it next, only to get voice mail.

Annoyed, I snapped my phone shut and huddled further into my own embrace to stay warm. We still had time. Besides, Seth not being at the store was a good thing. It meant he was on his way.

Yet, when seven and the start of the game arrived, he still wasn't there. I tried his cell again, then looked longingly at the doors. I wanted to see the beginning of the game. Seth might never have watched hockey, but I had and liked it. The continual movement and energy held my attention more than any other sport, even if the fights sometimes made me squirm. I didn't want to miss this, but I'd also hate for Seth to walk up and not know what to do when I wasn't where I said I'd be.

I waited fifteen more minutes, listening to the sounds of the game echoing toward me, before I finally faced the truth.

I had been stood up.

Such a thing was unheard of. It hadn't happened in . . . over a century. I felt more stunned than embarrassed or angry by the revelation. The whole thing was just too weird to fathom.

No, I decided a moment later, I was mistaken. Seth had been reluctant, yes, but he wouldn't just refuse to come, not without calling. And maybe . . . maybe something bad had happened. He could have been hit by a car for all I knew. After Duane's death, one could never predict when tragedy might hit.

Yet, until I had more information, the only tragedy I faced now was missing the game. I called his cell again, this time leaving him a message with my number and whereabouts. I would come outside and retrieve him if needed. I went into the game.

Sitting alone made me feel conspicuous, driving home the sadness of my situation. Other couples sat nearby, and a group of guys kept eyeing me, occasionally nudging one of their number who wanted to come talk to me. Being hit on didn't faze me, but looking like I needed it did. I might choose not to date, but that didn't mean I couldn't do it when I wanted. I didn't like others perceiving me as desperate and alone. I felt that way enough sometimes without outside confirmation.

At the first break, I bought a corndog to console myself. While sifting through my purse for cash, I found the slip of paper with Roman's phone number. I stared at it while I ate, remembering his persistence and how bad I'd felt refusing him. My sudden painful abandonment fired the need to hang out with someone, to remind myself I really could have social contact when I wanted.

Common sense froze me briefly as I was about to dial, cautioning that I would be breaking my decades-long vow of not dating nice guys. There were more prudent ways to deal with an unused hockey ticket, that reasonable inner voice reminded me. Like Hugh or the vampires. Calling one of them would provide a safer interaction.

But . . . but they treated me like a sister, and while I loved them like family too, I didn't want to be a sister just now. And anyway, it wasn't like this was even a real date. This would be a simple matter of companionship. Plus, the same precautions it had provided for Seth—lack of interaction— applied for Roman too. It would be perfectly safe. I dialed the number.

"Hello?"

"I'm tired of holding on to your coat."

I could hear his smile on the other end. "I figured you'd thrown it away by now."

"Are you crazy? It's a Kenneth Cole. Anyway, that's not really why I called."

"Yeah, I figured."

"Do you want to come to a hockey game tonight?"

"When does it start?"

"Um, forty minutes ago."

A Seth-worthy pause.

"So, you just now thought to invite me?"

"Well . . . the person I was going with didn't exactly show up."

"And now you call me?"

"Well, you were so adamant about going out."

"Yes, but I'm . . . wait a minute. I'm your second choice?"

"Don't think of it like that. Think of it as more like, I don't know, you're stepping up to fulfill what someone else couldn't."

"Like the Miss America runner-up?"

"Look, are you coming or not?"

"Very tempting, but I'm busy right now. And I'm not just saying that either." Another pause. "I'll stop by your place after the game, though."

No, that wasn't how this was supposed to play out. "I'm busy after the game."

"What, you and your no-show have other plans?"

"I . . . no. I have to . . . put together a bookcase. It's going to take a while. Hard work, you know?"

"I excel at that handy-type stuff. I'll see you in a couple hours."

"Wait, you can't—" The phone disconnected.

I closed my eyes in a moment of exasperation, opened them, then returned to the action on the ice. What had I just done?

After the game, I skulked back home. The elation of winning couldn't overpower the anxiety of having Roman in my apartment.

"Aubrey," I said upon entering, "what am I going to do?"

She yawned, revealing her tiny, domestic-sized fangs. I shook my head at her.

"I can't hide under the bed like you. He won't fall for it."

Both of us jumped at the sudden knock at the door. For half a second, I did consider the bed before deigning to let Roman in. Aubrey studied him a moment, then—apparently being too overwhelmed at the sight of a sex god in our midst—darted off for my bedroom.

Roman, casually dressed, stood bearing a six-pack of Mountain Dew and two bags of Doritos. And a box of cereal.

"Lucky Charms?" I asked.

"Magically delicious," he explained. "Requisite for any sort of building project."

I shook my head, still amazed at how he had managed to weasel his way over here. "This isn't a date."

He cut me a scandalized look. "Obviously. I'd bring Count Chocula for that."

"I'm serious. Not a date," I maintained.

"Yeah, yeah. I get it." He set the stuff on the counter and turned to me. "So, where is it? Let's get this started."

I exhaled, uneasily relieved by his matter-of-fact manner. No flirtation, no overt come-ons. Just honest, friendly helpfulness. I'd get the shelf built, and then he'd be gone.

We tore into the huge box, dumping out loose shelves and panels, as well as an assortment of bolts and screws. The directions were short on words, mostly containing some cryptic diagrams with arrows pointing to where certain parts went. After minutes of scrutiny, we finally decided the large backboard was the place to start, laying it flat on the floor with the shelves and walls placed on top. Once everything was properly aligned, Roman picked up the screws, studying where they joined the various parts together.

He examined the screws, looked at the box, then turned back to the shelf. "That's weird."

"What is?"

"I think . . . most of these things usually have holes in the wood, then they include a little tool to put the screws in."

I leaned over the wood. No premade holes. No tools. "We've got to screw these in ourselves."

He nodded.

"I've got a screwdriver . . . somewhere."

He eyed the wood. "I don't think that'll work. I think we need a drill."

I felt awed at his hardware prowess. "I know I don't have that."

We hightailed it over to a big chain home store, walking in ten minutes before they closed. A harried salesclerk showed us to the drill section, then sprinted off, calling back a warning that we didn't have much time.

The power tools stared back at us, and I looked to Roman for guidance.

"Not a clue," he finally admitted after a span of silence.

"I thought you excelled at this 'handy-type stuff.'"

"Yeah . . . well . . ." He turned sheepish, a new look for him. "That was kind of an exaggeration."

"Like a lie?"

"No. Like an exaggeration."

"They're the same."

"No they aren't."

I let the semantics go. "Why'd you say it then?"

He gave a rueful headshake. "Partially because I just wanted to see you again. And the rest . . . I don't know. I guess the short answer is you said you had something hard to do. So I wanted to help."

"I'm a damsel in distress?" I teased.

He studied me seriously. "Hardly. But you are someone I'd like to get to know better, and I wanted you to see I've got more on my mind than just getting you into bed."

"So if I offered you sex here in this aisle, you'd turn me down?" The flippant remark came off my tongue before I could stop it. It was a defense mechanism, a joke to cover up how confused his earnest explanation had made me. Most guys did just want to get me into bed. I wasn't quite sure what to do with one who didn't.

My glibness succeeded in killing the pensive moment. Roman became his old confident and charming self, and I almost regretted the change I'd wrought, wondering what might have followed.

"I'd have to turn you down. We've only got six minutes

now. They'd kick us out before it was done." He snapped his attention to the drills with renewed vigor. "And as for my so-called handy skills," he added, "I'm a remarkably fast learner, so I wasn't really exaggerating. By the end of the night, I will excel."

Not true.

After arbitrarily picking out a drill and coming home, Roman set himself to aligning the bookcase's pieces and putting them together. He fit one of the shelves to the back-board, lined up his screw, and drilled.

The drill went through at an angle, missing the shelf entirely.

"Son of a bitch," he swore.

I moved in and yelped when I saw the screw sticking through the back of my bookshelf. We took it out and stared bleakly at the conspicuous hole left behind.

"Probably it'll be covered by books," I suggested.

He set his mouth in a grim line and attempted the same feat again. The screw made contact this time but was still at an obvious angle. He pulled it out again, finally inserting it correctly on his third try.

Unfortunately, the process only repeated as he continued. Watching hole after hole appear, I finally asked if I could try. He waved his hand in a defeatist gesture and handed me the drill. I fitted in a screw, leaned over, and drilled it in perfectly in my first attempt.

"Jesus," he said. "I'm completely superfluous. I'm the damsel in distress."

"No way. You brought the cereal."

I finished attaching the shelves. The walls came next. The backboard had small hash marks to help with alignment. With careful scrutiny, I tried to line it up cleanly along the edges.

It proved impossible, and I soon realized why. Despite my

perfect drilling, all of the shelves were affixed crookedly, some too far to the left or right. The walls could not fit flush with the backboard's edges.

Roman sat back against my couch, running a hand over his eyes. "My God."

I munched on a handful of Lucky Charms and considered. "Well. Let's just line them up as best we can."

"This thing'll never hold books."

"Yeah. We'll do what we can."

We tried it with the first wall, and though it took a while and looked terrible, it sufficed as serviceable. We moved on to the next one.

"I think I finally have to admit I'm not so good at this," he observed. "But you seem to have kind of a knack. A regular handywoman."

"I don't know about that. I think the only thing I have a knack for is barely scraping by with things I have to do."

"That was a world-weary tone if ever I heard one. Why? You got a lot of things you 'have to do'?"

I nearly choked on my laugh, thinking about the whole succubus survival scene. "You might say that. I mean, doesn't everyone?"

"Yes, of course, but you've got to balance them with things you want to do. Don't get bogged down with the have-to's. Otherwise, there's no point in being alive. Life becomes a matter of survival."

I finished a screw. "You're getting kind of deep for me tonight, Descartes."

"Don't be cute. I'm serious. What do you really want? From life? For your future? For example, do you plan on being at the bookstore forever?"

"For a while. Why? Are you saying there's something wrong with that?"

"No. Just seems kind of mundane. Like a way to fill the time."

I smiled. "No, definitely not. And even if it was, we can still enjoy mundane things."

"Yes, but I've found most people harbor dreams of a more exciting vocation. The one that's too crazy to ever actually do. The one that's too hard, too much work, or just too 'out there.' The gas station attendant who dreams of being a rock star. The accountant who wishes she'd taken art history classes instead of statistics. People put their dreams off, either because they think it's impossible, or because they'll do it 'someday.'"

He had paused from our work, his face serious once more.

"So what do you want, Georgina Kincaid? What is your crazy dream? The one you think you can't have but secretly fantasize about?"

Honestly, my deepest longing was to have a normal relationship, to love and be loved without supernatural complications. Such a small thing, I thought sadly, compared to his grandiose examples. Not crazy at all, just impossible. I didn't know if I wanted love now as a way of making up for the mortal marriage I'd destroyed or simply because the years had shown me that love could be a bit more fulfilling than being a continual servant of the flesh. Not that that didn't have its moments, of course. Being wanted and adored was an alluring thing, a thing most mortals and immortals craved. But loving and longing were not the same things.

Relationships with other immortals seemed a logical choice, but employees of hell proved nonideal candidates for stability and commitment. I'd had a few semisatisfying relationships with such men over the years, but they'd all come to nothing.

Explaining any of this, however, was not a conversation Roman and I were going to have anytime soon. So instead, I confessed my secondary fantasy, half-surprised at how much I wanted to. People didn't usually ask me what I wanted from life. Most just asked me what position I wanted to do it in.

"Well, if I weren't at the bookstore—and believe me, I'm very happy there—I think I'd like to choreograph Vegas dance shows."

Roman's face split into a grin. "There, you see that? That's the kind of wacky, off-the-wall thing I'm talking about." He leaned forward. "So what holds you back from bare breasts and sequins? Risk? Sensationalism? What others will say?"

"No," I said sadly. "Simply the fact that I can't do it."

"'Can't' is a—"

"I mean, I *can't* choreograph because I can't write routines. I've tried. I can't . . . I can't create anything, for that matter. Anything new. I'm not the creative type."

He scoffed. "I don't believe that."

"No, it's true."

Someone had once told me that immortals were not meant to create, that that was the province of humans who burned to leave behind a legacy after their short existence. But I'd known immortals who could do it. Peter was always concocting his original culinary surprises. Hugh used the human body as a canvas. But me? I had never been able to do it as a mortal either. The lack was in me.

"You don't know how hard I've tried to do creative things. Painting classes. Music lessons. I'm a dismal failure at worst, a copycat of another's genius at best."

"You've been pretty adept with this building project."

"Another person's design, another person's directions. I excel at that part. I'm smart. I can reason. I can read people, interact with them perfectly. I can copy things, learn the right moves and steps. My eyes, for example." I pointed to them. "I can apply makeup as well or better than any of the department store girls. But I get all my ideas and palettes from others, from pictures in magazines. I don't make up anything of my own. The Vegas thing? I could dance in a show and be perfect. Seriously. I could be the star of any revue—following another's choreography. But I couldn't write any moves myself, not in any major or significant way."

The wall was done. "I don't believe it," he argued. His passionate defense both surprised and charmed me. "You're bright and vivacious. You're intelligent—extremely so. You have to give yourself a chance. Start small, and go from there."

"Is this the part where you tell me to believe in myself? The sky is the limit?"

"No. This is the part where I tell you it's getting late, and I need to go. Your shelf is finished, and I have had a lovely evening."

We stood up and lifted the bookcase, leaning it against my living room wall. Stepping back, we studied it in silence. Even Aubrey appeared for the inspection.

Each shelf sat at a crooked angle. One of the sidewalls almost lined up straight with the backboard's edge, the other had a quarter-inch margin. Six holes were visible in the backboard. And most inexplicably of all, the whole thing seemed to lean slightly to the left.

I started laughing. And I couldn't stop. After a moment of shock, Roman joined me.

"Dear Lord," I said finally, wiping tears away. "That's the most horrible thing I've ever seen."

Roman opened his mouth in disagreement, then reconsidered. "It just might be." He saluted. "But I think it'll hold, Captain."

We made a few more mirthful comments before I walked him to the door, remembering to give him his coat back. In spite of his jokes, he seemed more genuinely disappointed about our shelf failure than I did, like he had let me down. Somehow, I found this more appealing than his perfectly timed lines or charming bravado. Not that I didn't love those too. I studied him as we said goodbye, thinking about his "chivalry" and passionate belief in me following my heart's desire. The lump of fear I always carried around people I liked softened a little.

"Hey, you never told me your crazy dream."

The aqua eyes crinkled. "Not so crazy. Just still trying to score that date with you."

Not so crazy. Just like mine. Companionship over fame and glamour. I took the plunge.

"Well, then . . . what are you doing tomorrow?"

He brightened. "Nothing yet."

"Then come by the bookstore just before closing. I'm giving a dance lesson." The dance lesson would have lots of people. It would be a safe compromise for us.

That smile faltered only slightly. "A dance lesson?"

"You have a problem with that? Are you changing your mind about going out?"

"Well, no, but . . . is it like the Vegas thing? You covered in rhinestones? Because I could probably get into that."

"Not exactly."

He shrugged, the charisma on high-beam. "Well. We'll save that for the second date."

"No. There's no second date, remember? Just the one, then that's it. We don't see each other anymore. You said so. Super-secret Boy Scout . . . whatever."

"That might have been an exaggeration."

"No. That would be a lie."

"Ah." He winked at me. "I guess those two aren't the same then after all, eh?"

"I—" My words halted at the logic.

He gave me one of his roguish bows before sweeping away. "Farewell, Georgina."

I went back inside, hoping I hadn't just made a mistake, and found Aubrey sitting on one of my shelves. "Whoa, be careful," I warned. "I don't think that's structurally sound."

Although it was late, I didn't feel tired. Not after this wacky evening with Roman. I felt wired, his presence affect-

ng both my body and mind. Inspired, I shooed Aubrey off
he bookcase and started transferring my stacks. With each
ew weight addition, I expected collapse, but the thing held.

When I got to my Seth Mortensen books, I suddenly remembered the cataclysm that had sparked this whole
evening. Anger kindled in me once more. I'd heard nary a
word from the writer the entire time. The getting-hit-by-a-
car thing might still be a possibility, but my instincts
doubted it. He had stood me up.

Half of me considered kicking his books in retaliation,
but I knew I could never do that. I loved them too much. No
need to punish them for their creator's shortcomings. Long-
ngly, I picked up *The Glasgow Pact*, suddenly anxious to
ead my next five-page installment. I left the rest of my
books unshelved and settled on the couch, Aubrey at my
feet.

When I reached the stopping point, I discovered something incredible. Cady was developing a love interest in this
one. It was unheard of. O'Neill, ever the charming ladies'
man, got around all the time. Cady remained virtuously
pure, no matter the number of sexual innuendoes and jokes
she traded across the table with O'Neill. Nothing tangible
had happened thus far in the book, but I could read the inevitable signs of what was to come with her and this investi-
gator they'd met in Glasgow.

I kept reading, unable to leave that plotline hanging. And
the further I read, the harder it was to stop. I soon took a secret, irrational satisfaction at breaking the five-page rule.
Like I was somehow getting back at Seth.

The night wore on. Cady went to bed with the guy, and
O'Neill became uncharacteristically jealous and freaked out,
despite his usual surface charm. Holy shit. I left the couch,
put on pajamas, and curled up in my bed. Aubrey followed. I
kept reading.

I finished the book at four in the morning, bleary-eyed

and exhausted. Cady saw the guy a few more times as she and O'Neill wrapped up their mystery—as enthralling as ever, but suddenly less interesting compared to the interpersonal developments—and then she and the Scotsman parted ways. She and O'Neill returned to Washington, D.C., and the status quo resettled.

I exhaled and set the book on the floor, unsure what to think, mainly because I was so tired. Still, in a valiant effort, I got up from bed, found my laptop, and logged into my Emerald City e-mail. I sent Seth a terse message: *Cady got some. What's up with that?* Then, as an afterthought: *By the way, the hockey game was great.*

Satisfied I'd registered my opinion, I promptly fell asleep . . . only to be awakened a few hours later by my alarm clock.

Chapter 10

Jesus. What had I been thinking? I had to work today. Not only that, I had to work in ten minutes. I had no time for "real" clothing or makeup. With a sigh, I shape-shifted form, my robe giving way to gray slacks and an ivory blouse, hair and makeup suddenly done to my normal, immaculate perfection. Brushing my teeth and adding perfume could not be faked, and after performing those tasks, I grabbed my purse and sprinted out.

When I reached my lobby, the desk clerk called out to me.

"Got something for you." He handed over a flat parcel.

Still conscious of the time, I quickly tore at the wrapping and stifled a gasp at what I found. *Black Velvet Paint by Number Kit,* read the package. A subheading proclaimed: *Create Your Own Masterpiece! Contains Everything You Need to Paint Just Like a Real Artist!* The "masterpiece" I could create depicted a desert landscape with a giant cactus to one side and a howling coyote on the other. An eagle soared in the sky, and a ghostly, disembodied Native American head floated nearby. Terribly stereotyped and cheesy.

A small piece of paper had been taped to it. *Start small,* the note said. *Love, Roman.* The writing was so perfect as to be unreal.

I was still chuckling when I got to work. In my office, I settled in front of the computer and discovered a second morning surprise: another e-mail from Seth. It had been sent at five in the morning.

Georgina,

A few years ago, while writing *Gods of Gold,* I met a woman at a class I took on South American archaeology. I don't know how it is for women; it's probably not even always the same for us men. But for me, when I meet someone I'm attracted to, time stands still. The planets come into alignment, and I stop breathing. The angels themselves descend to sit upon my shoulders, whispering promises of love and devotion while less heavenly creatures whisper promises of an earthier, baser nature. I guess that's part of being a man.

Anyway, that was what happened with this woman. We fell pretty hard for each other and dated off and on for a very long time. Some days we wouldn't be able to leave each other's side for more than a minute, and then later, months would go by without any sort of contact. I have to confess, this latter behavior was more my fault than hers. I mentioned before that Cady and O'Neill are demanding. During phases when I was hot into my writing, I wouldn't be able to think about or do anything else that didn't involve my novel. I knew it hurt her—knew she was the kind of person who wanted to settle down and start a family, live a quiet and committed life. I was not that kind of person—I'm not even sure I am now—but I liked the idea of always having someone around, someone reliable who I could call up when *I* was finally ready to make time. It really wasn't fair to do that to her, always leave her hanging like that. I should have ended things early on, but I was too selfish and too comfortable.

One day, after not having spoken to her in a few months, I called her up and was astonished to hear a man answer the phone. When she came on the line, she told me she'd met someone else and wouldn't be able to see me anymore. To say I was shocked would be an understatement. I started rambling, going on and on about how much I cared for her, how she couldn't throw away what we had. She took it all pretty nicely, considering what a psycho I must have sounded like, but in the end, she closed things by saying I shouldn't have expected her to wait forever. She had her own life to live.

The reason I share this embarrassing tale from the canon of Seth Mortensen is twofold. First, I need to apologize to you for what happened tonight. In spite of my grumblings, I really did intend to meet you. A couple hours before the game, I ran home to get something and suddenly thought of a solution to the snag that had been blocking me all day. I sat down to write, only planning to spend an hour on it. As you might be guessing by now, it took a lot longer than that. I got so caught up that I completely forgot about the game—and about you. I never heard my phone ring. I wasn't aware of anything else except getting the story out on paper (or rather, my screen).

This, I'm afraid, is a problem I frequently have. It happened with my ex, it happens with my family, and unfortunately, it happened with you. Don't even get my brother started about how I nearly missed his wedding. The worlds and people in my head are so alive to me that I lose track of the real world. Sometimes I'm not even convinced Cady and O'Neill's world isn't the real one. I never mean to hurt people, and I feel terrible afterward, but it is a failing I can't seem to overcome.

None of this justifies abandoning you last night, but I hoped this might offer some insight into my unbalanced worldview. Please understand how very sorry I am.

My second reason for the memoir is to address your comment about Cady "getting some." In thinking about her and O'Neill, I decided that Cady wasn't the kind of person who would wait around forever either. Now, don't get me wrong: I don't think Cady and my ex-girlfriend have a lot in common. Cady isn't looking to settle in the suburbs and pick out curtains with O'Neill. But, she is a bright and passionate woman, who loves life, and wants to live it. A lot of people were upset to see her break out of her devoutly chaste, puppy-at-O'Neill's-side role, but I think she had to do it. Let's face it: O'Neill takes her for granted, and he needed a wake-up call. Now, does this mean steps are being made to finally bring them together, as so many readers have asked? Naturally, as their creator, my lips are sealed on that, but I can say this: I have a lot more books with them in mind, and readers tend to lose interest when protagonists hook up.

—Seth

P.S.—By the way, I bought the condo. Mistee was so excited that she took me on the spot, and we made love all over the granite countertops.

P.P.S.—All right, I'm making up that last part. Like I said, I'm a man. And a writer.

My eyes still heavy with sleep, I sluggishly pondered the letter's message. Seth had had a serious girlfriend. Wow. That shouldn't have surprised me, especially considering the sex scenes he wrote. I mean, he couldn't have pulled them all out of imagination. Still, it was hard to picture introverted Seth participating in all the social exchanges normally required of a long-term relationship.

And then the other part, his reasons for not showing. What to think of those? He was right in saying his burst of inspiration was no excuse for what he had done. The explanation did take away some of the sting, however, moving him from rude to simply thoughtless. No, maybe thoughtless was too harsh. Scattered, that was it. Perhaps scattered wasn't such a bad thing, I mused, since ignoring the real world allowed him to work on the written one. I just didn't know.

I pondered all this for the rest of the morning, my anger from last night growing cold in the wake of time passing and my speculation on a brilliant writer's mind. By the time lunch rolled around, I realized I had gotten over the hockey mishap. He had not intended the neglect, and it wasn't like my night had turned out too badly after all.

Around late afternoon, Warren came trolling around.

"No," I said immediately, recognizing the look in his eyes. I hated his presumption, yet always found myself eerily drawn to it. "I'm in a terrible mood."

"I'll make you feel better."

"I told you, I'm too bitchy."

"I like you bitchy." The succubus feeding instinct began waking up. I swallowed, annoyed at it and my own weakness. "And I'm really busy. There are . . . things . . . I should do . . ." My excuse sounded halfhearted, though, and Warren apparently recognized that.

He walked over to me and knelt by my chair, running a hand over my thigh. I wore thin, silky slacks, and the feel of his fingers stroking me through that smooth material was almost more sensual than on bare skin.

"How was your date the other night?" he murmured, moving his mouth up to my ear and then my neck.

I arched my head obligingly, in spite of my best resistance, liking the way his mouth grew fiercer against my skin, his teeth just teasing me. He was far from being a boyfriend but was still the closest I had to any sort of consistent relationship. That meant something. "Fine."

"Did you fuck him?"

"No. I slept alone, alas."

"Good."

"He's coming back tonight, though. For the dance lesson."

"Really?" Warren unbuttoned the top two buttons of my blouse, revealing a pale pink lace bra. His fingertips traced the shape of one of my breasts, following its inner curve down to where it met the other one. Then he moved his hand up to that breast, playing with the nipple through the lace. I closed my eyes, surprised at my swelling desire. After helping Hugh close the contract with Martin, I wouldn't have thought I'd need a fix so soon. Yet, the hunger tugged ever so slightly within me, mingled with lust. Pure instinct. "We'll introduce him to Marla."

Marla was Warren's wife. The thought of passing Roman off on her was too funny.

"You sound jealous," I teased. I pulled Warren toward me, and he responded by pushing me on top of the desk. I moved my hands down to unfasten his pants.

"I am," he grunted. Leaning over, he pulled the bra down to bare my breasts and lowered his mouth to one of the nipples. He hesitated. "Are you sure you didn't fuck him?"

"I think I'd remember something like that."

A knock sounded at the door, and Warren hastily sprang away from me, pulling up his pants. "Shit."

I, too, sat up and returned to my chair. With Warren's eyes on the door, I quickly used some more shape-shifting to neaten myself up and rebutton my blouse. Satisfied we were both decent, I called, "Come in."

Seth opened the door.

I clamped down on my jaw, lest it drop open in astonishment.

"Hi," said Seth, looking back and forth between Warren and me. "I didn't mean to interrupt."

"No, no, you aren't," Warren assured him, clicking into public relations mode. "We were just having a quick meeting."

"Not a very important one," I added. Warren gave me a droll look.

"Oh," said Seth, still appearing like he wanted to bolt. "I just came by to see if maybe . . . you wanted lunch. I . . . e-mailed you about what happened."

"Yeah, I read it. Thanks."

I smiled at him, hoping to silently communicate that all was forgiven. The worried look on his face was so heart-wrenching that I felt certain his conscience had suffered more than my ego last night.

"Excellent idea," boomed Warren. "Let's all go get some lunch, shall we? Georgina and I can meet again later."

"I can't."

I reminded him about how short-staffed we were and how I was needed for coverage. He scowled when I finished.

"Why haven't we hired anyone?"

"I'm working on it."

Warren ended up just taking Seth out—something the writer seemed highly uneasy about—and I was left alone, feeling abandoned. I would have half liked to hear what else Seth had to say about writing taking over his life. I might have even liked getting laid. Neither was to be. Ah, the injustices of the universe.

I apparently had one karmic favor left, however. Around four, Tammi—the red-haired girl from Krystal Starz—showed up to solve my staffing problem. As suggested, she brought a friend. After a quick interview, I felt satisfied by their competency. I hired them on the spot, pleased to have one task taken off my list.

When the store finally closed later, those few hours of sleep were catching up with me more fiercely. I felt in no mood to teach a dance lesson.

Realizing I needed to change, I closed the office door and shape-shifted my outfit for the second time that day. It felt like cheating, as always. For dancing I selected a sleeveless dress, clingy through the bodice and flowing through the skirt—just right for twirls. Colored in blending hues of peach and orange, I hoped the dress would warm my mood up. I also hoped no one had noticed I hadn't carried a change of clothes in with me this morning.

On the overhead speakers, I heard one of the cashiers make the announcement that the store had closed, just as another knock sounded on my door. I called an entry, wondering if it might be Seth again, but Cody appeared this time.

"Hey," I said, forcing a smile. "Are you ready for this?"

I had taught Cody to swing dance a year or so ago, and he had picked it up remarkably well, probably half due to vampire reflexes. As a result, I had—against his better judgment—recruited him to be my coteacher in these impromptu lessons for the staff. He kept claiming he was no good, but in both lessons so far, he'd proven remarkably efficient.

"What? Dancing? Yeah. No problem."

I glanced around, ascertaining we were alone. "Any more weird occurrences?"

Cody shook his head, blond hair framing it like a lion's mane. "No. It's been pretty quiet. Maybe I was overreacting."

"Better safe than sorry," I advised, feeling like somebody's clichéd grandmother. "What are you doing after this?"

"Meeting Peter at a bar downtown. You want to come with us?"

"Sure." We'd all be safer as a group.

The door pushed open, and Seth stuck his head inside. "Hey, I—oh, I'm sorry," he stammered, catching sight of Cody. "I didn't mean to interrupt."

"No, no," I said, waving him inside. "We were just talking." I gave Seth a curious look. "What are you still doing here? Are you staying for the lesson?"

"Er, well I, that is, Warren invited me to . . . but I don't think I'll actually dance. If that's okay."

"Not dance? What are you going to do then, watch?" I demanded. "Be like a voyeur or something?"

Seth gave me a sage look, appearing for the first time in a while like the guy who had written the comic observations about real estate agents and old girlfriends. The guy I'd once engaged in a stumbling flirtation with.

"I'm not that desperate. Not yet, anyway. But it's really safer if I don't dance. For those around me."

"That's what I used to say until she made me try it," remarked Cody, clapping me on the shoulder. "Just wait until you've been in Georgina's capable hands. You'll never be the same."

Before any of us could acknowledge that suggestive comment, Doug appeared behind Seth, outfitted as his grunge band self rather than assistant manager self.

"Hey, are we getting this party started or what? I came back here today just for this lesson, Kincaid. You better make the trip worth my while. Hey, Cody."

"Hey, Doug."

"Hey, Seth."

"Hey, Doug."

I groaned. "All right. Let's do this."

We left en masse for the café, where tables were being moved to give us space. I introduced Cody and Seth along the way. They shook hands briefly, the young vampire looking at me meaningfully when he realized just which Seth this must be.

"You sure you aren't going to dance?" I asked the writer, still puzzled by his obstinacy.

"Nope. Just doesn't feel right."

"Yeah, well, after the shitty day I've had, running this shindig doesn't feel right to me either, but we all endure. Put on the happy face and go, you know?"

Seth looked like he didn't know, only giving me a small, bemused smile. A moment later, that smile dimmed slightly. "You said you got the e-mail . . . did it . . . do you . . ."

"It's fine. Forget about it." His bizarre social habits might not mesh with mine, but I couldn't stand seeing him worry anymore about last night. "Honestly." I patted his arm, gave him my Helen of Troy smile, then turned my attention to the scene upstairs.

Most of the staff who'd worked today milled around, along with a few others who, like Doug, had come back. Warren and his wife waited with them, and so did Roman.

He approached with a smile when he saw me, and I felt a faint wave of lust sweep me, independent of any succubus feeding. As good-looking as ever, he wore black slacks and a teal shirt that gleamed like his eyes.

"Group date, huh?"

"For my safety. I've always found it best to keep a few dozen chaperones on hand."

"You'll need a few dozen more in that dress," he warned in a low voice, those eyes molesting me from head to toe.

I flushed, taking a few steps away from him. "You'll have to wait your turn, like everyone else."

Turning away from him, I inadvertently made eye contact

with Seth. He had obviously overheard the brief exchange. My blush deepening, I fled both of them for the center of the floor, Cody in tow.

Putting on the so-called "happy face," I pushed my long day out of my mind and grinned at my coworkers' whoops and cheers. "All right, gang, let's get going. Doug's in kind of a hurry and wants to finish this up as quickly as possible. I understand that's pretty standard for him in a lot of matters—especially romantic ones." This elicited both positive and negative catcalls from the crowd, as well as an obscene gesture from Doug.

I reintroduced Cody, who was less comfortable with the attention than I was, and began sizing up the group. We had more women than men, per usual, and a wide range of skill levels. I split couples up accordingly, putting especially adept women with other women since I felt confident they could dance the male part for this practice and switch effortlessly later. I didn't have such faith in everybody; some of them still struggled to follow a beat.

Consequently, I started the lesson by reviewing from last time, turning on the music and making everyone practice basic steps. Cody and I monitored, making minor adjustments and suggestions. My tension from the long day eased slightly as I worked the crowd. I loved swing dancing, had loved it when it first emerged in the early twentieth century, and had been thrilled when its revival came around recently. I knew it was going out of style again, which was part of the reason I wanted to pass on the knowledge to others.

Not knowing Roman's level of expertise, I'd placed him with Paige, a pretty skilled dancer. After watching them a minute or so, I shook my head and approached.

"You hustler," I chastised. "You acted all nervous about dancing, but in reality, you're a pro."

"I've done it a few times," he admitted modestly, taking her into a turn I hadn't taught them yet.

"Stop that. I'm splitting you guys up. Your skills are needed elsewhere."

"Oh come on," pleaded Paige. "Let me keep him. It's about time we had a man around here who knows what he's doing."

Roman cut me a glance. "She said it, not me."

I turned my eyes heavenward and reassigned them to new partners.

After a bit more supervising, I grew satisfied with the whole group's prowess, convinced I'd see little change. Deciding to move on, Cody and I taught them lindy kicks next. Not surprisingly, chaos soon broke out. The gifted in the group picked the move up right away, those who had struggled previously continued to struggle, and some who had performed fine with the basic steps and turns now fell completely apart.

Cody and I moved through the dancers, doing damage control, offering our words of wisdom.

"Keep the tension in your wrist, Beth—not too much, though. Don't hurt yourself."

"Count, damn it! Count! The beats are still the same as before."

"Keep facing your partner . . . don't lose track of her."

My role as teacher consumed me, and I loved it. Who cared about vampire hunters and the eternal struggles of good and evil?

I caught sight of Seth sitting off to the side, just as he'd vowed. "Hey, voyeur, still just want to watch?" I chided, breathless and excited from running all over the makeshift dance floor.

He shook his head, a faint smile playing across his features as he studied me. "Plenty to see from here."

Standing up from his chair, he leaned forward in a familiar sort of way, startling me when his hand reached out and pushed up a dress strap that had slipped off my shoulder down to my arm.

"There," he pronounced. "Perfect."

Goose bumps rose on my flesh at his touch, his fingers warm and gentle. For just a moment, a look I hadn't seen before crossed his face. It made him look less like the distracted writer I'd come to know and more . . . well, *male*. Admiring. Considering. Maybe even predatory. The look was gone as quickly as it had come, though I still felt taken aback.

"Keep an eye on that strap," warned Seth mildly. "You've got to make him work for it." He inclined his head slightly toward some dancers, and I followed the motion to see Roman walking one of the baristas through a complex step.

I admired Roman's graceful moves a moment before turning back to Seth. "It's not that hard. I can teach you." I held up a hand by way of invitation.

He looked as though he might agree but shook his head at the last second. "I'd make a fool of myself."

"Ah yes, and sitting here alone, while everyone else dances *and* we're short of men—yes, that doesn't make you look foolish at all."

He gave a soft laugh. "Maybe."

When no other explanation came, I shrugged and returned to the dance floor, continuing my instruction. Cody and I added a couple new tricks, assisted in more practice, and finally stood off to the side admiring our pupils. "Think they'll be ready for the Moondance?" he asked.

The Moondance Lounge was a ballroom dance club that hosted monthly swing dance nights. We considered this group's appearance there to be the ultimate triumph of graduation.

"One more lesson, I think. Then we can take them out in public."

An arm caught me around the waist, pulling me onto the dance floor. I recovered my footing quickly, falling in step with Roman as he spun me into an intricate turn. A few people nearby stopped to watch.

"It's my turn to be teacher's pet," he admonished. "I've hardly seen you all night; I don't think this counts as a date."

I let him lead me around flamboyantly, curious as to just how good he really was. "You're always changing what you want," I complained. "First you just want to go out, now you say you actually want to be alone with me. You need to pick a story and stick with it. Be more specific."

"Ah, I see. No one told me that." He led me into a reverse whip, and I followed through flawlessly, earning a grudging look of approval from him. "I don't suppose there's a Georgina Kincaid Instruction Manual around somewhere to help me avoid these embarrassing blunders in the future."

"We sell them downstairs."

"Oh yeah?" He began improvising steps now, and I enjoyed the challenge of second-guessing where he would go. "Is there a page on how to woo the fair Georgina?"

"Page? Hell, there's a whole chapter."

"Required reading, I'd imagine."

"Definitely. Hey, thanks for the paint by number."

"I expect to see that on your wall the next time I'm over."

"With that horrible Native American stereotype? The next time you see it will be on the ACLU's hit list."

He spun me out into a flourish-filled ending, much to the delight of everyone else. They had long since stopped dancing to watch me make a spectacle of myself. I felt slightly self-conscious but shrugged it off, savoring the moment, taking Roman's hand to bow luridly to my coworkers' applause.

"Get ready," I announced, "because that's going to be next week's exam."

Cheers and laughter continued, but as they faded and the group dispersed for the night, Roman persisted in holding on to my hand, his fingers laced with mine. I didn't mind. We walked around, making small talk and saying goodbyes.

"You want to go get a drink?" he asked me, once we were momentarily alone.

I turned toward him, standing close, studying those gorgeous features. In the now-warmed-up room, I could strongly smell his perspiration mingled with cologne, and it made me want to bury my face in his neck.

"I want to . . ." I began slowly, wondering if alcohol and raw animal lust would be a wise combination with someone I wanted to avoid sleeping with.

Looking beyond him, I caught Cody's eye. He was talking earnestly with Seth, which I found odd. Suddenly, I remembered my earlier promise to go meet the vampires at the bar.

"Damn," I muttered. "I don't think I can." Still holding Roman's hand, I led him over to Cody and Seth. They stopped talking.

"I feel left out," joked Cody a moment later. "I saw you do some stuff just now that you never taught me."

"You were supposed to have been doing it for homework." I cocked my head in consideration. "Have you met Roman, Cody? Or you Seth?" I made quick introductions around, and they all politely shook hands, guy-style.

Once that was done, Roman settled his hand comfortably on my waist. "I'm trying to get Georgina to have a drink with me. But I think she's playing hard to get."

Cody smiled. "I don't think she's playing."

I looked apologetically at Roman. "I told Cody I'd meet him and another friend tonight."

The young vampire made a wave of dismissal. "Forget about it. Go have fun."

"Yeah, but—" I cut myself off and made significant eye contact with him à la Jerome and Carter. I didn't want Cody to go off alone, lest he be targeted by the vampire hunter, but I could hardly say that in front of the others. "Take a cab," I said at last. "Don't walk."

"Okay," he said automatically. Too automatically.

"I mean it," I warned.

"Yes, yes," he muttered. "Do you want to call it for me?"

I rolled my eyes at him, then suddenly remembered Seth's presence. Feeling kind of embarrassed with him standing there while we all made plans, I wondered if I should offer to invite him along or send him with Cody.

As though reading my mind, Seth bluntly declared, "Well, I'll see you guys later." He turned around and left before any of us could answer.

"Is he mad or something?" asked Cody after a moment.

"I think that's just the way he is," I explained, not sure I'd ever understand the writer.

"Weird." Roman turned back to me. "Ready to step out?"

Seth quickly left my mind. Roman and I walked over to a small restaurant across the street from Emerald City, sitting together on one side of a booth. I ordered my vodka gimlet, and he got brandy.

When our drinks arrived, he asked, "Should I be jealous of anyone back there?"

I chuckled. "You don't know me well enough or have any claims on me to worry about jealousy yet. Don't jump the gun here."

"I suppose not," he agreed. "Still, famous writers and suave, young dance partners are certainly exalted company."

"Cody's not that young."

"Young enough. Is he a close friend?"

"Close enough. Not romantically close, if that's what you're still driving at." Roman and I had snuggled together in the booth, and I gave him a playful poke in the ribs. "Quit worrying about my acquaintances. Let's talk about something else. Tell me about the world of linguistics."

I meant it half-jokingly, but he complied, explaining his specialty—classical languages, ironically enough. Roman knew his material well, speaking about it with the same wit and cleverness used in his flirtations. I followed these explanations avidly, enjoying the opportunity to engage in a topic few others knew anything about. Unfortunately, I had to taper my participation, lest I show just how well versed in the subject I truly was. It might look a little weird if a bookstore manager knew more about an area of study than someone who had made a career out of it.

Throughout this whole gripping discourse, Roman and I stayed in contact—arms, hands, and legs touching. He never tried to kiss me, for which I was grateful, as that would have been walking into dangerous territory. We were really on an ideal date for me: stimulating banter and as much physical contact as a succubus could safely handle. Our flirty conversation flowed effortlessly, like reading from a script.

Our drink flew by in an eye blink, and before I knew it, we stood back outside, parting ways and making arrangements for another date. I attempted my protests, but both of us could see how weak they were. He kept claiming I owed him a real, unchaperoned outing. Standing there with him, warmed by his presence, I felt surprised at how badly I wanted that date. The thing about sparing nice guys was that I always ended up lonely. Looking up at Roman, I decided then that I wanted to put off being lonely again—just for a little while.

So I agreed to go out again, ignoring the mental warning bells this decision set off. His face lit up, and I thought he would definitely try a mouth kiss now. My heart thumped loudly at the prospect, scared and eager.

Apparently my previous neurotic rants about not getting too close hit home, however. He merely held my hand, finally brushing his lips across my cheek in a kiss that was barely a kiss. He wandered off into the streets of Queen Anne, and a moment later, I walked the half-block back to my apartment.

When I reached my door, I discovered a note taped to it. My name, done in beautiful, heavily inked calligraphy, lay scrawled across the surface. An apprehensive coldness ran through me. The note read:

> *You are a beautiful woman, Georgina. Beautiful enough, I think, to even tempt angels into falling—something that doesn't happen nearly as often as it should anymore. Beauty such as yours is effortless, however, when you can make it anything you like. Your large friend, unfortunately, doesn't have such luxury, which is a damned shame after what happened today. Fortunately, he works in the right business to correct any damage to his appearance.*

I stared at the note like something that might bite me. It bore no name, of course. Ripping it off the door, I hurried into my apartment and picked up the phone. I dialed Hugh's number without hesitation. With the references to "large" and "right business," he was the only one the note could be referring to.

His phone rang and rang before giving way to an answering machine. Annoyed, I dialed his cell number.

After three rings, an unknown female voice answered.

"Is Hugh Mitchell there?"

There was a long pause. "He . . . can't talk right now. Who is this, please?"

"This is Georgina Kincaid. I'm his friend."

"I've heard him talk about you, Georgina. This is Samantha."

The name didn't mean anything to me, nor did I have the patience for this runaround. "Well, can I please talk to him then?"

"No . . ." Her voice sounded strained, upset. "Georgina, something bad happened today . . ."

Chapter 11

Hospitals are creepy places, cold and sterile. A true reminder of the tenuous nature of mortality. The thought of Hugh here made me nauseous, but I squelched the feeling as best I could, sprinting through the halls to the room Samantha had named.

When I reached it, I found Hugh lying calmly in a bed, his large body clad in a gown, his skin bruised and bandaged. A blond figure sat next to the bed with him, holding his hand. She turned in surprise when I burst into the room.

"Georgina," Hugh said, giving me a weak smile. "Nice of you to stop by."

The blond woman, presumably Samantha, studied me uneasily. Slim and doe-eyed, she tightened her grip on Hugh's hand, and I figured this must be the twenty-year-old from work. Her unnatural breasts verified as much.

"It's all right," he told her reassuringly. "This is my friend Georgina. Georgina, Samantha."

"Hi," I told her, offering my hand. She took it. Hers was cold, and I realized then that her nervousness was not so much at meeting me as general concern over what had happened to Hugh. It was touching.

"Sweetie, would you excuse Georgina and me for a bit? Maybe go get yourself a drink from the cafeteria?" He spoke gently and kindly to her, a tone he rarely used with the rest of us on our pub nights.

Samantha turned to Hugh anxiously. "I don't want to leave you alone."

"I won't be alone. Georgina and I just need to talk. Besides, she's a, uh, black belt; nothing will happen to me."

I made a face at him behind her back as she considered. "I suppose that's all right . . . you'll call my cell if you need me, right? I'll come right back."

"Of course," he promised, kissing her hand.

"I'll miss you."

"I'll miss you more."

She rose, gave me another uncertain look, and retreated out the door.

I watched her go a moment before taking her chair beside Hugh. "Very sweet. I think I'm getting cavities."

"No need to be bitter. Just because you can't form meaningful attachments with mortals."

His jest hurt a lot more than it probably should have, but then, I still had Roman on the brain.

"Besides," he continued, "she's a little upset about what happened today."

"Yeah, I imagine so. Jesus. Look at you."

I surveyed his wounds in greater detail. Hints of stitches appeared beneath some bandages, and dark blotchy bruises blossomed here and there.

"Could be worse."

"Could it?" I wondered archly. I'd never seen any immortal sustain so much injury.

"Sure. First, I could be dead, and I'm not. Second, I heal just like you do. You should have seen me this afternoon when they brought me in. The trick now will be to get me out of here before someone notices just how fast I'm recovering."

"Does Jerome know about this?"

"Of course. I called him earlier, but he'd already felt it. I expect him to show up any time now. Did he call you?"

"Not exactly," I admitted, hesitant to bring up the note quite yet. "What happened? When you were attacked?"

"I don't remember a lot of details." Hugh shrugged slightly, an awkward maneuver for one lying down. I suspected he'd already gone through this story with a number of others. "I stepped out for coffee. I was the only one in the parking lot, and while coming back to my car, this . . . person, I guess, just jumped out and attacked me. No warning."

"You guess?"

He frowned. "I never really got a good look. He was big, though, I could peg that much. And strong—really strong. A lot stronger than I would have thought."

Hugh himself was no weakling. True, he didn't work out or do much with his body, but he had a big frame and a lot of density to fill that frame out.

"Why did he stop?" I asked. "Did someone find you guys?"

"Nah, I don't know why he quit. It was all beating and slashing one minute; the next, he's gone. Took about fifteen minutes before someone else came along and helped me."

"You keep saying 'he.' You think it was a guy?"

He attempted another shrug. "I don't really know. Just an impression I got. Could have been a hot blonde for all I know."

"Yeah? Should I question Samantha?"

"You shouldn't be questioning anyone, according to Jerome. Did you ever talk to Erik?"

"Yeah . . . he's looking into some things for me. He also

reaffirmed that vampire hunters can't kill you or me, nor has he ever heard of anything that can."

Hugh turned thoughtful. "This person didn't kill me."

"Do you think he was trying?"

"He was certainly trying to do something. Seems like if he could have killed me, he would have."

"But he couldn't," a voice behind me pointed out, "because, as I've said, vampire hunters can only inconvenience you, not kill you."

I turned, startled at hearing Jerome's voice. It startled me further to see Carter with him.

"Leave it to Jerome to play devil's advocate," joked the angel.

"What are you doing here, Georgina?" demanded the demon icily.

My mouth gaped, and it took me a moment to speak. "How . . . how did you do that?"

Carter stood there dressed as disreputably as ever. Whereas Doug and Bruce looked like they were in a grunge band, the angel looked like the band had kicked him out. He gave me a lopsided grin. "Do what? Come up with a clever pun referencing Jerome's demonic status? The truth is, I usually keep a stash of them on hand and—"

"No. Not that. I can't feel you . . . can't sense you . . ." I could see Carter with my eyes, but I could not feel that powerful signature, aura, or whatever, that normally radiated from an immortal. Turning to Jerome suddenly, I realized he was the same. "Or you. I can't sense either of you. I couldn't the other night either."

Angel and demon exchanged glances over my head. "We can mask it," said Carter at last.

"What, like a light switch or something? You can turn it on and off?"

"It's a bit more complicated than that."

"Well, this is news to me. Can we do it? Hugh and I?"

"No," both Jerome and Carter answered together. Jerome elaborated, "Only higher immortals can do it."

Hugh weakly attempted to sit up. "Why . . . are you doing it?"

"You never answered my question, Georgie," Jerome pointed out, obviously avoiding the subject. He glanced at the imp. "I told you not to contact the others."

"I didn't. She just came."

Jerome turned his gaze back on me, and I fished the mysterious note out of my purse. I handed it to him, and the demon read it expressionlessly before handing it over to Carter. When the angel finished, he and Jerome looked at each other again in that annoying way of theirs. Jerome deposited the note into an inner pocket of his suit jacket.

"Hey, that's mine."

"Not anymore."

"Don't tell me you're going to stick to your party line about this being a vampire hunter," I shot back.

Jerome's dark eyes narrowed shrewdly at me. "Why wouldn't I? This person mistook Hugh for a vampire, but as you've already observed, Nancy Drew, Hugh could not be killed."

"I think this person knew Hugh wasn't a vampire."

"Oh? Why do you say that?"

"The note. The person who wrote it mentions my shape-shifting. He knows I'm a succubus. He probably knows Hugh's an imp."

"His knowing you're a succubus explains why he didn't attack you. He knew he couldn't kill you. He wasn't sure about Hugh, however, so he took his chances."

"With a knife." Again, I remembered: *How do you know if a demon is lying? His lips are moving.* "I thought the story was that this was some amateur vampire hunter arbitrarily going after people with a stake because he didn't know any better. Instead, this person somehow knows about me and took on Hugh with a knife."

Carter stifled a yawn and joined in on Jerome's game. "Maybe this person's learning. You know, expanding their choice of weapons. After all, no one stays an amateur for long. Even new vampire hunters wise up eventually."

I jumped on the one detail here no one had addressed yet. "And even children know that vampires don't come out in daylight. What time were you attacked, Hugh?"

A strange look crossed the imp's face. "Late this afternoon. When the sun was up."

I looked exultantly at Jerome. "This person knew Hugh wasn't a vampire."

Jerome leaned against a wall, appearing unfazed as he picked nonexistent pieces of lint from his slacks. He looked more like John Cusack than ever today. "So? Mortals get delusions of grandeur. He kills one vampire and decides to do his part against the rest of the evil forces inhabiting this city. That changes nothing."

"I don't think it was a mortal."

Both Jerome and Carter, looking at other things in the room, now snapped their heads toward me. "Oh?"

I swallowed, slightly flustered under that scrutiny. "I mean . . . you guys prove higher immortals can go around without being sensed, and no one's been able to sense anything from this guy. Plus, look at Hugh's damage. Erik said mortals can't really do substantial—" I bit off my words, realizing my error.

Carter laughed softly.

"Damn it, Georgie." Jerome straightened like a whip. "I told you to let us handle this. Who else have you talked to?"

Whatever cloaking Jerome had been doing vanished, and I suddenly became aware of the power crackling around him. It reminded me of one of those sci-fi movies when a door opens into outer space, and all the debris gets sucked out as a result of the vacuum. Everything in the room seemed to be drawn into Jerome, toward his swelling power and might. To my immortal perceptions, he became a glowing bonfire of terror and energy.

I cringed against Hugh's bed, resisting the urge to shade my eyes. The imp put a hand on my arm, though whether it was for my comfort or his own, I didn't know. "No one. I swear it, no one else. I just asked Erik some questions . . ."

Carter took a step toward the furious demon, face angelically calm. "Easy there. You're sending up a beacon to any immortal in a ten-mile radius."

Jerome's eyes stayed fixed on me, and I felt true fear for the first time in centuries in the focus of all that intensity. Then, like the light switch I'd joked about earlier, it all vanished. Just like that, Jerome stood before me completely incognito for all arcane intents and purposes. Like a mortal. He exhaled heavily and rubbed a spot between his eyes.

"Georgina," he said at last. "Contrary to whatever you believe, this is not all some elaborate attempt to vex you. Please stop going against me. We're doing what we're doing for a reason. Your best interests really are at heart here."

My catty nature wanted to ask if demons had hearts, but something else struck me as more pressing. "Why the 'we' here? I assume you mean him." I nodded toward Carter. "What could involve both a demon and an angel and make them skulk around hiding their presence? Are you guys afraid of something?"

"Skulking?" Carter sounded jovially indignant.

"Please, Georgie," intoned Jerome, patience obviously at a breaking point, "leave well-enough alone. If you really want to do something useful, you will avoid dangerous situations like I advised before. I can't make you stay in protected company, but if you persist in being a nuisance otherwise, I can find a convenient place to stash you until this all blows over. This is not about anyone's 'side,' and you only run the risk of muddling up matters you don't understand."

I unconsciously squeezed Hugh's hand for support. I did not want to think about what sort of "convenient place" Jerome had in mind.

"Do we understand each other?" the demon asked softly.

I nodded.

"Good. You will be of most assistance to me by keeping yourself safe. I have too many things to worry about now without adding you to the list."

I nodded again, not trusting myself to speak. His small display had had its intended effect on temporarily cowing me, though some niggling part of me knew I would be unable to "leave well-enough alone" once I walked out of here. It would be best to keep that knowledge to myself.

"That will be all, Georgie," Jerome added. I heard the dismissal.

"I'll walk you out," offered Carter.

"No thanks." But the angel followed in my wake anyway.

"So how'd it go with Seth Mortensen?"

"Okay."

"Just okay?"

"Just okay."

"I hear he's living here now. And spends a lot of time at Emerald City."

I eyed him askance. "Where'd you hear that?"

He only grinned. "So? Tell me about it."

"There's nothing to tell," I snapped, uncertain why I was even discussing this. "I've talked to him a few times, toured him around. We don't really click. We can't communicate."

"Why not?" Carter wanted to know.

"He's a hardcore introvert. Doesn't talk much. Just watches. Besides, I don't want to encourage him."

"So you're increasing his silence."

I shrugged and pushed the button for an elevator.

"I think I know a book that might help you. I'll dig it out and let you borrow it."

"No thanks."

"Don't knock it. It'll improve your communication skills with Seth. I saw it on a talk show."

"Aren't you listening? I don't want to improve things."

"Ah," said Carter sagely. "You don't go for introverts."

"I—no, that's not it. I don't have a problem with introverts."

"Then why don't you like Seth?"

"I do like him! Damn it, stop this."

The angel quirked me a grin. "It's all right to feel that way. I mean, past evidence shows you tend to go for showy, flirty guys anyway."

"What's that supposed to mean?" I immediately thought of my attraction to Roman.

Carter's eyes flashed mischievously. We were at the hospital's exit now. "I don't know. You tell me, Letha."

I had nearly walked out the door, but his comment jerked me back. I spun around so fast, my hair whipped around and hit me in the face. *"Where did you hear that name?"*

"I have my sources."

A great nebulous emotion swelled up in my chest, something I couldn't entirely identify. It fell somewhere on the continuum of hate and despair, not really subscribing to either one. Hotter and hotter it grew within me, making me want to scream at Carter and that smug, knowing look on his face. I wanted to beat my fists against him or shape-shift into something horrific. I didn't know where he'd learned that name, but it woke up some sort of sleeping monster within me, something that had been tightly coiled up.

He continued watching me coolly, undoubtedly reading my thoughts.

Slowly, I became aware of my surroundings. The chilly

corridors. The anxious visitors. The efficient staff. I calmed my breathing and fixed the angel with a scathing look.

"Don't you ever call me that again. Ever."

He shrugged, still smiling. "My mistake."

I turned smartly on my heels and left him there. I stormed out to my car and didn't even realize I was driving until I was halfway across the bridge, tears leaking from the corners of my eyes.

Chapter 12

"**M**an, if Jerome had threatened to stash me somewhere, I wouldn't be out snooping around."

"I'm not snooping. I'm just speculating."

Peter shook his head and took the cap off a beer. I sat with him and Cody in their kitchen, the day after Hugh's attack. A ham and pineapple pizza had just arrived, and Cody and I dug into it while the other vampire merely watched.

"Why can't you just accept this for what it is? Jerome's telling the truth. It's a vampire hunter."

"No. No way. None of this adds up. Not the goofy way Jerome and Carter are acting. Not Hugh's attack. Not that fucked-up note I got."

"I figured you get screwy love notes all the time. 'My heart bleeds for you, Georgina.' Written in actual blood. Stuff like that."

"Yeah, nothing like self-mutilation to turn a girl on," I muttered. I gulped some Mountain Dew and returned to my pizza. Really, as far as caffeine and sugar went, Mountain

Dew was nearly as good as one of my mochas. "Hey, why aren't you eating any of this?"

Peter held up his beer bottle by way of explanation. "I'm dieting."

I peered at it. *Golden Village Low-Carb Ale.*

I froze, mid-bite. Low-carb?

"Peter . . . you're a vampire. Aren't you by definition always on a low-carb diet?"

"It's no use," Cody chuckled, speaking up for the first time. "I've already had this argument with him. He won't listen."

"You wouldn't understand." Peter eyed our pizza wistfully. "You can make your body look like anything you want."

"Yeah, but . . ." I looked to Cody. "Can he really even put on weight? Aren't immortal bodies, I don't know, unchangeable? Or timeless? Or something?"

"You'd know more about it than me," he said.

"We eat other things." Peter rubbed his stomach self-consciously. "Not just blood. It all adds up."

This had to be weirdest thing I'd heard since Duane's death. "Stop it, Peter. You're being ridiculous. Next thing, you'll be down at Hugh's asking for liposuction."

He brightened. "Do you think that would help?"

"No! You look fine. You look the same as you always have."

"I don't know. Cody's been getting all the attention whenever we go out. Maybe I should get more blond put into the spikes."

I refrained from pointing out that Peter had been almost forty when he'd become a vampire, his hair heavily receding. Cody had been very young—barely twenty—and bore tawny, leonine good looks. Immortals who were formerly human stayed fixed at the age and appearance immortality had taken over. If the two vampires still frequented clubs and college bars, I didn't doubt Cody had more luck.

"We're wasting time," I exclaimed, wanting to derail Peter from this whole image thing. "I want to figure out who attacked Hugh."

"Christ, you have a one-track mind," he snapped. "Why can't you just wait to find out?"

Good question. I didn't know why. Something inside me was tugging to get to the truth of this, to do what I could to protect my friends and myself. I just couldn't stand passively by.

"It couldn't have been a mortal. Not from the way Hugh described the attack."

"Yeah, but no immortal could have killed Duane. I already told you that."

"No *lesser* immortal," I pointed out. "But a higher immortal . . ."

Peter laughed. "Oh-ho, you are pushing the envelope now. You think there's some vindictive demon out there?"

"They'd certainly be capable."

"Yeah, but they have no motivation."

"Not nece—"

A funny sensation suddenly spread over me, tingly and gentle and silvery. I was put in mind of the fragrance of lilacs, the tinkling of small bells. I looked sharply at the others.

"What the—" began Cody, but Peter was already moving toward the door. The signature we all felt was similar to Carter's in certain ways but lighter and sweeter. Less powerful.

A guardian angel.

Peter opened the door, and Lucinda stood there primly, her arms clasped tightly around a book.

I nearly choked. It would figure. As a general rule, I didn't

nteract with many angels in the area, Carter being the ex-
eption because of his relationship with Jerome. Still, I
new who the locals were, and I knew Lucinda. She wasn't a
rue angel like Carter. Guardians were more like the heav-
nly equivalent of Hugh: former mortals who served and ran
rrands for all eternity.

I had no doubt Lucinda performed all sorts of good deeds
n a daily basis. She probably worked in soup kitchens and
ead to orphans in her free time. Whenever she was around
s, however, she became a prissy little bitch. Peter shared my
entiment.

"Yes?" he asked coolly.

"Hello, Peter. Your hair is very . . . interesting today," she
bserved diplomatically, not moving from the doorway.
May I come in?"

Peter scowled at the hair comment but had too many good
osting instincts drilled into him to not wave her inside. He
night tease me about mortal hobbies, but the vampire had
 meticulous sense of propriety and etiquette bordering on
bsessive-compulsive disorder.

She swept inside, proper in an ankle-length plaid skirt
nd high-necked sweater. Her short blond hair curled under
n a perfect bob.

I was a different story. Between my plunging neckline,
ltratight jeans, and fuck-me heels, I felt like I might as well
ie down on the floor and spread my legs. The demure look
he gave me clearly implied she was thinking the same
hing.

"Charming to see you all again." Her tone was crisp, for-
nal. "I'm here to deliver something from Mr. Carter."

"*Mr.* Carter?" asked Cody. "Is that his last name? I always
hought it was his first."

"I think he just has one name," I speculated. "Like Cher
r Madonna."

Lucinda said nothing to our bandying. Instead, she handed me a book. *Men Are from Mars, Women Are from Venus: The Classic Guide to Understanding the Opposite Sex.*

"What the hell is that?" exclaimed Peter. "I think I saw it on some talk show."

I suddenly remembered walking out with Carter in the hospital and how he'd claimed to own a book that would help me with Seth. I tossed it on the counter disinterestedly.

"Carter's fucked-up sense of humor in action."

Lucinda flushed deep crimson. "How can you use such language so carelessly? You sound like you're . . . like you're in a locker room!"

I smoothed down my tank top. "No way. I'd never wear this in a locker room."

"Yeah, it isn't even in school colors," said Peter.

I couldn't resist toying with the guardian. "If I were in a locker room, I'd probably have on a short cheerleader skirt. And no underwear."

Peter continued playing off me. "And you'd do that one cheer, right? The one with your hands splayed against the shower wall and ass sticking out?"

"That's me," I agreed. "Always ready to take one for the team."

Even Cody flushed at our crassness. Lucinda was practically purple.

"You—you two have no sense of decency! None at all."

"Oh whatever," I told her. "Back at the country club, or wherever you and the rest of the choir hang out, you probably wear a shorter version of that skirt all the time. With knee socks. I bet the other angels really go for the schoolgirl look."

If Lucinda were any one of my friends, a comment like that would have only escalated into more sarcasm and snide remarks. The guardian, however, merely stiffened and chose to rely on deadpan self-righteousness.

"We," she declared, "do not carry on in such an unseemly manner with each other. *We* act with decorum. *We* treat each other with respect. *We* do not turn on each other."

This last one came with a brief eye-glance toward me.

"What was that for?"

She tossed her hair, what little of it there was. "Oh, I think you know. We've all been hearing about your little vigilante act. First that vampire, then the imp. Nothing about you people surprises me anymore."

Now my face flushed. "That's bullshit! I was cleared of Duane a long time ago. And Hugh . . . that's just stupid. He's my friend."

"What does friendship mean among your kind? He's just as bad. From what I heard, he received a great deal of amusement telling anyone who would listen about your little whip and wings getup. Oh, and by the way, if you don't mind my observation, I think that has to be the most degrading thing I've ever heard. Even for a succubus." She arched a glance toward the book I had tossed to the counter. "I'll tell Mr. Carter you, uh, received the book."

With that, she turned neatly and left, closing the door behind her.

"Sanctimonious bitch," I muttered. "And how many people know about that demon girl thing anyway?"

"Forget her," said Peter. "She's a nobody. And an angel. There's no telling what they'll do."

I scowled. And then, it hit me. I couldn't believe I'd never thought of it before. Maybe Lucinda needed more credit.

"That's it!"

"What's it?" mumbled Cody through a mouthful of nearly cold pizza.

"An angel killed Duane and attacked Hugh! It's perfect.

You were right in saying a demon would have no reason to take our side out. But an angel? Why not? I mean a real one, not a guardian like Lucinda."

Peter shook his head. "An angel could do something like that, but it'd be too petty. The great cosmic good-versus-evil battle is bigger than one-on-one matches. You know that. Taking out one agent of evil at a time would be a waste of resources."

Cody considered. "What if it was a renegade angel? Someone not following the rules of the game."

Peter and I both turned to the younger vampire in surprise. He'd been more or less avoiding our speculation this evening.

"There's no such thing," his mentor countered back. "Is there, Georgina?"

I felt both vampires' eyes turn to me, waiting for my opinion. "Jerome says there are no bad angels. Once they're bad, they become demons, not angels anymore."

"Well, that kills your theory then. An angel doing something bad would fall and not be an angel anymore. Then Jerome would know about him."

I frowned, still intrigued by Cody's use of the word "renegade" over "fallen." "Maybe angel sin is like human sin . . . it's not always 'bad' if the person thinks they're doing 'good.' This one hasn't gone over yet."

We all pondered this a moment. Humans continually labor under the delusion that there really is a precise set of rules on what sin is and is not, rules that one might break without even realizing it. In reality, most people know when they do wrong. They feel it. Sin is more of a subjective matter than an objective one. Back in the days of the Puritans, corrupting souls had been no problem for a succubus since almost anything sexual and pleasurable felt wrong to those men. Nowadays, most people don't regard premarital sex as wrong, hence no sin is committed. Succubi have been forced to become more creative over the years if they want to get an energy fix *and* corrupt a soul.

Still, by that logic, it was possible that a renegade angel who believed he or she was doing good might not cross into the realm of sin. If there was no sin, then there could be no fall. Or could there be? The whole concept strained the mind, and Peter apparently thought so too.

"So what's the difference? What makes an angel fall? We're staking a lot here on a technicality."

I could have concurred until I recalled something else. "The note."

"Note?" asked Cody.

"The note that was on my door. It said I was beautiful enough to tempt angels into falling."

"Well, you do look pretty good." When I raised an eyebrow, Peter said grudgingly, "Okay, that is kind of suspicious . . . but it's almost too suspicious. Why would someone overtly leave a calling card?"

Cody nearly jumped out of his seat. "It's some kind of psycho angel who likes playing mind games. Like in those movies where killers carve clues into their victims, so they can watch the police puzzle things out."

I shuddered at that image as I thought over what I knew about angels in general, which really was nothing. Unlike our side, the powers of good did not have the same cryptic hierarchy of supervisors and geographic networks, no matter the stories about cherubim and seraphim. After all, we were the ones who had invented middle management, not them. I always had the impression that most angels and denizens of good operated like private investigators or field agents, completing assorted angelic missions in a very loosely organized way. Such an open venue would provide ample chance for someone to surreptitiously tackle a side agenda.

Angelic involvement would also explain the subterfuge, I reflected. Their side was embarrassed. Typical, really. Little embarrassed our side anymore. They, however, would be shamefaced to admit one of theirs had turned rogue, and Carter, being so chummy with Jerome, had conned the demon into keeping quiet about the whole matter. All of his sarcasm and attempts to mock me were only more weak efforts at saving face.

The more I considered this far-fetched theory, the more I liked it. Some disgruntled angel, wanting to be heroic, decided to turn vigilante and take on the forces of evil. The renegade angel theory would explain how any of us could be legitimate targets, as well as shed light on why no one could sense this being since we now knew higher immortals could hide their presence.

Which made me wonder why exactly Jerome and Carter were also masking their presence. Were they hoping to catch this angel unaware? That, and . . .

"Why'd this person let Hugh live then?" I looked from vampire to vampire. "An angel could take out any of us. Hugh said he wasn't winning, and no one interrupted. The attacker just got bored and took off. Why? Why kill Duane but not Hugh? Or me, for that matter, since this person knows what I am."

"Because Duane was an asshole?" suggested Peter.

"Personality aside, we all weigh in just as heavily on the evil side. Hugh maybe even more so."

Indeed, Hugh was in his prime as far as immortals went. He no longer held a novice's inexperience like Cody, nor had the imp grown world-weary and bored like Peter and I had. Hugh knew enough now to be good at his job, and he actually liked what he did. He should have been a prime target for any angelic vigilante wanting to make the world a better place.

Cody agreed with Peter. "Yeah. Evil or not, some of us are more likable than others. Maybe an angel could respect that."

"I doubt an angel would find any of us likable—"

I cut myself off. One angel did like us. One angel hung out with us a lot. One angel who seemed to be everywhere Jerome was lately when these attacks happened. One angel who knew us personally, who knew all of our habits and weaknesses. What better way was there to track and study us than to infiltrate our drinking group and pretend to be a friend?

The idea was so explosive, so dangerous, I felt ill at ease just giving shape to the thought. I certainly couldn't utter any of it aloud. Not yet. Cody and Peter hardly believed the angel theory at all. I doubted they'd jump on board if I started accusing Carter.

"You okay, Georgina?" Cody queried when I lapsed into silence.

"Yeah . . . yeah . . . fine." I caught a glimpse at the time on the stove and jumped up from my chair, head still reeling. "Shit. I've got to get back to Queen Anne."

"What for?" asked Peter.

"I have a date."

"With who?" Cody grinned slyly at me, and I blushed in response.

"Roman."

Peter turned to his apprentice. "Which one is that?"

"The hot dancing guy. Georgina was all over him."

"I was not. I like him too much for that."

They laughed. As I picked up my coat, Peter asked: "Hey, I don't suppose you could do me a favor sometime?"

"What?" My mind still clung to the mystery winding

around us. That, and Roman. He and I had talked on the phone a few times now since the last date, and I was growing more and more amazed at just how well we clicked.

"Well, you know how they've got those computer programs in salons that will show you what you'll look like with different colors and cuts? I was thinking you could be like a living one. You could morph into me and show me what I'd look like with different hairstyles."

Silence hung in the room for a full minute as Cody and I stared at him.

"Peter," I told him at last, "that's the stupidest idea I've ever heard."

"I don't know." Cody scratched his chin. "For him, it's not bad."

"We have too many other issues to deal with right now," I warned, having no patience to humor Peter with niceties. "I'm not wasting my energy on your vanity."

"Come on," pleaded Peter. "You're still brimming from that good virgin guy. You can spare it."

I shook my head, slinging my purse over one shoulder. "Succubus 101. The farther a transformation takes me from my natural form, the more energy it expends. Cross-gender changes are a pain in the ass; cross-species ones are even worse. Playing salon with you would burn through most of my stash, and I've got better things to waste it on." I eyed him dangerously. "You need some serious counseling for body image and insecurity, my friend."

Cody regarded me with new interest. "Cross-species? Could you, like, turn into a Gila monster or . . . or . . . a sand dollar or something?"

"Good night, boys. I'm out of here."

As I departed, I could just barely hear Peter and Cody debating if it would take more energy for me to change into a really small mammal or a human-sized reptile.

Vampires. Honestly, they're like children sometimes.

I drove home in record time. I remembered to shape-shift my heels into sandals and walked up to my building's door just as Roman did.

Seeing him banished any lingering thoughts of angels and conspiracies.

He had told me to dress casually for this evening, and while he had done the same, he still managed to make jeans and a long-sleeved T-shirt look like runway fashion. I apparently had the same effect on him because he caught me up in a giant bear hug and kissed my cheek.

"Hey, gorgeous," he murmured into my ear, holding on to the embrace a bit longer than necessary.

"Hey, yourself." I disentangled my body from his and smiled up at him.

"You're so short," he noted, cupping my cheek in his hand. "It's cute."

Those eyes threatened to engulf me, and I hastily turned away before I did something stupid. "Let's go." I paused. "Um, where are we going?"

He led me to his car, parked just down the street. "Since you seem to be so good with your feet, I thought I'd take us somewhere to test the rest of your bodily coordination."

"Like a hotel room?"

"Damn. Am I that obvious?"

Several minutes later, he pulled into a dilapidated establishment with a blinking neon sign reading BURT'S BOWLING ALLEY. I stared in open distaste, unable to hide my feelings.

"This is your choice of date? A bowling alley? Not even a nice one at that."

Roman seemed unconcerned about my lack of enthusiasm. "When was the last time you actually went bowling?"

I suspected it had been back in the 1970s. "Not in a very long time."

"Exactly. You see," he began conversationally as we went inside and approached the counter, "I've got you figured out. You claim you don't want to get serious with anyone, but I still get the impression you go out a lot. Size ten, please."

"Six and a half."

The cashier gave us each a pair of unsavory-looking shoes, and I felt grateful germs posed no threat to me. Roman handed over some cash, and she gestured us down to our designated lane.

"Anyway, like I was saying, regardless of your intentions, you must still end up dating quite a bit. I don't know how you couldn't with the attention you attract."

"What's that supposed to mean?" I sat down by our lane and took off my Birkenstocks, still eyeing the rental shoes askance.

Roman paused in his own shoe-tying and gave me a long, steady look. "Oh come on, you can't be that oblivious. Men check you out all the time. I always see it when I'm with you. Walking through the bookstore, going to that bar the other night. Even here, in this place. In just walking over from the counter, I saw at least three guys stop and watch you."

"Is there a point here somewhere?"

"Eventually." He stood up, and we walked over to a rack of communal bowling balls. "With all that attention, guys must ask you out all the time, and you must give in sometimes, just like you did with me. Right?"

"I guess."

He paused in his ball selection and gave me another one of those breathtaking, soul-searching looks. "So tell me about your last date."

"My last date?" I somehow didn't think Martin Miller counted.

"Your last date. I mean a real date, not like a casual grabbing a drink thing. A date where the guy gave his best shot at planning an itinerary he thought would get you into bed."

I tested the weight of a fluorescent orange and green swirled ball, racking my brain. "The opera," I said at last. "And dinner at Santa Lucia's."

"Nice spread. And the one before that?"

"Jesus, you're nosy. Um . . . let's see, I think it was the opening of an art exhibit."

"Undoubtedly paired with dinner at some restaurant where stiff waiters say 'thank you' after you make a selection, right?"

"I guess."

"Just as I thought." He hoisted a navy blue ball into the crook of his arm. "This is why you're resistant to dating, why you don't want to get serious with anyone. You're such a hot commodity that plush, five-star dates are par for the course. They're ordinary. Men try to throw out all the stops for you, but after a while, you get bored with them." His eyes danced mischievously. "Therefore, I will differentiate myself from those losers by taking you to places your little elitist feet would never dream of touching. The salt of the earth. Back to basics. The way dating was meant to be: two people, more concerned with each other than their posh venue."

I walked with him back to our lane. "You just took an awfully long time to say you think I want to go slumming."

"Don't you?"

"No."

"Then why are you with me?"

I eyed that gorgeous appearance and thought about the conversation we'd had the other night on classical languages. Looks and intellect. Hard to beat. "You're hardly slumming it."

He smiled at me and changed the subject. "That's your choice?"

I looked down at the ball's psychedelic color pattern. "Yeah. This night is already turning surreal enough. Figured I might as well get the full experience. Maybe we'll drop some acid later."

Roman's eyes crinkled with amusement, and he cocked his head toward the lane. "Let's see what you can do with it."

I stepped up uncertainly, trying to remember how I used to do this. All up and down the alley, I could see other players walking up and throwing with ease. Shrugging, I stood at the line, drew my arm back, and threw. The ball flew out jerkily, sailed about four feet, hit the lane with a loud *crack*, and then promptly entered the gutter. Roman walked up beside me, and we silently watched the ball complete its journey.

"Are you always that rough with balls?" he asked finally.

"Most men don't complain."

"I imagine not. Try making contact with the floor before you let it go this time."

I gave him a sharp look. "You aren't one of those guys that gets off from showing women how much better you are at stuff, are you?"

"Nope. Just offering friendly advice."

My ball returned, and I followed his instructions. The ball's impact proved quieter that way, but I still ended up in the gutter.

"All right. Show me what *you* can do," I grumbled, sitting down huffily into a chair.

Roman strode up to the lane, movements graceful and flowing like a cat's. The ball poured from his hand like water from a pitcher, sailing smoothly down and hitting nine pins. When his ball returned, he threw it effortlessly once more and took out the obstinate tenth.

"This is going to be a long night."

"Cheer up." He chucked my chin. "We'll get you through

this. Try it again, and aim more toward the left. I'm going to get us some beers."

I threw to the left as advised but only succeeded in hitting the left gutter. On my second throw, I tried greater moderation and managed to hit one pin on the far left. I whooped in spite of myself.

"Nicely done," cheered Roman, setting two mugs of cheap beer down on the table. I hadn't drunk anything not from a microbrewery in over a decade. "It's all about baby steps."

That certainly turned out to be true as our evening progressed. My pin count increased slowly, though I soon developed the nasty habit of creating splits on my first throw. I showed no aptitude for picking them up, despite Roman's best explanations. To his credit, he gave good, nonthreatening advice, as well as some hands-on instruction.

"Your arm goes like this, and the rest of you leans like this," he explained, standing behind me with one hand on my hip and the other on my wrist. My flesh warmed at his touch, and I wondered if his actions were truly driven by altruism or were an excuse to get his hands on me. I exercised such techniques regularly in succubus work. It drove men wild, and now I knew why.

Ruse or no, I didn't tell him to stop.

I hit my peak in the second game, even managing one strike, though my performance declined in the third round as beer and fatigue took over. Sensing this, Roman called our bowling adventures closed, lauding my progress as highly impressive.

"Do we have to go to a dive now for dinner, in order to keep with this dream-date slumming fantasy you've got going?"

He put his arm around me as we walked out to the car. "I guess that depends if you've succumbed to my wily charm or not."

"If I say yes, will you take me somewhere good? Sometimes the posh places do work, you know."

We ended up at an upscale Japanese restaurant, much to my satisfaction. Taking our time, we savored both food and conversation, and again Roman's knowledge and wit impressed me. This time we discussed current issues, sharing opinions on recent news and culture, things we liked, things that drove us crazy, etc., etc. I discovered Roman had traveled quite a bit and held strong views on world politics and affairs.

"This country is so in love with itself," he complained, sipping sake. "It's like one big mirror. It just sits all day and looks at itself. When it can be bothered to look away, it's only to tell others 'do this' or 'be just like me.' Our military and economic policies bully people outside our borders, and inside, conservative groups bully other citizens. I hate it."

I listened with interest, intrigued at this side of a normally light and easygoing guy. "So do something about it. Or leave."

He shook his head. "Spoken like a comfortable citizen. The old 'if you don't like it, you can just leave' policy. Unfortunately, it's a lot harder than that to cut yourself off from your roots." Leaning back, he forced levity with a small grin. "And I do do things here and there. Small acts. My own battle against the status quo, you know? Attend the occasional protest. Refuse to buy products made with third world labor."

"Avoid fur? Eat organic food?"

"That too," he chuckled.

"Funny," I said after a moment's silence. Something had just struck me.

"What?"

"This whole time, we've talked about current things. No sharing of traumatic childhoods, college days, exes, or whatever."

"So what's funny about that?"

"Nothing really. It's just that the human mating process usually seems to dictate everyone share their histories."

"You want to do that?"

"Not really." I actually hated that part of dating. I always had to edit my past. I hated the lying, having to keep track of my stories.

"I think the past plagues us enough without muddling it into our present. I'd rather look forward, not backward."

I studied him curiously. "Does your past plague you?"

"Very much so. I fight every day to not let the past overtake me. Sometimes I win, sometimes it does."

God only knew mine did the same. It was odd to talk to someone about this, someone who felt the same way. I wondered how many people in the world walked around with invisible baggage, hiding it from others. Even while packing said baggage, I'd always kept it concealed. I had a driving need to keep up surface appearances—hence the so-called "happy face." I'd smiled and nodded through the worst times of my life, and when that superficial reaction had not been enough, I'd finally just run—even though it cost me my soul.

I smiled slightly. "Well then. I'm glad you and I stick to the present."

He tweaked my nose. "Me too. In fact, my present is looking pretty damned good right now. Maybe my future too, if I keep weakening your resolve."

"Don't push it."

"Aw, come on. Admit it. You find my outrage at the powers-that-be endearing. Maybe even erotic."

"I think 'entertaining' would be a better word. If you want outrage, you should spend time with Doug, my coworker. You guys have a lot in common. By day he cleans up and plays respectable assistant manager, by night he's the lead singer of this wacky band, registering his discontent against society through music."

Roman's eyes flickered with interest. "Does he play around here?"

"Yup. He'll be at the Old Greenlake Brewery this Saturday. Me and some of the other staff are going."

"Oh yeah? What time should I meet you?"

"I don't recall inviting you."

"Don't you? Because I could have sworn you just named a day and place. Sounded like a passive invitation to me. You know, the kind where it'd be my job to say 'mind if I come along,' and then you say 'yeah, no problem,' and so it goes. I just skipped a few steps."

"Most efficient of you," I observed.

"So . . . mind if I come along?"

I groaned. "Roman, we can't keep going out. It was cute at first, but it was only supposed to be one date. We've already gone past that. People at work think you're my boyfriend." Casey and Beth had informed me recently what a "hottie" I had.

"Do they?" He looked very happy about this.

"I'm not joking here. I mean it when I say I don't want to get serious with anyone right now."

And yet, I didn't really mean it. Not in my heart. I'd spent centuries cutting myself off from any sort of meaningful attachment with another person, and it hurt. Even when I had purposely cultivated relationships with nice guys in my succubus glory days, I had immediately dropped them and disappeared post-sex. In some ways, my life now was even harder. I avoided the guilt of stealing a nice man's life energy, but I never had true companionship either. No one who cared exclusively for me. Sure, I had friends, but they had their own lives, and those who got too close—like Doug—had to be pushed away again for their own good.

"Don't you believe in casual dating? Or even male-female friendships?"

"No," I answered decisively. "I do not."

"What about the other males in your life? That Doug guy? The dance instructor? Even that writer? You're friends with them, aren't you?"

"Well, yeah, but that's different. I'm not attracted—"

I bit off my words, but it was too late. Roman's face bloomed with hope and pleasure. He leaned toward me, touching my cheek with his hand.

I swallowed, terrified and thrilled by how close he was. Beer and sake had made me fuzzy in body and mind, and I made a mental promise not to drink the next time we went out. Not that we were going out again . . . right? Alcohol confused my senses, made it harder to differentiate between the succubus feeding instinct and pure, primal lust. Either one was dangerous around him.

And yet . . . in that moment, lust wasn't even really the issue. He was. Being with him. Talking to him. Having someone in my life again. Someone who cared about me. Someone who understood me. Someone I could go home to. And with.

"What time should I meet you?" he murmured.

I looked down, suddenly feeling warm. "It's a late show . . ."

His hand slid from my cheek to the back of my neck, intertwining with my hair and tipping my face toward his. "You want to hang out beforehand?"

"We shouldn't." My words all seemed long and drawn-out, like I was swimming in molasses.

Roman leaned over and kissed my ear. "I'll be at your place at seven."

"Seven," I repeated.

His lips moved to kiss the part of my cheek closest to my ear, then the cheek's center, then just below my mouth. His lips hovered so close to mine; my whole body concentrated on that proximity. I could feel the heat from his mouth, like it had its own private aura. Everything moved in slow motion. I wanted him to kiss me, wanted him to consume me with his lips and his tongue. I wanted it and feared it, yet felt powerless to act either way.

"Can I get you something else?"

The waiter's mildly embarrassed voice shattered my numbing haze, snapping me back to reason, reminding me what would happen to Roman even with a kiss. Not too much, true, but enough. I broke out of his grasp and shook my head. "Nothing else. Just the check."

Roman and I spoke little after that. He drove me home and made no advances when he walked me to the door, only smiling kindly as he chucked me under the chin again and reminded me he'd be by at seven on Saturday.

I went to bed restless and aching for sex. The alcohol helped me fall asleep easily, but when I awoke in the morning, lying in bed in a drowsy state, I could still remember how it had felt to have his lips so close to mine. The lustful yearning returned with a vengeance.

"This is no good," I complained to Aubrey, rolling out of bed.

I had three hours before work and knew I needed to do something other than daydream about Roman. Remembering that I had never followed up with Erik, I decided I should pay him a visit. The vampire hunter theory was more or less obsolete as far as I was concerned, but he might have found something else of use. I could also ask him about fallen angels.

Considering the whole "stashing" threat, I probably should have experienced more concern about going back to Arcana, Ltd. Still, I felt more or less safe. One thing I had learned about the archdemon was that he was not a morning person. He didn't really need rest, of course, but it was a mortal luxury he'd taken to wholeheartedly. I expected him to still be asleep, wherever he was, with no way of knowing what I planned to do.

Dressing and eating breakfast, I soon hit the road to Lake

City. I found the shop effortlessly now, feeling dismay once more at its barren look and empty parking lot. Yet, when I entered, I saw a dark shape leaning over a corner of books, too tall to be Erik. Pleasure at the thought of Erik getting more business coursed through me until the figure straightened and fixed me with a sardonic, gray-eyed expression.

"Hello, Georgina."

I swallowed. "Hello, Carter."

Chapter 13

Carter picked up a book and leafed through it lazily. His stringy blond hair had been stuffed under a backward baseball cap, and his flannel shirt appeared to have seen better days.

"Looking for altar supplies?" he asked me without glancing up. "Or maybe here to brush up on your astrology?"

"It's none of your business why I'm here," I snapped back, too flustered at the sight of him to think of anything funny or even plausible.

The gray eyes looked up. "Does Jerome know you're here?"

"It's not his business either. Why? Are you going to tattle on me?"

My words came out boldly, though part of me kept thinking if Carter really was the one behind the attacks, I'd have a lot more to worry about than Jerome's wrath.

"Maybe." He closed the book, holding it between his palms. "Of course, I suspect the long-term entertainment value will be greater for me if I just keep quiet and let your schemes proceed uninterrupted."

"I don't know what 'schemes' you're talking about. Can't a girl go shopping without getting the third degree? You don't hear me grilling you about why you're here."

The truth was, I burned to know what he was doing. It didn't surprise me that he knew Erik—we all did—but finding him here in light of everything that had happened lately only furthered my suspicions.

"Me?" He held up the book he'd been glancing through. *Teach Yourself Witchcraft in 30 Days or Less.* "I need to make up for lost time."

"Cute," I acknowledged.

"Commendation from a master. I'm honored. Have I given you sufficient time to come up with an equally cute alibi?" He set the book down.

"Miss Kincaid." Erik shuffled into the room before I could answer. "I'm so pleased to see you. My friend just dropped off the earrings you asked for."

I stared, momentarily puzzled, and then I remembered the pearl necklace, as well as the earrings I'd offhandedly requested.

"I'm glad he was able to do it so quickly."

"Nice recovery," conceded Carter in an undertone.

I ignored him.

Erik opened a small box for me, and I peered inside. Three tiny strands of freshwater pearls, just like the ones from the necklace, dangled from the delicate copper wires of each earring.

"They're beautiful," I told him. I meant it. "Thank your friend. I have a dress these will look great with."

"That must be a relief," noted Carter, watching Erik ring the earrings up at the counter. "Proper accessories, I mean.

Cody tells me you're doing a lot of dating these days. I don't suppose you read the book I sent you."

I slid my credit card over to Erik. Cody had seen my male entourage at the dance lesson, but I'd only told him about my subsequent date with Roman yesterday.

"When did you talk to Cody?"

"Last night."

"Funny, so did I. And here you are today. Are you following me around?"

Carter's eyes danced merrily. "I was here first. Maybe you're following me around. Maybe you're starting to get into this dating thing and want to find a cunning way to come on to me."

I signed the credit card slip and handed it back to a quiet, listening Erik. "Sorry. I like my men to have a bit more life in them."

Carter chuckled quietly at my joke. Sex with other immortals gave me no energy payoff. "Georgina, sometimes I think you might be worth following around, just to hear what you'll say next."

Erik looked up. If he felt discomfort at being in the crossfire of two immortals, he did not show it. "Then perhaps you'd like to join us for tea, Mr. Carter? You were going to stay, weren't you, Miss Kincaid?"

I gave Erik one of my better smiles. "Yes, of course."

"Mr. Carter?"

"Thank you, but no. I've got things to do, and from the way I understand it, Georgina operates best one man at a time. It was nice seeing you as always, Erik. Thanks for chatting. As for you, Georgina . . . well, I'm sure I'll be seeing you very soon."

Something in those words chilled me. It took every ounce of my resolve to sound calm as I called out to him. "Carter?"

His hands touched the door. Pausing, he glanced back at me and arched an eyebrow in acknowledgment.

"Does Jerome know *you're* here?"

A slow, sly smile spread across the angel's face.

"Are you going to tattle on me now, Georgina? And here I thought we were making such progress. Perhaps we should have drawn out the small talk a bit more. You could have asked me if the weather would change soon, I might have commented how pretty you looked today, etc., etc. You know how it goes."

I blinked. His words this time invoked the note on my door.

You are a beautiful woman, Georgina. Beautiful enough, I think, to even tempt angels into falling . . .

Was he leaving me more clues? Toying with me in the way Cody had suggested? Or was I reading too much into this? Was he still just annoying Carter, bane of my existence, tormenting me like always? I honestly didn't know, but I still believed of all angels to be taking down evil immortals in the city, Carter had the most opportunity.

"How pretty am I then?" My voice caught slightly. "Pretty enough to fall for?"

The angel's lips twitched. "I knew you were coming on to me. See you later, Georgina, Erik." He opened the door and left.

I stood there, watching his retreating figure. "What was he doing here?"

Erik set a tray with two cups down on the small table. "Come now, Miss Kincaid. I keep your secrets. You can't expect me to do any less for him."

"No, I suppose not."

Nor, I thought as the old man went to get the teapot, did I want to risk endangering him by getting him caught up in immortal affairs. Well, at least caught up more than he already was.

He returned shortly and poured for us. "I had just put this on before you came in. I'm glad you're here to share it."

I tasted it. Another herbal blend. "What's this one called?"

"Desire."

"Fitting," I observed. Angels and conspiracies aside, I still hungered for Roman. "Did you find out anything?"

"I'm afraid not. I asked around but learned nothing more about vampire hunters, nor did I get any indication of one in the area."

"That doesn't surprise me." I sipped the tea. "I think something else is going on."

He said nothing, prudent as ever.

"I know you won't tell me why he was here, and I understand that . . ." I trailed off, determining how best to phrase my words. "But what do you . . . what do you think of him? Carter, that is. Has he done anything weird or seemed, I don't know, suspicious? Secretive?"

Erik gave me a droll look. "Begging your pardon, but I have a number of customers—yourself inclusive—who fit that description."

No doubt that was an understatement. "Well, then, I don't know. Do you trust him?"

"Mr. Carter?" Surprise registered across his features. "I've known him longer than I have you. If any of those 'suspicious and secretive' customers can be trusted, he is certainly first among them. I'd place my life in his hands."

No surprise there. If Carter could fool Jerome, he could surely fool a mortal as well.

Shifting gears, I asked: "Do you know anything about fallen angels?"

"I would think you are already familiar with that topic, Miss Kincaid."

I wondered if he referred to the company I kept or the old myth that succubi were demons. For the record, we aren't.

"Never ask a practitioner if you want to learn about a religion's history. Save those questions for outside scholars."

"Very true." He smiled, thinking as he brought the cup to his lips. "Well. Surely you know that demons are angels who turned away from the divine will. They rebelled, or as it is commonly referred to, 'fell.' Lucifer is generally accredited as being the first, and others left with him."

"That was in the beginning, though, right? One mass migration to the other side." I frowned, still wondering about the technicalities of when angels fell. "What about later? Was that the only time it happened? Just that once?"

Erik shook his head. "My impression is that it can happen still and has happened in the past. There are even documents suggesting—"

The door opened, and a young couple walked in. Erik rose and smiled at them.

"Do you have any books on tarot?" the girl asked. "For beginners?"

Did he ever. Erik had a whole wall of them. The interruption frustrated me, but I didn't want to disrupt a chance for him to do some business. I gestured him toward the couple, drinking the rest of my tea. He led them to the appropriate section, energetically explaining certain titles and questioning their needs in further detail.

I picked up my coat and purse, along with a box of the Desire tea. Erik watched me set a ten-dollar bill on the counter. "Keep the change," I told him.

Pausing from his discussion with the couple, he remarked to me, "Check . . . let's see, I believe it's the beginning of Genesis 6 . . . verse 2 or 4 perhaps? There might be something to help you in there."

"Genesis? Like in the Bible?" He nodded, and I glanced around the book-lined shelves. "Where is it?"

"I don't stock it, Miss Kincaid. I suspect your own resources will be more than adequate."

He returned to his customers, and I left, marveling at a

man who could pull up biblical verses by number but not have a copy on hand. Still, he was right about me having ample resources, and my shift started soon anyway.

I drove back to Queen Anne and found the street parking full. Digging my permit out from the glove box, I hung it on my rearview mirror and pulled into the tiny, private parking lot bordering an alley behind the bookstore. So many employees wanted to use the lot, I generally tried to avoid it when I could.

As I walked toward the store, I caught sight of two cars pulled hood to hood and a redheaded figure leaning over them. Tammi. I liked the teenager a lot, but she also had a tendency to chat. Not wanting to delay my biblical search, I stepped into some shadows and shape-shifted into a nondescript man she wouldn't know. I then walked on past her, barely getting a second glance as she jumped the car.

I changed back to my normal body once I was out of sight again. A momentary sense of windedness hit me, gone just as quickly as it had arrived. Cross-gender shape-shifting always took a bite out of me, which was why I had resisted Peter's silly haircut-modeling suggestion. I had probably just lost a few days' worth of my Martin-induced energy surplus. That left me with a couple weeks at least, but I felt the succubus feeding need stir slightly within me anyway, no doubt agitated by my perpetual longing for Roman.

The bookstore hummed with normal weekday business when I arrived. Immediately, I sought out our religion section. I had directed people to it on a number of occasions; I had even pulled select titles from it. What I had not done was pay close attention to just how many Bibles existed.

"Jesus," I muttered, staring at the various translations. There were Bibles for women and men respectively, Bibles for teens, illustrated Bibles, large-print Bibles, gold-embossed Bibles. At last I caught sight of the King James Version. I knew little about it, but at least I recognized the title.

Pulling it off the shelf, I flipped to Genesis 6 and read Erik's passage:

And it came to pass, when men began to multiply on the face of the earth, and daughters were born unto them,

That the sons of God saw the daughters of men that they were fair; and they took them wives of all which they chose.

And the LORD said, 'My spirit shall not always strive with man, for that he also is flesh: yet his days shall be an hundred and twenty years.'

There were giants in the earth in those days; and also after that, when the sons of God came in unto the daughters of men, and they bare children to them, the same became mighty men which were of old, men of renown.

Well. That cleared everything up.

I reread the passage a few more times, hoping to get something more out of it. I finally determined Erik must have given me the wrong chapter number. He'd been distracted, after all. This passage, by my estimation, had nothing to do with angels, falling, or even the cosmic battle of good and evil. What it did seem to be about, however, was human procreation. It didn't take a biblical scholar to figure out what "the sons of God came in unto the daughters of men" meant, especially when children followed in the next phrase. Sex had sold books back in the old days, just as it did now. I wondered if Erik had given me the passage number as a joke.

"Are you finding religion?"

I looked up first into a Pac-Man T-shirt, then into Seth's inquisitive face. "Found and lost it a long time ago, I'm afraid." I shut the book as he knelt down beside me. "Just looking up something. How are Cady and O'Neill today?"

"Making good progress on their latest case." He smiled fondly, and I found myself studying the amber-brown of his eyes. I'd had a few more e-mail exchanges with him in the last few days and enjoyed my mininovels, though our spoken conversation had seen little improvement. "I just finished a chapter and needed to take a break. Walk around, get something to drink."

"No caffeine, I presume." I had learned Seth didn't drink caffeinated beverages, which I found both frightening and unnatural.

"No. No caffeine."

"You shouldn't knock it. It might increase your writing output."

"Ah yes, that's right. You don't think my books come out fast enough."

I groaned, remembering the day I'd met him. "I think my own words came out a little too fast that first day."

"No way. You were brilliant. I'll never forget it."

His quizzical mask slipped briefly, just as it had at the dance lesson, and I once again saw male interest and appreciation cross his features. Crouching beside him, I again had a momentary sense of naturalness, like I normally had with Doug or one of the immortals. Something friendly and soothing. Like Seth and I had known each other forever. Maybe I had, in a manner of speaking, through his books.

And yet, at the same time, being this close to him proved disconcerting as well. Distracting. I began noticing things like the lean muscles in his arms and the way his messy brown hair framed his face. Even the gold sheen of light hitting his facial hair and the shape of his lips held my attention. Turning away, I felt the base thirst for life energy twitch in me, and I repressed the urge to reach out and touch his face. The outside shape-shifting had caused more damage than I realized. I still didn't really require a true refill of energy, but the succubus instinct was getting irritable. I needed to squelch it soon, but certainly not with Seth.

I stood up hastily, still holding the Bible, wanting to get away from him. He rose with me.

"Well," I began awkwardly when neither of us said anything for a few moments, "I need to get to work here."

He nodded, the interest in his face turning to apprehension. "I . . ."

"Hmm?"

Swallowing, he looked away briefly then back to me, his eyes now focused with determination. "So, I'm going to this party on Sunday, and I wondered if maybe . . . maybe if you weren't busy or weren't working, you could maybe, that is, maybe you'd want to come with me."

I stared, speechless. Had Seth Mortensen just asked me out? And hadn't . . . hadn't we just had a coherent conversation for once? Combined with me suddenly noticing how attractive he was, the very world seemed to be turning on its side. Worse still, I wanted to accept. Something about Seth suddenly felt natural and right, even if it wasn't like the roller coaster of excitement I felt with Roman. Somewhere in this bizarre, awkward relationship, I'd grown to genuinely like the writer independent of his novels.

But I couldn't accept. I knew I couldn't. I cursed myself for my initial flirtation; it had apparently stuck with him, despite my efforts to undo it and stay platonic. Part of me felt dismayed, part of me pleased. All of me knew what I had to do.

"No," I answered bluntly, still stunned.

"Oh."

I had no choice. No way could I have Seth attracted to me. No way could I risk anything but an arm's-length friendship with my favorite books' creator.

Realizing how rude I had sounded, I attempted a hasty recovery. I should have simply said I had to work, but instead, I found myself babbling on with a variant of what I had used on Doug over the years.

"You see . . . I'm not really interested in dating right now or getting involved with anyone. So, it's nothing personal, I mean, the party sounds great and all, but I just can't accept. I don't ever accept things like that, actually. Like I said, it isn't personal. It's just easier not to get involved. To not date. Um, ever."

Seth studied me for a long time, considering, and I was suddenly reminded of that first night when he looked much the same way while I explained my five-page rule with his books.

Finally, he said, "Oh. Okay. But . . . aren't you dating that guy? The really tall one with black hair?"

"No. We're not dating. Not really. We're just, uh, friends. Sort of."

"Oh," Seth repeated. "Friends don't go to parties together, then?"

"No." I hesitated, suddenly wishing I had a different answer. "They can maybe have coffee sometimes. Here in the bookstore."

"I don't drink coffee."

There was a sharpness to his voice. I felt like I'd been slapped. We stood there then in what was quite possibly among the top five most uncomfortable moments of my life. The silence stretched out between us. At last, I repeated my lame exit excuse: "I have to get back to work."

"Okay. See you around."

Just friends, just friends. How many times had I used that line? How many times had the lie been easier than facing up to the truth? I'd even used it on my husband so long ago, again hiding from the reality of a matter I didn't want to admit to when things had turned sour between us.

"Just friends?" Kyriakos had repeated, dark eyes staring at me.

"Of course. He's your friend too, you know. He just keeps me company when you're gone, that's all. It's lonely without you."

But I never told my husband how often his friend Ariston came to visit or how we always seemed to be finding excuses to touch each other. A casual brush here and there. His hand to help me up. Or the one day that still burned in my memory, when he had reached over me to grab a bottle, and his hand had grazed my breast. I'd given an involuntary gasp, and he'd lingered for a heartbeat before carrying on with his task.

And I didn't tell Kyriakos that Ariston made me feel like I had in the early days of my marriage, like I was clever, beautiful, and desirable. Ariston lavished me with the attention Kyriakos once had; Ariston loved the sharp wit that had once gotten me into trouble as an unmarried maiden.

As for Kyriakos . . . well, I assumed he loved those things too, but he didn't show it so much anymore. His father was making him work longer and longer hours, and when he finally got home, he would collapse into bed or seek the solitude of his flute. I hated that flute . . . hated it and loved it. I loathed that it seemed to hold his attention more than I did. Yet, on some nights, when I sat outside and listened to him play, I felt awed at his skill and that ability to create such sweetness.

But that didn't change the fact that I slept untouched more often than not. When I told him I'd never get pregnant that way, he'd laugh and tell me we had all the time in the world for children. This troubled me because I honestly— and irrationally—believed that having a baby would somehow fix everything between us. I ached for one, missing the way my little sisters had once felt in my arms. I loved the

honesty and the innocence of children and liked to think
might help guide one into becoming a good person. Nothing
seemed so sweet to me in those days as cleaning cuts, holding small hands, and telling stories. Furthermore, I had
reached a point where I needed to know that I *could* have a
baby. Three years of marriage was a long time to go without
a child in those days, and I'd seen the way others were starting to whisper that poor Letha might be barren. I hated their
simpering and sickeningly sugared pity.

I should have told Kyriakos everything that was on my
mind, every last detail. But he was so sweet and worked so
hard to provide for us, I couldn't bear it. I didn't want to
shake the contentment that ostensibly filled our household
just for my own self-gratification and need for attention. Besides, it wasn't like he always neglected my body. A bit of
coaxing, and I could sometimes get him to answer my desire. We'd come together in the middle of the night then, his
body moving in mine with the same passion he used in his
music.

Yet, looking at Ariston some days, I had the feeling he
wouldn't need any coaxing at all. And as empty days without
Kyriakos passed, that started to mean something.

Just friends, just friends. Standing there in the bookstore,
watching Seth walk away, I half wondered how anyone could
still use that line. But I knew why, of course. It was used because people still believed it. Or at least they wanted to.

When I returned downstairs—feeling sad, angry, and idiotic all at the same time—I stumbled upon a scenario guar-
anteed to make my day even weirder: Helena from Krystal
Starz stood there in front of the registers, gesticulating
wildly to the cashiers.

Helena here. On my turf.

Swallowing my confusion over Seth, I strode over in my
best managerial way, still carrying the Bible. "Is there something I can help you with?"

Helena spun around, making the crystals around her neck
tinkle as they hit each other. "It's her—she's the one. The one
who stole my staff."

I glanced behind the counter. Casey and Beth stood there,
looking relieved to see me. Tammi and her friend Janice
must have been somewhere else in the store, for which I was
grateful. Best to keep them out of this. I kept my voice cool,
ever-conscious of the customers observing.

"I'm sure I don't know what you mean."

"Don't start that with me! You know exactly what I mean.
You walked into my store, made a scene, and then lured
away my staff. They left without notice!"

"People have recently applied for jobs here," I responded
blandly. "I can't really keep track of where they used to
work. As assistant manager, however, I can empathize with
the inconvenience of employees who leave without giving
notice."

"Stop that!" Helena exclaimed, hardly resembling the
cool, collected diva from last week. "Do you think I can't
see through your lies? You walk in darkness, your aura
wreathed in fire!"

"What's on fire?"

Doug and Warren walked up, obviously attracted by the
mounting spectacle.

"Her," Helena proclaimed, pointing at me, using the New
Age raspy voice.

Warren eyed me curiously, as though actually assessing
for flames. "Georgina?"

"She stole my employees. Just came in and took them
like that. I could sue, you know. When I tell my lawyers—"

"Which employees?"

"Tammi and Janice."

I cringed, waiting to see what this new development
would unleash. Despite his many shortcomings, Warren did
have a smooth sense of customer service and professional-

ism. I worried what might ensue if my poaching received further investigation.

He frowned, trying to match faces with names apparently. "Wait . . . didn't one of them jump my car today?"

"Tammi did."

He snorted dismissively. "We're not giving them back."

Helena turned beet red. "You can't—"

"Ma'am, I am sorry for your inconvenience, but I can hardly pass back workers who have signed employment papers with us and are unwilling to work for you anymore. There's always turnover in retail. I'm sure you'll find someone soon."

She turned on me, still pointing. "I won't forget this. Even if I can't get you back for this, the universe will repay your cruel and twisted nature. You will die miserable and alone. Unloved. Friendless. Childless. Your life will have amounted to nothing."

So much for New Age love and kindness. I hardly feared her comments about dying, but the other adjectives dug in a little. *Miserable and alone. Unloved. Friendless. Childless.*

Warren, however, felt no such concerns for me. "Ma'am, Georgina's the last one I'd accuse of having a 'cruel' nature or leading a meaningless life. She holds this place together, and I trust her judgment implicitly—including the hiring of your former employees. Now unless you would like to make a purchase, I must ask you to leave before I'm forced to call the authorities."

Helena spouted off more curses and woes to us, no doubt entertaining the customers waiting in line. To my surprise, Warren continued holding his ground. He usually went out of his way to smooth customer relations and put our best foot forward, even at his employees' expense. Today he didn't apparently feel like humoring anyone. It was refreshing.

When Helena left, he retreated to his office without another word, and Doug and I stood there, astonishment quickly giving way to amusement.

"The things you cause, Kincaid."

"What? Don't peg that one on me."

"Are you kidding? Freaky witch women never showed up before you started working here."

"How would you know? I started before you." Checking my watch, I turned thoughtful. "You're still here for a while today, aren't you?"

"Yup. Lucky for you. Why?"

"No reason." I left him there and walked to the back offices. Instead of turning left for my office, however, I turned right into Warren's.

He sat at his desk, packing his briefcase, preparing to leave now that his car was ready. "Don't tell me she's back."

"No." I closed the door behind me. This made him look up. "I just wanted to thank you."

Warren eyed me shrewdly. "Kicking irrational customers out is part of my job."

"Yeah, but last time I didn't get praised. I had to apologize."

He shrugged, thinking of an incident from a year ago. "Well, that was different. You called an old woman a hypocritical, pathological Nazi neophyte."

"She was."

"If you say so." His eyes still watched my every move.

I walked over to him, setting the Bible down on his desk. Climbing onto his chair, I straddled his lap, making my tight red skirt ride up considerably, revealing the lace-covered tops of black thigh-highs underneath. I leaned in to kiss him, at first just running my teeth tauntingly over his lips, and then suddenly pressing my mouth in hard. He returned the kiss with equal fervor, hands automatically sliding up the backs of my thighs to cup my ass.

"Christ," he breathed when we broke apart slightly. One of his hands moved to my face, the other toyed with the thong I wore under my skirt. His fingers ran along its lacy edge and then pushed upward inside me, at first just delicately probing and then sliding up the full length. I was already wet from a sudden desire and breathed deeply as I savored those long, smooth strokes. Warren watched me with approval. "What's this all about?"

"What's what? We do this all the time."

"You never initiate it."

"I told you, I'm grateful."

That was true, actually. I had found his defense rather endearing. Also, still burning with Roman-lust and now maybe Seth-lust, I suddenly found Warren convenient in the wake of my grouchy succubus hunger.

The hand by my face wound up a lock of hair, and he turned pensive, although he didn't stop what he was doing between my legs. "Georgina . . . I hope . . . I hope you know what we do here in no way affects your job. You have no obligations—no danger of losing your position here if—"

I laughed out loud, surprised by this oddly considerate side. "I know that."

"I mean it—"

"I know that," I repeated, biting his lower lip with my teeth. "Don't go soft on me all of a sudden," I growled. "That's not what I'm here for."

He didn't interrupt again, and I let myself sink into the pleasure of contact. The feel of his tongue in my mouth, his hands brazenly exploring my body. After a long morning of sexual frustration, I just needed it from someone—anyone. He unbuttoned my blouse and tossed it to the floor, where it rested in a black, silken pile. My skirt and thong followed, leaving me only in thigh-highs, bra, and heels. All black.

He shifted his body, still in the chair, so that I could pull his pants off. Seeing him there—long, straight, and hard—

made me move his hand out of me. Fingers no longer satisfied me. I wrapped my legs more tightly around his hips, as much as the chair would allow. Then, without further warning, I thrust my body down, plunging him inside me. I arched my body so that I could take him deeper, then moved in steady, repeated thrusts. Looking back down, I watched him glide in and out. There was no sound in the room save that of flesh on flesh and our heavy breathing.

With penetration came a flood of feeling and sensations from him—different from the physical ones. As a less noble soul, his energy and presence did not knock me across the room like Martin's had. Succubi absorption depended on the victim's character. Strong, moral souls yielded more to the succubus and took a huge bite out of the guy. Corrupt men lost less and consequently gave less. Regardless of his energy or moral fiber, I did catch snippets of Warren's thoughts and emotions as I rode him. This was normal. They came through with his life force.

Desire certainly was foremost in his mind. Smug pride at being with a younger, attractive woman. Excitement. Surprise. He had little remorse about cheating on his wife—contributing to the lower energy yield—and even the brief fondness for me he'd displayed earlier gave way to raw lust. *So fucking hot. So wet. Love the way she rides me. Hope she comes and comes on top of me . . .*

I did, as it turned out. My movements becoming harder and fiercer as our bodies slapped together. My leg muscles clenching. Neck arched back again. Breasts hot and sweaty from where he'd clutched them. The orgasm reverberating through me. Spasms of pleasure growing fainter and fainter as my breathing slowly returned to normal.

And the energy fix wasn't bad either. It had leaked into me slowly throughout our building passion, starting off as fine glittering threads. Near the end, however, it had become strong and bright, pouring into me, reinvigorating my own life, fueling my immortality in a glorious climax that rivaled the physical one.

When we both had our clothes back on, I made moves for an exit. Small energy loss or no, Warren always felt exhausted and worn after we'd been together. He thought it was the result of his age going up against a younger, more active woman. I did nothing to change his attitude but usually tried to discretely leave, so he wouldn't feel self-conscious around me in his fatigue. I knew it bothered him to think he couldn't keep up with me.

"Georgina?" he called as I moved to the door. "Why are you carrying a Bible? You aren't trying to convert customers, are you?"

"Oh. That. Just researching something for a friend. It's applicable, actually. All about sex."

He wiped sweat off his brow. "After years and years of church, I think I'd remember any good sex scenes."

"Well, it's not so much a scene as a clinical description of procreation."

"Ah. Lots of those."

On impulse, I walked over to him and opened up Genesis 6. "See?" I pointed to the appropriate verses. "All these mentions of men taking women. They say it, like, three times."

Warren studied the book with a frown, and I remembered that he had not opened this place without a substantial background in literary study. "Well . . . it's repeated because here when it says 'men began to multiply on the face of the earth,' it's referring to human men."

I looked up sharply. "What do you mean 'human'?"

"Here. The 'sons of God' aren't human men. They're angels."

"What?" If I'd been holding the book, I would have dropped it. "Are you sure?"

"Positive. Like I said, years of church services. They use this term throughout the Bible." He flipped to Job. "See?

Here it is again. 'Now there was a day when the sons of God came to present themselves before the Lord, and Satan came also among them.' It's referring to angels—fallen angels in this case."

I swallowed. "What . . . what were they doing in Genesis then? With the 'daughters of men'? Were . . . were the angels having sex with human women?"

"Well, it says the women were 'fair.' Hard to blame them, huh?" He gave me an admiring sweep as he spoke. "I don't know. This isn't a point discussed a lot in church, as I'm sure you can imagine. Mostly we emphasized human sin and guilt, but I ignored that."

I continued to stare at the book, dumbfounded, yet suddenly ablaze with ideas and theories. Warren eyed me curiously when I didn't respond to his joke.

"Does that help you any?"

"Yes," I said, recovering myself. "It helps a lot."

I surprised him with a soft kiss on the lips, took the Bible, and left.

Chapter 14

"You called us together for biblical porn?"

Hugh turned away with disinterest from where the vampires and I huddled around my kitchen table. Barely a bruise showed on him anymore. Putting a cigarette to his lips, the imp produced a lighter from his coat pocket.

"Don't smoke in here," I warned.

"What do you care? Are you saying you didn't smoke throughout most of the twentieth century?"

"I'm not saying that at all. But I don't do it anymore. Besides, it's bad for Aubrey."

The cat, sitting on one of my counters, paused mid-bath at the sound of her name and eyed him askance. Hugh, glaring back, took a long drag on the cigarette before putting it out on the countertop next to her. She returned to her cleaning, and he paced around the apartment.

Beside me, Cody leaned over the table, studying my proffered Bible. "I don't get how these guys are actually angels. 'Sons of God' seems like a generic term for humans. I mean, aren't we all supposed to be children of God?"

"Present company excluded, of course," called Hugh from the living room. Then: "Jesus Christ! Where'd you get this bookcase? Hiroshima?"

"Theoretically we are," I agreed, ignoring the imp and answering Cody's question. I'd done a lot of biblical perusal since my earlier discovery today and was growing tired of looking at the book. "But Warren's right—that term is used throughout to refer to angels. Plus, the women here aren't called 'daughters of God.' They're called 'daughters of men.' They're human, their husbands are not."

"Could just be good old-fashioned sexism." Peter had finally taken the plunge and shaved his hair off. I did not find the look flattering at all, considering the shape of his head. "It's not like that'd be a new concept in the Bible."

"Nah, I think Georgina's right," said Hugh, returning to us. "I mean, we know something made angels fall. Lust is as good a reason as any, and it beats the hell out of gluttony or sloth."

"So what's the point then?" Peter wanted to know. "How does this relate to the not-just-a-vampire hunter?"

"Here." I pointed to verse 6:4. "It says, 'There were giants in the earth in those days; and also after that, when the sons of God came in unto the daughters of men, and they bare children to them, the same became mighty men which were of old, men of renown.' The key words here are 'in those days' and 'also after that.' It's saying angels have fallen for human women more than once. This answers our question about whether angels still fall anymore. They do."

Cody was nodding along with me. "Which backs up your theory that one is trying to fall right now."

"It doesn't sound like lust is going to be his catalyst, though," Hugh noted. "I think assault and battery will do it first."

"Unless it's lust for Georgina," suggested Peter dryly. "He seems to think you're pretty enough."

Something odd struck me at Hugh's observation. "Would assault and battery really do it, though? Especially of vampires and imps? It might be frowned upon by the other side, but I'm not convinced taking out evil agents would necessarily warrant an angel turning into a demon."

"Past evidence suggests the other side isn't exactly . . . flexible with transgressors," observed the imp.

"And ours is?" wondered Peter.

Cody gave me a sharp look. "Are you backing out of your own theory?"

"No, no. I'm suddenly reconsidering the falling bit, that's all. The 'rogue' or 'renegade' part might be more accurate."

"But your note did mention angels falling," Hugh pointed out. "Surely that's indicative of something? A meaningful clue and not just a bad attempt at humor?"

I thought about the note. Yes, Hugh was right. I felt certain the note's content played a role here; I just couldn't yet grasp what it meant.

"Bad humor is par for the course with angels," Peter reminded us. "At least if Carter's any indication."

I hesitated a moment, nervous about bringing up my secondary theory. They all seemed to be going along with the angel idea, however, so I figured it was now or never.

"Do you guys think . . . do you think it's possible Carter might be the one behind all of this?"

Three sets of eyes turned on me in astonishment.

Hugh spoke first. "What? Are you crazy? I know you two spar a lot, but Christ, if you think . . ."

"Carter's one of us," agreed Cody fiercely.

"I know, I know." I proceeded to explain the reasoning behind my accusation, citing his weird shadowing of me and subsequent conversation at Erik's.

Silence fell. Finally, Peter said, "All of that is strange. But I still can't buy it. Not Carter."

"Not Carter," agreed Hugh.

"Oh, I see. Everyone's quick to implicate me for Duane, but not perfect Carter?" My ire rose at their automatic solidarity, at the idea that Carter would be above reproach. "Why does he hang out with us then? Have you ever heard of an angel doing anything like that?"

"We're his friends," said Cody.

"And we're more fun," added Hugh.

"You can believe that if you want, but not me. Going from pub to pub with a demon and his cronies is the perfect setup for sabotage. He's been spying on us. You're just biased because he's such a good drinking buddy."

"And don't you think, Georgina," warned Peter, "there's just the slightest possibility that *you're* the one who's biased? I admit, this crazy angel theory makes more and more sense as time goes on, but where'd Carter come from?"

"Yeah," said Hugh. "Seems like you just sort of threw him in for no good reason. Everyone knows you two don't get along."

I stared disbelievingly at the three sets of angry eyes. "I have plenty of good reason. How do you explain him being at Erik's?"

The imp shook his head. "We all know Erik. Carter could have been there for the same reasons you were."

"What about the things he said?"

"What did he say really?" Peter asked. "Was he like, 'Hey Georgina, hope you got my note'? It's all pretty flimsy."

"Look, I'm not saying I have strong evidence, just that circumstantially—"

"I need to go," interjected Cody, standing up.

I gave him a cold look. Had I pushed them that far? "I understand if you don't agree with me, but don't just walk out."

"No, there's something I've got to do."

Peter rolled his eyes. "You're not the only one dating now, Georgina. Cody won't admit it, but I think he's got a woman stashed somewhere."

"A live one?" asked Hugh, impressed.

Cody put his coat on. "You guys don't know anything."

"Well, be careful," I warned automatically.

The tense mood was suddenly shattered, and no one seemed to be angry with me about suspecting Carter anymore. It was clear, however, that no one believed me about him either. They were dismissing my ideas like one does a child's irrational fears or imaginary friends.

The vampires left together, and Hugh followed soon thereafter. I wandered off to bed, still trying to put the pieces into place. The note writer had made a reference to angels falling for beautiful women; that had to be significant. Yet, I just couldn't reconcile it with this bizarre pair of attacks on Duane and Hugh, which had more to do with violence and brutality than beauty or lust.

When I got to work the next day, my e-mail inbox revealed a new message from Seth, and I feared some sort of follow-up to his date request from yesterday. Instead, he merely responded to my last message, which had been one in an ongoing conversation about his observations of the Northwest. The message's writing style and voice were as entertaining as ever, and he seemed for all the world not to have minded—or even noticed—my wacky rejection yesterday.

I verified this further when I went upstairs to buy coffee. Seth sat in his usual corner, typing away, oblivious to it being Saturday. I paused and said hello, getting a typically distracted response in return. He did not mention asking me to the party, did not seem upset, and indeed apparently didn't care at all about it. I supposed I should have been grateful that he'd recovered so quickly, that he wasn't pining or breaking his heart over me, but my selfishness couldn't help but feel a little disappointed. I wouldn't have minded making a slightly stronger impression on him, one that elicited some regret over my refusal. Doug and Roman, for example, hadn't let one rejection deter them. What a fickle creature I was.

Thinking of both of them reminded me I was meeting Roman later to go to Doug's concert. I grew heady at the thought of seeing Roman again, though apprehension tinged the feeling. I didn't like him having this effect on me, and I had thus far demonstrated no aptitude in refusing his advances. We were going to reach a critical point one of these days, and I feared for its outcome. I suspected that when it did come, I would wish Roman had bowed out of my pursuit so easily as Seth seemed to have.

Such worries vanished from my mind that evening when I admitted Roman into my apartment. He wore dress clothing all done in elegant shades of blue and silvery gray, every hair and fold perfectly in place. He flashed me one of those devastating smiles, and I made sure my knees didn't start knocking, schoolgirl style.

"You do realize this is a post-grunge, punk rock, ska-type of concert we're going to. Most everyone else will be in jeans and T-shirts. Maybe some leather here and there."

"Most good dates do end in leather." His eyes took in the sights of the apartment, lingering briefly on the bookcase. "But didn't you say this was a late show?"

"Yup. Starts at eleven."

"That gives us four hours to burn, love. You're going to have to change."

I looked down at my black jeans and red tank top. "This won't work?"

"That does wonderful things for your legs, I admit, but I think you're going to want a skirt or dress. Something like you wore swing dancing, only maybe . . . steamier."

"I'm pretty sure I've never heard the word 'steamy' applied to any of my wardrobe."

"I find that hard to believe." He pointed down my hall. "Go. The clock is ticking."

Ten minutes later I returned in a clingy, navy dress made of georgette. It had spaghetti straps and an asymmetrical hemline, jagged and ruffled, that rose high on my left leg. I had taken my hair out of its ponytail and now wore it long over my shoulders.

Roman looked up from where he'd been having meaningful, eye-to-eye communication with Aubrey. "Steamy." He pointed to the King James Bible sitting on my coffee table. It was open, like he'd been perusing. "I never took you for the churchgoing type."

Both Seth and Warren had made similar jokes. That thing was ruining my reputation.

"Just something I'm researching. It's only been moderately useful."

Roman stood up and stretched. "Probably because that's one of the worst translations out there."

I remembered the plethora of Bibles. "Is there a better one you'd recommend?"

He shrugged. "I'm no expert, but you'd probably get more out of one meant for research, not devotional use. Annotated ones. Ones that they use in college classes."

I filed the information away, wondering if the mystery verses might still have more to reveal. For now, I had a date to contend with.

We ended up at a small, hidden Mexican restaurant I'd never been to. The waiters spoke Spanish—as did Roman, it turned out—and the food had not been watered down for Americans. When two margaritas appeared on our table, I realized Roman had ordered one for me.

"I don't want to drink tonight." I recalled how flaky I'd been the last time we went out.

He stared at me like I'd just declared I was going to stop breathing for a change. "You have to be kidding. This place makes the best margaritas north of the Rio Grande."

"I want to stay sober tonight."

"One won't kill you. Take it with food, and you won't even notice." I stayed silent. "For Christ's sake, Georgina, just try the salt. One taste and you'll be hooked."

I reluctantly ran my tongue around the edge. It triggered a longing to taste tequila that rivaled my succubus urge for sex. Giving in against my better judgment, I took a sip. It was fantastic.

The food was too, not surprisingly, and I ended up having two margaritas, instead of just the one. Roman proved to be right about drinking with food, fortunately, and I only felt mildly buzzed. I did not feel out of control and knew I could handle things until the sobering up began.

"Two more hours," I told him as we left the restaurant. "Got something else in mind?"

"Sure do." He inclined his head across the street, and I followed his motion. *Miguel's*.

I racked my brain. "I've heard of that place . . . wait, they do salsa dancing there, don't they?"

"Yup. Ever tried it?"

"No."

"What? I thought you were a dancing queen."

"I'm not done with swing yet."

Truthfully, I was dying to try salsa. Like Seth Mortensen's books, though, I did not like to burn through too much of a good thing too fast. I still enjoyed swing and wanted to run it into the ground before I switched dances. Long life tended to make one savor things more.

"Well, now you'll just have to multitask." Taking my hand, he led me across the street.

I tried to protest but couldn't really explain my reasoning to him, and so, like the margaritas, I gave in fairly easily.

The club was warm and packed with bodies, and the music was to die for. My feet immediately began counting out beats as Roman paid our entrance fee and led me to the dance floor. Just like with swing, he turned out to be an expert at salsa, and I found myself easily catching on after a few practices. I might not have demonstrated much talent for standing my ground against margaritas, but I had been dancing for centuries. The skill was fused into me.

Salsa turned out to be a lot sexier than swing. Not that swing wasn't sexy, mind you, but salsa had a dark, sinuous edge about it. One couldn't help but focus on the closeness of the other person's body, the way hips moved together. I now knew what Roman had meant about steamy.

After about a half hour, we took a break, and he led us to the bar. "Mojitos now," he told me, holding up two fingers for the bartender. "In keeping with our Latin theme tonight."

"I can't . . ."

But the mojitos appeared without my counsel and turned out to be pretty damned good. We finished them faster than we should have, so we could get back out on the floor.

By the time we had to leave for Doug's concert, post-grunge, punk rock, ska-type music didn't sound so good anymore. I was exhilarated from dancing, hot and sweaty, and I'd gone through another mojito and a tequila chaser. I knew I'd found a new passion in salsa and silently cursed Roman for what would probably become a dancing addiction, even though I had exalted in the movement. His body had moved with a seductive grace, brushing against mine in a way that left me quivering and aching.

We stumbled out into the street, holding hands, breathless and laughing. The world spun around me slightly, and I decided it was probably just as well we'd left when we did. My motor controls had stopped operating at normal levels.

"Okay, where'd we park?"

"You've got to be kidding," I told him, jerking him around the corner where I could see the soft glow of a yellow taxi. "We have to take a cab."

"Come on, I'm not that bad."

But he had the wisdom to protest no further, and we caught the taxi up to the brewery in Greenlake. People milled in and out of the building; there had been two other performances before Doug's. As I had feared, our posh dancing clothing looked hopelessly out of place among the rough and tumble ware of the college-aged, but it no longer seemed the big deal it had when Roman picked me up.

"Don't get caught up in fashion games," he advised as we squeezed our way inside the packed brewery. "These kids probably think we're old, nark conformists or something, but really, they're just conforming in their own ways. They're conforming to nonconformity."

I scanned for the bookstore crew, hoping they'd secured a table. "Oh no. You don't wax political when you're drunk, do you?"

"No, no. I just get tired of people always trying to fit a mold, trying to toe some line, regardless if it's right or left. I'm proud to be the best-dressed person in this room. Make your own rules, that's what I say."

I spotted Beth and dragged Roman over to a table on the other side of the room. Other bookstore natives sat with her: Casey, Andy, Bruce—and Seth. My stomach sank.

"Nice dress," said Bruce.

"We saved you a seat." Casey indicated a chair. "I didn't realize you'd have a . . . friend."

The chair situation held little concern for me. All I could feel were Seth's eyes on me, his face thoughtful but neutral. Flushing, I felt like a complete idiot and wished I could just turn around and leave. After refusing him with my stupid tirade about not dating, here I was, hand in hand, drunk off my ass with Roman. I couldn't even imagine what Seth must think of me now.

"Not a problem," Roman declared, oblivious to my churning emotions and unfazed by my colleagues' bemused attention. He sat down in the chair, pulling me onto his lap. "We'll share."

Andy made a bar run, bringing back beers for all of us except Seth who, just like with caffeine, chose to abstain. Roman and I explained where we'd been, lauding salsa as the world's new greatest pastime, thus earning demands from the others that I start up a second wave of dance lessons.

Doug's group soon came on stage, and we all cheered appropriately at the sight of Doug-the-assistant-manager turned Doug-the-lead-singer of Nocturnal Admission. Beer kept coming, and while continuing to drink was probably the stupidest thing I could have done, I was beyond the point where I could reasonably stop. Besides, I had too many other things to worry about. Like avoiding eye contact with a thus-far-silent Seth. And savoring the feel of being on top of Roman, his chest against my back and arms around my waist. His chin rested on my shoulder, giving him easy access to whisper in my ear and occasionally run his lips by my neck. The hardness I felt underneath my thighs suggested I wasn't the only one getting something out of this seating arrangement.

Doug came to talk to us during a break, covered in sweat but thoroughly ecstatic. He took in the sight of me plastered on Roman. "You're a little overdressed, aren't you, Kincaid?" He reconsidered. "Or under. Hard to say."

"You're one to talk," I shot back, finishing my . . . second . . . or was it third . . . beer.

Doug wore tight, red vinyl pants; combat boots; and a long, purple velvet jacket left open to expose his chest. A ragged top hat perched jauntily on his head.

"I'm part of the entertainment, babe."

"So am I, babe."

Some of the others chuckled. Doug's expression turned disapproving, but he said nothing to me, instead making some comment to Beth about the number of people who had turned out for the show.

I entered that weird sort of tunnel vision that occurs sometimes with alcohol, where I became so consumed with my own buzzing, swirling perceptions that the conversation and noise around me blurred to an indistinct drone, and faces and colors faded out to an irrelevant background separate from my existence. Indeed, all I really felt was Roman. Every nerve in me was screaming, and I wished the hands he rested on my stomach would slide up to touch my breasts. I could already feel my nipples hardening under the thin fabric and wondered what it'd be like to turn around and ride him like I had Warren . . .

"Restroom," I suddenly exclaimed, clambering ungracefully off Roman. It was weird how one's bladder could turn from tolerable to unbearable so quickly. "Where's the restroom here?"

The others looked at me strangely, or so it seemed to me. "Back there," pointed Casey, her voice sounding far away despite her close proximity. "You okay?"

"Yeah." I pushed a slipping strap up. "I just need to use the restroom." *And get away from Roman,* I silently added, *so I can think about things clearly.* Not that that last feat would probably be possible in my current state.

Roman started to rise, as drunk and fumbling as me. "I'll go with you—"

"I will," offered Doug hastily. "I need to get back there anyway before the next set."

Taking my arm, he wound us through the people toward a

less-populated back hallway. I staggered slightly as we went, and he slowed his pace to help.

"How much have you had to drink?"

"Before or after I got here?"

"Holy shit. You are trashed."

"You got a problem with it?"

"Hardly. How do you think I spend most of my nights off?"

We paused outside the ladies' restroom. "I bet Seth thinks I'm a lush."

"Why would he think that?"

"You don't see him drinking. He's such a fucking purist. Him and his stupid no caffeine and no alcohol shit."

Doug's dark eyes flickered in surprise at my language. "Not all nondrinkers despise drinkers, you know. Besides, Seth's not the one I'm worried about. I'm more concerned about Mr. Happy Hands out there."

I blinked, confused. Then: "You mean Roman?"

"You've come a long way from refusing to date to practically making out in public."

"So?" I countered hotly. "Can't I be with someone? Aren't I entitled to do something for a change that's actually something I want to do, not something I have to do?" My words came out with more bitter truth—and volume—than intended.

"Of course," he soothed, "but you aren't yourself tonight. You're going to do something stupid if you're not careful. Something you'll regret later. You should ask Casey or Beth to take you home—"

"Oh, you're a piece of work," I exclaimed. I knew I was being irrational, that I'd never have turned on Doug sober, but I couldn't stop. "Just because I won't go out with you, just because I choose to fuck Warren or someone else, then you have to step in and try to keep me pure and untouched. If you can't have me, then no one can, is that it?"

Doug blanched, and a few passersby stared at us. "Christ, Georgina, no—"

"You're such a fucking hypocrite," I yelled at him. "You have no right to tell me what to do! No fucking right."

"I'm not, I—"

I didn't listen to what else he had to say. Turning, I stormed into the ladies' restroom, the only place I could go to escape these men. When I'd finished and gone to wash my hands, I looked up in the mirror. Did I look trashed? My cheeks were pink, some of the waves in my hair a little limper than when I'd started the evening. And I was sweating. Not too trashed, I decided. I could be a lot worse.

I felt hesitant to leave the restroom, fearing Doug waited for me. I didn't want to talk to him. Another woman came in with a lit cigarette, and I bummed one off her, smoking it in its entirety while I crouched in a corner to kill time. When I heard the band kick up again, I knew it was safe.

I walked out of the restroom and ran straight into Roman.

"Are you okay?" he asked, his hands catching me around the waist to steady me. "I was worried when you didn't come back."

"Yeah . . . I'm fine . . . er, no, I don't know," I admitted, leaning into him, wrapping my arms around him. "I don't know what's going on. I feel so strange."

"It's all right," he told me, patting my back. "Everything's going to be all right. Do you need to leave? Is there anything I can do?"

"I . . . don't know . . ." I pulled away slightly, looking up into his eyes. Those blue-green depths were drowning me, and suddenly, I didn't care.

I don't know who started it—it could have been either of us—but suddenly we were kissing, there in the middle of the hallway, arms pulling each other tighter, lips and tongues working furiously. The alcohol enhanced my base physical response yet numbed my awareness of succubus energy absorption. It must have still been working in spite of my inability to sense it, however, because Roman abruptly pulled away from me, looking aghast.

"Weird . . ." He put a hand to his forehead. "I feel . . . dizzy all of a sudden." He hesitated a moment then shook it off, pulling me toward him again. Just like all the others. They never caught on that it was me doing it, me hurting them, so they still came back for more.

His pause had been what I needed to gain some tiny sense of clarity in my drunken cloud. What had I done? What had I let myself become tonight? Every interaction with Roman had pushed me past another boundary. First I'd said we wouldn't date. Then I'd confined us to limited dates. Tonight I'd sworn I wouldn't drink, and now I could barely stand up from all the booze. Kissing was another taboo I had just broken. And it would only lead to the inevitable . . .

In my mind's eye, I could see us after sex. Roman would sprawl, pale and exhausted, drained of his life. That energy would crackle through me like an electric current, and he would stare at me, weak and confused, unable to comprehend what he no longer had. Depending on how much I stole from him, he would lose years off his life. Some sloppy succubi had even been known to kill victims by drinking too much life too fast.

"No . . . no . . . don't."

I pushed him away, unwilling to see that future realized, but his arm still held me. Looking beyond him, I suddenly caught sight of Seth coming down the hallway. He froze when he saw us, but I was too preoccupied to pay any attention to the writer.

I was a hair's breath away from kissing Roman again, from taking him somewhere—anywhere—where we could be alone and naked, where I could do all the things I'd fantasized doing with him. Another kiss . . . another kiss, and would not be able to stop. I wanted it too much. I wanted to be with someone *I* wanted. Just once after all these years.

And that was exactly why I couldn't do it.

"Georgina . . ." began Roman confusedly, hands still on me.

"Please," I begged, my voice a whisper, "let me go. Please let me go. You have to let me go."

"What's wrong? I don't understand."

"Please let me go," I repeated. "Let me go!" The sudden volume of my own voice startled me, giving me a small boost of will to break from his grasp. He reached toward me, saying my name, but I stepped back. I sounded hysterical, like a crazy woman, and Roman was looking at me rightfully so. "Don't touch me. Don't. Touch. Me!"

My anger was more at myself, at my life, than it was at him. A terrible rage and frustration, amplified by alcohol, coursed through me at the universe. The world wasn't fair. It wasn't fair that some people had perfect lives. That beautiful civilizations should fall to dust. That babies should be born with only a handful of breaths. That I should be trapped in this cruel joke of an existence. An eternity of making love without love.

"Georgina . . ."

"Don't touch me. Ever again. Please," I whispered hoarsely, and then, I did the only thing left to me. Escape. I ran. I turned from him and ran down the hall, away from Roman, away from Seth, away from the main seating area. I didn't know where I was going, but it would keep me safe. Would keep Roman safe. I might not be able to heal my own pain, but I could prevent any more from coming to him.

My poor coordination and desperation made me run into people who responded with varying degrees of politeness to my mania. Was Roman behind me? I didn't know. He'd drunk at least as much as I had; his coordination couldn't be any better. If I could just be alone, I could shape-shift or go invisible and get out of here . . .

I burst through a door, and a wave of cool night air suddenly engulfed me. Gasping, I looked around. I stood in the back parking lot. It was packed with cars, and a few people smoking pot lingered around, most not paying attention to me. The door I'd come through opened, and I turned, expecting Roman. Instead, I saw Seth, looking anxious.

"Stay away from me," I warned.

He held up his hands, palms forward in an appeasing gesture as he approached me slowly. "Are you okay?"

I took two steps back, fumbling for my purse. "I'm fine. I just have to . . . have to get away from here . . . get away from him." I pulled out my cell phone, intending to call one of the vampires. It slipped from my hands, dodged my attempts to catch it, and hit the asphalt with a sickening crack. "Oh shit."

Kneeling down, I picked up the phone, looking with dismay at the gibberish on the display. "Shit," I repeated.

Seth knelt by me. "What can I do?"

I looked up at him, his face swimming in my blurred vision. "I have to get out of here. I have to get away from him."

"Okay. Come on. I'll take you home."

Seth took my arm, and I had a faint recollection of being led a few blocks to some dark-colored car. He helped me inside and drove away. Leaning back, I sank into the motion of the drive, letting it pull me under, the backward and forward of inertia, backward and forward, backward and forward . . .

"Pull over."

"What?"

"Pull over now!"

He complied, and I opened the door, expelling the contents of my stomach onto the street outside. When I had finished, Seth waited a moment before asking, "Are you okay to keep going?"

"Yeah."

But a few minutes later, I made him pull over and repeated the process.

"This . . . car ride is killing me," I gasped once we were on the road again. "I can't stay in the car. The motion . . ."

Seth's brow furrowed, and he suddenly made a hard right that nearly set me to throwing up inside the car. "Sorry," he said.

We drove a few more minutes, and I was on the verge of asking him to pull over again when the car stopped. He helped me out, and I looked around, not recognizing the building in front of us. "Where are we?"

"My place."

He ushered me inside, straight to a bathroom where I promptly knelt and paid homage to the toilet, again releasing more liquid than I had realized was in me. I felt distantly aware of Seth behind me, pulling my hair out of the way. Dimly, I remembered that higher immortals like Jerome and Carter could be affected by alcohol as little or as much as they liked, choosing to sober up at will. Bastards.

I don't know how long I knelt there before Seth gently helped me to my feet. "Can you stand?"

"I think so."

"It's . . . uh . . . in your hair and on your dress. I think you'll want to change."

I looked down at the navy georgette and sighed. "Steamy."

"What?"

"Never mind." I started pulling the straps down so I could get out of the dress. His eyebrows rose, and he hastily turned away.

"What are you doing?" he asked in a forcibly normal voice.

"I need to shower."

Naked, I stumbled over and turned on the water. Seth, still not looking at me, retreated to the door. "You won't fall or anything?"

"I hope not."

I stepped into the water, gasping at its heat. I leaned against the tiled wall and just let the heavy stream power-wash me, the shock momentarily rousing my wits. Looking up, I saw that Seth was gone, the bathroom door closed. I sighed and shut my eyes, wanting to sink to my knees and pass out. Standing there, I thought again about Roman, about how good it had felt to kiss him. I didn't know what he would think of me now, not after how I'd acted.

When I turned off the water and stepped out, the bathroom door opened a crack. "Georgina? Use these."

A towel and an oversize T-shirt were tossed through before the door closed again. I dried myself off and put on the shirt. It was red and had a picture of Black Sabbath on it. Nice.

The activity took its toll, however, and a wave of nausea rolled over me again. "No," I moaned, making for the toilet.

The door opened. "Are you okay?" Seth came in and pulled my hair back once more.

I waited but nothing came. Finally, I stood uneasily. "I'm all right. I need to lie down."

He led me out of the bathroom and into a bedroom with an unmade queen-sized bed. I collapsed onto it, pleased to be flat and stationary, even though the room continued to spin. He sat down gingerly on the bed's edge, watching me uncertainly.

"I'm sorry about this," I told him. "Sorry you had to . . . do all this."

"It's okay."

I closed my eyes. "Relationships suck. This is why I don't date. You just hurt people."

"Most good things come with the risk of something bad," he observed philosophically.

I remembered the letter he'd sent me, about the long-term girlfriend he'd neglected for his writing. "Would you do it again?" I asked. "Go out with that one girl? Even if you knew things would turn out exactly the same?"

A pause. "Yes."

"Not me."

"Not me what?"

I opened my eyes and looked up at him. "I was married once." It was the kind of drunken admission one made fully aware that it would never have been spoken sober. "Did you know that?"

"No."

"No one does."

"It didn't work out then?" Seth asked when I didn't say anything for a minute.

I couldn't help a bitter laugh. Didn't work out? That was an understatement. I had been weak and foolish, giving into the same physical urges that had nearly led me into disaster with Roman. Only with Ariston, I couldn't claim drunkenness for that slip. I had been dead sober, and honestly, I think I'd been planning it for a long time anyway. We both had.

He'd come over one day for another visit, only this time we didn't talk much. I think we were past conversation by then. We'd both been restless, pacing and standing, making small talk that neither of us really listened to. My attention was on his physical presence—on his body and the powerful muscles in his arms and legs. The air was so thick with sexual tension it was a wonder we could move at all.

I walked to the window, staring at nothing as I listened to him pacing the rest of the house. A moment later he returned, this time standing behind me. His hands suddenly rested on my shoulders, the first deliberate touch he'd ever made. His fingers burned me like a brand, and I shivered, making his hold tighten as he stepped closer to me.

"Letha," he said in my ear, "you know . . . you know I think about you all the time. I think about what it would be like to . . . be with you."

"You're with me now."

"You know that's not what I mean."

He turned me around to face him, and his gaze was like hot oil running over my body, slick and scorching. Trailing his hands up my neck, he cupped my face for a moment. He leaned down and held his mouth a breath away from mine. Then, his tongue darted out and lightly ran over my lips, the barest of caresses. My lips parted, and I leaned forward to take more, but he stepped away with a small smile. One of his hands moved down to my shoulder, to the clasp that held my gown together, and unfastened it. The fabric slid off me, pooling around me on the floor, so I stood naked before him.

His eyes blazed, taking in every part. I should have felt embarrassed or shy, but I didn't. I felt wonderful. Desired. Adored. Wanted. Powerful.

"I would do anything, anything at all to have you right now," he whispered. His hands traveled down my shoulders to the sides of my breasts, to my waist, and then my hips. My mother had always said my hips were too skinny, but under his hands, they felt lush and sexy. "I would kill for you. I would go to the ends of the earth for you. I would do anything at all that you ask. Anything just to feel your body against mine and your legs wrapped around me."

"No one's ever said anything like that to me." I was surprised at how calmly my voice came out. Inside, I was melting. I would hear variations of his promises for the next millennium or so, from a hundred different men, but at the time, the words were fresh and new.

Ariston's lips turned up in a rueful smile. "Kyriakos must say things like that all the time." There was an arch tone to his voice, reminding me that even though the two men were longtime friends, there had always been a rivalry underscoring that friendship.

"No. He makes love to me with his eyes."

"I want to use a lot more than my eyes."

In that moment, I suddenly understood the power women had over men. It was surprising and exhilarating. Never mind issues of property and politics; it was in the bedroom that women ruled. With flesh and sheets and sweat. The knowledge filled me, rushing through me with an arousal stronger than any aphrodisiac could produce. I thrived on it, liking this newfound clout. I think it was this revelation that would later make the powers of hell cast me as a succubus.

I reached out trembling hands to him and began removing his tunic. He stood still as I undressed him, but every inch of him quivered with heat and longing. His breathing came heavy and fast as I studied his body now, noticing all the ways it was the same as Kyriakos' and all the ways it was different. I moved my fingertips over him, lightly touching the tanned flesh, the well-defined muscles, the nipples. Then my hands moved lower, below his stomach, wrapping around the long, hard length they found there. Ariston emitted a soft groan but did not move toward me yet. He was still waiting for my consent.

I raised my eyes from my fondling hands and looked into his face. He really would have done anything for me. That awareness increased my need for him.

"You can do anything you want to me," I told him finally.

I made it sound like a concession, but truthfully, I *wanted* him to do anything he wanted. My words broke the spell that had been holding us apart. It was like a dam bursting. Like exhaling after holding your breath for too long. A rush. A release. My body nearly tumbled into his, like it had been straining and straining at bindings that had finally been cut. Touching him made me realize we should have been touching long before this.

He jerked me into a harsh kiss, jamming his tongue into my mouth as his hands moved under me to grab the backs of my thighs. In one motion, he hoisted me up and pressed my back against the wall. My legs wrapped around his hips, needing him closer to me, and then with one hard thrust, he was inside. I don't know if I was too tight or he was too big—maybe both—but it hurt in a sort of pleasurable way. I let out a surprised cry, but he didn't stop to see if I was okay. The passion had seized him, that animalistic urge locked deep into our blood that ensures the continuation of our species. He focused only on his own pleasure now as he pushed into me, over and over, harder and harder, seeming to thrive on every moan and scream that crossed my lips. I wouldn't have thought I could find release in such rough sex, but I did—more than once. Each time, it came as a great, consuming wave of sensation, starting deep within me and spreading throughout my body, rubbing every nerve, covering every piece of me until I was completely saturated. Then the wave would explode into glittering fragments, leaving me warm and tender and breathless. Like being shattered then remade. It was exquisite. Each of these orgasms seemed to drive him more urgently until his own climax came. This time, I was the one thriving on his release, digging my nails into his back as tightly as I could, holding on to him, bringing the episode to a shuddering, gasping end.

And yet, it wasn't the end because in only a little while, he was ready again. He took me to my bed and this time put me on my knees, leaning into me from behind. "I've heard the old women say this is the best position for conceiving a child," he whispered.

I had only a moment to ponder this before he was in me

again, still rough and demanding. I considered his words as he pumped away, that maybe he would be the one who gave me a child after all, not Kyriakos. The realization made me feel strange, eager yet regretful.

Ariston felt no such regret when we lay back on the blankets later in the afternoon, both of us exhausted and spent as warm sun spilled in over us through the window.

"The lack could be in Kyriakos," he explained. "Not you. With as many times as I've had you today, you can't help but get pregnant." He sucked my earlobe and wrapped his arms around me from behind, letting his hands rest on my breasts. "I've filled you up, Letha."

His voice was low and proprietary, like he'd just gained something more tangible than sex. Suddenly I wondered who really did have the power in the bedroom after all.

I lay against him, wondering what I had done and what I wanted to do now. How did one go back to being a wife after being someone else's goddess? I never got to decide, however, because the next thing I heard was Kyriakos calling me from the front of the house, home too early. Ariston and I both sat up, startled. My fingers fumbled as I tried to get the blankets off me, tangling in the fabric. My dress. I needed to find my dress. But it wasn't here, I realized. I'd left it in the other room. Maybe, I thought desperately, I could get to it before Kyriakos found us. Maybe I could move fast enough.

But it turned out I couldn't.

In the present, all I said to Seth was: "Yeah. It didn't work out. Not at all. I cheated on him."

"Oh." A pause. "Why?"

"Because I could. It was stupid."

"That's why you don't date?"

"Everything about that hurt too much. No good justified the bad."

"You can't know that the next one will turn out badly. Things change."

"Not for me." I closed my eyes to hide the tears welling up. "I'm going to pass out now."

"Okay."

He might have left or he might have stayed; I didn't know. I simply slept, lost in black, numbing sleep.

Chapter 15

Sometimes you wake up from a dream. And sometimes, every once in a while, you wake up in a dream. That's what happened to me. I opened my eyes, head throbbing, vaguely aware of something warm and fuzzy in my arms. Bright sunlight made me squint at first, but when I could finally focus, I realized I was looking straight into the faces of Cady and O'Neill.

I shot upright, a motion my head did not approve of at all. Surely I was mistaken. Surely, no . . . there they were. Before me, next to the bed I sat in, was a large oak desk surrounded by bulletin boards and white boards. Pinned to the bulletin boards were magazine cutouts, faces and faces of people who reflected every nuance of the characters described in Seth's books. One section was even labeled NINA CADY, displaying at least twenty different cutouts of slim blondes with cropped, curly hair, while another section— marked BRYANT O'NEILL—displayed brooding, thirty-something men with dark hair. Some of the cutouts were from major ads I recognized, though I'd never before connected the resemblance to Seth's characters. Other minor characters from the books also had places on the display, though less noticeably so than the leads.

Scrawls of notes and words filled the white boards, most done in a bizarre shorthand type of flow chart that made no sense to me. *Working Title: Azure Hopes—fix later; Add Jonah Chap. 7; Clean up 3-5; C&O in Tampa or Naples? Check stats; Don Markos in 8* . . . On and on the scrawls went. I stared and stared at them, realizing I was seeing the skeleton foundation of Seth's next novel. Part of me whispered I should look away, that I was ruining something, but the rest of me was too fascinated at glimpsing the way a novel and its world came to life.

Finally, the smell of frying bacon made me turn from Seth's desk, forcing me to piece together how I'd arrived here. I cringed, recalling what an idiot I'd been around Doug, Roman, and even Seth, but my hunger won out in temporarily allaying my remorse. It seemed odd that I should feel hungry after what I'd put my stomach through last night, but like Hugh's beating, I could bounce back quickly.

Disentangling myself from the covers and the teddy bear I'd unknowingly been holding, I made my way to the bathroom to rinse my mouth and study my appearance: wild-haired and downright adolescent looking in the T-shirt. I didn't want to waste the energy to shape-shift, however, and trotted out of the bathroom, following the sounds of sizzling against a background of "Radar Love" by Golden Earring.

Seth stood in a modern, well-lit kitchen, tending a skillet on a stove. The color scheme was bright and cheery, maple wood cupboards and beams accented with cornflower blue paint on the walls. Seeing me, he turned down the music and gave me a solicitous look. His shirt today displayed Tom and Jerry.

"Good morning. How are you feeling?"

"Surprisingly well." I made my way to a small, two-person

table and sat down, tugging the shirt to cover my thighs. "My head seems to be the only casualty thus far."

"You want something for it?"

"No. It'll clear up." I hesitated, detecting something through the smell of salty, greasy meat. "Is that . . . coffee?"

"Yup. Want some?"

"Regular?"

"Yup." He walked over to a pot, poured a mug of steaming coffee, and brought it to me, along with a cute sugar and creamer set.

"I thought you didn't drink this stuff."

"I don't. I just keep it on hand in case caffeine-crazed women wake up in my bed."

"That happen a lot?"

Seth smiled mysteriously and returned to the stove. "Are you hungry?"

"Famished."

"How do you like your eggs?"

"Over hard."

"Nice choice. You want bacon too? You're not a vegetarian or anything?"

"I'm an honest carnivore. I want the works . . . if that's not asking too much." I felt kind of sheepish about him waiting on me, considering everything else he'd already done. He didn't appear to mind.

The works turned out to be more than I'd imagined: eggs, bacon, toast, two kinds of jam, coffee cake, and orange juice. I ate it all, thinking about how jealous Peter would be, still confined to his low-carb diet.

"I'm in a food coma," I told Seth afterward, helping with the dishes. "I'll need to go back to bed and sleep it off. Do you eat like this every day?"

"Nah. Just when aforementioned women are hanging out. It ensures they don't leave too quickly."

"Not a problem, considering this is all I have to wear."

"Not true," he told me, pointing toward his living room. Looking up, I saw my dress—clean—hanging on a hanger. The sheer, bikini-cut panties I'd worn under it had been looped around the hanger's head. "It said dry-clean, but I took a chance on putting it on extra-gentle cycle in the wash. It came out okay. So did the, uh, other thing."

"Thanks," I replied, unsure as to how I felt about him washing my underwear. "Thanks for everything. I really appreciate what you did for me last night—you must think I'm a total freak—"

He shrugged. "It's no problem. But"—he glanced at a nearby clock—"I may need to run out on you soon. Remember that one party? It starts at noon. You can still hang out here."

I turned to the same clock. Eleven forty-seven.

"Noon! Why didn't you wake me up sooner? You'll be late!"

He shrugged again, infinitely unconcerned. "I figured you needed the sleep."

Setting down the towel I'd been holding, I darted to the living room and grabbed my dress. "I'll call a cab. You go. Don't worry about me."

"Seriously, it's no problem," he argued. "I can give you a ride home even, or . . . well, if you wanted, you could come with me."

We both froze awkwardly. I didn't really feel up to going to some strange party. What I needed to do was get home and do damage control with Roman and Doug. Yet . . . Seth had been terribly nice to me, and he had wanted me to go to this thing before. Didn't I owe him? Surely I could do this for him. An afternoon party probably wouldn't even last that long.

"Would we need to pick up anything?" I asked at last. "Wine? Brie?"

He shook his head. "Probably not. It's for my eight-year-old niece."

"Oh. So no wine then?"

"Yeah. And I think she's more into Gouda anyway."

I looked at the dress. "I'll be overdressed. You got anything I can put on over this?"

Seven minutes later, I sat in Seth's car, driving toward Lake Forest Park. I had the georgette dress back on, along with a man's plaid flannel shirt in shades of white, gray, and navy. The shirt was open save for a couple buttons. I had French-braided my hair in lieu of shape-shifting it into place and now frantically applied cosmetics from my purse as I rode. I suspected I had a sort of Ginger-Rogers-Joins-Nirvana look going.

We arrived at the suburban house I'd dropped Seth off at a few weeks ago. Pink balloons fluttered from the mailbox, and a mother in jeans and a sweatshirt waved goodbye as a small girl disappeared into the house. Said mother then returned to the massive, soccer team–carrying vehicle running in the driveway.

"Whoa," I said, taking it all in. "I've never been to anything like this before."

"You must have when you were little," Seth amended, parking across the street.

"Well, yeah," I lied. "But it's a different experience at this age."

We approached the front door, and he entered without knocking. Immediately, four small, blond female forms slammed into him, grappling onto his limbs, nearly knocking him over.

"Uncle Seth! Uncle Seth!"

"Uncle Seth's here!"

"Is that for me? Is that for me?"

"Desist, before I have to break out the tear gas," Seth told them mildly, unclasping one who threatened to rip his left arm off.

One of them, all blond curls and giant blue eyes like the others, caught sight of me. "Hi," she said boldly, "who are you?" Before I could answer, she tore out of the foyer, yelling, "Uncle Seth brought a girl!"

Seth made a face. "That's Morgan. She's six." He pointed to a clone of her. "This is McKenna, her twin. Over here's Kayla, four. This one"—he paused to lift up the tallest of the four, a motion that made her cackle gleefully—"is Kendall, the birthday girl. And I imagine Brandy's here somewhere, but she's too civilized to assault me like the rest."

A living room extended beyond the foyer, and another blond girl, a few years older than Kendall, watched us over the back of a couch. Other assorted children—the party guests, I presumed—ran and screamed beyond her. "I'm here, Uncle Seth."

Seth set Kendall down and tousled Brandy's hair, much to her chagrin. She wore the affronted dignity only one on the edge of adolescence could have. Morgan returned shortly thereafter with a tall, blond woman in tow. "See? See?" exclaimed the little girl. "I told you."

"Do you always create such a scene?" the woman asked, giving Seth a quick hug. She looked happy but exhausted. I could understand why.

"I should be so lucky. My fans aren't half this ravenous. Andrea, this is Georgina. Georgina, Andrea." I shook her hand as a slightly shorter, younger version of Seth entered the room. "And that's my brother, Terry."

"Welcome to our chaos, Georgina," Terry told me after I'd been introduced. He glanced at all of the children, his own and others, running around the house. "I'm not sure I fully understand Seth's wisdom in bringing you here. You'll never come back."

"Hey," exclaimed Kendall to me, "isn't that the shirt we got Uncle Seth for Christmas?"

An awkward silence fell among us adults as we all tried to look somewhere else. Finally, Andrea cleared her throat and said, "All right, guys, let's fall into line and get some games going."

I had expected a child's birthday party to be wild, but what proceeded to pass that afternoon surpassed even my imaginings. Equally impressive was the way in which Seth's brother and sister-in-law managed to control the herd of screaming, jumping creatures that somehow seemed to be everywhere in the house at once. Terry and Andrea handled them all with efficient good nature while Seth and I did little more than watch, occasionally fielding random questions tossed our way. The entire experience stunned me as a by-stander; I could hardly imagine coping with it on a regular basis. It was fascinating.

At one point, catching his breath, Terry saw me alone and struck up a conversation.

"I'm glad you could come," he said. "I didn't know Seth was seeing anyone."

"We're just friends," I clarified.

"Still. It's nice to see him with someone flesh and blood. Someone he didn't make up."

"Is it true he nearly missed your wedding?"

Terry grimaced by way of confirmation. "My best man, if you can believe that. Showing up two minutes before the ceremony began. We were on the verge of starting without him."

I could only laugh.

He shook his head. "If you continue hanging out with him, make sure you keep him in line. My brother may be brilliant, but by God, he needs a keeper sometimes."

After party games came cake, and after cake came presents. Kendall lifted Seth's up expertly and shook it. "Books," she declared.

Brandy, older and therefore quietest of the group, glanced at me and explained, "Uncle Seth always gets us books."

This did not seem to faze Kendall any. She tore open the package and crowed delightedly over three books of pirate stories contained within.

"Pirates, huh?" I asked Seth. "Is that politically correct?"

His eyes danced. "She wants to be one."

As the party wound down and guests were retrieved by parents, Kendall beseeched Seth to read stories, and I followed him, the nieces, and other stragglers into the living room while the girls' parents attempted to clean up in the kitchen. Seth read in the same compelling way he had at his signing, and I curled up in an armchair, content to just listen and watch. I was therefore startled when Kayla's small form scrambled up and sat on my lap.

Youngest of the girls, she could shriek with the best but tended to speak very little. She studied me with her globes of eyes, touched my French braid with interest, and then snuggled into me to listen to Seth. I wondered if she understood any of what he was saying. Regardless, she was soft and warm and smelled like little girl. Unconsciously, I ran my fingers through the fine, corn silk strands of hair and soon began weaving it into a braid similar to mine.

When Seth finished a story, McKenna noticed what I was doing. "Me next."

"No, me," ordered Kendall eagerly. "It's my birthday."

I ended up braiding for all four of the younger girls. Brandy shyly demurred. Not wanting four copies of me, I elected other styles for the girls, herringbones and plaits that delighted them. Seth continued to read, occasionally glancing up at me and my handiwork.

By the time we were ready to leave, I felt drained physically and emotionally. Children always made me feel a little wistful; being in close contact like this made me downright sad in a way I couldn't explain.

Seth said goodbye to his brother while I lingered near the door. As I did, I noticed a small bookcase beside me. Studying the titles, I picked out *Burberry's New Annotated Bible: Old and New Testaments*. Remembering what Roman had said about the King James Version being a bad translation, I opened this one up to Genesis 6.

The wording was nearly identical, a little cleaner and more modern sounding here and there, but mostly unchanged. With one exception. In verse 4, the King James Version had read: "There were giants in the earth in those days; and also after that, when the sons of God came in unto the daughters of men . . ." This version, however, said: "The Nephilim were on the earth in those days and also afterwards, when the sons of God went to the daughters of men . . ."

Nephilim? A superscript number appeared by the word, and I followed it to the appropriate footnote.

The word "nephilim" is sometimes translated as "giants" or "fallen ones." Sources vary in accounts of these angelic offspring, citing them sometimes simply as neighbors to the Canaanites and other times as Titan-like creatures reminiscent of Greek heroes (Harrington, 2001).

Frustrated, I looked up the Harrington reference in the book's bibliography, finding it linked to *Biblical Arcana and Myth* by Robert Harrington. I memorized the title and author, slipping the Bible back into its place just as Seth turned to go.

We drove in silence, the sky graying early as Seattle's winter loomed nearer. I might normally have interpreted the quiet in the car as awkward or weird, but I found it comfortable as my mind pondered the nephilim reference. I needed to get a hold of the Harrington book, I decided.

"They didn't have ice cream," Seth suddenly noted, interrupting my thoughts.

"Huh?"

"Terry and Andrea. They had cake with no ice cream. You want to get some ice cream?"

"Not enough sugar for you already?"

"They just go together, that's all."

"It's only about fifty out," I warned as he pulled up next to an ice cream parlor. Ice cream in inclement weather seemed odd to me. "And it's windy."

"Are you kidding? In Chicago, a place like this wouldn't even be open this time of year. This is balmy."

We went inside. Seth ordered a double cone of mint chocolate chip. I ordered a more adventurous double of blueberry cheesecake and mocha almond swirl. Sitting at a table by the windows, we ate our sugary confections in more silence.

Finally, he said, "You're quiet today."

I turned on him in wonder, pausing in my mental dissection of nephilim. "That's a switch."

"What is?"

"Usually I think you're too quiet. I have to talk and talk to keep things going."

"I've noticed. Er, I didn't mean that like it came out. That sounded bad. You talking is a good thing. You always know what to say. Exactly the right thing at exactly the right time."

"Not last night. I said horrible things last night. To Doug and Roman both. They'll never forgive me," I lamented.

"Sure they will. Doug's a good guy. I don't really know Roman, but . . ."

"But what?"

Seth suddenly looked embarrassed. "I imagine you're easy to forgive."

We looked at each other for a moment, and warmth flushed my cheeks. Not blood boiling, get naked and jump someone warm, but just cozily warm. Like being wrapped in a blanket.

"That looks terrible, you know."

"What does?"

He pointed at my cone. "That combination."

"Hey, don't knock it until you try it. They actually go pretty well together."

He looked doubtful.

I slid my chair over by him and offered him a bite. "Make sure you get both flavors."

He leaned in for the bite and managed both the blueberry cheesecake and mocha almond swirl. Unfortunately, a piece of the blueberry cheesecake scoop fell off onto his chin in the process. I instinctively reached out to stop it, sliding it back to his mouth. He just as automatically nabbed the wayward piece with his tongue, licking it off my fingers.

A blast of eroticism coursed through me, and looking into his eyes, I knew he'd shared it too. "Here," I said hastily, reaching for a napkin, ignoring the desire to return my fingers to his mouth.

Seth wiped his chin with it, but for once, he didn't let his self-consciousness get the better of him. He stayed where he was, leaning close to me.

"You smell amazing. Like . . . gardenias."

"Tuberose," I corrected automatically, dazed by how close he was to me.

"Tuberose," he repeated. "And incense, I think. I've never smelled anything like it." He leaned a hair closer.

"It's Michael by Michael Kors. You can get it at any high-end department store." I nearly groaned as the words left my flustered lips. What an idiotic thing to say. My nervousness made me flippant. "Maybe Cady could start wearing it."

Seth was all seriousness. "No. This is you. Only you. It would never smell exactly the same on anyone else."

I shivered. I wore this perfume because it was reminiscent of what other immortals sensed in my unique signature, my aura. *This is you.* With just a few casual words, I felt as though Seth had uncovered some secret part of me, looked into my soul.

We sat there then, chemistry burning between us like crazy, neither of us acting. I knew he would not try to kiss me as Roman had. Seth was content simply to look at me, to make love to me with his eyes.

Suddenly the wind caught the door to the tiny restaurant, forcing it open as a huge gust swept in. Wisps of hair blew into my face, and I slammed my hands down on the napkins that flew up from our table. Other items in the parlor had less success as more napkins and scraps of paper drifted around, and a cup of plastic spoons fell off the counter, spilling its contents on the floor. The clerk behind the counter ran to the door, fighting against the wind to make the latch catch. When he'd finally done so, he glared at the door resentfully.

With the moment—whatever it was—shattered, Seth and I picked up our things and left shortly thereafter. I asked him to drop me off at the bookstore. I hoped Doug would be there to apologize to, plus I wanted to get ahold of that Harrington book.

"You want to come in and hang out? Say hi to anybody?" I somehow felt reluctant to leave Seth now, in spite of all the things I needed to do.

He shook his head. "Sorry. I've got to go. I'm meeting someone."

"Oh." I felt kind of foolish. He could have a date now for all I knew. And why shouldn't he? It wasn't like I was his only social connection, especially after my no-dating spiel. I

was foolish to be reading so much into the ice cream encounter, especially since I was supposedly crazy about Roman.
"Well. Thanks again for everything. I'll make it up to you."

He waved his hand dismissively. "It wasn't anything. Besides, you paid me back by going to the party."

Now I shook my head. "I didn't really do anything there."

Seth only smiled. "See you around."

I stepped out of the car and suddenly stuck my head back
in. "Hey, I should have asked you this earlier. Do you have
my book signed yet? *The Glasgow Pact?*"

"Oh . . . man. No. I can't believe I forgot about that. It's
still at my place. I'll sign it and bring it soon. I'm sorry." He
looked sincerely contrite.

"Okay. It's no problem." I should have ransacked his
condo for it.

We said goodbye again, and I turned into the bookstore.
If I remembered my schedule right, Paige should have
opened and Doug should be here now as the late manager.
Sure enough, he stood at the information desk, looking on
while Tammi helped a customer.

"Hey," I said, walking up to him, uneasiness filling me as
I recalled my harsh words. "Can I talk to you for a minute?"

"No."

Whoa. I'd expected him to be upset . . . but this?

"You need to call your friend first."

"I—what?"

"That one guy," Doug explained. "That plastic surgeon
that hangs out with you and Cody."

"Hugh?"

"Yeah, that's the one. He's called, like, a hundred times,
leaving messages. He's been worried about you." His expression turned both soft and wry as he took in my dress and
flannel ensemble. "So have I."

I frowned, wondering at Hugh's urgency. "Okay. I'll call
him now. Come talk to me later?"

Doug nodded, and I started to pull out my cell phone until I remembered I'd broken it last night. Retreating to the back office instead, I sat on the desk's edge and called Hugh.

"Hello?"

"Hugh?"

"Jesus Christ, Georgina. Where the hell have you been?"

"I, er, nowhere . . ."

"We've been trying to get ahold of you all last night and today."

"I wasn't at home," I explained. "And my cell phone broke. Why? What's going on? Tell me there hasn't been another one."

"Afraid so. Another murder this time, no more friendly beatings. When we couldn't reach you, the vampires and I thought he'd got you too, even though Jerome said he could feel that you were fine."

I swallowed. "Who . . . who was it?"

"Are you sitting down?"

"Sort of."

I braced myself, ready for anything. Demon. Imp. Vampire. Succubus.

"Lucinda."

I blinked. "What?" All my theories of an avenger of evil shattered. "But that's impossible. She's—she's—"

"—an angel," Hugh finished for me.

Chapter 16

"Georgina?"

"I'm still here."

"Pretty fucked up, huh? I guess this kills your angel theory."

"I'm not so sure."

My initial feeling of dismay was being replaced by a new idea, one that had been percolating in the back of my mind ever since I read the biblical passage at Terry and Andrea's. I wondered now . . . wondered exactly what we were dealing with, if it was an angel after all. The words in Genesis came back to me: *There were giants in the earth in those days . . . the same became mighty men which were of old, men of renown . . .*

"What's Jerome saying about all of this?"

"Nothing. What'd you expect?"

"Everyone else is okay, though?"

"Fine, last I knew. What are you going to do? Nothing stupid, I hope."

"I have to go check on something."

"Georgina . . ." Hugh warned.

"Yeah?"

"Be careful. Jerome's in a terrible mood over all of this."

I laughed harshly. "I can imagine."

An awkward silence hung on the line.

"What else aren't you telling me?"

He hesitated a moment longer. "This . . . this is a surprise to you, right? This Lucinda thing?"

"Of course it is. Why wouldn't it be?"

Another pause. "It's just . . . well, you've got to admit it's kind of weird, first Duane . . ."

"Hugh!"

"And then, I mean, when no one could contact you . . ."

"I told you, my cell phone broke. You can't be serious about this."

"No, no. It's just . . . I don't know. I'll talk to you later."

I disconnected.

Lucinda dead? Lucinda, with her plaid skirt and bob? It was impossible. I felt terrible; I'd just seen her the other day. Sure, I'd called her a sanctimonious bitch, but I hadn't wanted this. Any more than I'd wanted Duane dead.

Yet, the connections Hugh had drawn were weird, weirder than I liked to admit. I'd argued with both Duane and Lucinda, and they'd died shortly thereafter. But Hugh . . . how did he fit in? *Some friend. From what I heard, he received a great deal of amusement telling anyone that would listen about your little whip and wings getup.* I remembered Lucinda's jibe. I had indeed had a small flare-up with the imp just before his attack. A small flare-up and a small attack, considering he had lived.

I shivered, unsure as to what this meant. Doug walked in.

"You get everything straightened out?"

"Yeah. Thanks." We stood there uncomfortably for a moment until I finally unlocked the floodgates of my guilt. "Doug, I—"

"Forget it, Kincaid. It's nothing."

"What I said, I shouldn't have. I was—"

"Wasted. Trashed. Flat on your ass drunk. It happens."

"Still, I had no right. You were trying to be nice, and I turned complete psycho bitch on you."

"You weren't that psycho."

"But definitely a bitch?"

"Well . . ." He hid a smile, not meeting my eyes.

"I'm sorry, Doug. I'm really sorry."

"Quit it. I can't take much more of this sentimentality."

I leaned over and squeezed his arm, resting my head slightly on his shoulder. "You're a good guy, Doug. A really good guy. And a good friend. And I'm sorry . . . sorry for a lot of things that have—or haven't—happened between us."

"Hey, forget about it. It's nothing between friends, Kincaid." A pregnant pause hung between us; he was still clearly uncomfortable with this exchange. "Did . . . did everything turn out all right? I lost track of you after the show. That outfit you have on doesn't reassure me any."

"You'll never believe whose shirt this is," I teased, subsequently telling him the whole tale of getting sick with Seth and the follow-up birthday party.

Doug was pushing hysterics by the time I finished, albeit in a relieved sort of way. "Mortensen's a good guy," he finally said, still laughing.

"He says the same thing about you."

Doug grinned. "You know he's—oh, man. I forgot, what with all those phone calls." Turning to the desk, he sifted through papers and books, finally producing a small white envelope. "You got a note. Paige said she found it last night. I hope it's good news."

"Yeah, me too."

But I had my doubts when I saw it. I took it gingerly, like something that might burn me. The paper and calligraphy were identical to the last one's. Opening up the envelope, I read:

So you're interested in fallen angels, are you? Well, there'll be a hands-on demonstration tonight. It should prove more informative than your current endeavors and won't require you screwing your boss in order to get help with extrapolation—not that watching you make a whore of yourself didn't have its moments.

I looked up, meeting Doug's curious eyes. "No worries," I told him lightly, folding the note up and placing it in my purse. "This is old news."

Hugh's report implied Lucinda had been killed last night, and this note had been slipped to me beforehand, according to Doug. The warning had gone unheeded. This person apparently didn't have a good grasp of my schedule, or they hadn't wanted me to actually act beforehand. It was more like a scare tactic.

Whatever their point in giving me a heads-up on Lucinda, it was nothing compared to the other reference in the note. The thought that someone had watched me have sex with Warren made my skin crawl.

"Where are you off to now?" Doug asked.

"Believe it or not, I need to find a book."

"You're in the right place."

We went back out to the information desk, where Tammi stood. It pleased me to see Doug training her in this post; we'd need people available for all jobs when the holidays came.

"Practice time," I told her. "Tell me where we keep this book."

I gave her the name, and she looked it up in the computer, frowning at the results. "We don't. We can order it for you."

I scowled, suddenly understanding why people seemed so pissed off when I told them that. "Great," I muttered. "Where am I going to get it tonight?" Erik probably stocked it, but he'd be closed by now.

"I hate to recommend this," joked Doug, "but a library might have it."

"Maybe . . ." I eyed a clock, unsure how late the local branches stayed open.

"Um, Georgina?" began Tammi carefully. "I know a place that has it. And that's still open."

I turned to her in surprise. "Really? Where—no. No. Not there."

"I'm sorry." Her blue eyes pleaded with me to forgive her for such tidings. "But there were three copies in stock the last time I was there. They couldn't have sold out."

I groaned, rubbing my temples. "I can't go in there. Doug, you want to run an errand for me?"

"I've got to close," he admonished. "What place are you avoiding?"

"Krystal Starz, home of 'freaky witch woman.' "

"You couldn't pay me to go there."

"You could pay me," noted Tammi, "but I'm closing too. If it makes it any easier, she's not there all the time."

"Yeah," added Doug helpfully. "No manager is always on-duty. She must have other staff to cover her."

"Unless they're short-staffed," I muttered. The irony.

I left the store and got into my car for the journey to Krystal Starz. As I drove, I reflected on the two pieces of information I'd gleaned today.

First, the nephilim reference. The King James translation had mentioned angelic offspring, even mentioned them as being abnormal, but I had never considered the possibilities half-angel children might present. The annotation in Terry and Andrea's translation had elaborated only slightly more on such creatures, but it had been enough to spring a lock in my head. Who better, I thought, to take on both angels and demons than some sort of bastard demigod?

Of course, the whole discovery of the nephilim had come about as a spin-off to the verse Erik had given me about fallen angels. I could be running away with a blind lead here when really the culprit was just a regular immortal, albeit an unstable one, slaying members of both sides. After all, I still hadn't ruled Carter out of the realm of suspects, nor had I figured out why said killer would finish the job with Duane and Lucinda but let Hugh live.

My other piece of data today, the new note, offered little I hadn't already known. I'd simply found it too late for it to be of preemptive use. And if some voyeur was following me around, there was nothing I could do about that either.

Yet, it led to the obvious question: Why was this person following me around? Evidence suggested I was the only one receiving such attention, the only one receiving notes. And again, there was the niggling truth: Everyone I'd fought with had later become a victim . . .

When I had almost reached Krystal Starz, I pulled off onto a deserted street. Unbeknownst to Tammi and Doug, I already had a simple solution for facing Helena. Stripping out of the dress and Seth's shirt, lest they be consumed, I shape-shifted, taking on the guise of a tall, willowy Thai woman in a linen dress. I sometimes used this body to hunt in.

The New Age bookstore was quiet when I entered, with only a couple of browsing customers. I saw the same boyish acolyte from before manning the register, and blessing upon blessing, I couldn't see Helena anywhere. Even disguised, I still had no desire to run into that nutcase.

Smiling at the young man behind the counter, I approached and asked where I could find the book. Grinning back like an idiot—this was a very attractive form, after all—he led me to a certain section in their cryptic cataloging system, immediately finding the book. As Tammi had said, the store stocked three copies.

We returned to the register to cash out, and I sighed in relief, thinking I was going to make it out of here unscathed. No such luck. The back door leading to the conference room opened, and Helena glided out as though conjured, clad in a flowing fuchsia gown, laden with her usual ten pounds of necklaces. Damn it. It was like the woman really did have a sixth sense or something.

"Things are well, Roger?" she asked the clerk, using her raspy show voice.

"Yes, yes." He bobbed his head eagerly, apparently thrilled that she'd call him by first name.

Turning to me, she gave me one of her diva smiles. "Hello, my dear. How are you this evening?"

Remembering that this persona had no grudge with her, I forced a smile and answered politely, "Good, thank you."

"I imagine so," she told me gravely as I handed cash to the boy, "because I sense excellent things about your aura."

I widened my eyes in what I hoped was a laywoman's awe. "Really?"

She nodded, pleased at an appreciative audience. "Very bright. Very strong. Lots of color. You have good things in store for you." This message was a far cry from the one she'd given me at Emerald City, I thought. Seeing my book, she eyed me sharply, probably because it was dense and filled with research, as opposed to most of the fluff she sold. "I'm surprised. I would have expected you to be reading up on how to focus your gifts more. Maximize your full potential. I have several titles I can recommend if you're interested."

Didn't this woman ever stop with the sales pitching? "Oh, I'd love to," I oozed back, "but I only brought enough cash for this." I gestured to the bag now in hand.

"I understand," she told me gravely. "Let me show you anyway. So you'll know what to come back for next time."

Torn, I contemplated which would cause me the most discomfort: going along with her or starting a feud in yet another body. Noticing a clock, I saw that the store closed in fifteen minutes. She couldn't waste that much of my time.

"Okay. I'd love to."

Beaming, Helena led me across the store, another victim in her thrall. As promised, we looked at books on utilizing the strongest parts of the aura, a few books on crystal channeling, and even one on how visualization could help bring about the things we most wanted. This last one was so painful, I wanted to beat myself in the head with it to end my suffering.

"Don't underestimate the power of visualization," she whispered. "You can control your own destiny, set your own paths, rules, and stakes. I can sense great potential in you, but following these principles can help you unlock more— all the things you'd want for a happy and fulfilling life. Career, home, husband, children."

An image of Seth's niece curled in my lap suddenly came unbidden to me, and I hastily turned away from Helena. Succubi bore no children. No such future waited for me, book or no.

"I need to go. Thanks for your help."

"Of course," she responded demurely, handing me a list she'd conveniently written the titles—and prices—upon. "And let me give you some brochures for our upcoming programs and events."

It didn't end. She finally released me once I was sufficiently laden with paper, all of which I dumped into the trash bin in the parking lot. Lord, I hated that woman. I supposed Helena the schmoozing con artist was better than Helena the raving lunatic who had been at Emerald City, but really, it was a tough call. At least I'd obtained the book, which was all that mattered.

I pulled off at one of my favorite Chinese places on the way home, back in my normal shape. Carrying Harrington's book in, I ate General Tso's chicken while reading the entry on nephilim:

Nephilim are first referenced in Genesis 6:4, where they are sometimes referred to as "giants" or "fallen ones." Regardless of the word's translation, the nephilim's origin is clear from this passage: they are the semi-divine offspring of angels and human women. Genesis 6:4 refers to them as "mighty" and "men of renown." The rest of the Bible makes little reference to the nephilim's angelic siring, but encounters with giants and men of "great stature" are frequently recorded in other books, such as Numbers, Deuteronomy, and Joshua. Some have speculated that the "great wickedness" prompting the flood in Genesis 6 was actually a result of the nephilim's corrupting influence on mankind. Further apocryphal readings, such as 1 Enoch, elaborate on the plight of the fallen angels and their families, describing how the corrupted angels taught "charms and enchantments" to their wives while their offspring ran wild throughout the earth, slaughtering and causing strife among humans. The nephilim, gifted with great abilities much like those of the ancient Greek heroes, were nonetheless cursed by God and neglected by their parents, consigned to wander the earth all their days without peace until eventually destroyed for the sake of mankind.

I looked up, feeling breathless. I had never heard of anything like this. I had been right in telling Erik practitioners were the worst to ask about their own histories; surely this was something someone should have told me about before. Angelic offspring. Were nephilim real? Were they still around?

Or was I really just chasing a dead end here, following a distracting lead when I should have restricted my search to immortals of my caliber or above, like Carter? After all, these nephilim were half-human; they couldn't be all that powerful.

After paying the bill, I walked out to my car, opening my fortune cookie as I went. It was empty. Charming. A light rain misted around me, and fatigue crept in around my edges, not surprising considering the last twenty-four hours.

I couldn't find a parking spot when I arrived in Queen Anne, which indicated some sort of sporting event or show going on nearby. Grumbling, I parked seven blocks away from home, vowing to never again lease an apartment that only had street spots. The wind Seth and I had felt earlier was fading, normal since Seattle was not a wind-prone city. The rain picked up in intensity, however, further darkening my mood.

I was halfway home when I heard footsteps behind me. Pausing, I turned to look back but saw nothing save slick pavement, blearily reflecting streetlights. No one was there. I turned back around, starting to pick up my pace until I did a mental head slap and simply turned invisible. Jerome was right; I did think like a human too much.

Still, I didn't like the street I'd chosen back; it was too deserted. I needed to cut over and walk the rest of the distance on Queen Anne Avenue itself.

I had just turned the corner when something impacted me hard on my back, knocking me forward six feet, startling me so much that I shifted back to visible.

I tried to turn around, flailing at my attacker, but another blow hit me in the head hard, knocking me to my knees. The sense I had was of being struck by something hand and arm shaped, but it packed a punch, more like a baseball bat. Again, my attacker hit me, this time across one of my shoulder blades, and I cried out, hoping someone would hear me.

Another strike swiped the side of my head, the force pushing me over onto my back. I squinted up, trying to catch sight of who was doing this, but all I could dimly discern was a dark, amorphous shape, bearing down on me fast and hard as another blow made contact with my jaw. I could not get up from that onslaught, could not fight against the pain descending on me harder and thicker than the rain around me.

Suddenly, brilliant light filled my vision—light so brilliant it hurt. I was not alone in my assessment. My attacker recoiled, letting me go, and I heard a strange high-pitched scream emitted above me. Attracted by some irresistible lure, I looked toward the light. A white-hot pain seared my brain as I did, my eyes taking in the figure moving toward us: beautiful and terrible, all colors and none, white light and darkness, winged and armed with a sword, features shifting and indiscernible. The next scream I heard was my own, the agony and ecstasy of what I had seen scorching my senses, even though I could no longer see it. My vision had gone white-whiter-whitest until all was black, and I could see nothing at all.

Then, silence fell.

I sat there sobbing, hurting physically and spiritually. Footsteps came, and I felt someone kneel beside me. Somehow, despite my blindness, I knew it was not my attacker. That person had long since fled.

"Georgina?" a familiar voice asked me.

"Carter," I gasped out, throwing my arms around him.

Chapter 17

I woke to the sound of Aubrey purring in my ear. Sensing my consciousness, she moved closer and licked the part of my cheek near my earlobe, her whiskers gently rubbing against my skin. It tickled. Squirming slightly, I opened my eyes. To my astonishment, light, color, and shapes came through to me—albeit in a blurred, distorted manner.

"I can see," I muttered to Aubrey, trying to sit up. Immediately, myriad aches and pains screamed all over my body, making the motion difficult. I lay stretched out on my couch, an old afghan tossed over me.

"Of course you can see," Jerome's cold voice informed me. Aubrey fled. "Though it'd serve you right if you couldn't. What were you thinking, looking at an angel in full form?"

"I wasn't," I told him, squinting at his dark-clad shape pacing in front of me. "Thinking, that was."

"Obviously."

"Lay off," came Carter's laconic voice from somewhere behind me.

Straightening up and peering around, I made out his fuzzy form leaning against a wall. Peter, Cody, and Hugh also stood nearby in the room. It was a regular, dysfunctional family reunion. I couldn't help but laugh.

"And you were there, and you were there . . ."

Cody sat down beside me, his features materializing into sharp focus as he leaned in to study my face closer. Gently, he ran a finger along one of my cheekbones, frowning. "What happened?"

I sobered up. "Is it that bad?"

"No," he lied. "Hugh was worse." The imp made a nondistinct noise across the room.

"I already know what happened," snapped Jerome. I didn't need to see the demon's face in detail to know he was glaring at me. "What I don't understand is *why* it happened. Did you actually try to come up with the most dangerous situation possible? 'Hmm, let's see . . . dark alley, no one around . . . ' That sort of thing?"

"No," I shot back. "I wasn't thinking of that. I wasn't thinking of anything except getting home." I related the evening's events to the best of my ability, beginning with the footsteps, ending with Carter.

When I'd finished, Hugh sat down in an armchair across from me, pensive. "Pauses, huh?"

"What?"

"The way you tell what happened . . . you got hit, pause, then another one, pause, then another one. Right?"

"Yeah, so? I don't know. Isn't that how fights work? Punch, draw back, get ready for another? Besides, we're talking about breaks of, like, a second or so. Not real breathing time."

"There was nothing like that for me. I had slashing too. It was an onslaught. A stream of blows, continuously. It defied understanding or ability. Definitely supernatural."

"Well, so was this," I countered. "Believe me, I couldn't fight against it. It wasn't some mortal mugging, if that's what you're suggesting." Hugh simply shrugged.

Silence fell, and I gave the imp a sidelong glance to the best of my limited vision's ability. "They're looking meaningfully at each other, aren't they?"

"Who?"

"Carter and Jerome. I can feel it." I turned to Carter, suddenly wondering if my trip last night had been for naught. "I don't suppose you salvaged the shopping bag I had on me?"

Walking over to my kitchen counter, the angel produced a bag and tossed it to me. My depth perception still off, I missed, and the bag bounced off the couch onto the floor. The book slipped out. Jerome snatched it up in an instant and read the title.

"Fuck me, Georgie. Is this why you were out skulking in dark corners? This is what you nearly got killed for? I told you to lay off the vampire hunter investigating—"

"Oh come on," cried Cody, jumping up in my defense. "None of us believe that anymore. We know there's an angel doing this—"

"An angel?" I heard heavy amusement and even a scoff in the demon's words.

"No mortal did that to me," I agreed hotly. "Or to Hugh. Or to Lucinda. Or to Duane. It was a nephilim."

"A nephi-what?" asked Hugh, startled.

"Isn't that a character on *Sesame Street*?" Peter spoke up for the first time.

Jerome stared silently at me for a moment, then finally demanded, "Who told you about that?" Not waiting for an answer, he turned toward the angel. "You know you're not supposed to—"

"It wasn't me," retorted Carter mildly. "I'm guessing she figured it out on her own. You don't put enough faith in your own people."

"I did find out on my own, though I had help."

I briefly detailed my string of leads, how one had led to another, from Erik to the book at Krystal Starz.

"Shit," muttered Jerome, after listening to my spiel. "Fucking Nancy Drew."

"Okay," said Peter, "compelling chase or no, you still haven't told us what a nephilopogus is."

"Nephilim," I corrected. Hesitantly, I looked at Jerome. "Can I?"

"You're asking me for permission? How quaint."

Taking that as acquiescence, I began uncertainly, "Nephilim are the offspring of angels and humans. Like in that passage in Genesis. Where the angels fell and took human wives? Nephilim are the result. They have certain abilities . . . I don't know all of them . . . strength and power . . . like Greek heroes . . ."

"Or like major nuisances," added Jerome bitterly. "Don't forget that."

"How so?" Hugh asked.

I continued when Jerome didn't. "Well . . . what I read said they used to cause strife and slaughter among humans."

"Yeah, but this one's not going after humans," pointed out Peter.

Carter shrugged. "They're unpredictable. They don't play by anyone's rules, and honestly, we're not really sure what this one's intentions are. It's playing a game, that's for sure, what with its attacks on random immortals and that note it sent Georgina."

"Two notes," I corrected. "I got another one just before Lucinda died, but I was with Seth all night and didn't read it until the next day."

Hugh and the vampires turned to stare at me.

"You were with Seth all night?" asked Cody, astonished.

"Which one's he again?" Hugh asked.

"The writer," provided Peter.

The imp regarded me with new interest. "What'd you do 'all night' then?"

"Can we not discuss Georgina's love life right now, fascinating though it may be?" Jerome gave me a speculative look. "Unless, of course, this Seth person is someone of strong moral character and principle whose life energy you plan on stealing soon in support of the greater cause of evil and its goals."

"Right on the first, not on the rest."

"Damn it. I need a drink."

"Help yourself."

Jerome wandered over to my liquor cabinet and sifted through its contents.

"So how can we spot this nephilim?" asked Cody, getting us back on track.

I glanced uncertainly at Carter and Jerome. I didn't know any of the technicalities.

"You can't," the angel announced cheerfully.

"They can hide their signature too, then. Like higher immortals."

He nodded back at me. "Yes, they have the worst characteristics of both their parents. Ample power and pseudo-angelic abilities, mixed with rebelliousness, a love of the physical world, and poor impulse control."

"How much power?" I wanted to know. "They're half-human, right? So half the power?"

"That's the clincher." Jerome looked much more cheerful with a glass of gin in hand. "It varies wildly, just as each angel has a different level of power. One thing is clear: Nephilim inherit a lot more than half their parent's power, though they can never exceed it. It's still plenty—which is why I've been trying to knock sense into all of you to stay clear. A nephilim could easily blow one of you out of the water."

"But not one of you." Peter spoke the words more as a

statement than a question, despite the uncertain note lacing his voice.

Neither angel nor demon responded, and another piece clicked into place for me.

"That's why you guys are going around with your signatures masked. You're hiding from it too."

"We're merely taking appropriate precautions," Jerome protested.

"It ran from you," I reminded Carter. "You must have been stronger than it."

"Probably," he agreed. "I was more concerned with you, so I didn't get a good sense. An angel in full form will freak most beings out—it'll kill a mortal—so I could have been stronger than it or not. Hard to say."

I didn't like that answer, not at all. "What were you doing there anyway?"

The angel's trademark sarcastic smile appeared. "What do you think? I was following you around."

I started. "What? Then I was right . . . that day at Erik's . . ."

"Afraid so."

"My God," said Peter, amazed. "You really were on to something, Georgina. At least about him stalking you."

I felt semivindicated, even if Carter obviously didn't seem to be the culprit anymore. Hugh had been right in accusing me of bias. I had really wanted Carter to be the responsible party for all these attacks, as a sort of payback for all the times he'd mocked me. His timely intervention in the alley only muddled my opinion of him now.

Carter explained, "After realizing that first note was probably from this nephilim, I thought it'd be prudent to pop in once in a while since our friend here seems to have an especial interest in you. My intention was to catch him or her off-guard, not to help you, though I'm happy to have been able to. Plus, that day at Erik's . . ."

He looked over at Jerome. The demon threw his arms in

the air. "Sure? Why not? Tell them. Tell them everything. They already know too much."

"Erik?" I prompted.

"This thing, this nephilim . . ." Carter paused thoughtfully. "This being knows a surprising amount about us and about the immortal community."

"Well . . . it's like you said, right?" asked Peter. "This nephilim would find one of us and follow him or her around."

"No. I mean, yes, that's possible, but evidence indicates this one knows much more than simple surveillance might give it . . ."

"For Chrissake," Jerome snapped, "if you're going to tell them, tell them. Stop speaking in riddles." The demon turned to us. "He's saying this nephilim is working with a leak. Someone's feeding it information about the immortal community here."

Cody caught the insinuation just as I did. "You think Erik's doing it."

"He's the strongest suspect," admitted Carter apologetically. "He's been here for decades, and he has the talent to sense immortals."

"And to think, he spoke so well of you," I murmured, feeling aghast. "Well, you're wrong. It's not him. Not Erik."

"Don't get huffy about it now, Georgie. He's not our only lead, just the most likely."

"And I don't like it any more than you," the angel added. "But we can't dismiss any possibilities. We need to neutralize this nephilim threat soon. It's out of hand; we'll get outside involvement before long, and that's always a pain."

"Then why aren't you letting us help you?" I cried. "Why all the secrecy?"

"Are you deaf? It's for your own protection. This thing could blast you to Armageddon!" Jerome downed the rest of his gin in a flurry.

I didn't buy it. There was more than just our safety at stake here. Jerome still hadn't come clean. "Yes, but—"

"The committee meeting is over," he interrupted me icily. "Would the rest of you excuse Georgina and me?"

Oh shit. I looked desperately at my friends, hoping they might stay and defend me, but they all scurried out. Cowards, I thought. None of them would cross Jerome when he spoke like that. Okay, I wouldn't have either in their shoes.

Carter, I noticed, did not leave. The directive apparently did not apply to him.

"Georgie," began Jerome carefully, once the others were gone, "you and I seem to be facing off more often than not lately. I don't like it."

"It's not exactly facing off," I noted, squirming uneasily, recalling his display of power at the hospital and threat to "stash" me somewhere. "We're just having differences of opinion lately."

"Differences that can get you killed."

"Jerome, this can't possibly just be about—"

"No more."

A wall of power slammed into me, throwing me back against the couch. It was like one of those carnival rides where people stand along the sides of a round room that spins faster and faster until inertia pins everyone's limbs to the walls. Moving became agony. Even breathing was a struggle. I felt like Atlas, bearing the brunt of the world's weight.

Jerome's voice boomed inside my head, and some brave part of me cursed his parlor tricks, even as the rest of me recoiled.

I need you to listen to me for once without constantly interrupting. You cannot keep poking around here. Doing so calls attention to yourself, and you already have a lot more of it on you from this nephilim than I would like. I neither need nor want a new succubus. I've grown accustomed to you, Georgina. I do not want to lose you. I am more lenient with you than I should be, however. You get away with things no other archdemon would allow. I haven't minded indulging you thus far, but things can change—especially if you continue to be insubordinate. I can have you transferred somewhere else, away from this cozy delusion of a human life you've established. Or I can call Lilith in and report your behavior to her directly. I'm sure she'd be happy to do a little retraining with you.

My heart stopped at the mention of the Succubus Queen. I had met her only once, when I first joined the ranks. That encounter, rather like seeing Carter in all his angelic glory, was not an experience I wanted to repeat anytime soon.

Do you understand?

"Y-yes."

Are you sure?

The pressure increased, and it was all I could do to manage a weak nod. The psychic cage abruptly dropped, and I slumped forward, taking in deep breaths. I could still feel where his power had touched me, rather like a tactile version of the afterimage one sees with a camera flash.

"I'm glad you understand, and I'm sure you'll also understand if I don't entirely believe you. It's part of the nature of our side."

"Is this . . . is this the part where you stash me somewhere?"

He chuckled softly. Menacingly. "No. Not yet at least. Frankly, I think you just need a little supervision to stay out of trouble. I'm also not entirely convinced you and the nephilim merely have a passing relationship."

A retort was on my lips, but I bit it off, my skin still burning.

"I'd have one of your friends do it, but I don't doubt you

could wrap any of them around your smallest finger. No, you need babysitting by someone who won't bend, who won't fall for your tricks."

"Tricks? Who then?" For a minute, I half thought he referred to himself until I noticed Carter's smug smile. Oh man. "You can't be serious."

"It'll ensure you toe the line, Georgie. What's more, it will keep you alive."

"You're practically our best lead at the moment," Carter explained. "This nephilim has some interest in you, even though that interest seems to have shifted a bit from note-passing to assault."

"Carter will be ready if it tries to finish what he interrupted. He can also shield your apartment from prying eyes."

"But it'll sense him when we go out—" I tried weakly.

"No more than you can now," Carter reminded me. "And I'll be invisible. A ghost at your side. An angel on your shoulder, if you will. You won't even know I'm around."

"Jerome, please, you can't do this—"

"I can, and I will. Unless, like I said, you want me to have a chat with Lilith?"

Damn him. The threat of Lilith was stronger than any potential stashing, and he knew it.

"Good. If there's no further discussion then, I'll take my leave and let you two get situated." Jerome glanced between us, dark eyes resting on me a moment. "Oh, by the way. Do check yourself out in a mirror at some point."

I scowled, thinking of Cody's scrutiny of my injuries. "Thanks for reminding me."

"What I'm reminding you of is that you're a succubus. Those bruises are a manifestation of believing you're human. You are not. You have to feel them, but you don't have to wear them."

With that, the demon vanished in an eye blink, leaving a faint smell of brimstone in his wake that I suspected was pure showmanship.

"So, do I get the couch?" Carter asked me cheerfully.

"Go to hell." I left the room to go check out my reflection.

"Hardly a nice way to treat your new roommate."

"I didn't ask for your—"

I stopped halfway down the hallway. I'd spent the last couple of weeks suspecting Carter of murder and other terrible things; I'd spent the last half-century hating him as a person. Yet he'd just saved my life, and I hadn't uttered one word of thanks.

I turned toward him, dreading what I now had to say.

"I'm sorry."

He wore a look similar to the one Jerome had had when I asked his permission earlier. "Really? For just now?"

"For not thanking you earlier. For saving me out there. I mean, I'm not happy about you shacking up here, but I am grateful for what you did then. And I'm sorry, too, if I haven't exactly been . . . nice to you."

The angel's expression was unreadable. "Glad to have helped."

Not knowing what else to say, I turned and kept walking.

"What are you going to do now?" he asked.

I paused again. "Look at the damage and then go to bed. I'm tired. And I hurt."

"Aw, no slumber party games or popcorn? No make-overs?"

"Don't take this personally, but you could use a make-over. You look like a refugee. Why . . ." I swallowed and rephrased my words as I studied him. "When I saw you out there, on the street, you were . . . you were so beautiful. The most beautiful thing I've ever seen." My voice came out as a whisper.

Carter's face turned grave. "Jerome's the same way, you

know. In his true form. Just as beautiful. Angels and demons come from the same stock. He chooses that John Cusack wannabe shape by choice."

"Why? Why does he do that? And why do you choose to look like a junkie or a bum?"

The edges of the angel's lips turned slightly upward. "Why does a woman who claims she wants to avoid the attention of nice men choose a form that makes everyone around her do a double take and stare?"

I swallowed again, lost in the far reaches of his eyes, but not in the same way I had been lost in Roman's or Seth's eyes. It was more like the angel could see all the way through me, through all of my facades, down to my soul or what remained of it.

With great effort, I broke that scrutiny, turning back toward my bedroom.

"No one is punished forever," he told me gently.

"Yeah? That's not what I hear. Good night."

I went into my bedroom, closing my door behind me. Just before it clicked, I heard Carter call, "So, who's making breakfast?"

Chapter 18

Around ten the next morning, the phone jolted me out of a dream I'd been having about jellyfish and mint chocolate chip ice cream. Rolling over, I picked it up, discovering in the process that I ached a lot less than I had last night. Immortal healing in action.

"Hello?"

"Hey, it's Seth."

Seth! Yesterday's events rushed back to me. The birthday party. The ice cream. The perfume. I again wondered who he'd had to meet after dropping me off at the bookstore.

"Hi," I gushed, sitting up. "How are you?"

"Not bad. I'm, uh, over at Emerald City, and I didn't see you . . . they said it's your day off."

"Yeah, I'll be back tomorrow."

"Okay. So, um, do you want to maybe do something today? Lunch? Or a movie maybe? Unless you have other plans . . ."

"No . . . not exactly . . ." I bit my lip, silencing the immediate acceptance that wanted to spring forth.

I still had that strange, inexplicable attraction and sense of comfortable familiarity with Seth. I would have liked to hang out with him more, but I had already tried walking the line of friendship and dating with Roman, only to have that blow up in my face. It would be far better never to get started with Seth, despite my longings. Besides, I hadn't forgotten about my angelic bodyguard; I didn't really want him tagging along. Best to keep Carter indoors as long as possible.

"But I'm sick."

"Really? I'm sorry."

"Yeah, you know . . . just that kind of run-down feeling." It wasn't entirely a lie. "I don't really feel up to getting out today."

"Oh. Okay. Do you need anything? Do you want me to bring you any food maybe?"

"No . . . no," I hastily assured him, banishing images of Seth feeding me chicken soup while I lounged around in cute pajamas. Christ. This was going to be harder than I thought. "I don't want you to have to keep taking care of me. Thanks, though."

"I don't mind. I mean, no problem."

"I should be in tomorrow, if this doesn't get worse . . . so I'll see you then. Maybe we can have coffee. Or rather, I'll have coffee and you can . . . not have coffee."

"Okay. I'd like that. Not having coffee, I mean. Would you mind . . . that is, can I check on you later? Call you again?"

"Sure." The phone was safe enough.

"Okay. If you need anything before then . . ."

"I know how to reach you."

We said our goodbyes and disconnected, and I clambered out of bed to see what mischief Carter had managed this morning. I found the angel sitting on a stool by my kitchen counter, feeding Aubrey sausage with one hand while he held some sort of breakfast sandwich in the other. An enormous McDonald's bag sat on the counter near him.

"I made breakfast," he told me, eyes on Aubrey.

"Don't give her that," I chastised. "It's bad for her."

"Cats don't eat kernels of dry food in the wilderness."

"Aubrey couldn't survive in the wilderness."

I scratched her head, but she was more interested in licking the grease off her chops. Opening the bag, I found a variety of sandwiches and hash brown patties.

"I didn't know what you'd want," Carter explained as I pulled out a Bacon, Egg, & Cheese Biscuit.

I bit into it, melting at that scrumptiousness, grateful weight gain and cholesterol were nonevents for me. "Hey, wait. Did you actually go to McDonald's?"

"Yup."

I swallowed the food. "You just left? Just now?"

"Yup."

"What kind of bodyguard are you? What if the nephilim came back and attacked me?"

He eyed me and shrugged. "You look okay to me."

"You're not very good at this."

"Who was on the phone?"

"Seth."

"The author?"

"Yeah. Wanted to hang out today. I told him I was sick."

"Poor guy. You're breaking his heart."

"Better that than something else." I finished the sandwich and went for a second one. Aubrey watched me hopefully.

"So what are we doing today?"

"Nothing. At least, I'm not going out, if that's what you mean."

"You aren't going to attract nephilim attention that way." He glanced around my apartment and grimaced when I didn't respond. "It's going to be a long day then. I hope you at least have cable."

We spent the rest of the morning more or less staying out of each other's way. I let him use my laptop, and he got caught up in surfing eBay. What he could be looking for, I had no idea. As for me, I stayed in my pajamas after all, tossing a robe over them and deeming that good enough. I attempted to call Roman once, knowing I'd need to face him eventually, but I only managed to leave a voice mail message. I hung up with a sigh, opting to curl up on the couch with a book Seth had recommended in one of his e-mails.

Just as I was starting to think I'd recovered from the dense breakfast and needed lunch, Carter suddenly peered over the top of the laptop, like a hound sniffing the wind.

"I have to go," he told me abruptly, standing up.

"What? What do you mean?"

"Nephilim signature."

I bolted upright from my lounging position. "What? Where?"

"Not here."

With that, he blinked out of sight.

I sat there, looking around uneasily. Whereas earlier I'd felt stifled by his presence, his sudden disappearance became a gaping hole in my environment. I was exposed. Vulnerable. When he didn't return in a few minutes, I tried unsuccessfully to pay attention to my book, finally giving up after I'd reread the same sentence five times.

Still wanting lunch, I called and ordered a pizza, making sure I included enough for Carter. Doing this wasn't the best of ideas on my part since it meant opening the door eventually. When I did, I expected no less than an army of nephilim outside. Instead, I only found a bored-looking pizza guy, demanding $15.07.

I munched on the pizza and tried to watch television with little luck. Turning to the laptop, I checked my e-mail and found that Seth had sent me a funny letter, much more eloquent than our earlier conversation, per usual. It only provided temporary distraction, and I was on the verge of breaking out the paint-by-number kit when Carter blinked back into my living room.

"What the hell was that? Where have you been?"

The angel regarded me with a calm, wry smile. "Easy there, haven't you ever heard of respecting boundaries in a relationship? It was in that book you were so quick to discard."

"Cut it out. You can't just say 'nephilim signature' and then disappear like that."

"I can actually. I have to." He found the cold pizza on my counter and bit into a piece. Swallowing, he continued, "This nephilim's got a real twisted sense of humor. Every once in a while, it likes to unmask . . . flash us, so to speak. This time it came from West Seattle."

"You can detect that from this far away?"

"Jerome and I can. We never catch the creep, but we have to check it out anyway. Leads us on a merry chase."

The implications seemed obvious to me. "So you leave me? What if it's a setup? What if it flashes you over there and then zaps back to me while all the attention's away?"

"It can't just 'zap' around. Nephilim don't move like higher immortals do; they're constrained by the same limitations as you, fortunately. This one would have to get in a car and drive back over here, just like everyone else, which would hardly be a speedy process. You're protected by miles of traffic congestion."

"Weird."

"Like we said, they're unpredictable. They like breaking rules, shaking up the status quo just to see what we'll do."

"Weird," I repeated. "Does it even know you're there? That it's making you drop everything and come?"

"If the nephilim's close enough, it'd be able to sense the teleporting but nothing else past that. As long as we're masked, our identities, strength, and whatever stay hidden.

So, if it is lurking, it knows two higher immortals came to check it out, but not much more than that."

"And it just watches and waits," I concluded. "Kind of twisted. Lord, these things are a pain in the ass."

"Tell me about it. They 'do not go gently into that good night.'"

I blinked at the poetic reference. "Wait . . . that's what's going to happen? You're going to kill . . . er, destroy it or something?"

Carter cocked his head toward me curiously. "What'd you think would happen? Ten years and parole?"

"I . . . don't know. I just figured . . . wow. I don't know. Are you into that? The whole smiting thing? I mean, I suppose you guys vanquish evil on a regular basis, huh?"

"We smite, as you so cutely term it, when we have to. Demons tend to be more into it than we are. In fact, Nanette even offered to come up and take care of this nephilim," he recalled, referring to Portland's archdemoness. "But I told Jerome I'd help."

"Wouldn't Jerome want to do it himself?"

"Do you refuse backup when it's offered?" he asked me, answering my question with a question which, really, was no answer at all. Thinking about it, he laughed softly. "Of course, I forget, Georgina rushes in where angels fear to tread."

"Yeah, yeah, I know how that quote really goes." I stood up and stretched. "Well, if the excitement's over, I think I'll take a bath."

"Wow. The harsh lifestyle of a succubus. I wish I had your job."

"Hey, our side's always recruiting. You might need to be a little prettier to be an incubus, though. And a little more charming."

"Untrue. Mortal women go for jerks. I see it all the time."

"Touché."

I left him and took my bath, afterward finally giving up my pajamas for jeans and a T-shirt. I returned to the living room, turned on the television, and found *The African Queen* just starting. Carter closed the laptop and watched with me. I'd always liked Katharine Hepburn but couldn't help marvel at what a dull day this was turning out to be. Avoiding going outside wouldn't do me any good in the long term since I'd have to drag Carter around with me tomorrow anyway when I went to work. My self-imposed enclosure today only prolonged the inevitable. In light of this, I considered breaking the cabin fever by seeing if he wanted to go to dinner after the movie. He shot up before I could speak, once more sensing a nephilim signature.

"Twice in one day?"

"It happens."

"Where now?"

"Lynnwood."

"This guy gets around."

But I was speaking to empty air; Carter had disappeared. Sighing, I turned back to the movie, feeling a little more at ease after the angel's last explanation. The nephilim was in Lynnwood, trying to be a nuisance to Jerome and Carter. Commuting time was rapidly approaching, and Lynnwood was no small jump away. No nephilim would beat the angel back. As Carter had pointed out, I was safe for the time being. I had no need to panic.

Yet, I nearly jumped out of my skin anyway when I heard the phone ring a few minutes later. Nervously, I picked up the receiver, imagining a nephilim blasting out of it.

"Hello?"

"Hey. It's me again."

"Seth. Hi."

"Hope I'm not bothering you. I just wanted to see how you are . . ."

"Better," I told him sincerely. "I liked your e-mail."

"Did you? Cool."

Our normal silence fell. "So . . . did you get a lot of writing done today?"

"I did actually. About ten pages. That never sounds like a lot, but—"

A knock sounded at the door, and a chill ran down my spine. "Can-can you hang on?"

"Sure."

Hesitantly, I prowled toward the door like a cat burglar, as though slow and drawn-out movements would actually do something against an insanely powerful supernatural being. Reaching the door, I carefully peered out the peephole.

Roman.

Exhaling with relief, I opened the door, resisting the urge to throw my arms around him. "Hi."

"Are you talking to me?" asked Seth through the phone.

"Hi," Roman told me, looking just as uncertain as I felt. "Can . . . I come in?"

"Er, no I'm not, I mean, yes you can, and yes I am talking to you now." I stepped aside so Roman could enter. "Look Seth, can I, um, call you back? Or maybe . . . I'll just see you tomorrow, okay?"

"Uh, yeah. I guess. Everything okay?"

"It's fine. Thanks for calling."

We hung up, and I gave Roman my full attention.

"Seth Mortensen, famous author?"

"I've been sick today," I explained, using the same excuse I'd given Seth. "He just wanted to check on me."

"Terribly considerate of him." Roman put his hands in his pockets and paced.

"We're just friends."

"Of course you are. Because you don't date, right?"

"Roman—" I cut off the onslaught that wanted to rush out, switching to safer territory. "Can I get you anything? Soda? Coffee?"

"I can't stay. I was passing through and got your message. I just thought I'd . . . I don't know what I was thinking. It was stupid."

He turned as if to leave, and I frantically reached out, grabbing his arm. "Wait. Don't. Please."

He turned to face me, looking down from his lofty height, the normally good-humored face grave today. Fighting my natural reaction at such proximity, I felt surprised when his expression softened, and he noted, mildly astonished, "You really aren't feeling well."

"W-what makes you say that?" I had shape-shifted my bruises away as Jerome had suggested and whatever smarting pain I felt was no longer visible.

Gingerly, he reached out and stroked my cheek, fingers becoming bolder. "I don't know . . . you're just . . . kind of pale, I guess."

I started to point out I wasn't wearing makeup and then realized I wanted to appear sick. "Probably a cold."

He let his hand drop. "Is there anything I can do for you? I don't like . . . seeing you like this . . ."

Lord, how bad did I look? "I'm fine. I just need rest. Look, about the other night—"

"I'm sorry," he interrupted. "I shouldn't have pushed you—"

I stared, amazed. "You didn't do anything. It was me. I was the nutjob. I'm the one who couldn't handle things."

"No, it was my fault. I knew how you felt about getting serious, and I still kissed you."

"I did as much kissing as you. That wasn't the problem. Me freaking out was the problem. I was drunk and stupid. I shouldn't have done that to you."

"It's no problem. Really. I'm just glad you're okay." A faint smile glimmered on his handsome features, and I remembered Seth saying I was easy to forgive. "Look, since we both feel we're at fault, maybe we can make it up to each other. Go out sometime this week and—"

"No." The calm certainty in my voice startled both of us.

"Georgina—"

"No. Roman, we aren't going out anymore . . . and I don't think we can really pull off friends either." I swallowed. "It'd be better if we just make a clean break—"

"Georgina," he exclaimed, eyes widening. "You can't be serious. You and I—"

"I know. I know. But I can't do this. Not now."

"You're breaking up with me."

"Well, we weren't ever really going out . . ."

"What happened to you?" he demanded. "What happened to you at some point in your life that made you so terrified of getting close to another person? What makes you run like this? Who hurt you?"

"Look, it's complicated. And it doesn't matter. That past is gone, remember? I just can't do this with you now, okay?"

"Is there someone else? Doug? Or Seth?"

"No! There's no one. I just can't be with you."

We went around and around, rephrasing the same points in different ways, our emotions growing and growing. It felt like forever, but really only a few minutes passed as he pressed and I refused. He never turned angry or pushy, but his dismay was clearly apparent, and I felt certain I'd cry as soon as he left.

Finally, glancing at the time, he ran a hand ruefully through his dark hair, turquoise eyes luminous with regret. "I have to go. I want to talk to you more—"

"No. I don't think we should. It's better. I've really liked being with you . . ."

He laughed harshly, walking toward the door. "Don't say that. Don't sugar coat things."

"Roman . . ." I felt horrible. Anger and grief were written all over his face. "Please understand—"

"See you around, Georgina. Or maybe not."

He had barely slammed the door when tears spilled down my cheeks.. Going to my bedroom, I lay down on my bed, ready for a good cry that never came. No more tears issued forth, in spite of my mixed feelings of despair and relief. Part of me wanted to call Roman back right now, make him return to me; the other part coolly warned I now had clear reason to cut Seth off as soon as possible before things escalated.

Good Lord, why did it seem I was always hurting people I cared about? What was it about me that made me repeat this cycle over and over? Roman's devastated face still hovered in my mind, but I took comfort in the fact that he hadn't been traumatized as much as Kyriakos. Not nearly as much.

The discovery of my affair with Ariston had led to condemnation from both our families and an impending divorce coupled with the loss of my dowry. I think I might have been able to handle that scorn, even the hateful looks. What I could not handle was the way Kyriakos had been stripped of all life and caring. I almost wished he would turn angry and lash out at me, but there was nothing like that within him. Nothing at all. I had destroyed him.

After several days of separation, I found him sitting on one of the rocky outcroppings overlooking the water. I tried to engage him in conversation a number of times, but he wasn't responding to any of it. He would only stare out at that expanse of blue, face dead and expressionless.

I stood by him, my own emotions writhing inside me. I had reveled in being a forbidden object of desire with Ariston, but I also wanted to be one of love with Kyriakos. I couldn't have it both ways apparently.

I reached out to wipe the tears from his cheeks, and he slapped my hand away. It was the closest he had ever come to hitting me.

"Don't," he warned, leaping up. "Don't ever touch me again. You sicken me."

I felt my own tears now, even if his anger meant he was still alive. "Please . . . it was a mistake. I don't know what happened."

He laughed hollowly, a terrible, mirthless sound. "Don't you? You seemed to know perfectly well at the time. So did he."

"It was a mistake."

He turned his back to me and walked over to the edge of the cliff, staring out at the sea. He spread his arms out and tipped his head back, letting the wind blow over him. Gulls cried nearby.

"Wh-what are you doing?"

"I am flying," he told me. "If I keep flying . . . right over this edge, I will be happy again. Or better yet, I won't feel anything at all. I won't think about you anymore. I won't think about your face or your eyes or the way you smile or the way you smell. I won't love you anymore. I won't hurt anymore."

I approached him, half-afraid my presence would make him go over. "Stop it. You're scaring me. You don't mean any of this."

"Don't I?"

He looked at me, and there was no more anger or cynicism. Only grief. Sorrow. Despair. Depression blacker than a moonless night. It was terrible and frightening. I wanted him to snap at me again, to yell at me. I would have even let him hit me, if only to see some sort of heat in him. There was none of that, though. Only darkness.

He gave me a sad, bleak smile. The smile of one already dead.

"I will never forgive you."

"Please . . ."

"You were my life, Letha . . . but no more. No more. I have no life now."

He walked away, and even as my heart broke, I exhaled in relief to see him moving away from the cliff. I wanted to run after him but gave him his space instead. Sitting down in his spot, I drew my knees up and buried my face in them, half wishing I was dead.

"He'll come back here, you know," a voice suddenly said behind me. "The pull is too strong. And next time, he may go over."

I jerked my head up, startled. I hadn't heard anyone approach. I didn't recognize the man who now stood there, odd in a town where everyone knew everyone else. He was slim and well-groomed, dressed in clothes more elegant than I usually saw around here.

"Who are you?"

"They call me Niphon," he said with a small bow. "And you are Letha, Marthanes' daughter, formerly wife of Kyriakos."

"I still am his wife."

"But not for long."

I turned my face away. "What do you want?"

"I want to help you, Letha. I'd like to help you with this mess you've gotten yourself into."

"No one can help me. Not unless you can undo the past."

"No. No one can undo the past. I can make people forget it, though."

I slowly turned back to him, assessing his bright eyes and dapper manner. "Stop joking. I'm not in the mood."

"I assure you, I am most earnest."

Staring at him, I suddenly somehow knew he was telling the truth, as impossible as it was to believe. Later I would learn that Niphon was an imp, but at the time, I had only sensed that he had a strange air about him, the whispering of power that promised he really could do what he said.

"How?"

His eyes gleamed, not unlike Hugh's when he was on the edge of a major deal. "To erase the memory of what you've done is no small feat. It carries a price."

"Can you make me forget too?"

"No. But I can make everyone else forget. Your family, your friends, the town. *Him*."

"I don't know . . . I don't think I could go back to them then. Even if they didn't remember, I still would. I couldn't face Kyriakos like that. Unless . . ." I hesitated, wondering if it might not be better never to come in contact with them again. "Can you make them forget me altogether? Make it like I've never been born?"

Niphon drew a sharp, excited breath. "Yes, oh yes. But a favor like that . . . a favor like that carries an even higher price . . ."

He'd explained it to me then, what I'd have to give in return to completely blot me from the minds of those I'd known. My soul was a given. I'd carry it as long as I walked the earth, but it would have a lease on it, so to speak. That was the standard price for any hellish deal. But hell wanted more of me: my eternal service in the corruption of souls. I would spend the rest of my days seducing men, fulfilling their fantasies for my own gain and for those whom I served. It was an ironic fate, considering what had brought me to this point.

To aid me, I'd gain the ability to take any form I chose, as well as the power to enhance my own charm. And of course, I'd have eternal life. Immortality and invulnerability. For some, that might have been benefit alone.

"You'd be good. One of the best. I can sense it within you." Imps had the ability to look into a person's soul and nature. "Most people think desire is only in the body, but it's here too." He touched my forehead. "And you would never die. You would stay young and beautiful forever, until the earth perishes."

"And after that?"

He smiled. "That's a long way off, Letha, whereas your husband's life is at stake now."

That had been what sold me. The knowledge that I could save Kyriakos and give him a new life, a life free of me where he would have a chance to be happy once more. A life where I could slink away from my disgrace and maybe even be rightfully punished. My soul—which I barely understood anyway—seemed a small price. I'd agreed to the bargain, first shaking on it, then putting my mark on paperwork I couldn't read. Niphon left me, and I returned to town. It was eerily simple.

When I returned, it was exactly as he had promised. The wish had already been carried out. No one knew me. Passing people—people I'd known my entire life—gave me the glances reserved for strangers. My own sisters walked by me without recognition. I wanted to find Kyriakos, to see if it was the same for him, but I couldn't muster the courage. I didn't want him to see my face, not ever again, even if he didn't recognize it. So I spent the day wandering, trying to accept the fact that I was gone to these people. It was harder than I thought it would be. And sadder.

When nightfall came, I retreated again to the outskirts of town. I had nowhere to stay, after all. No family or friends. Instead, I sat in the dark, watching the moon and stars, wondering what I was supposed to do now. The answer came quickly.

She rose almost from the ground, at first appearing as nothing more than a shadow, then gradually coalescing into the shape of a woman. The air vibrated with power around her, and suddenly I felt suffocated. I backed up, terror filling every part of me, my lungs unable to take in air. Wind rose from nowhere, whipping my hair and flattening the grass around me.

Then, she stood before me, and the night was still again. Lilith. Queen of the Succubi. Lady of the Night. The First Woman.

Fear like I had never known swept over me—and lust. I had never been attracted to a woman before, but Lilith has that effect on everyone. It is fixed in her being. No one can resist her.

She wore a tall, slim shape that night, willowy and lovely. Her skin was the pale white of the aristocracy of that time— a white never achieved by those of us who worked outside regularly. Her hair was a raven's wing of black, falling in gleaming waves to her ankles. And her eyes . . . well, let me just say there's a reason the old myths call succubi "flame-eyed." Her eyes were beautiful and deadly, promising anything you could ever want or desire if only you would let her help you. I still can't remember what color they were, but I could not look away from them that night.

"Letha," she crooned, approaching me. The air shimmered around her, and I actually trembled now from my desire. I wanted to run but instead sank to my knees, both from respect and the inability to stand. She came to me and tipped my chin so that I had to look in those eyes again. Sharp, black nails dug painfully into my skin, and it felt wonderful. "You will be my own daughter now, spreading discord and passion for the rest of your days. You will be both punisher and tester, a creature of both dreams and nightmares. Mortals will do anything for you, just for a touch. You will be loved and desired until the earth is dust."

I whimpered at her proximity, and then she moved closer still, lifting me up so I stood before her. Those glorious lips came to mine, and that kiss shot orgasmic pleasure through my body. My cries were lost, smothered in that kiss. I closed my eyes, unable to look at her and unable to break away. I soaked into that ecstasy pulsing over and over in my body. And yet, as I let that bliss consume me, something else happened too.

My mortality was being stripped away.

It felt like disintegrating, like I had become ashes in the wind. I wondered if that was how death felt. Like you were nothing. Gone. Then, just as quickly, I was put back together, myself once more. But I could feel the power burning through me now, different from the life that filled humans. My immortality shone like a star in the night, cold and pure. No longer would old age threaten. No longer would sickness haunt me. No longer would my flesh be passionately driven by the knowledge that time was short, that I had to leave my mark on the world. That I had to pass on my blood.

I opened my eyes, and the onslaught of pleasure disappeared. So did Lilith. I stood alone in the darkness, quivering with my newfound power. And with that power, I could feel something more: an itch in my flesh. An itch that told me my skin could become anything I wanted it to be with only a thought. I was reborn. I was empowered.

And I was hungry . . .

"What's wrong?"

Blinking back tears, I looked up at Carter. He stood in the doorway to my bedroom, pushing a lock of hair out of his eyes, face concerned.

"Nothing," I muttered, burying my face in my pillow. "No nephilim?"

"No nephilim." An awkward pause followed. "Look . . . are you sure you're okay? Because you don't look okay."

"I'm fine. Didn't you hear me?"

He still wouldn't give up, though. "I know we're not that close, but if you need to talk—"

"Like you'd understand," I scoffed, venom in my voice.

"You've never had a heart. You don't know what it's like, so don't even pretend like you do."

"Georgina."

"Go. Away. Please."

I turned back toward my pillow, waiting for another protest, but none came. When I dared a peek, the angel was gone.

Chapter 19

Carter brought me daffodils the next morning. I had no idea where he could have found them this time of year. He'd probably teleported to another continent.

"What are these?" I demanded. "You aren't coming on to me after all, are you?"

"I'd bring roses for that." For the first time since I'd known him, the angel looked embarrassed. "I don't know. You seemed upset last night. I thought . . . I thought these might cheer you up."

"Thanks . . . that's nice, I guess. About last night . . . when I snapped at you . . ."

He shook it off. "Don't worry about it. We all have moments of weakness. It's how we recover from them that really counts."

I put the daffodils in a vase, considered putting them on the counter. Roman's bouquet, now wilting, was already there, and the red carnations I'd bought the night Duane had died had long since been thrown away. It seemed unfair to give Roman's flowers competition, so I put Carter's on the windowsill in my bedroom.

After that, the days fell into a comfortable routine. Carter and I never became best friends, but we managed a sort of pleasant equilibrium. We hung out together, watched movies together, and even on occasion cooked together. The angel turned out to be pretty dapper in the kitchen; I was still inept.

At work, he followed me around, as invisible and unobtrusive as promised. I wasn't sure what he did during my shifts. He gave me the impression he wandered the store, people-watching. Maybe even browsing books. I also knew he spent a good deal of time waiting in my office, even if I wasn't there, hoping another nephilim note might appear. None came. The occasional nephilim flashings did, however, and Carter would disappear for a while without even telling me, either giving me a brief feathery touch on the cheek to indicate his return or speaking a few quick words inside my mind.

I also started having coffee with Seth before my shifts. He had been waiting for me that first day back with a white chocolate mocha, and to my surprise, one for himself as well. "Bruce made it decaf for me," he had explained.

The gesture had been too cute to refuse, so I'd sat and talked with him that day, and the next, and the next . . . It was hardly cutting him off as I'd intended, but I did stay pretty firm in refusing any other attempts at socializing outside of work. The coffee encounters seemed good enough for him, fortunately, and an interesting dynamic soon developed.

Since I was still depressed over Roman, I moved and acted sluggishly, talking very little, too caught up in my own personal misery. Seth must have sensed a bit of this, and rather than let our coffee conversations die in the water, he took the lead in discussion—a notable change for him. It seemed a bit forced at first, but once he grew more comfortable, I found he truly could speak as well as he wrote. I marveled at the shift and enjoyed our time together, finding my heartache over Roman soothed a bit.

He's really nice, Carter noted one morning after I'd left Seth to go work the information desk. *I don't know why you spend so much time mooning over that other guy when you've got one like this.*

It isn't as simple as Seth being nice or not, I snapped back, still feeling a little weird about the mind-to-mind communication higher immortals employed so readily. *And it's not like I'm looking for a new guy anyway. Besides, you didn't even know Roman. How can you talk?*

I know that you didn't know him for that long. How much could have really developed between you guys?

Plenty. He was really funny. And smart. And good looking.

I suppose relationships have been built on less. Still, I'm putting my money on Seth.

Go away. I have to work.

Angels. What did they know?

While walking home from the bookstore on my fourth day at work with Carter, he asked, *You want to go see Erik?*

I frowned, thinking. I had worked the early shift today and had to go back tonight to teach the staff's final dance lesson. I had two hours before that happened and had figured the angel and I would continue our newly formed habit of watching old movies together.

"What do you have in mind?" I asked aloud, once we were safely inside my apartment.

He materialized beside me. "I want to test the waters. We've had no nephilim activity in a while. No notes. No attacks. Yet, we know it's still around because I keep getting those little flashings. Why? What's its game?"

I pulled a can of Mountain Dew out of my refrigerator and sat on a stool. "And you haven't ruled out Erik as a leak."

"No, I haven't. Like I said before, I don't want it to be Erik, but he is probably the biggest mortal source of immortal information around."

"And," I concluded drearily, "if he communicates with the nephilim, he might know some of its plans. What are you going to do, shake him down for information? Because I don't want to be around for that."

"I don't work that way. I can tell if people are lying, but I'm not particularly good at . . . oh, how shall I put this, teasing information out of them. As you noted recently, I'm not exactly charming. You, however, excel at charm."

I didn't like where this was going. "What do you want me to do?"

"Nothing out of the ordinary, I promise. Just talk to him like you normally would. Like you were following up on your last conversation. Allude to nephilim if you can, and see what happens. He likes you."

"What will you do?"

"I'll be there, just invisible."

"We're going to be cutting it close to drive back here in time for the dance lesson."

"Not true. I'll teleport you."

"Ugh." I had had higher immortals do that for me a handful of times over the years. It was not pleasant.

"Come on," he urged, sensing my reluctance. "Don't you want to put this nephilim business to an end?"

"All right, all right, let me change clothes. I'm still not convinced we won't be cramming at the end."

He made some Jerome-like comments about my desire to adorn myself the old-fashioned way, but I ignored him. When I was ready, we both turned invisible, and he gripped my wrists. There was a feeling, only a millisecond long, like wind rushing over me, and then we stood inside a corner of Erik's store. A faint wave of nausea, similar to what I'd had while drinking heavily, rolled up in me and quickly faded.

Seeing no one around, not even Erik, I turned visible. "Hello?"

A few moments later, the old shopkeeper stuck his head out from the back room. "Miss Kincaid, my goodness. I didn't hear you come in. It's a pleasure to see you again."

"Likewise." I gave him a prizewinning succubus smile.

"You're dressed up tonight," he told me, taking in my dress. "Special occasion?"

"I'm going dancing after this. In fact, I can't stay long."

"Yes, of course. Do you have time for tea then?"

I hesitated a moment, and Carter spoke in my head: *Yes.*

"Yes."

Erik went to put on water, and I cleared off our table, both of us falling into usual roles. When he returned with the tea, I learned it was yet another of his themed herbals, this time called Clarity.

I complimented him on it, smiling the whole time, doing my best to play up the charming part. I even made a bit of small talk before finally plunging ahead with my mission objective.

"I wanted to thank you for your help last time with the scripture reference," I explained. "It helped me understand the whole fallen angel bit, but I confess . . . it sort of sent me off in a weird direction."

"Oh?" His bushy gray eyebrows rose as he brought the cup to his lips.

I nodded. "In mentioning angels falling . . . it also mentioned those who married and had offspring. Who had nephilim."

Boy, you don't waste time, Carter noted dryly.

The old man nodded along with me, as though I had made a perfectly ordinary observation. "Yes, yes. Fascinating topic, the nephilim. Quite a controversial subject among biblical scholars."

"How so?"

"Well, some adherents don't like to acknowledge that angels, the holiest of the holy, would engage in such base activities, fallen or no. That their half-divine bastards might be walking the world is more startling still. It makes a lot of faithful very angry."

"But is it true then? That there are nephilim out there?"

Erik gave me one of his canny smiles. "Once again, you ask me questions I'm surprised you don't know the answer to."

See? This is what he does to me too. Evades the question.

You and Jerome do it to us all the time, I shot back to the angel.

To Erik I replied, "Well, like I've said before, my scope is rather limited." He only chuckled, and I pushed the issue. "So? Are they, or aren't they out there?"

"You sound like someone chasing extraterrestrials, Miss Kincaid. Ironic, since some conspiracy theorists claim alien sightings are actually nephilim sightings and vice versa. But to reassure you—or not, perhaps—yes, they are indeed out there."

"Aliens or nephilim?" I joked, trying to keep the conversation light, though I knew he had meant nephilim. I already knew they existed, but I was glad to hear him reaffirm it so readily. Surely if he wanted to hide being a nephilim's ally, he would have been more evasive.

"Both, actually, if you spent extensive time around my previous place of employment."

I laughed out loud, recalling how Krystal Starz did indeed stock books on how to commune with beings from outer space. "I'd forgotten about that. You know, I've actually had a few run-ins with your former boss recently."

Erik's eyes sharpened. "Have you? What happened?"

"No big deal. Just professional differences, I guess. I poached a few of your old coworkers—Tammi and Janice?—from her. Helena wasn't very happy."

"No. I imagine she wouldn't be. Did she do anything?"

"Came to my work and made a lot of noise, gave me some doom and gloom predictions. No big deal."

"She's an interesting woman," he observed.

"That's an understatement." I realized we'd gotten sidetracked and half expected Carter to chastise me for it. He didn't. "So, do you know of any way to spot a nephilim? Anticipate where it'll be next?"

Erik gave me a strange look, not responding right away. I felt my stomach lurch a little. Maybe he did know more about our nephilim. I hoped not.

"Not really," he finally said. "Identifying immortals isn't so easy."

"But it can be done."

"Yes, of course, but some are better at hiding than others. Nephilim especially have reason to stay hidden since they're continually pursued."

"Even when not being nuisances?" I asked, surprised. Neither Carter nor Jerome had mentioned that.

"Even then."

"That's kind of sad."

I remembered the blurb from Harrington's book, recalling how both heaven and hell had rejected the nephilim. Maybe I'd be really pissed off in that case too, wanting to cause trouble and let both sides know I didn't approve of their policies.

Erik had little more to offer on nephilim, and our conversation digressed further and further. An hour went by to my surprise, as I would have expected Carter to stop me by now. Making my own excuses, I apologized to Erik, telling him I needed to get going. I bought some of the tea as usual, and he urged me to come back anytime, also as usual.

When I got to the door, he called hesitantly, "Miss Kincaid? About nephilim . . ."

I felt gooseflesh rise on me. He did indeed know something about all of this. Damn it.

"Remember, they're immortal. They've been around for a long time, but unlike other immortals, they have no agendas or divine plots to carry out. Many try to simply live meaningful and even ordinary lives."

I pondered this weird piece of information as I walked outside, imagining a nephilim commuting to a day job. Hard to juxtapose that with the horrific images I had otherwise been fostering.

Evening had long since fallen, and the parking lot was empty. Turning invisible, I waited for Carter to take us out. And waited. And waited.

"Well? What's the holdup?" I murmured.

No answer.

"Carter?"

No answer.

Then it hit me: Carter had left on another nephilim hunt. I was alone. Great. What was I supposed to do? I had no car, and regardless of what the angel had said about me being safe when he did this sort of thing, I felt uneasy standing out here alone in the dark. I stepped back inside the store, visible. Erik looked up at me with surprise.

"Do you mind if I wait here for a ride?"

"Not at all."

Of course, now I had to get a ride. Pulling out my new cell phone, I debated who to call. Cody would be the ideal choice, but he lived far south of the bookstore and I was north. He would already be on his way to the dance lesson, and coming up here would only ensure we were both late. I needed someone who lived close by, but I didn't know anybody except . . . well, Seth lived in the University District.

That wasn't too far away from Lake City. The tricky part was whether he was actually at his home or still in Queen Anne.

Taking the plunge, I called his cell.

"Hello?"

"It's Georgina. Where are you at?"

"Um, home . . ."

"Great. Would you mind giving me a ride?"

Fifteen minutes later, Seth arrived at Erik's. I'd half expected Carter to show back up in that time, but there'd been no sign of him. Thanking Seth, I slid into his car. "I really appreciate you doing this. My ride kind of flaked out on me."

"I don't mind." He hesitated and gave me a sidelong glance. "You look beautiful."

"Thanks." I had on a red sleeveless dress with a corset-like top.

"It could use a flannel shirt, though."

It took me a moment to remember the ensemble I'd worn to his brother's, a moment longer still to recall I'd never given him the shirt back.

"I'm sorry," I told him after I pointed the same thing out to him. "I'll bring it back soon."

"Not a problem. I'm still holding your book hostage, after all. Fair is fair. Feel free to wear it some more, so it smells like you and that perfume."

He abruptly shut up, apparently fearing he'd said too much, which was probably true. I wanted to laugh the comment off, ease his embarrassment a little, but instead all I could imagine was Seth holding the flannel shirt to his face, inhaling deeply, because it smelled like me. The image was so sexy, so utterly provocative, that I turned slightly away from him, looking out the window to hide my feelings and suddenly heavy breathing.

What a shameless strumpet I was, I decided as the rest of the car ride proceeded in dead silence. Crying over Roman one minute, suddenly wanting to jump into bed with Seth the next. I was fickle. I gave out mixed signals to men, flitting from one to another, beckoning with one hand and pushing away with the other. Admittedly, the Martin energy ride was fast coming to an end, so most males were starting to look pretty good again, but still . . . I had no shame. I didn't even know who or what I wanted anymore.

When Seth parked but refused to come in with me to Emerald City, I felt guilty, knowing he thought that I thought he must be a pervert or something for the perfume comment. I couldn't let that go, couldn't stand the thought of him feeling bad over me. Especially when the perfume remark had been kind of a turn-on. I had to fix things.

I leaned toward him, hoping the corset top would do half my work for me in smoothing the matter over. "Do you remember that one scene in *The Glass House*? The one where O'Neill walks that waitress home?"

He raised an eyebrow. "Um, I wrote that scene."

"If I recall, doesn't he say something about what a shame it is to abandon a woman in a low-cut dress?"

Seth stared at me, expression unreadable. Finally, a not-so-dazed smile flickered onto his face. "He says, 'A man who leaves a woman alone in a dress like that is no man at all. A woman in a dress like that doesn't want to be alone.'"

I looked back at him meaningfully. "Well?"

"Well, what?"

"Don't make me spell it out. I'm in this dress, and I don't want to be alone. Come inside with me. You owe me a dance, you know."

"And you know I don't dance."

"You think that'd stop O'Neill?"

"I think O'Neill kind of goes off the deep end sometimes. He doesn't know his limits."

I shook my head in exasperation and turned away.

"Wait," Seth called. "I'm coming."

"Cutting it close, aren't you?" Cody asked me later when we arrived in the café of the now closed bookstore, practically running.

I gave him a quick hug, and he and Seth nodded cordially at each other before the author blended off into the crowd of staff. "It's a long story."

"Is it true?" Cody whispered in my ear, leaning toward me. "Is Carter hanging around right now?"

"No, actually. He was, but then he just bailed on me. That's why I'm late. I had to call Seth to pick me up."

The young vampire's serious mien relaxed. "I'm sure that was a big sacrifice for both of you."

Ignoring the jibe, I rounded up the troops so the lesson could get under way. As we had observed last time, most were about as ready as they would ever get. We didn't teach anything new, choosing instead to review old techniques, making sure the basics were solid. Seth, as he had stated, did not dance. He had a harder time resisting, however, as most of the staff knew him well by now. Many of the women tried to entreat him. He remained obstinate.

"He'd dance if you asked him," Cody told me at one point.

"I doubt it. He's been refusing all night."

"Yeah, but you're persuasive."

"Carter implied the same thing. I don't know when I got this reputation as Miss Congeniality."

"Just ask him."

Rolling my eyes, I walked over to Seth, noticing his gaze was already on me.

"All right, Mortensen, last chance. Are you ready to make the switch from voyeur to exhibitionist?"

He inclined his head toward me curiously. "Are we still talking about dancing?"

"Well, that depends, I suppose. I heard someone once say that men dance the same way they have sex. So, if you want everyone here to think you're the kind of guy who just sits around and—"

He stood up. "Let's dance."

We stepped out, and despite his bold declaration, his nervousness came through loud and clear. His palm was sweaty as he grasped my hand, his other hand almost too hesitant to fully rest its weight on my hip.

"Your hand swallows mine up," I teased him gently, easing mine inside his. "Just relax. Listen to the music, and count the beats. Watch my feet."

As we moved, I had the impression he had done the basic step before. He had no trouble remembering the pattern. His problem was coordinating his feet with the music, a behavior which came instinctually to me. I could tell he literally counted beats in his head, forcefully lining them up with his feet. Consequently, he spent more time looking down than at me.

"Are you going to come with us when we go out?" I asked conversationally.

"Sorry. I can't talk and count at the same time."

"Oh. Okay." I did my best to hide a smile.

We continued on this way, in silence, until the lesson ended. It never became a natural process for Seth, but he never missed any steps, paying attention to them with steadfast determination and diligence, sweating profusely the entire time. Standing so close to him, I could again feel something akin to static in the air between us, heady and electric.

I made the rounds with Cody as things closed down, telling everybody goodbye. Seth was one of the last to leave, approaching Cody and me as we walked out the back door.

"Nice job tonight," Cody told him.

"Thanks. My reputation was on the line." Seth turned to me. "I hope I redeemed myself with the whole dancing-sex comparison."

"I suppose there were a couple of notable similarities," I observed, holding a straight face.

"A couple? What about attention to detail, heavy exertion, lots of sweat, and single-minded determinedness to get the job done and done well?"

"Mostly I was thinking you just don't talk during sex." Mean perhaps, but I couldn't resist.

"Well, my mouth has better things to do."

I swallowed, my own mouth dry. "Are we still talking about dancing?"

Seth told us good night and left.

I watched him go wistfully. "Anyone else here feel like swooning?"

"I sure do," came Carter's jovial voice behind us.

Cody and I both jumped.

"Christ," I exclaimed. "How long have you been back?"

"No time for small talk. Hang on, kids."

After giving a quick glance around to ascertain we were alone, the angel suddenly grabbed our wrists. I felt that nauseating, rushing feeling again, and the next thing I knew, we stood in a very elegantly decorated living room. I had never seen this place before, but it was beautiful. Coordinated leather furniture adorned the room, expensive-looking art hung on the walls. Opulence. Style. Magnificence.

The only problem was, the entire place had been trashed. Slashes marred the posh furniture, tables had been knocked over, and the art was either askew or defiled or both. On one wall, a huge symbol I didn't recognize had been spray-painted: a circle with one line crossing it vertically and another cutting through at an angle, left to right. The glamour mixed with such desecration left me utterly dumbfounded.

"Welcome to Château Jerome," Carter announced.

Chapter 20

"My apologies for the abrupt transport," Carter continued. "Jerome started freaking out that I'd left you alone for so long."

"I've never 'freaked out' in my life—er, existence, er whatever," mused Jerome, strolling into the room. Studying him, I could believe his words. Dressed immaculately as ever, he held a martini in one hand and looked utterly at ease amid the disarray.

"Nice place," I told him, still aghast at the damage done to such beauty. "Fixer-upper?"

The demon's eyes flashed with amusement at my joke. "I do so love having you around, Georgie." He sipped his drink. "Yes, it is a little rough around the edges right now, but no worries. It'll clean up. Besides, I have other domiciles."

Jerome had always been very tight-lipped about where he lived, and I suspected it was only Carter's intervention that allowed us to even remain here right now. The demon would have never invited us. Walking over to a large bay window, I beheld a magnificent view of Lake Washington, the Seattle skyline glittering beyond it. Based on the angle of my view, I would have wagered money we were in Medina, one of the more elite Eastside suburbs. Only the best for Jerome.

"So what happened?" I finally asked when it became apparent no one else intended to broach the subject. "Was this a nephilim attack, or did you just throw a party that got out of hand? Because honestly, if it's the last one, I'm going to be really pissed we weren't invited."

"No such fears," Carter told me, smiling. "Our friend the nephilim did a little redecorating, kindly flashing us when it was over. That's why I abandoned you at Erik's. I would have given you some warning, but when I felt it over here . . ." He looked meaningfully at Jerome. The demon scoffed in response.

"You what? Thought I was in danger? You know that's not possible."

Carter made a nondescript noise of disagreement. "Yeah? What do you call that?" He inclined his head toward the spray-painted symbol.

"Graffiti," responded Jerome disinterestedly. "It means nothing."

I walked away from the breathtaking window and its pricey view, looking the symbol up and down. I'd never seen anything like it, and I was familiar with a lot of characters and markings from all types of places and times.

"It must mean something," I countered. "Seems like a lot of trouble for nothing. Otherwise, he could have just written 'you suck' or something like that."

"Maybe that's in one of the other rooms," suggested Cody.

"A punch line worthy of Georgie. You're learning more than dancing."

Ignoring the demon's attempt to change the subject, I

turned to Carter for answers. "What is it? You must know what it means."

The angel studied me speculatively a moment, and I realized I'd never appealed to him before for serious help. Until our recent roommate stint, most of our interactions had been downright antagonistic.

"It's a warning," he said slowly, not looking at his demonic counterpart. "A warning of impending disaster. The real phase of a battle about to begin."

Jerome's finely suppressed control snapped. He slammed the glass down on an off-kilter table, face flushing. "Christ, Carter! Are you insane?"

"It doesn't matter, and you know it. Everything's going to come out anyway."

"No," hissed the demon icily, "not everything."

"Then you tell them." Carter made a grandiose gesture toward the symbol. "You explain and make sure I don't say too much."

Jerome glared at him, and they locked eyes in their usual way. I'd seen it happen countless times, but upon reflection, I felt pretty sure I'd never actually seen them at such odds with each other before.

"It might have meant those things at one time," Jerome admitted at last, exhaling in an effort to calm himself. "But not anymore. As I said, it's meaningless now. An archaic scrawl. A charm which, without anyone to believe in it anymore, holds no power."

"Then why use it at all?" I wondered aloud. "More of the nephilim's bizarre sense of humor?"

"Something like that. It's to remind me who we're dealing with—as if there was any possible way I could forget." Picking up his sloshed martini, Jerome finished it in one gulp. Sighing, suddenly looking tired, he glanced at Carter. "You can tell them about the other ones if you want."

The angel's face registered mild surprise at the concession. He looked back up at the marred wall. "This symbol is the second in a set of three. The first is the declaration of battle—a way to sort of psyche out your enemy with what's to come. It looks just like this but with no diagonal. The last symbol marks victory. It has two diagonals and is displayed after the enemy is defeated."

I followed his gaze. "So, wait . . . if this is the second, does that mean you've seen the first already?"

Jerome walked out of the room and returned a moment later, handing me a piece of paper. "You're not the only one who gets love notes, Georgie."

I opened it up. The paper was the same kind used for my notes. Displayed on it, in heavy black ink, was a copy of the symbol on Jerome's wall without the diagonal. The first symbol, the declaration, according to Carter.

"When did you get this?"

"Just before Duane died."

I thought back through the weeks. "That's why you didn't push me too hard when he died. You already had a good idea who was responsible."

The demon shrugged by way of answer.

"Wait a minute then," exclaimed Cody, coming to look over my shoulder at the note. "If this is the first warning . . . are you saying that everything that's happened—Duane, Hugh, Lucinda, Georgina—has been part of the 'psyching out'?" The vampire grew incredulous when neither of the higher immortals responded. "What more can there be? What is this 'real phase'? I mean, he's already attacked or killed, what, four immortals?"

"Four *lesser* immortals," I supplied, suddenly catching on. I looked back and forth between Jerome and Carter. "Right?"

The angel gave me a tight-lipped smile. "Right. You guys

have been the practice round before the big hit." He gave Jerome another pointed look.

"Stop it," the demon snapped back. "I'm not a target here."

"Aren't you? No one spray-painted this on my wall."

"No one knows where you live."

"You're not exactly in the yellow pages yourself. You're the mark here."

"It's a moot point. It can't touch me."

"You don't know that—"

"I do know that, and you know it too. There is absolutely *no* way it can be stronger than me."

"We need backup after all. Call Nanette—"

"Oh yes," laughed Jerome harshly. "No one would notice if I pulled her from Portland. Do you have any idea what a red flag that would throw up? People would start noticing, start asking questions—"

"So what if they do? It's no big deal—"

"Easy for *you* to say. What would you know about—"

"Please. I know enough to know that you're being overly paranoid about . . ."

The two went back and forth at each other, Jerome adamantly denying there was any problem, Carter maintaining that they needed to take appropriate precautions. As noted earlier, I had never seen the two of them in such open disagreement. I didn't like it, especially as their voices began to rise in volume. I didn't want to be around if they came to blows or displays of power, having already seen too much of their strength in the last few weeks. Slowly, I backed up out of the living room toward a nearby hallway. Cody, catching my mood, followed.

"I hate it when Mom and Dad fight," I commented as we retreated away from the divine bickering, seeking a safer locale. Looking in doorways, I saw a bathroom, a bedroom, and a guest room. Somehow I didn't imagine the demon hosted too many overnight guests.

"This looks promising," observed Cody as we turned in to an entertainment room.

More leather seating surrounded a massive, absurdly thin plasma screen hanging on the wall. Sleek, beautiful speakers stood in strategic spots around us, and a substantial glass case displayed hundreds of DVDs. This room, like the others, had been sacked. Sighing, I threw myself on to one of the ripped chairs while Cody checked out the sound system.

"What do you think of all this?" I asked him. "The new developments, I mean, not the entertainment setup."

"What's to think? It seems straightforward to me. This nephilim character warms up with lesser immortals and now decides to take on the higher ones. Sick and twisted, but well, that's the way it is. On the bright side, maybe we're out of danger now—no offense to Jerome or Carter."

"I don't know." I tipped my head back, thinking. "Something still isn't right to me. There's something we're missing. Listen to them in there. Why is Jerome being such an idiot about all of this? Why won't he listen to Carter?"

The young vampire glanced up from his perusal of the movies and gave me a sly smile. "I never thought I'd see the day when you advocated for Carter. You must have gotten really chummy this last week."

"Don't get any romantic delusions," I warned him. "God knows I have enough of that on my plate already. It's just that, I don't know. Carter's not as bad as I used to think."

"He's an angel. He's not bad at all."

"You know what I mean, and you've got to admit, he has a point. Jerome should be taking appropriate measures. This thing trashed his place and left warnings—even if they're obsolete charms or whatever. Why is Jerome so convinced he's safe?"

"Because he thinks he's stronger than it is."

"How would he know though? Neither of them have gotten a good feel for it—even Carter didn't the night he saved me."

"Jerome doesn't seem like the type to dismiss things without a reason. If he says he's stronger, then I'd—holy shit. Check this out." His serious spiel melted into laughter.

Getting up, I walked over and knelt beside him. "What?"

He pointed to the bottom row of DVDs. I read the titles. *High Fidelity. Better Off Dead. Say Anything. Grosse Pointe Blank.* All John Cusack movies.

"I knew it," I breathed, thinking of the demon's coincidental resemblance to the actor. "I knew he was a fan. He's always denied it."

"Wait'll we tell Peter and Hugh," crowed Cody. He pulled *Better Off Dead* off the shelf. "This one's his best."

I pulled out *Being John Malkovich,* my tense mood momentarily relaxed. "No way. This one is."

"That one's too weird."

I glanced up at the plasma screen, a huge gash slashing across its surface. "Normally I'd suggest we have a showdown to settle the point, but somehow I don't think there'll be any viewings for a while here."

Cody followed my gaze and grimaced at the massacre. "What a waste. This nephilim's a real bastard."

"No doubt," I agreed, standing up. "It's no wonder—"

I froze. Everything froze. *A real bastard.*

"Georgina?" asked Cody curiously. "You all right?"

I closed my eyes, reeling. "Oh my God." *A real bastard.*

I thought then about the entire trail of nephilim events, how from the very beginning Jerome had been warning us away. Ostensibly, his actions had been to keep us safe, but there had been no reason not to explain nephilim to us, no real danger to us in understanding the nature of our adversary. Yet Jerome had stayed tight-lipped about it, growing irrationally angry when any of us got too close. When Cody had first posited the "rogue angel" theory, I had written the secrecy off to embarrassment from the other side. Yet, it wasn't their side that had something to hide. It was ours.

Click, click. Once started, the dominoes in my head tumbled forward in a rush. I thought about Harrington's book: *the corrupted angels taught "charms and enchantments" to their wives while their offspring ran wild . . .* Charms. Like the obsolete one on Jerome's wall. *It's to remind me who we're dealing with—as if there was any possible way I could forget,* he had explained offhandedly.

Carter had told me demons generally get into hunting down nephilim. Nanette had wanted to come and help with this one, but Jerome wouldn't let her, thus minimizing those involved. Carter he had kept on hand for the kill, however. *Wouldn't Jerome want to do it himself?* I had wondered, but the angel had evaded answering.

Still the dominoes fell. *Nephilim inherit a lot more than half their parent's power, though they can never exceed it.* Jerome's words to us last week, again spoken casually, just after my attack. Only minutes ago, I had wondered at his confidence at being stronger than the nephilim, questioning how he could be so certain. But of course he could be. Divine genetics had already dictated the parameters.

"Georgina? Where are you going?" Cody exclaimed as I strode out of the room, back toward the still-roaring argument down the hallway.

"Look," Carter was saying, "it won't hurt anything to just—"

"It's yours," I cried to Jerome, attempting to stare him down—difficult, since he was taller than me. "The nephilim is yours."

"My problem?"

"No! You know what I mean. Your child. Your son . . . or daughter . . . or whatever."

Silence descended, and Jerome stared at me with those piercing black eyes, boring right into my soul. I expected at any moment to be blasted across the room. Instead, all he asked was, "So?"

Startled at his mild response, I swallowed. "So . . . so . . . why didn't you just tell us? From the beginning? Why such secrecy?"

"As you can perhaps imagine, this is not a topic I enjoy bringing up. And contrary to popular belief, I do feel entitled to some privacy."

"Yes, but . . ." Now that it was out, I didn't know what to say or think or do. "What will happen? What are you going to do?"

"The same thing I've been planning on doing. We will find this creature and destroy it."

"But it . . . he or she . . . is yours . . ."

I, who had so jealously and longingly watched Paige's growing pregnancy and Seth's bevy of nieces, could not even begin to fathom calmly announcing the murder of one's offspring.

"It doesn't matter," the demon said simply. "It's a liability, a danger to the rest of us. My connection to it is irrelevant."

"You . . . you keep saying 'it.' Are you so detached that you can't even . . . you know, call it by name or gender? What is it anyway? A son or a daughter?"

He hesitated a moment, and I detected a faint trace of unease in that cool mask. "I don't know."

I stared. "What?"

"I wasn't there when it was born. When I found out she . . . my wife . . . was pregnant, I left. I knew what would happen. I was neither the first—nor the last—to take a mortal wife. Plenty of nephilim had been born and destroyed by that point. We all knew what they were capable of. The right thing to do when it was born would have been to destroy it right then." He paused, once more perfectly expressionless. "I couldn't do it. I left, so I wouldn't have to deal with it, so I wouldn't have to make that choice. It was a coward's way out."

"Did you . . . ever see her again? Your wife?"

"No."

Speechless, I wondered what she must have been like. I barely understood Jerome now as a demon, let alone before he fell. He hardly ever showed any sort of emotion or affection for anyone; I couldn't imagine what kind of a woman would have so overcome him that he would turn his back on all he held sacred. And yet, despite that love, he had still left, never to see her again. She would have been dead for millennia by now. He had left to save their child, only to once again be faced with holding its life in his hands. The whole thing was heartbreaking, and I wanted to do something—hug the demon, maybe—but I knew he wouldn't thank me for my sympathy. He was already too embarrassed at us finding out about all of this.

"So you've never seen it? How do you know for sure this one is yours?"

"The signature. When I feel it, I feel half of my own aura and half of . . . hers. No other creature could have that combination."

"And you've felt that every time?"

"Yes."

"Wow. Yet you know nothing else about it."

"Correct. As I said, I was gone long before it was born."

"Then . . . then it would make sense that you really are a target," I told him, gesturing to the wall. "Even independent of all this. The nephilim has especial reason to be pissed off at you."

"Thanks for the unconditional support."

"I didn't mean it like that. I just meant . . . the nephilim already have good cause to be angry. Everybody hates them and tries to kill them. And this one . . . well, people spend thousands of dollars on therapy to get over bad experiences with their fathers. Imagine what kind of neuroses would develop after several thousand years."

"Are you suggesting a family counseling session, Georgie?"

"No . . . no, of course not. Although . . . I don't know. Have you tried talking to it? Reasoning with it?" I remembered Erik's comment about nephilim just wanting to be left alone. "Maybe you could work something out."

"All right, this conversation is growing more absurd, if that's possible." Jerome turned to Carter. "You want to take them home now?"

"I'm staying with you," the angel stated flatly.

"Oh, for Christ's sake, I thought we settled this—"

"He's right," I piped up. "The warning phase is over. I'm safe now."

"We don't know—"

"And besides, this wasn't so much about my safety anyway as having Carter keep me from finding out the truth about your family problems. It's too late now, and I'm tired of having a shadow. You keep him, and we'll all sleep easy, even if it is overkill."

"Eloquently put," chuckled Carter.

Jerome still protested, and we bickered a bit more about it, but in the end, the decision rested in Carter's hands. Jerome had no power to order him around; indeed, if Carter wanted to follow the demon indefinitely, there was nothing Jerome could do, not really. They weren't going to wage any epic battles with each other, no matter how annoyed they currently seemed.

Carter did agree to teleport us back, though I suspected it

was more of a kind gesture to make sure Cody and I could never find Jerome's place again. After he'd taken the vampire home, Carter transported me to my living room, hesitating before he disappeared again.

"It is better this way, I think," he told me. "Me staying with Jerome. I know the nephilim can't be stronger than him . . . but there's still something weird going on. I'm not convinced you're out of danger either, but whatever's going on with you is something entirely different." He shrugged. "I don't know. There are a lot of hard calls here; I wish Jerome would let us get a little outside help. Not too much, of course. Just something. Anything."

"Don't worry," I assured him. "I'll manage. You can't be everywhere at once."

"Isn't that the truth. I'll have to ask this nephilim how it does it when this is over."

"You can't question the dead."

"No," he agreed grimly. "You can't." He turned as if to depart.

"It's weird . . ." I began slowly. "The whole idea of Jerome loving someone. And falling because of it."

He gave me one of those canny, creepy smiles. "Love doesn't make angels fall, Georgina. If anything, love can have quite the opposite effect."

"So, what? If Jerome fell in love again, he could turn back into an angel?"

"No, no. It's not quite that simple." Seeing my baffled look, he chuckled and gave my shoulder a quick squeeze. "Watch out for yourself, Daughter of Lilith. Call if you need help."

"I will," I assured him as he blinked out, not that ever actually getting a hold of higher immortals was easy. Jerome could sense if I was hurt, but he was a lot harder to call for a casual chat.

I went to bed shortly thereafter, fatigued by everything

that had happened, too tired to worry about nephilim attacking me in my sleep. I worked the closing shift tomorrow, and it was my last day before another two days off. I needed the break.

I woke up later the next morning, still alive. While walking into the bookstore, I ran into Seth, armed with his laptop, ready for another day of writing. Recalling the dance lesson with him put my nephilim concerns temporarily at bay.

"Got my book?" I asked as he held the door open for me.

"Nope. Got my shirt?"

"Nope. I like the one you're wearing, though." His themed T-shirt today displayed the logo for the musical *Les Miserables*. "My all-time favorite song comes from that."

"Really?" he asked. "Which one?"

" 'I Dreamed a Dream.' "

"That's a really depressing song. No wonder you don't want to date."

"So what's your favorite then?" I had asked Roman my stock question, but not Seth.

" 'Ultraviolet' by U2. You know it?"

We approached the espresso counter. Bruce was there, and he started making my mocha before I even ordered. "I know some of their other stuff, but not that one. What's it about?"

"Love, of course. Like all good songs. The pain of love juxtaposed with its redemptive power. A bit more optimistic than yours."

I remembered Carter's comment from last night. *Love doesn't make angels fall.*

Seth and I sat down to talk, conversation now flowing smoothly between us. Hard to believe there had ever been any awkwardness, I thought. He was so comfortable.

Finally, knowing I had to work sometime, I dragged myself away to check on the rest of the staff and then retreat to my office. I only intended to check my e-mail, however; I felt sociable today and wanted to work the floor. Tossing my purse on the desk, I started to sit in my chair when I saw a too-familiar white envelope with my name on it.

My breath caught. So much for being off the nephilim's radar. Trembling, I lifted the envelope up, opening it with clumsy fingers.

Miss me? I imagine you've been kept pretty busy with your immortal friends, making sure everyone is safe and accounted for. I imagine you've been just as busy with your oh-so-fascinating personal life, barely sparing a thought for me. Cruel, considering all I've done for you.

I wonder, though, do you worry just as much about the mortals in your life as you do the immortals? Admittedly, mortal deaths are so much less meaningful. After all, what's fifty less years compared to the centuries of an immortal? Mortals hardly seem worth the fuss, yet you put on a good face of caring for them. But do you really? Or are they just a diversion for the long stretch of your own centuries? What about your boyfriend? Is he another toy, another hobby to pass the time? Does he really mean anything to you?

Let's find out. Convince me he does today. You have until the end of your shift to ascertain his safety. You know the rules—keep him in safe places, keep others around him, etc., etc. I'll be with you, watching. Convince me you really care, and I'll spare him. Make me believe. Fail—or involve any of your immortal contacts—and no amount of "safekeeping" will do him any good.

I dropped the note, hands cold. What kind of fucked-up game was this? It made no sense. The nephilim told me in one breath to keep someone safe, yet implied in the next that t didn't matter, that there was no safety. It was stupid, another stirring of the waters, shaking up the status quo just to watch what I'd do. Looking around uneasily, I wondered: Was the nephilim here now? Was Jerome's disgruntled offspring lurking invisibly beside me, smirking at my distress? What should I do?

Finally, and perhaps most importantly, just who the hell was my boyfriend anyway?

Chapter 21

I had no boyfriend. Despite all the uncertainties in m
world, that at least was one thing I could feel confide
about. Unfortunately, this nephilim apparently had a mo
optimistic view of my love life.

"I don't know who you're talking about," I shouted to n
empty office. "Do you hear me, you son of a bitch? I don
know who you're fucking talking about!"

No one responded.

Paige, passing by a moment later, stuck her head insid
"Did you call me?"

"No," I grumbled. She wore a dress that clung distinct
to her swelling belly. It didn't help my mood any. "Just tall
ing to myself." I closed the door after she left.

My immediate impulse was to run for help. Carte
Jerome. Somebody. Anybody. I couldn't deal with th
alone.

Fail—or involve any of your immortal contacts—and
amount of "safekeeping" will do him any good.

Damn it. I didn't even know who "he" was. Frantically, I tried to figure out who among my mortal acquaintances could have been mistaken by the nephilim as something more. As if it wasn't hard enough being my friend already.

Surprisingly—or perhaps not—my thoughts promptly strayed to Seth. I thought about our recent rapport. Censored and proper certainly, but still warm. Still right and natural. Still occasionally making me catch my breath when we touched.

No, that was stupid. My fascination with him was shallow. His books made me suffer from hero worship, and our friendship had become a sort of rebound from Roman. Whatever crush or minor attraction he'd had for me had to be fading fast. He'd shown no other indications of more-than-friends feelings, and my distancing had to be having an effect. Besides, he still kept disappearing for mysterious meetings, probably for some girl he was too shy to tell me about. It was presumptuous of me to even consider him in a boyfriend category.

Yet . . . would the nephilim know any of that? Who knew what the bastard was thinking? If it had observed Seth and me having our coffee chats, it might assume anything. Fear clenched me, making me want to immediately run upstairs and check on Seth. But no. That would be a waste, for now at least. He was writing, in public, surrounded by people. The nephilim would not attack him in such a setting.

Who else then? Warren perhaps? That voyeur nephilim had watched us have sex. If that didn't count as some sort of relationship, I didn't know what did. Of course, the nephilim would have also observed that Warren and I almost never interacted in any other intimate way. Poor Warren. Sex with me had already wiped him out; it would be beyond cruel if he became a target for the nephilim's bizarrely misplaced humor. Fortunately, I had already seen Warren come in

today. He was busy in his office, but perhaps that sti
counted as safe. Alone he might be, but any screams from
nephilim attack would immediately draw attention.

Doug? He and I had always had a perky flirtation. Cer
tainly one might consider his sporadic pursuit of me indica
tive of something more than friendship. Yet, in the last fev
weeks, he and I hadn't talked very much. I'd been too dis
tracted by the nephilim attacks. Those, and Roman.

Ah, Roman. There it was, the possibility that had bee
hovering in the back of my mind. The reality I'd been avoid
ing because it meant contacting him, breaking the silence I
tried so hard to maintain. I didn't know what was betwee
us, other than a scorching attraction and the occasional tu
of solidarity. I didn't know if it was love or the start of lov
or whatever. But I knew I cared about him. A lot. I misse
him. Cutting myself off completely had been the safest wa
to recover, to get over my longing and move on. I feare
what reinitiating contact could do.

And yet . . . because I cared about him, I could not let th
nephilim prey upon him. I could not risk Roman's life in th
because, really, he probably was the most likely candidat
Half the bookstore staff still considered us an item; why n
the nephilim? Especially in light of how touchy-feely we
been on a number of outings. Any stalking nephilim woul
be well justified in reading that as romantic attachment

I picked up my cell phone and called him with bate
breath. No answer.

"Shit," I swore, listening to his voice mail. "Hi Roma
it's me. I know I wasn't, uh, going to call you anymore, b
something's come up . . . and I really need to talk to you. A
soon as possible. It's really weird, but it's really importa
too. Please call me." I left him both my cell and the book
store numbers.

I disconnected, then sat and pondered. Now what did

lo? On impulse, I glanced at the staff directory and dialed
Doug's home number. He had the day off.

No answer, just like Roman. Where was everybody?

Shifting my attention back to Roman, I tried to figure out
where he would be. Work, most likely. Unfortunately, I didn't
know where that was. What a negligent pseudo-girlfriend I
was. He'd said he taught at a community college. He referred to it all the time, but it was always "at school" or "at
the college." He'd never mentioned the name.

I turned to my computer and did a search for local community colleges. When the search returned several hits for
Seattle alone, I swore again. More existed outside of the city
too, in the suburbs and neighboring sister cities. Any of them
could be possibilities. I printed out a list of all of them, with
phone numbers, and stuffed the paper in my purse. I needed
to get out of here, needed to take this search to the field.

I opened my office door to leave and flinched. Another
identically written note hung on my door. I peered around in
the offices' hallway, half hoping to see something. Nothing. I
pulled the note down and opened it.

*You're losing time and men. You've already lost the
writer. You'd best get a move-on with this scavenger hunt.*

"Scavenger hunt indeed," I muttered, crumpling the note.
"You're such an asshole."

But . . . what did he mean about losing the writer? Seth?
My pulse quickened, and I raced up to the café, earning a
few startled looks along the way.

No Seth. His corner was empty.

"Where's Seth?" I demanded of Bruce. "He was just
here."

"He was," concurred the barista. "Then he suddenly packed
up and left."

"Thanks."

I definitely needed to get out of here. I found Paige in
New Books.

"I think I need to go home," I told her. "I'm getting a migraine."

She looked startled. I had the best track record for attendance of any employee. I never called in sick. Yet, for that very reason, she could hardly refuse me. I was not a worker who abused the system.

After she'd assured me I should go, I added, "Maybe you can get Doug to come in." That would kill two birds with one stone.

"Maybe," she said. "I'm sure we'll manage, though. Warren and I are here all day."

"He's here all day?"

When she reiterated that he would indeed be there, I felt somewhat relieved. Okay. He was off the list.

As I walked home to my apartment, I called Seth's cell phone.

"Where are you?" I asked.

"Home. I forgot some notes I needed."

Home? Alone?

"Do you want to get breakfast with me?" I asked suddenly, needing to get him out.

"It's almost one."

"Brunch? Lunch?"

"Aren't you at work?"

"I went home sick."

"Are you sick?"

"No. Just meet me." I gave him an address and hung up.

As I drove to the rendezvous, I tried Roman's cell again. Voice mail. I pulled out the community college phone numbers and started with the first one on the list.

What a pain. First, I had to start with campus information and try to get to the right department. Most community colleges didn't even have linguistics departments, though almost all had at least one introductory class taught through some other related area—like anthropology or humanities.

I made it through three colleges by the time I reached Capitol Hill. I breathed a sigh of relief, seeing Seth waiting outside the place I'd indicated. After I parked and paid the meter, I walked up to him, trying to smile in some semblance of normality.

It apparently didn't work.

"What's wrong?"

"Nothing, nothing," I proclaimed cheerfully. Too cheerfully.

His look implied disbelief, but he let the matter drop. "Are we eating here?"

"Yup. But first we have to go see Doug."

"Doug?" Seth's confusion deepened.

I led him to an apartment building next door and climbed to Doug's floor. Music blared from inside his apartment, which I took as a good sign. I had to beat on the door three times before anyone answered.

It wasn't Doug. It was his roommate. He looked stoned.

"Is Doug here?"

He blinked at me and scratched his long, unkempt hair.

"Doug?" he asked.

"Yeah, Doug Sato."

"Oh, Doug. Yeah."

"Yeah, he's here?"

"No, man. He's . . ." The guy squinted. Lord, who got high this early in the day? I hadn't even done that back in the 1960s. "He's practicing."

"Where? Where do they practice?"

The guy stared at me.

"Where do they practice?" I repeated.

"Dude, did you know you have, like, the most perfect tits I've ever seen? They're like . . . poetry. Are they real?"

I clenched my teeth. "Where. Does. Doug. Practice?"

He dragged his eyes from my chest.

"West Seattle. Over by Alki."

"Do you have an address?"

"It's by . . . California and Alaska." He blinked again. "Whoa. California and Alaska. Get it?"

"An address?"

"It's green. You can't miss it."

When no other information came, Seth and I left. We went to the restaurant I had indicated. "Poetry," he reflected along the way, amused. "Like an ee cummings poem, I'd say."

I was too preoccupied to process what he was saying, my mind racing. Even waffles with strawberries couldn't keep me from worrying about this idiotic scavenger hunt. Seth attempted conversation, but my answers were vague and distracted, my mind clearly not with him through the meal. When we finished, I unsuccessfully tried Roman again, then turned to Seth.

"Are you going back to the bookstore?"

He shook his head. "No. I'm going home. I realized I need too much of my research to write this scene. Easier to stay in my own office."

Panic blazed through me. "Home? But . . ." What could I say? Tell him that if he stayed at home, he might be in danger of attack by a sociopathic, supernatural creature?

"Stay with me," I blurted out. "Run errands with me."

His polite complacency finally broke. "Georgina, what in the world is going on? You go home sick when you're not. You're clearly agitated about something, desperately so. Tell me what this is about. Is something wrong with Doug?"

I closed my eyes for a second, wishing this was all over. Wishing I was somewhere else. Or someone else. Seth must think I was out of my mind.

"I can't tell you what's wrong, only that something is. You have to leave it at that." Then, hesitantly, I reached out and squeezed his hand, turning my eyes pleadingly toward his. "Please. Stay with me."

He tightened his grip on my hand and took a step forward, face concerned and compassionate. For a moment, I forgot about the nephilim. What did other men matter when Seth looked at me like that? I had the urge to embrace him and feel his arms enclose me.

I almost laughed. Who was I kidding? I didn't need to worry about leading him on. I was the one getting hooked here. I was the one in danger of escalating this relationship. I needed to stop procrastinating on my "clean break" with him.

I hastily broke apart and lowered my eyes. "Thank you."

He offered to drive to West Seattle, freeing me up to keep calling colleges. I had nearly finished by the time we reached the intersection of Alaska and California. He slowed slightly, and we both peered around, searching for a green house.

You can't miss it. It was a stupid piece of advice. What constituted green anyway? I saw a sage house, a forest green house, and a color that could have been green or blue. Some houses had green trim, green doors, or—

"Whoa," said Seth.

A small, run-down house painted a glaring shade of mintish lime stood there, nearly obscured by two much nicer houses.

"You can't miss it," I muttered.

We parked and walked toward it. As we did, the sounds of Doug's band clearly emanated from the garage. When we reached the open door, I saw Nocturnal Admission in full glory, Doug belting out lyrics in that amazing voice of his. He cut off abruptly when he saw me.

"Kincaid?"

His fellow band members looked on quizzically as he jumped down and sprinted over to me. Seth discretely took a few steps away, studying some nearby hydrangea bushes.

"What are you doing here?" asked Doug, not offended so much as astounded.

"I called in sick," I said stupidly. What did I do now?

"Are you sick?"

"No. I—I had something to do. Still do. But I'm . . . I'm worried about leaving the store. How long will you be here? Can you fill in for me after this?"

"You came here to ask me to cover for you? Why'd you call in sick? Are you finally running away with Mortensen?"

"I—no. I can't explain it. Just promise me, after this, you'll swing by the store and see if they need help."

He was staring at me with a look Seth had been shooting me all afternoon. One that sort of implied I needed a tranquilizer.

"Kincaid . . . you're freaking me out here . . ."

I looked up at him with the same baleful expression I'd used on Seth. Succubus charisma in action. "Please? You still owe me, remember?"

His dark eyes frowned in understandable consternation. At last he said, "Okay. But it'll be a few hours before I can go."

"That's all right. Just go there straight afterward. No stops. And don't . . . don't tell them you saw me. I'm supposed to be sick. Make up some reason to go there."

He shook his head in exasperation, and I thanked him with a quick hug. As Seth and I departed, I saw Doug glance at Seth questioningly. Seth shrugged, answering the other man's silent inquiry with shared confusion.

I made more phone calls as we drove away, finishing my college list and leaving yet another desperate message for Roman.

"What now?" asked Seth when I lapsed into silence. Hard to say what he thought of my harassment of both Roman and Doug.

"I . . . I don't know."

I had reached the end of my options. Everyone was accounted for except Roman, and I had no way to reach him. The clock was ticking. I didn't know where he lived. I thought he'd mentioned Madrona once, but that was a big area. I could hardly start knocking on all those doors. The nephilim had said I had until the end of my shift. Despite bailing on work, I assumed that still meant nine o'clock. I had almost three hours left.

"I guess I'll pick up my car and go back home."

Seth dropped me off at the restaurant and followed me back to Queen Anne. A traffic light stopped him, so I made it to my apartment about a minute before he did. On my door was another note.

Nice job. You'll probably end up alienating all of these men with your erratic behavior, but I admire your pluck. One left to go. I wonder how fast on his feet your dancer truly is.

I was crumpling this note up when Seth reached me. I pulled my key out of my purse and feebly attempted to put it in my lock. My hands shook so badly, I couldn't do it. He took the key from me and opened the door.

We entered, and I collapsed on to the couch. Aubrey slithered out from behind it and jumped on my lap. Seth sat nearby, taking in my apartment—including my prominently displayed collection of his books on the new shelf—then returned his worried gaze to me.

"Georgina . . . what can I do?"

I shook my head, feeling helpless and defeated. "Nothing. I'm just glad you're here."

"I . . ." He hesitated. "I hate to tell you this, but I've got to leave in a little while. I'm meeting someone."

I looked up sharply. Another of those mysterious meetings. Curiosity temporarily replaced my fear, but I couldn't question him. Couldn't ask if he was meeting some woman. At least he said he was meeting *someone*. He wouldn't be alone.

"You'll be with . . . them . . . for a while then?"

He nodded. "I could come back late tonight, if you wanted. Or . . . maybe I could cancel."

"No, no, don't worry about it." By then, it would all be over.

He stayed awhile longer, again attempting conversation I couldn't participate in. When he finally stood up to leave, I could see anxiety written all over him and felt terrible I'd involved him in this.

"This will all be resolved tomorrow," I told him. "So don't worry. I'll be back to normal then. I promise."

"Okay. If you need anything, let me know. Call me, no matter what. Otherwise . . . well, I'll see you at work."

"No. I have tomorrow off."

"Oh. Well. Do you mind if I stop by?"

"Sure. Go ahead." I would have agreed to anything. I was too tired to hold to my earlier notion of distancing. I'd worry about that later. Honestly. One thing at a time.

He left reluctantly, no doubt baffled when I told him to spend a lot of time with whoever he was meeting. As for me, I paced all over my apartment, not knowing what to do. Maybe I couldn't get ahold of Roman because the nephilim had already found him. That would hardly be fair since I'd never even had a chance to genuinely warn him, but this nephilim didn't really seem like the type to care about right or wrong.

Struck by inspiration, I called Information, realizing I'd missed the obvious way to find him. It didn't matter. Unlisted.

Two hours before my shift would have ended, I left Roman another message. "Please, please, *please* call me," I begged. "Even if you're really mad at me for what happened. Just tell me you're out there and okay."

No return call came. Eight o'clock rolled around. With one hour remaining, I left him another message. I could feel hysteria creeping in. God, what was I going to do? All I did do was continue pacing, pondering how soon would be too soon to call Roman one more time.

Five minutes before nine, utterly frantic, I grabbed my purse, desperate to leave my apartment and do something. Anything. Time was almost up.

What would happen? How would I know if I'd successfully jumped through the nephilim's hoops? When I saw Roman's murder plastered across the paper tomorrow? Would there be another note? Or maybe some gruesome token? What if the nephilim hadn't even meant any of the people I'd considered? What if it was someone completely out of the realm of—

I opened my door to leave and gasped.

"Roman!"

He stood there, mid-knock, as surprised to see me as I was him.

I dropped my purse and ran to him, flinging myself at him in a fierce embrace that nearly toppled him. "Oh God," I breathed into his shoulder, "I'm so glad to see you."

"I guess," he replied, pulling slightly away to look down at me, his turquoise eyes concerned. "Lord, Georgina, what's wrong? I've got like eighty messages from you—"

"I know, I know," I told him, still not letting go. Seeing him stirred up all the old, queasy feelings I had thought were buried. He looked so good. He smelled so good. "I'm sorry— it's just, I thought something had happened to you . . ."

I hugged him again, catching sight of my watch as I did so. Nine o'clock. My shift was over, as was the nephilim's ridiculous game.

"Okay, it's all right." He patted me awkwardly on the back. "What's going on?"

"I can't tell you." My voice shook.

His mouth opened to protest, but he reconsidered. "Okay. Let's take this slow. You're pale. Let's go get something to eat. You can explain all this then."

Yeah, that would be a fun conversation. "No. We can't do that . . ."

"Come *on*. There's no way you can leave me all those desperate messages and then start playing the 'we need space' game. Seriously, Georgina. You're a wreck. You're shaking. I wouldn't want you to be by yourself anyway if I'd found you like this, let alone after those calls."

"No. No. No going out." I sat down on the couch, needing to let him go, reluctant to do so. "Let's stay here."

Still looking distressed, Roman fetched me a glass of water, then sat down by me, holding my hand. As time passed, I calmed down, listening as Roman talked about inconsequential things in an effort to make me feel better.

For his part, he was quite nice about my psycho phone calls. He continued trying to tease out an explanation, but when I remained evasive, only saying I had cause to worry about him, he stopped pushing—for now. He continued cheering me up, telling me funny things as well as his usual political soliloquies, complaining about the irrational rules and hypocrisy of the powers that be.

By late in the evening, I was relaxed again, left only with embarrassment for the way I'd behaved. Damn, I hated that nephilim.

"It's getting late. You going to be okay if I go?" he asked, standing with me near my living room window, overlooking Queen Anne Avenue.

"Probably better than if you stay."

"Well, that's a matter of opinion," he chuckled, running a hand over my hair.

"Thanks for coming by. I know . . . I know . . . it seems crazy, but you've just got to trust me on this one."

He shrugged. "I don't really have a choice. Besides . . . it's kind of nice to know you were worried about me."

"Of course I was. How could I not be?"

"I don't know. You aren't easy to read. I couldn't figure out if you really liked me . . . or if I was just something to pass the time. A diversion."

Something in his words rang a bell in my head, something I should have paid attention to. Instead I was more caught up in how close he suddenly stood to me, how his hand ran down my cheek to my neck and to my shoulder. He had long, sensuous fingers. Fingers that could do a lot of good in a lot of good places.

"I do like you, Roman. If you don't believe anything else I tell you, believe that."

He smiled then, a smile so full and beautiful, it made my heart melt. God, I had missed that smile and his funny, breezy charm. Moving his hand back up to my neck, he pulled me toward him, and I realized he was going to kiss me again.

"No . . . no . . . don't," I murmured, squirming out of his grasp.

He backed off from the kiss, still holding on to me as he exhaled, disappointment all over his face. "Still worried about that?"

"You can't understand. I'm sorry. I just can't . . ."

"Georgina, nothing traumatic happened the last time we kissed. Short of your reaction, I mean."

"I know, but it's not that simple."

"Nothing happened," he repeated, an unfamiliar hardness in his voice.

"I know, but—"

My mouth hung there mid-sentence as I replayed his words. *Nothing happened.* No, something had happened that night at the concert, kissing in the back hallway. I'd seen

Roman stagger from the kiss. But me . . . what had happened to me? What had I felt? Nothing. A kiss that intense, a kiss with someone strong, a kiss with someone I wanted so badly should have triggered something. Even with a low energy yield like Warren, a deep kiss would wake up my succubus instinct, start to connect us, even if no significant transfer took place. Kissing Roman like that—especially when he ostensibly had a reaction—should have resulted in some kind of feeling on my end. Some sensation. Yet, there had been nothing. Nothing at all.

I had written it off to too much alcohol at the time. But that was ridiculous. I drank all the time before getting a fix. Alcohol could muddle my senses—as it obviously had that night—but no amount of intoxication could completely negate the sensation of anima transfer. Nothing could. I had been too trashed to realize the truth. Alcohol or no, I would always feel something from sexual or intimate physical contact unless . . .

Unless I was with another immortal.

I jerked away from Roman, breaking his hold on me. His expression registered surprise, immediately replaced by sudden understanding. Those beautiful eyes sparkling dangerously, he laughed.

"Took you long enough."

Chapter 22

"**Y**ou faked it . . . faked being affected by me," I realized, shock making my words come out thick and faltering.

Still chuckling, he took a step toward me, and I cringed, frantically trying to find a way to run, to get out of my own apartment. What had moments ago seemed safe and inviting now became close and stifling. My apartment was too small, the door too far away. I couldn't breathe. The amusement on Roman's face shifted to astonishment.

"What's the matter? What are you afraid of?"

"What do you think I'm afraid of?"

He blinked. "Me?"

"Yes, you. You kill immortals."

"Well, yeah," he admitted, "but I'd never hurt you. Never. You know that, don't you?" I didn't answer. "Don't you?"

I backed up farther, not that I had anywhere to go. I was faced in such a way as to only keep moving toward my bedroom, not toward the front door. That wasn't likely to do any good.

Roman still seemed floored at my reaction. "Come on, I can't believe this. I would never do anything to you. I'm half in love with you. Hell, do you know what a wrench you've already thrown into this operation?"

"Me? What have I done?"

"What have you done? You've wrapped my heart around your little finger, that's what you've done. That day . . . when you solicited me at the bookstore? I couldn't believe my luck. I'd been watching you all week, you know, trying to learn your habits. Christ, I'll never forget the first day I saw you. How feisty you where. How beautiful. I would have gone to the ends of the earth for you right then and there. And later . . . when you wouldn't go out with me after the signing? I couldn't believe it. You were originally going to be my first target, you know. But I couldn't do it. Not after I'd talked to you. Not after I'd realized what you are."

I swallowed, curious in spite of myself. "What—what am I?"

He took a step toward me, a rueful half-smile on his handsome face. "A succubus who doesn't want to be a succubus. A succubus who wants to be human."

"No, that's not true . . ."

"Of course it is. You're like me. You don't play by the rules. You're tired of the system. You don't let them push you into the role they've dictated for you. God, I couldn't believe it, watching you. The more you seemed interested in me, the more you tried to back off. You think that's normal for a succubus? It was the most amazing thing I'd ever seen—not to mention the most frustrating. That's why I finally decided to call you out today. I couldn't decide if you'd really cut me off for my own good or were just interested in someone else now—like Mortensen."

"Wait—that's why you arranged that stupid little game today? For your own fucking ego gratification?"

Roman shrugged haplessly, still looking self-satisfied. "It

sounds so shallow when you put it like that. I mean, okay, it was pretty stupid. And maybe a little childish. But I had to know where your affection stood. You can't imagine how touching it was to see you so worried about me—not to mention the fact that you checked on me first. That was the real kicker: I got priority over the others."

I almost protested that I'd actually worried about Seth first, having only called Roman beforehand because I thought Seth was already accounted for. Fortunately, I had enough sense to keep my mouth shut on that issue. Better to let Roman think he'd proven his point.

"You have issues," I said instead, perhaps unwisely. "Making me jump through hoops like that. Me and the other immortals."

"Perhaps. And I am sorry for any discomfort I caused you, but as for the others?" He shook his head. "It's good for them. They need it, Georgina. I mean, doesn't it piss you off? What they've done to you? You're obviously not happy with your lot, but do you think the folks in charge are going to let you change things? No. No more than they're going to give me or my kind a break. The system is flawed. They're locked in their fucking 'this is good' and 'this is evil' mentality. No gray area. No mutability. That's why I go around and do what I do. They need the wake-up call. They need to know they aren't the be all and end all of sin and salvation. Some of us are still fighting."

"Go around . . . How often do you do this? This killing thing?"

"Oh, not that often. Every twenty to fifty years or so. Sometimes a century. Doing it sort of cleanses me for a while, and then, over the years, I'll start getting pissed off at the whole system again and stake out a new place, a new set of immortals."

"Is it always the same pattern?" I remembered Jerome's symbols. "The warning phase . . . then the main attack phase?"

Roman brightened. "Well, well, haven't you done your homework. Yes, it usually works that way. Take out a few lesser immortals first. They're easy targets, even if I always feel a little guilty about it. Really, they're as much victims of the system as you and I are. Still, messing with them freaks out the higher immortals, and then the stage is set to move on to the main attraction."

"Jerome," I stated grimly.

"Who?"

"Jerome . . . the local archdemon." I hesitated. "Your father."

"Oh. Him."

"What's that supposed to mean? You don't sound like he's a big deal."

"In the grand scheme of things, he's not."

"Yeah . . . but he's your father . . ."

"So? Our relationship—or lack thereof—doesn't really change anything."

Jerome had said almost the exact same thing about Roman. Baffled, I sat down on the arm of a nearby chair since it appeared my imminent destruction wasn't quite so imminent after all. "But isn't he . . . isn't he the 'real target'—the higher immortal you're here to kill?"

Roman shook his head, face turning serious. "No. That's not how the pattern works. After I move on from the lesser immortals, I focus in on the local bigwig. The real power-house in the area. That tends to unsettle people more. Better psychological effect, you know? If I can take out the big man on campus, then they worry no one is safe."

"So, that would be Jerome."

"No, it's not," he countered patiently. "Archdemon or no, my illustrious father is not the ultimate power source around here. Don't get me wrong; I'm getting a nice bit of satisfaction from pissing in his territory, so to speak, but there's someone else who dwarfs him. You probably don't know him. It's not like you'd have reason to hang out with him or anything."

Stronger than Jerome? That only left—

"Carter. You're going after Carter."

"Is that his name? The local angel?"

"He's stronger than Jerome?"

"Considerably." Roman gave me a curious look. "Do you know him?"

"I . . . know of him," I lied. "Like you said, I don't hang out with him or anything."

In reality, my mind raced. Carter was the target? Mild, sardonic Carter? I could hardly believe he was more powerful than Jerome, but then, I knew almost nothing about him. I didn't even know what he did, what his job or mission in Seattle was. Yet, one thing that was obvious to me—and only me, apparently—was that if the angel really did outclass Jerome, then Roman couldn't do anything to him, not if the rule about nephilim power not exceeding parental power held true. Roman shouldn't technically be able to harm either angel or demon.

I chose not to mention this to him, however—or the fact that I knew Carter better than Roman believed. The more delusional he was, the more of a chance we had to do something about him.

"Good. I didn't really figure a succubus would be too friendly with an angel, but with you, it's hard to tell. You may have a sharp tongue, but you still manage to gather a lot of admirers." Relaxing slightly, Roman leaned against a wall, crossing his arms over his chest. "God knows I've already gone out of my way to avoid your friends."

Anger helped me overcome my fear. "Oh really? What about Hugh?"

"Which one's he?"

"The imp."

"Ah, yes. Well, I had to keep setting an example, didn't I?

So, yeah, I messed with him a little. He'd been impertinent to you. But I didn't kill him." He looked at me in what I supposed was meant to be an encouraging type of way. "That was for your benefit."

I stayed silent. I recalled how Hugh had looked in the hospital. Impertinent?

"And what about the others?" he pushed. "That annoying angel? The vampire that threatened you? I wanted to break his neck on the spot. I got rid of them for you. I didn't have to do that."

I felt ill. I wanted no deaths on my hands. "Most considerate of you."

"Come on, give me a break here. I had to do something, and really, once I'd met your vampire friend at the dance lesson, I couldn't bring myself to do anything to him at all. You put me in a really tight spot. I was running out of victims."

"Sorry for the inconvenience," I snapped, ire rising at his pathetic show of compassion. "Is that why you took it easy on me that night?"

He frowned. "What do you mean?"

"You know what I mean!" Thinking back to my attack, it all made perfect sense. It had occurred after I'd been to Krystal Starz, the day after I'd run out on Roman at the concert. A perfect excuse for him to be angry and seek retaliation. "Remember? The day after Doug's concert? After I'd been with Seth?"

Understanding washed over Roman's features. "Oh. That."

"That's all you have to say?"

"It was a bit juvenile, I admit, but you can hardly blame me. It wasn't easy watching you cozy up to Mortensen after freaking out on me like that. I'd watched you go home with him the night before. I had to do something."

I sprang up from my seat, old apprehension returning. "You had to do something? Like beat the crap out of me in an alley?"

Roman raised an eyebrow. "What are you talking about? I told you I would never hurt you."

"Then what are *you* talking about?"

"I'm talking about that ice cream place. I'd followed you two around earlier in the day, and when I saw how cute you were getting over dessert, I got jealous and blew the door open. Juvenile, as I said."

"I remember that . . ." I trailed off stupidly, recalling how the door had blown open at the parlor, letting the outside wind wreak havoc in the small store. Wind like that was certainly uncharacteristic here, yet I had never suspected supernatural influence. He was right; it had been juvenile.

"So what's the alley thing you're talking about?" he prompted.

I snapped out of my memory. "Later . . . that night. I'd been running errands, and you . . . or someone . . . attacked me on the way home."

Roman's face turned cold, his eyes sharpening to aqua steel. "Tell me. Tell me everything. Exactly what happened."

I did, explaining my lead to the Harrington book, subsequent trip to Krystal Starz, and walk home in the dark. I edited the part about my rescuer, however. I didn't want Roman to know I had more than a casual acquaintance with Carter, lest the nephilim think I might be a deterrent to his plans. The more he thought I had no interest in the angel, the more likely I would be able to get out some kind of warning.

Closing his eyes, Roman leaned his head against the wall when I finished, sighing. Suddenly, he looked less like a dangerous killer and more like a tired version of the man I'd come to know and nearly love. "I knew it. I knew noninterference was too much to ask."

"What . . . what do you mean?" A strange feeling crawled down my spine.

"Nothing. Forget it. Look, I'm sorry about that. I should have taken precautions beforehand to protect you. I knew too . . . the next day? When I came by and you cut things off between us? I could tell you had been hurt, even through your shape-shifting. I could tell it was supernaturally inflicted too, but I never suspected . . . I thought it was some other immortal—one of your own circle—you'd tangled with. You had sort of a residual effect on you . . . the faint traces of someone else's power . . . like a demon's . . ."

"But that's not—oh. You mean Jerome."

"Daddy dearest again? Don't tell me . . . don't tell me he did something to you too." Roman's brief lapse into mildness faded, replaced by something more sinister.

"No, no," I said hastily, recalling Jerome's psychic slap, pinning me to the couch. "It wasn't like that. It was more of a show of power that I caught the edge of. He wasn't the one who hurt me. He'd never hurt me."

"Good. I'm still not happy about what happened in the alley, mind you, but I'll have a little chat with the guilty party and make sure it never happens again. When I saw you that day, I had half a mind to take out all the immortals in the area. The thought of someone hurting you . . ." Closer and closer he came to me. Hesitantly, he squeezed my arm. I didn't know whether to recoil or reach out to him. I didn't know how to reconcile my old attraction with this new terror. "You have no idea how much I care about you, Georgina."

"Then how . . . in the alley—"

Before I could follow that thought to completion, another suddenly poked its head up at Roman's words. *When I saw you that day.* He had visited me the day after the attack, coming over while Carter investigated a nephilim signature. But that was impossible. I couldn't remember where that particular signature had occurred, but it had not been close by. Roman could not have flashed Carter and then made it over to my apartment so quickly.

I knew noninterference was too much to ask for. I'll have a little chat with the guilty party.

I understood then why Roman felt he could take on Carter, why having less power than the angel would pose no concern. The realization sank into me like lead, heavy and cold. I'm not sure what look crossed my face, but Roman's suddenly softened with compassion.

"What's the matter?"

"How many?" I whispered to him.

"How many what?"

"How many nephilim are in the city?"

Chapter 23

"Two," he said after a moment's hesitation. "Just two."

"Just two," I repeated flatly, thinking *oh shit*. "Is that including you?"

"Yes."

I rubbed my temples, wondering how I could warn Jerome and Carter that we had two nephilim to deal with now. No one had mentioned that possibility.

"Someone should have known that," I muttered, more to myself than to Roman. "Someone should have sensed it . . . there would have been two different nephilim signatures. That's how Jerome knew it was you. You have a unique signature—no one else has it."

"No one else," Roman agreed with a smirk, "except my sister."

Oh shit.

"Jerome didn't mention more than one—ah." I blinked in sudden understanding. Jerome, by his own admission, hadn't actually been around for the birth. "Twins? Or . . . more?"

The archdemon could have fathered quintuplets for all I knew.

Roman shook his head, still highly amused at my deductions. "Only twins. Just the two of us."

"So this is a family act then? You two hit the road together, going from town to town, wreaking havoc . . ."

"Nothing so glamorous, love. Usually it's just me. My sister tries to keep a low profile—spends more time on her job and living her life. She doesn't really get caught up in grand machinations."

"Then how'd you rope her into this one?" Again, I thought about Erik's words, how most nephilim simply wished to be left alone.

"She lives here. In Seattle. We're on her turf, so I talked her into going in on the final kill with me. She wasn't really into any of the stuff with the lesser immortals."

"Except beating on me," I pointed out.

"I am sorry about that. I think you pissed her off."

"I don't even know her," I exclaimed, wondering which was worse: a nephilim in love with me or a nephilim holding a grudge.

He just smiled. "I wouldn't be so sure of that." He reached out to touch me, almost casually, and I backed away, making his smile slip. "Now what's wrong?"

"What do you mean? You think you can just dump this on me and then expect things to be all peachy between us?"

"Well, why not? Honestly, what have you got left to worry about?" I opened my mouth to protest, but he continued before I could speak: "I've already told you, I'm not going to hurt you or any of your friends. The only person left on my list is someone you don't even know or care about. That's it. End of story."

"Oh yeah? What'll happen then? After you kill Carter?"

He shrugged. "Then I leave. I'll find someplace to hang

out for a while. Probably teach again." He leaned toward me, holding my gaze. "You could come with me, you know."

"What?"

"Think about it." He spoke eagerly, excitement growing with each word. "You and me. You could settle down and do all the things you like to do—your books, your dancing— without any immortal politics to muck your life up."

I scoffed. "Hardly. It's not like I can stop being a succubus. I still need sex to survive."

"Yes, yes, I know you'd still have to tag the occasional victim, but think about the times in between. You and me. Together. Being with someone you don't have to worry about hurting. Being with someone simply for the pleasure of it, not for survival. No superiors to harass you about meeting your quotas."

Seth came to mind just then, part of me idly wondering what it'd be like to be with him "just for pleasure."

Shifting back to my harsh reality, I told Roman, "I can't just run off. Seattle is my post. I have people to answer to; they wouldn't let me leave."

Cupping my face in his hands, he whispered, "Georgina, Georgina. I can protect you from them. I have the power to hide you. You can live your own life. No more answering to the bureaucracy above. We can be free."

Those hypnotic eyes hooked me like a fish on a line. For centuries, I had lived out immortality achingly alone, bouncing from one short-term relationship to another, ending any connection that got too deep. Now, Roman was here. I was attracted to him, and I didn't have to push him away. I couldn't hurt him through physical contact. We could be together. We could wake up together. We could live out eternity together. I would never have to be lonely again.

Longing surged up within me. I wanted it. Oh God, I wanted it. I didn't want to hear Jerome chastise me for my "all lowlifes, all the time" seduction policy. I wanted to come home and tell someone about my day. I wanted to go out dancing on the weekends. I wanted to take vacations together. I wanted someone to hold me when I was upset, when the ups and downs of the world pushed me too far.

I wanted someone to love.

His words blazed through me, piercing my heart. I knew, however, they were only that: words. Eternity is a long time; we couldn't hide forever. Eventually we'd be found, or when Roman finally got destroyed on one of his "protest" missions, I'd be exposed and have a lot of angry demons to answer to. He was offering me a child's dream, an impractical fantasy with a short-lived, doomed run.

Furthermore, running off with Roman meant complying with the outcome of this insane plot of his. Logically, I could understand his angst and desire to lash back. I felt for his sister—even if she inexplicably hated me—who simply wanted to live an ordinary life. I had seen slaughter and bloodshed over the years, the extinction of entire populations of people whose names and cultures no one remembered today. To live with that over and over throughout these long millennia, to always be on the run, hiding simply because of an accident of birth . . . yes, perhaps I would be pissed off too.

Yet, I still could not see that as sufficient reason for the random killing of immortals, simply to "prove a point." The fact that I knew these immortals personally made it worse. Carter's attitude still unnerved me, yes, but he had saved my life, and my days with him hadn't been unbearable. If anything, Roman should laud the angel. The nephilim's biggest complaint was that immortals stayed locked into archaic sets of rules and roles, but Carter had broken the mold: an angel who chose friendship with his hypothetical enemies. He and Jerome typified the kind of rebellious, nonconforming lifestyle so advocated by Roman.

Too bad that didn't seem to be enough to dissuade the nephilim. I wondered if I could.

"No," I told him. "I can't do it. And you don't have to do it either."

"Do what?"

"This plot. Killing Carter. Just let him go. Let it all go. Violence only begets more violence, not peace."

"I'm sorry, love. I can't. There's no peace for my kind."

I reached out and touched his face. "You call me that, but do you really mean it? Do you love me?"

He caught his breath, and I suddenly realized he could be just as hypnotized by my eyes as I was by his. "Yes. I do."

"Then do this for me if you love me. Walk away. Walk away from Seattle. I . . . I'll go with you if you do."

I hadn't realized I'd meant it until the words escaped my lips. Running off was a child's fantasy, true, but it would be worth it if I could avert what was to come.

"You mean it?"

"Yes. As long as you can keep me safe."

"I can keep you safe, but . . ."

He stepped away from me and paced around, running a hand through his hair in consternation.

"I can't walk away," he finally told me. "Almost anything in the world I would do for you, but not this. You can't imagine what it's been like. You think immortality's been cruel to you? Imagine what it's like always running, always watching your back. I have just as much trouble settling down as you. Thank God for my sister. She's the only one I have, the only mainstay in my life. The only one I loved—until you, at least."

"She can come with us . . ."

He closed his eyes. "Georgina, when my mother was still alive—millennia ago—we lived in a camp with some of the other nephilim and their mothers. We were always running, always trying to stay ahead of those pursuing us. One night . . . I'll never forget it. They found us, and I swear, Armageddon itself could never be so terrible. I don't even know who did it—angels, demons, or whatever. I mean, when it comes down to it, they're all the same really. Beautiful and terrible."

"Yes," I whispered. "I've seen them."

"Then you know what they can do. They swept in and just destroyed everyone. It didn't matter who. Nephilim children. Humans. Everyone was considered a liability."

"But you escaped?"

"Yes. We were lucky. Most weren't." He turned back to look at me. His heartache made my eyes burn. "Do you see now? Do you see now why I have to do this?"

"You only further the bloodshed."

"I know, Georgina. For Christ's sake, I know. But I have no choice."

I saw in his face then that he hated being a part of that bloodshed, part of the same destructive behavior that had haunted his childhood. But I also saw that he was inextricably tied to that. He could not escape it. He had lived too long, so much longer than me. The years of fear and anger and blood had twisted him. He had to see this game played out.

I fight every day to not let the past overtake me. Sometimes I win, sometimes it does.

"I have no choice," he repeated, face desperate. "But you do. I still want you to come with me when I'm done."

A choice. Yes, I did have a choice. A choice between him and Carter. Or did I? Was there anything I could do to save Carter at this point? Did I want to save Carter? For all I knew, Carter had slaughtered countless nephilim children over the years in the name of good. Maybe he deserved the punishment Roman wanted to mete out. What were good and evil, really, but stupid categories? Stupid categories that restricted people and punished or rewarded them based on how they responded to their own natures, natures they really didn't have any way to control.

Roman was right. The system was flawed. I just didn't know what to do about it.

What I needed was time. Time to think about all of this, time to figure out a way that would save angel and nephilim both, if such a feat were possible. I didn't know how to buy that time, though, not with Roman standing there staring at me, aflame with his romantic notion of running off together.

Time. I needed time and had no idea how to get it. I had no powers to help in a situation like this. If Roman decided I was a threat, I would be unable to fight against him. *A nephilim could easily blow one of you out of the water.* I could not pull divine strings and contracts like Hugh, had no superhuman reflexes and strength like Cody and Peter. I was a succubus. I changed shape and had sex with men. That was it.

That was it . . .

Chapter 24

"Well?" Roman asked softly. "What do you think? Will you go with me?"

"I don't know," I replied, looking down. "I'm afraid." A tremulous note hung in my voice.

He turned my face toward his, obviously concerned. "Afraid of what?"

I looked at him through my lashes. It was a demure action. Vulnerable, even. Hard to resist. I hoped.

"Of . . . of them. I want to . . . but I don't think . . . I don't think we could ever be free. You can't hide from them, Roman. Not forever."

"We can," he breathed, putting his arms around me, his heart swelling at my fear. I didn't resist at all, letting him press his body up against mine. "I told you. I can protect you. I'll find the angel tomorrow, and we'll leave the next day. It's that easy."

"Roman . . ." I stared up at him, my eyes wide, the look of one overcome with some emotion. Hope, maybe. Passion. Wonder. I saw my expression mirrored in his own, and when he leaned down to kiss me, I didn't stop him this time. I even kissed him back. It had been a long time since I'd kissed simply for the sake of kissing, for the feel of his tongue gently pushing into my mouth, lips caressing mine as his hands held me tightly to him.

I could have kissed like that forever, just enjoying the physical sensation, devoid of any succubus feeding. It was magnificent. Intoxicating, even. There was no fear. Roman wanted more than kissing, however, and when he pulled me down, right onto my living room carpet, I didn't stop him then either.

Obvious heat and yearning filled his body. Yet, he moved carefully and slowly over me, showing a restraint that surprised and impressed me. I slept with so many guys that yielded right away to their own needs that it was downright astonishing to have someone apparently concerned with my fulfillment.

No way was I complaining.

He kept his body against mine, so there was no space between us as he continued kissing me. Eventually he moved from my mouth to my ear, tracing it with his tongue and lips before shifting to my neck. My neck has always been one of my more erogenous places, and I exhaled a trembling breath as that clever tongue slowly stroked the sensitive skin, making gooseflesh rise. I arched my body into his, letting him know he could have expedited things if he wanted, but he seemed to be in no hurry.

Down, down he moved, kissing my breasts through the delicate charmeuse of my shirt until the fabric was wet and clung to my nipples. I sat up so he could pull the shirt off me entirely. While he was at it, he slid off the skirt too, so I was left only in panties. Still focused on my breasts, however, he continued kissing and touching them, varying between soft feathery kisses and hard, biting ones that threatened to leave flowering purple bruises. At last he slid down, trailing his tongue along the smooth skin of my stomach, pausing when he finally reached my thighs.

Meanwhile, I was a wreck, aching and desperate to touch his body in return. But when I reached for him, he gently pushed my wrists to the floor. "Not yet," he admonished.

I guess that was just as well since I was supposed to be doing something with time here. Buying it, right? Yeah, that was it. I was delaying so I could figure out a plan. A plan that I'd get to . . . later.

"Magenta," he observed, running his fingers along the panties. They were flimsy, barely a collection of scraps of lace and sheer material. "Who'd have guessed?"

"I almost never wear any clothes in the pink and magenta family," I admitted, "but for some reason I love lingerie in those colors. And black, of course."

"It suits you. You can shape-shift these on anytime, right?"

"Yeah, why?"

He reached out and, with one deft motion, ripped them off. "Because they're in my way."

Bending down, he pushed my thighs apart and buried his face between them. His tongue moved slowly over the edges of my lips and then darted forward to stroke my burning, swollen clit. Moaning, I lifted and ground my hips into him, trying to get more of my aching need fulfilled. Once again, he pushed me back to the floor, taking his time, letting his tongue circle and tease me, driving me into higher and higher pleasure. Every time I seemed about to peak, he would pull back and move his tongue down, letting it actually probe inside me where I was growing wetter.

When he finally let me come, I did so loudly and wildly, my body practically thrashing as he held me down and continued sucking and tasting through my spasms. By then, I was so sensitive and dizzy that his touch was almost too much. I heard myself begging him to stop, even as he made me come again.

Easing up, he released me and backed off, watching as the blissful spasms in my body slowed down. Between us, we had his clothes off in about two seconds, and he laid his body over mine, pressing bare skin against bare skin. When my hands slid down, grasping and stroking his erection, he sighed with palpable bliss.

"Oh God, Georgina," he breathed, eyes on mine. "Oh God. You have no idea how much I want you."

Didn't I?

I guided him toward me, sliding him inside. My body opened to him, welcoming him like a piece of myself I'd been missing, and he moved in and out of me with long, controlled strokes, watching my face and gauging how each angle and motion affected me.

I'm buying time, I thought sagely, but as he pinned my wrists to the floor, claiming ownership of my body with each thrust, I knew I lied to myself. This was about more than just buying time to warn Jerome and Carter. This was about me. It was selfish. I had continuously craved Roman over the last few weeks, and now I had him. Not only that, but it was exactly as he had said: there was no survival here, only pleasure. I had had sex with other immortals before but not in some time. I had forgotten what it was like to not have someone else's thoughts in my head, to simply luxuriate in my own sensations.

We moved with a practiced rhythm, like our bodies did this together all the time. Those controlled strokes grew more savage, less precise. Harder and fiercer he brought himself into me, like he was going to go through the floor. Someone was making a lot of noise, and I realized distantly that it was me. I was sort of losing track of what was around me, of coherent thought. There was only my body's response, the building force that consumed me and set me on fire and still made me demand more. I longed for completion and urged him on, bringing my body up to meet his and clenching the muscles around him.

He gasped as he felt me grow tighter. His eyes burned with a near-primitive passion. "I want to see you come again," he gasped out. "Come for me."

For whatever reason, it only took that command to finish me off, to plunge me over the edge of that dizzying ecstasy. I cried out more loudly, my throat long since gone hoarse. Whatever expression I wore, it was enough to drive him into his own finish. No sound came out as his lips parted, but he closed his eyes and held himself inside me after a final hard thrust, shaking with pleasure.

When he had finished, his body still trembling with the force of his orgasm, he rolled off me onto his back, sweaty and satisfied. I turned toward him, splaying my fingers on his chest, admiring the lean muscles and tanned flesh of his body.

"You're beautiful," I told him, taking a nipple into my mouth.

"You aren't so bad yourself," he murmured, stroking my hair. Perspiration rolled off my body too, making some of the strands damp and curl up more than usual. "Is this you? Your real shape?"

I shook my head, surprised by the question. I trailed my lips up to his neck. "I've only worn that body once since becoming a succubus. A long time ago." Pausing mid-kiss, I asked, "You want something different? I can be anything you want me to be, you know."

He grinned, flashing those white teeth. "One of the perks of loving a succubus, no doubt." Sitting up, he scooped me into his arms and then rose, slightly wobbly with the added weight. "But no. Ask me in another century, maybe, and I might have a different answer. For now, I've got a lot more to learn about this body."

He carried me off to my bedroom, where we made love in a slower, slightly more civilized manner, our bodies twining together like ribbons of liquid fire. With that initial animalism somewhat satisfied, we lingered longer now, exploring the different ways each person's body responded. We spent most of the night cycling through a pattern: slow and loving, fast and furious, rest, repeat. I grew exhausted somewhere around three and finally gave in to sleep, resting my head against his chest, ignoring the nagging worries in the back of my mind.

I woke up a few hours later, sitting bolt upright as the previous night's events came slamming back into me with sharper clarity. I'd gone to sleep in a nephilim's arms. Talk about vulnerability. Yet . . . here I was, still alive. Roman lay beside me, snug and warm, Aubrey at his feet. Both of them regarded me with tired, squinty eyes, wondering at my sudden motion.

"What's the matter?" he asked, stifling a yawn.

"N-nothing," I assured him. Removed from passion, I found myself able to think a bit more clearly. What had I done? Sleeping with Roman might have bought me time, but I was no closer to finding some way out of this crazy situation.

Lying there, I caught sight of Carter's daffodils, and they jolted me into a decision. The flowers themselves had only been part of a small act, but something about them made me realize I could not sit passively by and let Roman kill Carter. I had to act, no matter the risk, no matter the likelihood of failure. *We all have moments of weakness. It's how we recover from them that really counts.*

It didn't matter if I loved the nephilim and hated the angel, neither of which was entirely true. This was more about me, about the kind of person I was. I had spent centuries hurting men for my own survival, often devastatingly so, but I could not be a part of premeditated murder, no matter how noble the cause. I hadn't reached that stage of life. Not yet.

I blinked back sudden tears, overwhelmed by what I had to do. What I had to do to Roman.

"Then go back to sleep," he murmured, running a hand along my body, from waist to thigh.

Yes, I knew what I had to do. It was a long shot, hardly a solid plan, but I couldn't think of anything else to take advantage of Roman's current, off-guard mood.

"I can't," I explained, starting to get out of bed. "I have to work."

His eyes opened wider. "What? When?"

"I open. I need to be there in a half hour."

He sat up, dismayed. "You work all day?"

"Yup."

"I still had a few more things I wanted to do to you," he mumbled, sliding an arm around my waist to pull me back, cupping a breast in his hand.

I leaned back into him, feigning being caught up in passion. All right, I wasn't exactly feigning.

"Mmm . . ." I turned my face toward his, brushing our lips together. "I could call in sick maybe . . . not that they'd believe it. I'm never sick, and they know it."

"Fuck them," he mumbled, pushing me back down into the bed, his hands growing bolder. "Fuck them so I can fuck you again."

"Then let me up," I laughed. "I can't call in like this."

Reluctantly he released me, and I slid out of the bed, grinning back at him as I went. He watched me hungrily, like a cat sizing up prey. Honestly, I liked it.

That desire quickly melted into apprehension as I walked into the living room and picked up my portable phone. I had left all the room doors open, acting as casual and relaxed as possible, giving Roman no cause for alarm. Knowing he could probably hear me in the living room, I mentally rehearsed my words as I dialed Jerome's cell phone number.

Not surprisingly, however, the demon did not answer. Damn him. What good was our bond if I couldn't use it at will? Having anticipated this, I tried my next option: Hugh. If I got his cell's voice mail, I would be out of luck. I could not pull off my plan if I had to call his office number and wade through his arsenal of secretaries.

"Hugh Mitchell speaking."

"Hey, Doug, it's Georgina."

A pause. "Did you just call me Doug?"

"Look, I can't come in today. I think I've caught that bug that's been going around."

Roman wandered out of my bedroom, and I smiled at him as he made his way to my refrigerator. Meanwhile, Hugh tried to make sense of my nonsense.

"Uh, Georgina . . . I think you dialed the wrong number."

"No, I'm serious, Doug, so don't get smart with me. I can't come in, okay?"

Dead silence. Finally Hugh asked, "Georgina, are you all right?"

"No. I already told you that. Look, will you just pass it on?"

"Georgina, what's going on—"

"Well, I'm sure you'll figure out something," I continued, "but it'll have to be without me. I'll try to be in tomorrow."

I disconnected and looked up at Roman, shaking my head. "It would figure Doug was there. He definitely didn't believe me."

"Knows you too well, huh?" he asked, drinking a glass of orange juice.

"Yeah, but he'll cover for me, despite his complaining. He's good like that."

I tossed the phone onto the couch and approached Roman. Time for more distraction. I doubted Hugh would fully grasp the situation, but he would at least assume something wasn't right. As I had noted in the past, one couldn't live as long as an immortal did and be stupid. He would suspect something and hopefully hunt down Jerome. My job now was to keep the nephilim busy until the cavalry came.

"So what exactly was it you wanted to do to me?" I purred.

A number of things, as it turned out. We wound up back in my bedroom, and I discovered waiting out the time until Hugh could take action wasn't nearly as difficult as I had feared. Slight twinges of guilt tugged at me over enjoying Roman so much, especially now that I'd made my decision and called for help. He had murdered untold numbers of immortals and had designs on a near-friend. Still, I couldn't help my feelings. I was attracted to him—had been for a long time, even—and he was really, really good in bed.

"Eternity doesn't seem so bad with you in my arms," he murmured later, stroking my hair as I curled up against him. Turning my face toward his, I saw a somber expression in his eyes.

"What's wrong?"

"Georgina . . . do you . . . do you really want me to leave this angel alone?"

"Yes," I blurted out after a moment of surprise. "I don't want you to hurt anyone else."

He studied me for a long time before speaking. "Last night, when you asked me, I didn't think I could. I didn't think I could let it go. Now . . . after being with you . . . being like this. It just seems petty. Well, maybe petty isn't the right word. I mean, what they did to us was terrible . . . but maybe if I keep going after them, I let them win. I become what they say I am. I let them keep dictating the parameters of my life. I'd be conforming to nonconformity, I guess, and missing what's really important. Like loving and being in love."

"Wh-what are you saying?"

He cupped my cheek. "I'm saying, I'll do it, love. The past will not rule my present. For you, I'll walk away. You and me. We'll go today and leave all this behind. Get a home somewhere and start a life together. We can go to Vegas."

I turned rigid in his arms, my eyes widening. Oh God.

A knock sounded at my door, and I nearly jumped ten feet. Only about forty minutes had passed. *No, no,* I thought. It was too soon. Especially in light of this sudden turnabout. Hugh couldn't have acted so fast. I didn't know what to do.

Roman raised an eyebrow, curious more than anything else. "Expecting anyone?"

I shook my head, trying to hide the racing of my heart. "Doug's always threatened to come get me," I joked. "I hope he didn't finally decide to act on it."

Getting out of bed, I went to my closet, urging every nerve in my body to look nonchalant. I put on a deep red kimono, ran a hand self-consciously through my messy hair, and walked out to the living room, trying not to hyperventilate once out of Roman's sight. *Oh Lord,* I thought, approaching the door. *What am I going to do? What am I going to—*

"Seth?"

The writer stood outside, a bakery box in hand, his own face registering as much shock as mine undoubtedly did. I watched his eyes quickly slip up the length of me, and I suddenly became aware of how short my robe was and just how much the clinging silk revealed. His eyes snapped up to my face, and he swallowed.

"Hi. I . . . that is . . ."

One of my neighbors walked by, stopping and staring when he saw me in the robe. "Come in," I urged Seth with a grimace, closing the door behind him. Having expected a cavalcade of immortals, I felt more confused than ever now.

"I'm sorry," he managed at last, trying to keep his eyes from drifting to my body. "I hope I didn't wake you . . ."

"No . . . no . . . it's not a problem . . ."

Naturally Roman chose that moment to make an appearance, coming down the hall from my bedroom in only boxers. "So what's—oh hey, how's it going? Seth, right?"

"Right," said Seth flatly, looking from me to Roman and then back to me. In the wake of that gaze, I didn't care about nephilim, immortals, or saving Carter. All I could think of was how this must look to Seth. Poor Seth, who had done nothing but be nice to me since I'd met him, yet who nonetheless managed to get hurt over and over by my insensitivity—not to mention an unfortunate set of circumstances. I didn't know what to say; I felt as mortified as he apparently did. I did not want him to see me like this, all of my lies and inconsistent signals coming to light.

"Is that breakfast?" the nephilim asked cheerfully. He was the only one of us at ease.

"Huh?" Seth still looked stunned beyond words. "Oh yeah." He set the box down on my coffee table. "Keep it. It's a coffee cake. Maple pecan. As for me . . . I'm going to . . . I'm just going to leave now. I'm sorry to bother you. Really sorry. I knew it was your day off and just thought we could . . . I don't know. You'd said yesterday . . . well. It was stupid. I should have called. It was stupid. I'm sorry."

He started to turn, but the damage was done. Of all the possible scenarios, this would be the one in which short-spoken Seth chose to ramble. *I knew it was your day off.* Shit. Roman turned on me, the incredulity on his face transforming to fury before my eyes.

"Who," he gasped, voice barely coming out in his anger, "who did you call? Who the *fuck* did you call?"

I stepped backward. "Seth, get out of—"

Too late. A wave of power, not unlike the one Jerome had used on me, slammed against both Seth and me, thrusting us against my living room wall.

Roman strode up to us, glaring at me, his eyes like blue flame. "Who did you call?" he roared. I didn't answer. "Do you have any idea what you've done?"

Turning from us, he grabbed my phone and dialed. "I need you to get over here right now . . . .yes, yes, I don't fucking care. Leave it." He recited my address and disconnected. I didn't need to ask who he had called. I knew. The other nephilim. His sister.

Running a hand through his hair, Roman paced frantically around my living room. "Shit. *Shit*. You may have ruined everything!" he yelled at me. "Do you realize that? Do you realize that, you lying bitch? How could you do this to me?"

I didn't respond. I couldn't. Movement, even talking, was too hard in that psychic net. I couldn't even look at Seth. God only knew what he must think of all of this.

Ten minutes later, I heard another knock. If I had any sort of divine favor left, it would be Jerome and Carter, ready to come to my rescue. Surely even a succubus deserved a break now and then, I thought as I watched Roman open the door.

Helena walked in. Oh, man.

"About time," Roman snapped, slamming the door behind her.

"What's going—" She cut her words off, eyes widening at the sight of Seth and me. Turning back to Roman, she gave him and his boxers a once-over. "For crying out loud, what have you done now?"

"Someone's coming," he hissed, ignoring her question. "Right now."

"Who?" she demanded, hands on hips. There was no rasp in her voice now, and she looked amazingly competent. If I hadn't already been rendered speechless, the sight of her would have done it.

"I don't know," he admitted. "Probably our exalted sire. *She* called someone."

Helena turned and approached me, making terror sink into my bones as I realized my danger. Helena was the other nephilim. Crazy, swindling Helena. Helena, whom I had insulted on a number of occasions, mocked behind her back, and stolen employees from. The look on her face informed me she was considering all of those things as she stared me down.

"Drop the field," she snapped to Roman, and a moment later, Seth and I slumped forward, gasping, as the power released us. "Is he right? Did you call our father?"

"I . . . didn't call . . . anyone . . ."

"She's lying," Roman observed mildly. "Who did you call, Georgina?"

When I didn't answer, she walked over and slapped me hard, the impact making a loud *crack*. There was something oddly familiar about it, but then, there would be. Helena was the one who had beat me up that night on the street. I realized then she must have known it was me when I went to Krystal Starz, in spite of my disguise. Recognizing my signature, she had chosen to play with me, feeding me the lines about having a great future as she pushed titles and workshops on me.

"Always difficult, aren't you?" she scoffed. "For years, I've put up with you and others like you, those who mock my lifestyle and teachings. I should have done something about you a long time ago."

"Why?" I wondered aloud, gaining control of my voice again. "Why do you do it? You, of all people, who know about angels and demons . . . why do you tout the New Age bullshit?"

She eyed me scathingly. "Is it really? Is it bullshit to encourage people to seize control of their own lives, to view themselves as sources of power instead of getting caught up in all the guilt of what's right and what's wrong?" When I didn't answer, she continued, "I teach people to empower themselves. I teach them to let go of sin and salvation, to learn how to find happiness now—in *this* world. True, some of it is . . . embellished for the sake of creating wonder and awe, but what does that matter, if the ends are achieved? People walk away from my classes feeling like gods and goddesses. They find that within themselves, rather than selling out to some cold, hypocritical institution."

I couldn't even begin to formulate a response, and it occurred to me that Helena and Roman thought exactly alike, both of them dissatisfied with the system that had spawned them, each of them rebelling against it in different ways.

"I know what you think of me. I've heard what you say about me. I saw you throw away the materials I gave you that night, no doubt thinking I was just some crazy, babbling New Age crackpot. And yet . . . for someone so smugly confident, so critically self-righteous, you are one of the most unhappy people I've ever met. You hate the game, and yet you play it. You play it, and you defend it because you don't have the courage to do anything else." She shook her head, chuckling dryly. "I didn't have to be psychic to give you any of those predictions. You are gifted, but you waste it. You are wasting your life, and you will spend it miserable and alone."

"I can't change what I am," I told her hotly, stung by her words.

"Spoken like a slave to the system."

"Fuck you," I shot back. Having one's pride and self-identity shattered will often make a person irrationally angry, regardless if the point was well made. "Better a comfortable slave than some freakish divine bastard. It's no wonder your kind is being hunted to extinction."

She hit me again, this time packing nephilim power with the punch, not unlike that night in the alley. It hurt—a lot.

"You little whore. You have no idea what you're talking about."

She moved to hit me again but was stopped as Seth suddenly pushed himself in front of me. "Stop it," he exclaimed. "Stop it, all of—"

A blast of power—from Roman or Helena, I didn't know—pushed Seth across the room, to the other wall. I flinched. "How dare you—" began Helena, her blue eyes flashing angrily. "You, a mortal, who have no idea what you're—"

I was already moving before the words could even come out of her mouth. Seeing Seth abused sparked something in me, an angry response I knew to be hopeless but which I couldn't really prevent. I sprang at Helena, taking on the first shape that came to mind, no doubt thanks to seeing Aubrey earlier: a tiger.

The transformation only took a second but hurt like hell, as my human body expanded, feet and hands turning to heavy, clawed paws. I had the element of surprise, but only for a moment, as I slammed into her, knocking her slight body to the floor.

My victory was short lived. Before I could sink teeth into her neck, a hurricane-worthy force blew me from her into my china cabinet. The impact was ten times harder than the one that had pinned Seth and me earlier, and the pain jolted me back into my normal shape as glass and crystal broke behind me, pieces falling around me, cutting my skin.

I moved again, frantic, knowing the futility but needing to do something, too caught up in battle lust. I lunged at Roman this time, urging my body to take on the shape of . . . well, I didn't even know what. I had no specific form in mind, only features: claws, teeth, scales, muscles. Sharp.

Large. Dangerous. A creature of nightmares, a true demon of hell.

I never even came close to touching the nephilim, however. One or both of them anticipated me, mid-leap, throwing me back to land near Seth this time, his wide eyes watching me with terror and wonder. Bolts of power struck me, making me cry out in pain, shattering every nerve within me. My new shape's hide protected me only briefly, and then hurt and exhaustion made me lose control of the transformation. I slipped back into the slim, human body just as another net of power pinned me into place, ensuring I couldn't move anymore.

My entire shape-shifting attack had lasted all of a minute, and I now felt completely drained and worn, my reserve of Martin Miller power finally dried up. So much for bravery. *A nephilim could easily blow one of you out of the water.*

"Valiantly done, Georgina," chuckled Roman, wiping sweat off his brow. He had expended a great deal of power too, but he had a lot more of it to spend than I did. "Valiant, but foolish." Walking over, he looked me up and down and shook his head with bitter amusement. "You don't know how to ration your energy. You've burned yourself out."

"Roman . . . I'm so sorry . . ."

I didn't need him to tell me how low on energy I was. I could feel it. I wasn't just low, I was empty. Running on fumes, so to speak. Looking at my hands, I saw my appearance flicker slightly, shimmering almost like a heat mirage. That was bad. Wearing a body for long enough, even if it isn't your original, becomes ingrained after a few years, and I had had this one for fifteen. It was second nature to me. I thought of it as my own; it was what I always unconsciously returned to. Yet, I was fighting to hold on to it right now, to not slip back to the body of my birth. This was bad—very bad.

"Sorry?" Roman asked, and I saw on his face just how terribly I'd hurt him. "You can't even begin to imagine—"

We all felt it at the same time. Roman and Helena spun around to shoot each other alarmed looks, and then my front door blew open. The bonds holding me dropped as the nephilim redirected their power at the apocalypse coming through.

Brilliant light spilled inside, light so brilliant it hurt. Familiar light. The same terrible shape I'd seen in the alley appeared once more, only there were two of them this time. Mirror images. Indistinguishable. I didn't know who was who, but I remembered Carter's offhand observation from a week ago: *an angel in full form will freak most beings out—it'll kill a mortal . . .*

"Seth," I whispered, turning from that glorious spectacle to look at the writer. He was staring at it, brown eyes wide with awe and fear as the glory of it drew him in. "Seth, don't look at them." With my fleeting strength, I lifted a shimmering hand and turned his face toward mine. "Seth, don't look at them. Look at me. Only at me."

Somewhere beyond us, someone screamed. The world was blowing apart.

"Georgina . . ." breathed Seth, gingerly touching my face. "What's wrong with you?"

Focusing all of my will, I urged my body to fight and hold on to the shape he had first come to know me in. It was a losing battle. A dying one even. I could not survive much longer like this. Seth leaned closer to me, and I tuned out the sounds of chaos and destruction raging around us, instead focusing all the world, all of my perception, toward his face.

I had said Roman was beautiful, but he was nothing—nothing at all—compared to Seth in that moment. Seth, with those long-lashed, quizzical brown eyes, kindness made manifest in all of his actions. Seth, his messy hair and slightly unkempt facial hair, framing a face which could not hide his nature, the strength of his character shining out at me, his soul like a beacon on a foggy night.

"Seth," I whispered. "Seth."

He leaned toward me, letting me draw him closer and closer, and then, as heaven and hell raged beyond, I kissed him.

Chapter 25

Sometimes you wake up from a dream. Sometimes you wake up in a dream. And sometimes, every once in a while, you wake up in someone else's dream.

"If he wanted to carry me off and make me his love slave, I'd do it, so long as I got advance copies of his books."

My first words spoken to Seth as I passionately discussed his work. Seth's initial impression of me. Head held high, hair tossed over my shoulder. A flippant remark always at the ready. Grace under fire. A cool social confidence introverted Seth could never muster but envied. *How can she do that? Never miss a beat?* Later, my rambling explanation of the five-page rule, a goofy habit he found infinitely endearing. Someone else who appreciated literature, viewing it like fine wine. *Smart and deep. And beautiful.* Yes, beautiful. I saw myself now as Seth had seen me that night: the short skirt, the racy purple top, brilliant as a bird's plumage. Like some exotic creature, hopelessly out of place in the bookstore's dreary landscape.

All of this was in Seth, the past of his growing feelings for me mingling with the present, and I drank everything up.

Not just beautiful. Sexy. Sensual. A goddess made flesh whose every move hinted at passion to come. The dress strap slipping off my shoulder. Faint beads of perspiration on my cleavage. Standing in his kitchen, clad only in that ridiculous Black Sabbath shirt. *No underwear on under that. Wonder what it'd be like to wake up with her next to me, messy and untamed.*

It all spilled into me. More and more.

He would watch me at the bookstore. Loved watching me interact with customers. Loved that I seemed to know something about everything. The witty dialogue he pondered for his characters coming to my lips without hesitation. *Amazing. Never met anyone who talks like that in real life.* My bartering with the used book store owner. A charisma that drew in shy, quiet Seth, made me glow in his eyes. Made him feel more confident.

Still his feelings rushed through me. I had never felt anything like it. Certainly I had felt attraction and fondness in my victims, but never such love, not directed at me.

Seth thought I was sexy, yes. Desired me. But that raw lust juxtaposed with something softer too. Something sweeter. Kayla sitting on my lap, small blond head against my chest as I braided her hair. A brief shifting of the image as he momentarily considered his own daughter on my lap. *Fierce and witty on one hand, gentle and vulnerable on the other.* My inebriated state at his condo. A swell of protectiveness as he led me to bed, watching me hours after I'd gone to sleep. He thought no less of me for the weakness, for my lapse of control and judgment. It was a letting down of my walls for him, a sign of imperfection that made him love me more.

Further and further I drank, my desperate and weakened state unable to stop.

"Why doesn't she date?" Seth asked Cody. Cody? Yes, there he was, in the back of Seth's mind. A memory. Cody secretly giving Seth swing lessons, neither of them telling me, instead making up vague excuses for why they always had to be "somewhere." Seth, trying so hard to make his feet obey so he could dance with me and be closer to me. *"She's afraid,"* the vampire replied. *"She thinks love causes pain."*

Love causes pain.

Yes, Seth loved me. Not the crush I'd imagined. Not a superficial attraction I thought I'd dissuaded. It was more, so much more. I embodied everything in a woman he could ever imagine: humor, beauty, intelligence, kindness, strength, charisma, sexuality, compassion . . . His soul seemed to have recognized mine, drawn uncontrollably toward me. He loved me with a depth of feeling I could not even begin to tap into, though believe me, I tried. I wanted it. I wanted to feel it all, to suck up that burning within him. To consume it. Set myself on fire with it.

Georgina!

Somewhere far away, someone called to me, but I was too into Seth. Too into absorbing that strength within him, that strength fused with his feelings for me. Feelings brought on, amplified even, by kissing. Lips soft and eager. Hungry. Demanding.

Georgina!

I wanted to become one with Seth. I needed to. I needed him to fill me up . . . physically, mentally, spiritually. There was something there . . . something concealed inside him I couldn't quite reach, hovering in the background. A tantalizing piece of knowledge I should have long since recognized. *You are my life.* I needed to get in farther, reach out for more. Find out what was hiding from me. That kiss was my lifeline, my connection with something bigger than myself, something I had been aching for all my life but never known.

I couldn't stop. Couldn't stop kissing Seth. Couldn't stop. Couldn't—

"Georgina! Let go!"

Rough hands tore me away from Seth, like flesh ripping from my own body. I cried out in agony at the broken connection, fighting the hands that pulled me and held me. I clawed at my captor, needing to find out the secret lurking beyond that kiss, yearning for the completeness of that union with Seth—

Seth.

My hands dropped, and I blinked, bringing the world back into focus. Reality. I was no longer inside Seth's head; I was still in my apartment. A feeling of solidness settled in me, and I didn't have to look down to know my body had stopped its shifting, my form snapping back to a short, slim woman with honeyed brown hair. The girl I had been long ago was buried within me once more, never to come out if I could help it. Seth's life force now filled me to overflowing.

"Georgina," murmured Hugh behind me, letting his hands ease up on my arms. "Christ, you scared me."

Looking across the room, I saw Carter, bedraggled as usual, leaning over Seth's body.

"Oh God—" I sprang up and moved to them, kneeling beside the angel. Seth lay on the floor, skin pale and clammy. "Oh God. Oh God. Oh God. Is he . . . ?"

"He's alive," Carter told me. "Barely."

Stroking Seth's cheek, feeling the fine golden-red haze of his near-beard, I felt tears brimming in my eyes. His breathing came shallow and jagged. "I didn't mean to. I didn't mean to take so much . . ."

"You did what you had to do. You were in bad shape, could have died."

"And now Seth might . . ."

Carter shook his head. "No. He won't. He'll need recovery time, but he'll pull through."

I drew my hand back, half-afraid my touch might harm Seth more. Glancing around, I became aware of the disheveled state of my apartment. It looked worse than Jerome's. Smashed china and glass. Broken tables. Overturned chairs and couch. The unstable bookshelf in pieces at last. From the kitchen, Aubrey hunkered down under the kitchen table, wondering what was going on. I wondered myself. The nephilim were nowhere in sight. What had happened? Had I really missed it all? The epic, divine battle of the century, and I had missed it for a kiss? Admittedly, a really good kiss, but still . . .

"Where is . . . everyone else?"

"Jerome's off doing, uh, damage control with your neighbors."

"That doesn't sound good."

"Standard practice. Supernatural battles aren't exactly quiet, you know. He'll do a little mind erasing, make sure no authorities get notified."

I swallowed, afraid to ask my next question. "What about . . . what about the nephilim?"

Carter studied me, gray eyes holding me long and hard.

"I know, I know," I said at last, looking down, unable to return that gaze. "There's no ten years and parole, right? You destroyed them."

"We destroyed . . . one of them."

I looked up sharply. "What? What about the other one?"

"He got away."

He. My looming tears slipped out now; I could not control them. *For you, I'll walk away.* "How?"

Carter laid a hand on Seth's forehead as though taking vital stats and then turned back to me. "It all happened really fast. He masked and went invisible in the confusion, while we were taking on the other one. And honestly . . ." The angel looked at my closed front door, then at Hugh and me.

"What?" I whispered.

"I'm not . . . I'm not entirely convinced Jerome didn't let him get away. He wasn't expecting two. I wasn't either, though I should have, in retrospect. After killing the first one . . ." Carter shrugged. "I don't know. Hard to say what happened."

"Then he'll be back," I realized, fear and relief blending weirdly in me over the thought of Roman's escape. "He'll be back . . . and he won't be happy with me."

"I don't think that'll be a problem," the angel observed. Gently, he lifted Seth up and walked to my overturned couch. A moment later, it flipped over untouched, righting itself. Carter laid Seth on it and continued speaking. "He took a real beating—the other nephilim. A really bad beating. I can't believe he had the power left to hide himself from us; I still keep expecting to feel him again any minute. If he's smart, he's running as fast and far from us as he can right now, getting out of our range—out of any immortal's range—so he can drop his shields and rest."

"Then what?" asked Hugh.

"He's in bad shape. It'll take him a long time to recover. When he does, he knows he doesn't have the backup to return here again."

"He could still take on me," I noted, shivering as I remembered Roman's wrath toward me at the end. It was hard to believe we'd been wrapped in each other's arms, caught in the throes of passion, less than twenty-four hours ago.

"He could take you on," agreed Carter. "But he can't take me on. Or Jerome. He certainly can't take both of us on. That was what decided it, in the end. They didn't expect that. Us teamed together. It'll give him pause to just come bursting back here, even if you alone pose no threat."

I didn't find that reassuring in the least. I thought of Roman, passionate and rebellious, always eager to make a point against the system. That personality type lent itself well to revenge. I had tricked him, made love to him, and then betrayed him, resulting in the annihilation of his plans—and his sister. *Thank God for my sister. She's the only one I have, the only mainstay in my life.*

He might pause, as Carter had suggested, but not for long. Of that, I was certain.

"He'll be back," I whispered, more to myself. "Someday he'll be back."

Carter gave me a steady look. "Then we will deal with him then."

My front door opened, and Jerome entered. He looked neat and prim, hardly like he'd just been in an apocalyptic battle with his own offspring.

"Housekeeping all done?" asked Carter.

"Yes." The demon's eyes darted over to Seth. "He's alive?"

"Yes."

Angel and demon locked eyes then, and a tense moment of palpable silence hung between them.

"How fortuitously unexpected," Jerome murmured at last. "I could have sworn he was dead. Well. *Miracles* happen every day. I suppose we'll have to wipe him now."

I stood up. "What are you talking about?"

"Nice to have you back with us again, Georgie. You look lovely, by the way."

I glared at him, angry at his joke, knowing it was Seth's energy giving me the succubus glamour now. "What do you mean you have to 'wipe' him?"

"What do you think? We can't let him walk away after everything he's seen. I'll diminish a little of his affection for you while I'm at it; he's a liability to you."

"What? No. You can't do that."

Jerome sighed, putting on the look of one who suffered long and hard. "Georgina, do you have any idea what he was just exposed to? He has to be wiped. We can't let him know about us."

"How much of me will you take from him?" Pieces of

Seth's memories—my memories, now—glittered in my head like jewels.

"Enough so that he forgets he has any more than a passing knowledge of you. You've been even more negligent with your job than usual these last few weeks." I hardly thought that was Seth's fault; Roman had helped too. "Both of you will function much better if he finds some mortal woman to obsess on instead."

Don't you want to stand out in some way? Carter's taunting question from what seemed like an eternity ago whispered in my head. "You don't have to do this. You don't have to take me out with the rest."

"If I'm already in there, I might as well clear you too. There's no way he can just go on as usual after being exposed to denizens of the divine realms. Even you have to agree with that."

"Some mortals know about us," I argued. "Like Erik. Erik knows, and he keeps it to himself."

In fact, I realized suddenly, Erik had kept Helena's secret to himself as well. He had figured it out after working with her over the years but had never revealed the full truth, only doling out small clues for me.

"Erik is a special case. He has a gift. An ordinary mortal like this one couldn't handle it." Jerome walked over to my couch, looking at Seth dispassionately. "It's better this way."

"No. Please," I cried, running over to Jerome and pulling his sleeve. "Please don't."

The archdemon turned to me, dark eyes cold and shocked that I would dare grab hold of him like that. I knew then, cringing under that gaze, that something in our fond, indulgent relationship had changed forever—something small, but important nonetheless. I didn't know what had done it. Maybe it had been Seth. Maybe it had been Roman. Maybe it had been something else altogether. All I knew was that it had happened.

"Please," I begged, ignoring how desperate I must sound. "Please don't. Don't take me from him . . . out of his head like that. I'll do anything you want. Anything." I brushed a hand over my eyes, attempting to look calm and in control, knowing I was failing.

One eyebrow shifted ever so slightly on Jerome's face, the only hint that I had piqued his interest. The term "deal with the devil" had not arisen lightly; few demons could resist a bargain.

"What could you possibly offer me? The sex thing only worked on my son, so don't even think about trying it now."

"Yes," I agreed, voice growing stronger as I plunged forward. "It worked on him. It works on all sorts of men. I'm good, Jerome. Better than you know. Why do you think I'm the only succubus in this city? It's because I'm one of the best. Before I hit this funk . . . this, I don't know, whatever mood I've been in for a while now, I could have any man I wanted. And not just simply for their strength and life force. I could manipulate them. Make them do anything I asked, talk them into acts of sin they never would have dreamed of before meeting me. And they would do it. They'd do it, and they'd like doing it."

"Go on."

I took a deep breath. "You're tired of the 'all lowlifes, all the time,' right? Me being negligent? Well, I can change that. I can raise your stock higher than you've ever dreamed. I've done it before. All you have to do is let Seth go. Let him keep his memories intact. All of them."

Jerome studied me a moment, mind working. "All the 'stock' in the world won't do me any good if he runs around blathering about what he's seen."

"Then we'll see if he can handle it first. When he recovers and wakes up, we'll talk to him. If he doesn't look like he'll be able to cope with it all . . . well, then you can erase his memories."

"Who will make the call if he can cope or not?"

I hesitated, not wanting that decision in the demon's hands. "Carter will. Carter can tell if someone's telling the truth." I looked at the angel. "You'll know if it's okay, right? Okay for him to know . . . about us?"

Carter gave me an odd look, one I could not interpret. "Yes," he finally admitted.

"What about your end?" asked Jerome. "Will you hold it up—even if Carter decides he's unsafe?"

That was harsh. I had a feeling Jerome wouldn't negotiate on this one, but I was willing to risk it, so confident did I feel about Seth's capacity to process immortal activity. I opened my mouth, about to agree, when I caught Hugh shaking his head at me out of the corner of my eye. Frowning, he tapped his watch, mouthing something I couldn't understand at first.

Then, it clicked. Time. I had listened to the imp talk about his job enough to know the rules of negotiation: never make an open-ended deal with a demon. "If Seth keeps his memories, I'll walk the succubus straight and narrow for a century. If they have to be erased anyway, then I'll still do it for . . . a third of that."

"Half," countered Jerome. "We aren't mortal. Even a century is nothing on the face of eternity."

"Half," I agreed dully, "but no more than survival dictates. I'm not going to do this every day, if that's what you're thinking. I'll only get fixes as I need them, but they'll be strong ones. Very strong—loaded with sin. With men of good caliber, that'll be . . . oh, every four to six weeks."

"I want better than that. Extra credit. Every couple of weeks, whether you need it or not."

I closed my eyes, unable to fight anymore. "Every couple of weeks."

"Very well," said Jerome, a warning note in his voice. "But you will be held to this agreement unless *I* choose to terminate it for some reason. Not you. There will be no wiggling out for you."

"I know. I know, and I accept."

"Shake then."

He extended his hand to me. Not hesitating, I took it, and power crackled briefly around us.

The demon smiled thinly. "We have a deal."

Chapter 26

"Why so blue, Kincaid?"

I looked up from the information desk's computer screen to see Doug leaning lazily over the counter's edge. "Am I?"

"Sure. You have the saddest look on your face I've ever seen. It's breaking my heart."

"Oh. Sorry. Just tired, I guess."

"Well, then, get out of here. Your shift's over."

Glancing down, I read the time on the computer. Five-oh-seven. "I guess it is."

He eyed me askance as I rose listlessly from the chair and made my way out from behind the desk. "You sure you're okay?"

"Yeah. Like I said, just tired. I'll see you around."

I started to walk away. "Oh, hey, Kincaid?"

"Yeah?"

"You're friendly with Mortensen, aren't you?"

"Sort of," I conceded cautiously.

"Do you know what happened to him? He used to be

here, like, every day, and now he's been gone all week. It's freaking Paige out. She thinks we offended him or something."

"I don't know. We're not that friendly. Sorry." I shrugged. "Maybe he's sick. Or out of town."

"Maybe."

I left the store, stepping out into the dark autumn evening. Friday in Queen Anne brought people in droves, drawn by the area's assortment of activities and nightlife. Ignoring them, lost in my own thoughts, I walked over to my car, parked a block away. Immediately, a vulture in a red Honda slowed down and put her signal on, realizing my spot was about to be vacated.

"You ready for this?" Carter asked me, materializing in the passenger seat.

I fastened my seat belt. "Ready as I'll ever be."

We drove up to the University District in silence, a hundred questions on my mind. Since removing Seth from my apartment last week, the angel had told me not to worry, that he would see to the writer's recovery. I'd still worried anyway, of course, about both Seth and the deal I'd made with Jerome. I was about to become the single greatest source of chaos and temptation in Seattle; even Hugh's stellar track record wouldn't look so good . . . er, bad, anymore. I would be more than the slave Helena had claimed I was. The very thought made me ill.

"I'll be with you," Carter told me soothingly as we approached Seth's door minutes later. The angel flickered briefly in my vision, and I realized he'd gone invisible to mortal eyes, though not to mine.

"What does he know?"

"Not much. He's been awake more and more these last couple of days, and I've told him a little, but really . . . I think he's been waiting for you."

Sighing, I nodded and stared at the door. Suddenly I felt unable to move.

"You can do this," Carter said gently.

Nodding again, I turned the door handle and stepped inside. Seth's condo looked much the same as when I'd last been here, the kitchen still bright and cheery, the living room lined with boxes of unpacked books. Faint music drifted from the bedroom. I thought it was U2, but I didn't recognize the song. Moving toward the sounds, I reached Seth's bedroom, pausing in the doorway, afraid to cross the threshold.

He was in bed, half sitting up, propped up by pillows. In his hands he held *The Green Fairy Book,* looking to be about a third of the way through it. He looked up at my approach, and I nearly sagged in relief to see how much better he looked. His color was back, his eyes bright and alert. Only that facial hair looked ragged and unkempt, the result of no shaving for a week, I guessed. That answered my question about whether or not Seth had maintained the thin, neat beard on purpose.

He reached for a remote on the bedside table and turned the music off. "Hey."

"Hey."

I took a few more steps into the room, afraid to get any closer. "Do you want to sit?" he asked.

"Sure." Cady and O'Neill's faces scrutinized me from the bulletin board as I brought a chair alongside Seth. I sat down, looked at him, and then looked away, unable to handle the depth of those amber-brown eyes after seeing into his mind.

Our old silence fell between us, the progress we'd made in conversation banished to the winds. Seth would not take the lead this time. As Carter had observed, the writer was waiting for me. I looked back up, forcing myself to meet his eyes. I had to do this. I had to do the explaining here, but I

alked at it. It was ironic, I thought. Me, who half the time
iidn't know when to shut up. Me, famed for always having
ome catchy quip at the ready.

Knowing it would never get any easier, I took a deep
reath and let it all out, conscious of the weight of heaven at
ny back and the hell I'd just consented to stretching out be-
ore me.

"The truth is . . . the truth is, I don't really work in a book-
tore. I mean, I do, but that's not really why I'm here, what
ny purpose is. The truth is that I'm a succubus, and I know
ou've probably heard of us before—or think you've heard of
s before, but I doubt what you've heard is correct . . ."

On I went. I told him. I told him everything. The rules of
he succubus lifestyle, my dissatisfaction with it, why I
vouldn't date people I liked. I told him about other immor-
ils, angels and demons walking among us. I even explained
bout nephilim, hinting that Roman's presence in my apart-
nent had been part of a lure on my part, but mostly skim-
ning over the embarrassing circumstances Seth had found
s in. On and on, I talked, not even knowing what I said half
he time. I only knew I had to keep talking, keep trying to
xplain to Seth that which defied explanation.

I finally reached the end, my stream of discourse ex-
austed. "So. So, I guess that's it. You can believe it or not,
ut the forces of good and evil—as humans perceive them,
t least—are alive and well in the world, and I'm one of
hem. This city is filled with supernatural agents and enti-
ies; humans just don't realize it. It's probably just as well,
eally. Otherwise, if they knew too much about us, they
night find out how pathetic and fucked up our lives actually
re."

I shut up, thinking if Seth hadn't seen what he had al-
eady seen, he probably would have thought I was crazy.
Iell, even after it all, he still probably thought I was crazy.
Ie would be justified. Those brown eyes weighed me and

my words in silence, and an annoying wetness welled up i
my own eyes. I looked away to hide it, blinking rapidly, be
cause while succubi might be accused of doing all sorts c
bizarre things around mortal men, I was pretty sure cryin
wasn't one of them.

"You said . . . you said you used to be human." He spok
the words awkwardly, no doubt trying to grasp the whol
concept of mortal and immortal. "How then . . . how did yo
become a succubus?"

I looked back up at him. I could refuse him nothing i
that moment, no matter how painful.

"I made a bargain. I told you before that I was married . .
that I had cheated on my husband. The consequences of tha
were . . . not pleasant. I traded away my life—becoming
succubus—in order to repair the damage I had caused."

"You gave away eternity to fix one mistake?" Set
frowned. "That doesn't seem equitable."

I shrugged, highly uncomfortable with the topic. I ha
never spoken of it to anyone. "I don't know. It's done."

"Okay." He shifted slightly in bed, the soft swishing c
fabric the only sound between us. "Well. Thanks for tellin
me."

I recognized a dismissal when I heard one, and it dug int
me like a blade. That was it. Done. Seth was through wit
me. We were finished. After everything I had told him, ther
was no way things could return to how they'd been, but reall
wasn't that for the best?

I hurriedly stood up, suddenly not wanting to be there an
longer. "Yeah. Okay." I moved toward the door, suddenl
pausing to look back at him. "Seth?"

"Yeah?"

"Do you understand? Why I do what I do? Why w
can't—why we have to—" I couldn't finish the thought. "It
impossible. I wish it were different . . ."

"Yeah," he said quietly.

Turning, I fled his condo for my car. When I got into it, I buried my face into the steering wheel, sobbing uncontrollably. After a few minutes, gentle arms wrapped around me, and I turned toward Carter, crying into his chest. I'd heard reports of people who had angelic encounters, witnesses talking about the peace and beauty experienced by such moments. I'd never given any of it much thought, but as minutes passed, the terrible pain in my chest abated, and I grew calmer, finally lifting my head up to look at the angel.

"He hates me," I choked out. "Seth hates me now."

"Why do you say that?"

"After everything I just told him . . ."

"I suspect he's troubled and confused, yes, but I don't think he hates you. Love like that doesn't turn to hate quite so easily, though I'll admit the two intertwine sometimes."

I sniffled. "Did you feel it? His love?"

"Not like you did. I sensed it, though."

"I've never felt anything like it. I can't match that. I like him . . . like him so much. Maybe I even love him too, but not in the same way he loves me. I'm not worthy of that love."

Carter made a soft, chastising click. "No one is beyond being loved."

"Not even someone who just agreed to spend the next century hurting humans, corrupting souls, and leading them to temptation and despair? You must hate me for that. Even I hate me for that."

The angel watched me, expression steady and calm. "Why did you agree then?"

I leaned my head back against the seat. "Because I couldn't stand the thought of me . . . of that love being wiped out of his head . . . of not being remembered."

"Ironic, huh?"

I turned toward him, hardly surprised at anything anymore. "How much do you know about me?"

"Enough. I know what you got for becoming a succubus."

"I thought it was the right thing then . . ." I murmured, my mind's eye turning to a faraway time and place, another man. "He was so sad and so angry at me . . . he couldn't go on knowing what I'd done. I just wanted to be blotted from his mind forever. I thought it would be better if he—if everyone—forgot about me. Forgot I'd ever existed."

"And now you don't agree?"

I shook my head. "I saw him . . . years later, when he was an old man. I shape-shifted to the form he'd known me in—that was the last time I've worn that face, actually—and approached him. He looked right past me, though. Didn't know me at all. The time we'd had together. The love he'd had for me. All gone. Gone forever. It killed me. I felt like one of the walking dead after that.

"I couldn't let that happen. Not again. Not with Seth, after experiencing what he felt for me. Even if that love is ruined . . . marred by what he thinks of me now. Even if he never speaks to me again. It's still better than that love never having existed at all."

"Love is rarely flawless," Carter pointed out. "Humans delude themselves by thinking it has to be. It is the imperfection that makes love perfect."

"No riddles, please," I told him, suddenly feeling tired. "I just lost the one person I might have loved again after all these years. Really, truly loved too. Not just pure excitement either, like with Roman. Seth . . . Seth had it all. Passion. Commitment. Friendship.

"Not only that, but I've agreed to go on 'active duty' again as a succubus." I closed my eyes, swallowing the bile in my throat. I thought of all the nice guys in the world, men like Doug and Bruce. I did not want to be their downfall. "I really do hate it, Carter. You have no idea how much I hate it, no idea how much I don't want to do this anymore. But it's worth it. Worth it if Seth can keep his memories."

I looked over at the angel uncertainly. "He can, can't he?" Carter nodded, and I exhaled with relief. "Good. At least there's one spot of hope in all of this."

"Of course there is. There's always hope."

"Not for me."

"There's always hope," he repeated more firmly, a commanding note in his voice that startled me. "No one is beyond hope."

I could feel tears coming to my eyes again. Lord. I seemed to be crying all the time lately. "What about a succubus?"

"Especially a succubus."

He put his arms around me again, and I gave way to my sobs once more, a damned soul taking momentary respite in the embrace of a heavenly creature. I wondered if what he said was true, if it was possible that there was still hope for me, but then I remembered something that made me half laugh and half choke all at once.

Angels never lied.

Epilogue

"Casey's out sick," Paige told me briskly, putting on her coat. "So you'll probably have to cover for her on the registers."

"It's no problem." I leaned against her office wall. "Keeps things interesting, you know?"

Pausing, she gave me a brief smile. "I really appreciate you coming in like this—on such short notice." She patted her stomach absentmindedly. "I'm sure it's nothing, but I've had this pain all day—"

"No, it's fine. Go. You have to take care of yourself. You have to take care of both of you."

She smiled at me again, picking up her purse and walking to the door. "Doug's skulking around here somewhere if you need help, so make him do it. Hmm . . . there was one other thing I needed to tell you . . . Oh yeah—there's something for you in your office. I left it on your chair."

Butterflies shot through my stomach at her words. "W-what is it?"

"You'll have to see. I've got to go."

I followed Paige out of her office and turned uncertainly

into my own. The last thing left on my chair had been an envelope from Roman, one more piece in his twisted game of love and hate. *Oh God,* I thought. *I knew it wouldn't be as easy as Carter had said. Roman's back, starting it all up again, waiting for me to—*

I stared, swallowing a gasp. *The Glasgow Pact* sat on my chair.

Gingerly, I picked up the book, handling it like fine china. It was my copy, the one I had given Seth to sign over a month ago. I'd forgotten all about it. Opening up the inside cover, I saw lavender rose petals fall out. There were only a handful of them, but they were more precious to me than any of the bouquets I'd received this month. Trying to catch them, I read:

To Thetis,
Long overdue, I know, but very often the things we most desire come only after much patience and struggle. That is a human truth, I think. Even Peleus knew that.

—Seth

"He's back, you know."

"Huh?" I looked up from the baffling inscription to see Doug leaning against the door frame.

He nodded toward my book. "Mortensen. He's up in the café again, typing away as usual."

I closed the book, holding it tightly with both hands. "Doug . . . are you up on your Greek mythology?"

He snorted. "Don't insult me, Kincaid."

"Thetis and Peleus . . . they were Achilles' parents, right?"

"Indeed they were," he told me, smug with the confidence of his area of expertise.

For my part, I was simply puzzled. I didn't really get the inscription or understand why Seth would reference the Trojan War's greatest warrior.

"Do you know the rest?" Doug asked me expectantly.

"What? That Achilles was a dysfunctional psychopath? Yeah, I know that."

"Well, yeah, everyone knows that. I mean the really cool part. About Thetis and Peleus." I shook my head, and he continued, professor-like, "Thetis was a sea nymph, and Peleus was a mortal who loved her. Only, when he went to woo her, she was a real bitch about it."

"How so?"

"She was a shape-shifter."

I nearly dropped the book. "What?"

Doug nodded. "He approached her, and she turned into all sorts of shit to scare him off—wild animals, forces of nature, monsters, whatever."

"What . . . what'd he do?"

"He held on. Grabbed her and wouldn't let go through all of those terrible transformations. No matter what she turned into, he just held on."

"Then what?" I could barely hear my own voice.

"She finally turned back into a woman and stayed a woman. Then they got married."

I had stopped breathing somewhere around the word "shape-shifter." Still clutching the book, I stared off into space, a great winged feeling swelling in my chest.

"You all right, Kincaid? Christ, you've been weird lately."

I blinked, tuning back in to reality. The feeling in my chest burst out, launching into glorious flight. I started breathing again.

"Yeah. Sorry. I've just had a lot on my mind." Forcing levity, I added, "I'll do my best not to be too weird from now on."

Doug looked relieved. "Coming from you, that might be a long shot, but here's to hoping."

"Yes," I agreed, smiling. "Here's to hoping."

Please turn the page for an exciting
sneak peek of Richelle Mead's
second Georgina Kincaid novel,
SUCCUBUS ON TOP,
now on sale at bookstores everywhere!

Chapter 1

Demons are scary.

No matter what religion or walk of life you come from, this remains pretty constant. Oh sure, they have their absurd moments—especially in the circles I run with—but all in all, people have good reason to fear and avoid hell's diabolical servants. They're cruel and merciless, delight in pain and suffering, and torture souls in their free time. They lie. They steal. They cheat on their taxes.

Yet, in spite of all that, I couldn't help but think I was about to witness the most terrifying demonic act yet.

An awards ceremony. For me.

Horatio, Vice Demon of such-and-such division of Infernal Affairs, stood before me, trying to impart an air of solemnity to the moment and failing miserably. I suspected his sky blue polyester suit and matching paisley bow tie were largely to blame. The sideburns didn't help either. He probably hadn't left the inner circles of hell in about six centuries, back around the last time sky blue polyester was in style.

With a too-long clearing of his throat, he glanced back

and forth between those gathered, verifying we all paid attention. My supervisor Jerome stood nearby, looking utterly bored, occasionally glancing at his watch. Beside him, Horatio's impish assistant Kasper grinned from ear to ear. A briefcase sat on the floor near him, and he clutched an assortment of papers. The eager, sucking-up lapdog look on his face indicated a burning desire for promotion.

As for me . . . well, I was fighting a hard battle to look excited too—and failing. Which was unacceptable, of course. I'm a succubus. My entire existence relies on making people—men in particular—believe and see what they want to in me. I can switch from simpering virgin to sultry dominatrix in a heartbeat. All it takes is a bit of shape-shifting and a dash of playacting. I'd picked up the former ability when I traded away my human soul; I'd acquired the latter over time. After all, you can't spend centuries telling every guy, 'Yeah baby, you were the best I've ever had' and not learn a little something about schmoozing. Myths may paint us as ethereal, demonic creatures of pleasure, but honestly, being a succubus just comes down to a convincing poker face and a good sales pitch.

So, really, this awards thing shouldn't have been a problem for me. But Horatio wasn't making it easy to keep a straight face.

"Verily, it gives me great honor to be here today," he intoned in a nasally, baritone voice.

Verily?

"Hard work is what makes us great, and we gather here now to recognize one who has shown dedication and given her all to the Greater Evil. Such individuals are what make us strong, what will allow us to win in this immense battle when all tallies are counted at the end of time. Such individuals are worthy of our esteem, and we strive to reward their commitment, letting all know just how important it is to push hard against the odds and fight for our objectives in these difficult times."

He then added: "Whereas those who do not work hard are cast into the fiery pits of despair, to burn for all eternity and be ripped asunder by the hounds of hell."

I opened my mouth, on the verge of noting how that would be more cost effective than severance pay, but Jerome caught my eye and shook his head.

Meanwhile, Horatio had nudged Kasper, and the imp hastily handed over a gold embossed certificate. "It is therefore with great pleasure that I present unto you this Award of Achievement for Excellently Exceeding and Surpassing Requisite Succubus Quotas in this Most Recent Quarter. Congratulations."

Horatio shook my hand and handed me the certificate, which had been signed by about fifty different people.

This certifies that:

LETHA (alias Georgina Kincaid), Succubus in the Archdiocese of Seattle, Washington, United States of America, North America, Earth has hereby Excellently Exceeded and Surpassed Requisite Succubus Quotas in this Most Recent Quarter, demonstrating outstanding performance in seduction, damnation, and corruption of human souls.

Everyone looked at me when I finished reading, so I supposed they expected some kind of speech or something. Mostly I was wondering if I'd get in trouble for trimming this down to fit an eight by ten frame.

"Um, thanks. This is . . . cool."

That seemed to satisfy Horatio. He nodded smartly, then shot a glance to Jerome.

"You must be so proud."

"Exceptionally," murmured the archdemon, stifling a yawn.

Horatio turned back to me. "Keep up the good work. You might find yourself in line for promotion to the corporate level."

As if giving my soul away wasn't already bad enough. I forced a smile.

"Well. There's still so much to do here."

"Excellent attitude. Most excellent. You've done well with her." He gave Jerome a chummy pat on the back, something my boss did not look happy about at all. He didn't really like friendly pats. Or being touched, period. "Well, if there's nothing more, I should probably—oh, I nearly forgot."

Horatio turned to Kasper. The imp handed over something else to his master.

"These are for you. As a token of our appreciation."

He gave me a gift card for Applebee's, as well as some Blockbuster free rental coupons. Jerome and I both stared for a moment, dumbstruck.

"Wow," I finally said. The runner-up for this award probably got a gift card for Sizzler. Never doubt that second place really is the first loser.

Horatio and Kasper vanished. Jerome and I stood in silence for a few moments.

"You like riblets, Jerome?"

"Droll, very droll, Georgie." He strolled around my living room, pretending to study my books and artwork. "Nice job with the quota thing. Of course, it's easy to excel when you're starting at zero, huh?"

I shrugged and tossed the certificate on my kitchen counter. "Does it really matter? Still gets you the laurels. I figured you'd like that."

"Of course I do. In fact, I've been rather pleasantly surprised at just how well you've kept your promise."

"I always keep my promises."

"Not *all* of your promises."

My silence made him smile. "So what now? Going out to celebrate?"

"You know where I'm going. I'm going to Peter's. Aren't you?"

He avoided the question; demons excelled at that. "I thought perhaps other plans had arisen. Plans with a certain mortal. You do seem to be doing that an awful lot lately."

"It's none of your business what I do."

"All of your business is my business."

Again, I didn't answer. The demon stepped closer, dark eyes boring into me. For inexplicable reasons, he chose to look like John Cusack while walking the human world. That might seem like it would reduce his power to intimidate, but I swear, it only made things worse.

"How long are you going to keep up this farce, Georgie?" His words were a challenge, trying to draw me out. "You can't honestly think you have a future with him. Or that you two can stay chaste forever. For Christ's sake, even if you can keep your hands off him, no human male's going to stay celibate for long. Especially one with a large fan base."

"Did you miss the part where I said it's my business?"

Heat rose to my cheeks. Despite knowing better, I'd recently gotten myself involved with a human. I wasn't even entirely sure how it had happened since I've always gone out of my way to avoid that kind of thing. I guess you could say he sort of snuck up on me. One moment he was simply a warm and comforting presence at my side; the next I realized how intensely he loved me. That love had blindsided me. I hadn't been able to resist it and had decided to see where it might take me.

As a result, Jerome never failed to remind me of the potential disaster I courted daily in this romance. His opinion wasn't entirely unfounded. A small part of this was because I didn't have a good track record with serious relationships. The larger part was that doing much more than hand-holding with a human would inevitably lead to me sucking away some of his life. But hey, all couples have their stumbling blocks, right?

The demon smoothed down the jacket of his perfectly tailored black suit. "Just friendly advice. It makes no difference. I don't mind if you keep playing house with him—denying him a future, a family, a healthy sex life. Whatever. So long as you keep up the good work, it's all the same to me."

"Are you done with the pep talk? I'm late."

"One more thing. I thought you might like to know I just made some arrangements for a pleasant surprise. One you'll like."

"What kind of surprise?" Jerome didn't really do surprises. Not good ones, at least.

"Wouldn't be a surprise if I told you, now would it?"

Typical. I scoffed and turned away. "I don't have time for your games. Either tell me what's going on or leave."

"I think I'll leave. But, before I do, just remember something." He put his hand on my shoulder and turned me around to face him again. I flinched at his touch and his proximity. The demon and I were not as buddy-buddy as we had once been. "You only have one man who's a constant in your life, only one man you will always answer to. A hundred years from now, *he* will be dust in the earth, and *I* will be the one you keep coming back to."

It sounded romantic or sexual, but it wasn't. Not in the least. My tie to Jerome ran deeper than that. A binding and loyalty that literally went straight to my soul. A connection I was bound to for all eternity, at least until the powers of hell decided to assign me to a different archdemon.

"Your pimp routine is getting old."

He stepped back, undisturbed by my rancor. His eyes danced.

"If I'm a pimp, Georgina, what's that make you?"

There was an ostentatious poof of smoke, and Jerome disappeared before I could reply.

Fucking demons.

I stood alone in my apartment, turning over his words in my mind. Finally, remembering the time, I headed for the bedroom to change clothes. As I did, I passed Horatio's certificate. Its gold seal winked up at me. I flipped it over, face-down, suddenly feeling queasy. I might be good at what I did, but that didn't mean I was proud of it.

I ended up being only about fifteen minutes late for my friend Peter's shindig. He answered his door before I could even knock. Taking in his billowing white hat and *Kiss the Cook* apron, I said, "I'm sorry. No one told me *Iron Chef* was being filmed here tonight."

"You're late," he chided, waving a wooden spoon in the air. "So what, you win an award and think you can forget all about propriety now?"

I ignored his disapproval and swept inside. It was the only thing you could do with an obsessive-compulsive vampire.

In the living room, I found our other friends Cody and Hugh sorting large piles of cash.

"Did you guys rob a bank?"

"Nope," said Hugh. "Since Peter's trying to provide us with a civilized meal tonight, we decided a civilized pastime was required."

"Money laundering?"

"Poker."

From the kitchen, I could hear Peter muttering to himself about a soufflé. It sort of diminished my image of a bunch of shady characters huddled around a backroom card table. "I think bridge would be more appropriate."

Hugh looked doubtful. "That's an old-person's game, sweetie."

I had to smile at that. 'Old' was kind of a relative term

when most of us could boast centuries. I had long suspected that among my circle of lesser immortals—those who were not true angels or demons—I had more years than any of them, never mind my driver's license's optimistic claims to being twenty-eight.

"Since when do we even play games?" I wondered aloud. Our last attempt had involved a game of Monopoly with Jerome. Competing with a demon in a struggle for property and ultimate control is kind of futile.

"Since when don't we play games? Games of life, games of death. Games of love, of hope, of chance, of despair, and of all the myriad wonders in between."

I rolled my eyes at the newcomer. "Hello, Carter." I'd known the angel was lurking in the kitchen, just as Peter had felt me coming down the hall. "Where's your better half tonight? I just saw him. I thought he was coming too."

Carter strolled in and gave me one of his mocking smiles, gray eyes alight with secrets and mirth. He wore his usual transient ware, ripped jeans and a faded T-shirt. When it came to age, the rest of us couldn't even compare to him. The others and I had once been mortal; we measured our lives in centuries or millennia. Angels and demons . . . well, they measured their lives in eternity. " 'Am I my brother's keeper . . .' "

Classic Carter answer. I looked to Hugh who was, in a manner of speaking, our boss's keeper. Or at least a sort of administrative assistant.

"He had to take off for a meeting," said the imp, stacking twenties. "Some kind of team building thing in L.A."

I tried to imagine Jerome participating in a ropes course. "What kind of team building do demons do exactly?"

No one had an answer for that. Which was probably just as well.

While the money sorting continued, Peter made me a vodka gimlet. I eyed the bottle of Absolut on his counter.

"What the hell is that?"

"I ran out of Grey Goose. They're practically the same anyway."

"I swear, if you weren't already an abomination before the Lord, I'd accuse you of heresy."

When all the money was sorted, including my contribution, we sat around the vampires' kitchen table. Like everyone else in the known world right now, we started playing Texas Hold 'Em. I could play okay but faired far better with mortals than immortals. My charisma and glamour had less effect on this group, which meant I had to think harder about odds and strategy.

Peter scurried around during the game, attempting to play and watch his meal at the same time. It wasn't easy since he insisted on wearing sunglasses while playing, which then had to be removed while he checked the food. When I commented on how this would be my second fancy dinner in two nights, he nearly had a fit.

"Whatever. Nothing you had last night will even compare to this duck I've made. *Nothing*."

"I don't know about that. I went to the Metropolitan Grill."

Hugh whistled. "Whoa. I wondered where you got the glow from. When a guy takes you to the Met, you can't really help but put out, huh?"

"The glow's from a different guy," I said uncomfortably, not really wanting to be reminded of a tryst I'd had this morning, even if it had been pretty hot. "I went to the Met with Seth." The memory of last night's dinner brought a smile to my face, and I suddenly found myself rambling. "You should have seen him. He actually didn't wear a T-shirt for once, though I'm not sure it made a difference. The shirt he did have on was all wrinkled, and he couldn't really tie the tie. Plus, when I first got there, he had his laptop out on the table. He'd shoved everything else aside—napkins, wine-glasses. It was a mess. The waiters were horrified."

Four sets of eyes stared at me.

"What?" I demanded. "What's wrong?"

"You are," said Hugh. "You're a glutton for punishment."

Cody smiled. "Not to mention totally love struck. Listen to yourself."

"She's not in love with him," said Peter. "She's in love with his books."

"No I'm—" The words died on my lips, mainly because I wasn't sure what I wanted to argue. I didn't want them to think I only loved the books, but I wasn't entirely sure I loved Seth yet either. Our relationship had blossomed with remarkable speed, but sometimes, I worried what I actually loved was the idea of him loving me.

"I can't believe you guys are still doing the sexless dating thing," continued Hugh.

My temper flared. I'd already taken this from Jerome; I didn't need to hear it here too.

"Look, I don't want to talk about this if you guys are just going to nag me, okay? I'm tired of everyone telling me how crazy it is."

Peter shrugged. "I don't know. It's not that crazy. You always hear about these married couples who never have sex anymore. They survive. This would be almost the same thing."

"Not with our girl." Hugh shook his head. "Look at her. Who wouldn't want to have sex with her?"

They all looked again, making me squirm.

"Hey," I protested, feeling the need to clear up a point. "That's not the problem. He *wants* to, okay? He's just not going to. There's a difference."

"Sorry," said Hugh. "I'm just not buying it. He can't be with you in the clothes you wear and not crack. Even if he could, no guy could handle his woman seeing as much action as you do."

It was a well-worn point in my mind, the same Jerome had made, the one that worried me more than our ability to stay hands-free around each other. One of my greatest nightmares involved having a conversation akin to: *Sorry, Seth. I can't go out tonight. I have to go work this married guy I met, so I can get him to sleep with me, thus leading him farther and farther down the road to damnation while I suck away part of his life. Maybe when I'm done, you and I can catch a late movie.*

"I don't want to talk about this," I repeated. "We're doing just fine. End of story."

Silence fell, save for the sound of cards and money hitting the table. Glancing around, I saw Carter watching me levelly. Only he had stayed out of the Seth bashing. This didn't surprise me. The angel usually just listened until he could interject some sarcastic or esoteric quip. This used to infuriate me, but recent events had changed my attitude toward him. I still didn't fully understand him or know if I could trust him, but I had come to respect him.

Troubled by the scrutiny, I glanced back down and discovered I finally had a respectable hand after several rounds of shit. Three of a kind. Not the greatest but passable. I raised high, wanting to get the others out before more cards came into play and made my hand less passable.

My strategy worked on the vampires. The next card fell. Seven of spades. Hugh scowled and folded when I raised again. I waited for Carter to drop out as well, but instead, he re-raised further.

I hesitated only a moment before calling. As the last card was about to play, I puzzled over what the angel might have and whether I could beat it. A pair? Two pair? Ah. The last card came out. Another spade. There was now a strong possibility he had a flush. That would beat me. Still hoping I could bluff him out, I raised even more. He re-raised me again, more than doubling my initial bet.

That was a lot of money to add, especially considering

what I'd already put in. Centuries of investments kept me pretty comfortable, but that didn't mean I had to be stupid. What did he have? It had to be the flush. Balking, I folded.

With a pleased grin, he swept in the massive pot. When he tossed his hand over to the discard pile, the cards' edges caught, making them flip over. Two of diamonds. Eight of clubs.

"You . . . you bluffed!" I cried. "You had nothing!"

Carter wordlessly lit a cigarette.

I looked to the others for confirmation. "He can't do that."

"Hell, I've been doing it for half this game," said Hugh, borrowing Carter's lighter. "Not that it's done me any good."

"Yeah . . . but . . . he's, you know. An angel. They can't lie."

"He didn't lie. He bluffed."

Cody considered, twisting a piece of his blond hair around one finger. "Yeah, but bluffing is still dishonest."

"It's implied lying," said Peter.

Hugh stared at him. " 'Implied lying?' What the fuck does that mean?"

I watched Carter stack his money and made a face at him. You'd think an angel who hung around with employees of evil would be a good influence, but at times, he seemed worse than we were. "Enjoy your thirty pieces of silver, Judas."

He gave me a mock hat tip while the others argued on.

Suddenly, like a row of dominoes, conversation steadily dropped. Carter felt it first, of course, but he merely arched an eyebrow, as indifferent as ever. Then came the vampires with their heightened reflexes and sensitivity. They exchanged glances and looked toward the door. Finally, seconds later, Hugh and I sensed it as well.

"What is that?" Cody frowned, staring across the room. "It's sort of like Georgina but not."

Hugh followed the young vampire's gaze, face mildly speculative. "Incubus."

I had already known that, of course. The signatures we all carried differed by creature. Vampires felt different from imps just as imps felt different from succubi. If one knew an immortal well enough, one could also pick up on an individual's unique twinges. I was the only succubus who inspired sensations of silk and tuberose perfume. In a room full of vampires, I would have been able to quickly determine if Cody or Peter were present.

Likewise, I immediately knew there was an incubus approaching Peter's door, and I knew exactly which incubus it was. I would have known his signature anywhere, even after all this time. The fleeting feel of velvet on the skin. A whispered scent of rum, almond, and cinnamon.

Not even realizing I'd gotten up, I flung the door open, staring with delight at the same fox-faced features and mischievous eyes I'd last seen over a century ago.

"Hello, *mon fleur,*" he said.